THE GRAND II:
THE ROARING TWENTIES

Also by Katherine Hardy

The Grand

To Sheila
with my best
wishes

THE GRAND II:
THE ROARING
TWENTIES

A novelisation by
Katherine Hardy

Katherine Hardy

POCKET
BOOKS

LONDON · SYDNEY · NEW YORK · TOKYO · SINGAPORE · TORONTO

First published in Great Britain by Pocket Books, 1998
An imprint of Simon & Schuster Ltd
A Viacom Company

The Grand television series II
Copyright © Granada Television Ltd, 1998
Text © Karen Watkins, based on original scripts by Russell T.
Davies and Chris Thompson.

Simon & Schuster Ltd
West Garden Place
Kendal Street
London
W2 2AQ

SIMON & SCHUSTER AUSTRALIA
SYDNEY

A CIP catalogue record for this book is available from the British
Library.

1 3 5 7 9 10 8 6 4 2

ISBN 0-671-01596-6

Typeset by SX Composing DTP, Rayleigh, Essex
Printed and bound in Great Britain by Caledonian International
Book Manufacturing, Glasgow

Chapter One

The street was cold, dark, chillingly impersonal, its gloom broken by silver pools of street lamps that did more to accentuate the shadows than illuminate the street. Occasionally, a brighter radiance shimmered through uncurtained windows and doors. None brighter, or holding more promise of warmth and welcome, than the golden lights emanating from the grey-white, marbled façade of the Grand Hotel.

Inside, the concierge, Jacob Collins, presided over the foyer, calm, unruffled, his professional smile unwavering, even in the face of the blasts of icy air that gusted through the mahogany-trimmed, plush interior every time the door opened.

'Good evening.' He inclined his head as the Grand's resident guest, Esme Harkness, walked in with a grey-haired, distinguished-looking man. The concierge frowned disapprovingly at the liftboy, who was staring open-mouthed at the birdcage the man was carrying, its shape clearly distinguishable beneath a chenille cover.

'Mr Collins.' Esme rolled her eyes in exasperation as the concierge stepped back to allow her companion to manoeuvre the cage into the lift. There was just time for her to give him a wry smile before the doors closed.

'Jacob!' Stephen, the son of one of the Bannerman brothers who owned and managed the Grand Hotel, charged through the front doors, his coat flapping open behind him, his tie awry. 'The cars are outside. Tell the drivers to wait. I need ten minutes. Is Clive ready? Does he know we need him at the start? What time is it now? Did you order a third car? Adele's coming as well . . .'

'I did, sir,' Collins answered calmly in an attempt to stem Stephen's panic. 'Clive's fine, and it's twenty past seven.'

Stephen glanced at his watch. Tapping it impatiently, he wrenched it from his wrist. 'Thought so. Damn thing keeps stopping.'

'I can get it repaired, sir.'

'No. Tell the cars to wait . . .' He ran towards the stairs. Changing his mind, he turned back and handed the concierge his watch. 'Actually, if you would . . . How many cars?'

'Three, sir, just as you asked for.'

'God! I haven't even changed yet.' Racing up the stairs, he barged into his uncle.

'Hurry up,' Marcus shouted impatiently after him.

'I am.' Stephen disappeared around the corner of the landing.

'For God's sake, Collins, who's that boy?' Marcus demanded as he strode past the reception desk. 'He looks like a refugee from the twopenny papers. Your staff are supposed to welcome the guests, not drive them into the arms of the competition.'

'Frederick!' Collins reprimanded, casting a stern eye over the uniform of the footman on door duty.

Fred Willets looked suitably sheepish as he straightened his jacket and squared his shoulders.

'Detail, Mr Collins, detail,' Marcus lectured. 'That's

what caused the fall of the Roman Empire. The devil's in the detail. Are the cars ready?'

'They are, sir. Will Mrs Bannerman be joining you?'

'Of course. You know she will, so why do you ask?'

'Just to confirm, sir.'

'Is there a problem?'

'Not at all, sir,'

'If there is, you can tell her yourself.'

The lift doors opened behind them. Sarah Bannerman stepped out, smiling with the confidence that came with expensively tailored evening clothes, seductive French perfume, immaculately applied make-up and a perfect coiffure.

'You look wonderful,' Marcus complimented, a rare sincerity in his voice.

'Oh, yes? And how many women have you told that to today?' she countered playfully.

'Just you.'

'Then you're slipping. Mr Collins, fetch him a bath chair. He's past it. Stephen's running late, thank God, and as I'm being dragged into the wilds of Manchester, I need fortification.' She tapped her brother-in-law's arm with her fan. 'Champagne, and you're paying.'

'As a matter of fact, sir . . .' They both turned back. 'As I recall, sir, the Roman Empire was brought down by decadence. Simply that. Decadence,' Collins pronounced flatly.

Irritated by the obvious implication, Sarah continued to walk towards the bar, but Marcus stopped and smiled. Collins did not return the smile. The sight of Sarah flirting with her brother-in-law was becoming too familiar in his opinion. Her husband, John Bannerman, was much more than just his employer. He had earned the respect accorded him by the staff the hard way. Unlike his brother, Marcus, who had been devious and underhanded in his dealings with everyone since boyhood.

The tranquil, studied elegance of the hotel foyer did not extend behind the scenes. Below stairs, the house-keeper was presiding over an increasingly chaotic scene.

'I've got the list here.' Mrs Harvey had to shout to make herself heard above the racket the maids and porters were making. 'And I want this done with the minimum of fuss. Kate, Lynne, Brenda Potter, I want you moved out by eight o'clock. Linda, Jane Jenkins, Susan, you're to move your beds down to the old coal room . . .'

'We haven't got a Susan, Mrs Harvey,' Lynne informed the housekeeper, tartly.

'Who do I mean, then?' Mrs Harvey glared at Lynne, in an attempt to instil some deference for her position. 'You.' She pointed to a girl staggering beneath a bundle of blankets. 'What's your name? Sally? You're with Linda and Jane Jenkins. Kate, where do you think you're going?' she demanded as the senior maid picked up a pile of towels.

'Room eleven. They want towels, Mrs Harvey.'

'Good girl. Off you go. Guests come first.'

Kate lowered her head, to conceal a smile of triumph as she dived through the door. Mrs Harvey's voice echoed after her.

'Now I don't want any noise, and if your new bed-room hasn't got any ventilation, then make do – the men are coming to sort that out tomorrow . . .'

Charging up the back staircase, Kate raced past the first and second floors that housed the guest bedrooms. She didn't stop until she reached the top floor and the Bannermans' private quarters. Pausing outside a door at the end of the corridor, she pulled a couple of unruly red curls from beneath her mobcap and straightened her apron. Knocking, she opened the door without waiting for a 'come in'. Breezing past Stephen who was jabbing a cufflink into his shirt sleeve, she murmured, 'Excuse me, sir, towels.'

Still fiddling with the cufflink, Stephen kicked the door shut with the heel of his shoe.

'I could open a towel shop.'

'Had to think of something.' Dumping the towels besides the untouched set on the washstand, Kate smiled. 'Just wanted to say good luck. So there we are. Good luck.'

'I'm late. The wine merchant was due at two o'clock. What time did he turn up? Six! I've been running ever since. But it's all ready and waiting. You should see it, Kate, it's magnificent.'

'I might surprise you. Put me best frock on and tip up, demanding service.'

Stephen forgot his panic as he looked into her eyes. 'I wish you would.'

Wary of a sudden tenderness in his voice, and reluctant to think what it might mean, Kate opened the door and pushed him into the corridor. 'Oh aye? And I wish the back wall didn't need lime wash, but that's what I'll be doing. Go on, get going.'

Stephen barely had time to grab his dinner jacket before they both tumbled headlong and laughing, into the passageway. Kate fell silent when she saw the tall, disapproving figure of the hotel barman, Clive, standing in front of the lift.

'Sorry to disturb you, sir,' Clive apologised stiffly. 'I didn't know if you wanted me to head off, or wait for you, or what?'

'No, you're coming with me.' Stephen glanced at Kate. 'I've asked Clive to work at the bar, just for tonight.'

'I know, sir. We do talk to each other.'

'Yes, of course you do. Right, Clive, if you're ready. Into the fray.' Stephen led the way. Clive followed, but not until he'd shot an acid glance at Kate. She held her head high as she made her way to the servants' staircase. What right did Clive Jenkins have to judge her behaviour? What right at all?

Clive had difficulty keeping up with Stephen as he ran headlong down the three flights of stairs that led to the ground floor.

'Stephen, calm down,' John called, smiling, as his son appeared flushed and agitated in the foyer. 'It can't start until you arrive.'

'I suppose not,' Stephen acknowledged, slipping on his jacket.

John held out his hand. 'All the best.'

'Yes. Thanks.' Stephen shook it before looking round at the assembled crowd. His younger sister Adele was clinging to the arm of her latest handsome and empty-headed flame, Cassian. Marcus's wife, Ruth, was standing behind his father in a shapeless smock that looked drab in comparison with the sequin-encrusted evening dresses of the other women.

'At last.' Marcus walked out of the bar with Sarah trailing behind him. 'I thought I'd have to sack you on the first night.'

'You can't do that, Uncle Marcus,' Adele complained petulantly. 'Stephen's promised me the best table.'

The Grand II: The Roaring Twenties

'Actually all the tables are the same.' Stephen pulled his cuffs below his jacket sleeves and ran his fingers over his bow tie. 'Let's go, we're late. I thought Clive could come with us in the car.'

'They'll be joining us for breakfast next,' Marcus sniped.

'I'll walk, sir. It's only ten minutes.'

'Don't listen to him, Clive,' Sarah interposed. 'You're perfectly welcome.'

Ruth gave her husband a brittle smile. 'Off you go then, Marcus. Don't think about me, no, not once. Dance and drink, safe in the knowledge that I'll be here. Doing my job.'

'What job?' Marcus enquired irritably. 'You've never done a day's work in your life.'

Ruth patted her swollen stomach. 'He's my job. You made that perfectly clear on the day we married. I'm good stock.' She dropped her voice to cockney slang. 'Pleasure to serve you, sir.'

Embarrassed by the interchange between Marcus and Ruth, Sarah turned her back on them and kissed her husband's cheek.

'Enjoy yourself.'

'I will, John.' She took the arm Marcus offered.

Standing back, Ruth saw her husband smile at Sarah as they swept out through the doors. She clung to the banister for support as she began the long climb up to the third floor.

'You should go with them, sir,' Collins advised John.

'The captain stays with the ship. And it's Stephen's night. He doesn't want his father looking on.' He shook his head at the concierge. 'No doubt I'd disapprove.'

'I was thinking of your wife, sir. She might

appreciate the company.'

If John heard Collins, he gave no indication of it as he walked into the office and the pile of paperwork waiting for his attention.

'How many beds can you fit in one room?' Lynne asked in the singsong voice of a music-hall comedian as she, Brenda and Kate surveyed the cramped, windowless quarters the porters had carried their iron-framed bedsteads into.

'More than three,' Fred Willets answered as he and another porter struggled through the door with a fourth set of springs.

'It's like the black hole of Calcutta in here. It's bad enough having to share with her' – Lynne jabbed her thumb in Kate's direction – 'without having to move. I liked me old room. We had shelves.'

'You know full well we need your old room for storage,' Mrs Harvey rebuked, as she pushed her way past Kate and Brenda. 'Put it there,' she ordered Fred, who was still holding the fourth bed.

'I'm being pushed out for half a ton of disinfectant,' Lynne grumbled.

'I think you forget, disinfectant is every bit as important as people.'

Kate looked at the empty bed, as the boys heaved it next to hers. 'Who's going to sleep there?'

'New girl. She starts tomorrow. Right, that's your lot. I'm needed in the Lancaster Suite. Colin . . . what's your name . . . Frederick, out you come. I won't have boys in the girls' rooms.'

'I'll tuck them in for the night. How about it, Lynne?' Fred grinned suggestively.

'Out!' Mrs Harvey commanded imperiously, above the combined laughter of the girls. 'Listen to him.

The Grand II: The Roaring Twenties

Only been here a fortnight. Enough lip to feed the five thousand.' She opened the door wider. 'I said out!' She swept the boys before her and marched them down the corridor.

'And there was me thinking you ordered this specially, just in case his lordship comes visiting?' Lynne eyed Kate as she bounced on the spare bed.

'And he might do just that,' Kate retorted airily. 'He's besotted. There he is tonight, opening his own club, and look at me? Guest of honour.'

'Chasing after you every spare minute,' Lynne contradicted. 'We saw you. Stephen Bannerman and Kate, the chambermaid, dancing together.'

'Once. We danced once.'

'In public! With all his family watching. Do that in my house, and you're engaged,' Brenda pronounced authoritatively.

'Mind you, I've always thought, he's *too* good-looking, him. I went out with a good-looker once. Kissed like a fish.'

'Well, if that's the case with Stephen Bannerman, I wouldn't know.'

'You're useless, Kate,' Lynne declared as she tipped her clothes out of a paper bag on to the bed. 'Tell me, what's the point of sharing with her?' She looked to Brenda. 'She hasn't even got good gossip. I wanted to share with Big Lucy. She's been engaged three times. Two of them died and one went to Cardiff.' Fishing a tin of biscuits from the mess on her bed, she held it aloft. 'I'm labelling this. It's mine. You lot want biscuits, you can buy your own.'

Stephen was glad to exchange the blistering, sweat-soaked atmosphere of the packed bar of the Manhattan for the cool of the club office. Having shut out the insistent double beat of the Charleston, he closed his eyes. But he could still see the crowds demanding his time and attention. Leaning back, he stole a couple of blissful seconds of peace before tipping a bag of coins out on to the desk.

'Hiding?' Marcus pushed the door open.

'No. Looking for change. I'll have to get a bigger float tomorrow. They're spending money like there's a run on the bank.' He looked quizzically at his uncle. 'I still don't know why you chose me. I should be on the other side of the bar. There must be dozens of men you could have employed.'

'Hundreds,' Marcus corrected drily. 'And they're still waiting. You let me down, and you'll be replaced by morning.'

'Marcus. I don't know that I've said thank you. Not properly.'

'Oh shut up, and get busy.' Marcus opened the door. 'Make it work. Surprise me.'

Stephen sorted the silver from the copper. He bagged half the coins and locked them in the safe before following his uncle.

'They told me the owner was handsome. I didn't believe them.' Sarah waylaid Stephen as he passed her table.

'I'm the owner,' Marcus interrupted.

'The manager then.' Sarah grasped Stephen's hand. 'It's wonderful, darling. Everyone's saying as much.'

'Almost, it's not quite complete,' Stephen qualified.

'Care to dance, Mrs Bannerman?' Marcus asked. Stephen stood back and watched them move around the crowded floor. This was his new world. He might only be the manager, but this was the culmination of weeks of work. His, and no one else's. All the tables were full, packed with guests, drinking, laughing and enjoying themselves. He doubted that another couple could be squeezed on to the dance floor. Clive and the new boy he'd taken on, Jim, were hard-pressed to keep up with the demand for drinks. His domain, and a successful one.

Sarah saw her son standing back from the crowd. She tensed herself, willing with all her might that this time it really was going to be all right for Stephen. Then, the pressure of Marcus's hand resting on her waist brought the acute realisation of his proximity. She looked up. Her brother-in-law was studying her intently. His grip tightened. He didn't say anything, but then, he didn't have to.

Engrossed in the columns of figures set in the ledger in front of him, John took a few moments to realise he was being watched. He glanced up at the door. Ruth was leaning against the post.

'I thought you'd be asleep.' He laid his pen on the blotter.

'Oh, I'm supposed to be asleep, and all for the sake of this one. It's a wonder the human race survives, we're supposedly so delicate.'

'Sit down.' John placed a chair opposite his own, before reaching down a couple of glasses and a bottle of whisky from a cupboard above his head. 'I always keep a little something aside for these late nights.'

'Lonely nights in the office, while your brother runs wild. It occurs to me there's a certain danger, don't you think?'

John avoided her gaze as he poured the whisky. 'In what way?'

'Marcus. His relationship with someone very close to you.' She lifted her glass. 'Giving your son an establishment stocked to the ceiling with alcohol.'

John laughed in relief at the mention of Stephen. 'Yes, indeed, I'd rather not think about that.'

'It strikes me, John, that there's a lot of things you'd rather not think about. And *that's* how the human race survives.' She touched her glass to his. 'To the Grand Hotel. The kingdom of the blind. Good Lord!'

'What?' Alarmed by her sudden pallor, he wondered if she felt faint.

Ruth left her chair. Staring into the foyer through the glass panel set in the door she knocked her whisky over. John tore a sheet from the blotter and laid it over the mess before looking out.

'How marvellous.'

An elegantly dressed, elderly woman was talking to Collins at reception. The concierge saw them standing in the office, so walked over and knocked on the door.

'Excuse me, Mr Bannerman. Mrs Bannerman, a visitor for you, ma'am.'

'So there you are.' The visitor stood back and looked Ruth up and down.

'There's no use hiding. Let me see.' She stared at John as Ruth retreated into the office. 'Didn't even tell me she was expecting – I had to hear it second-hand. Still, I'm here now. I take it you have room for me? That is the purpose of this establishment.'

'Mrs Crawford, sir, Mrs Isobel Crawford.' Collins effected the introduction Ruth was obviously reluctant to make.

'My maternal grandmother,' Ruth explained briefly as she sank back on to the chair.

Isobel continued to stare at John. 'Is this him? Doesn't look like a bastard. I've heard you're a bastard, sir, they usually are. Still, if you've tamed her, best of luck to you. There's many failed.'

'No, I'm sorry, Mrs Crawford. Wrong Mr Bannerman.'

Ignoring John's assertion, Isobel laid her hand on Ruth's abdomen. 'What is that? Five months? And look at the time. You're up and about courting disaster. Come here.' She kissed Ruth's cheek, then surveyed the foyer. 'What is this exactly? How many rooms?'

'One hundred,' John disclosed, amused by the woman's directness. 'Plus the staff quarters.'

'Making a profit?'

'Yes. Not bad . . .'

'And it's yours,' she interrupted baldly. 'You're not in debt? Up to your neck in loans and favours?'

'No, not at all. I own it with my brother Marcus, he's the one—'

'Yes, I see, it works. Could almost be charming, if it weren't for the city that surrounds it. Give it a lick of paint and I'll be happy to call this home.'

Not quite knowing how to deal with Isobel Crawford's audacity, John looked to Ruth for support, but when she saw him watching her, she turned away.

Marcus noticed Jim opening a bottle of champagne at a neighbouring table. He did it quietly, with the minimum of fuss, as though he was accustomed to opening dozens of bottles every night. The host at the table held up an empty glass to Stephen, who was working behind the bar. Stephen smiled, shaking his head before handing the customer he'd been serving the whisky he'd just poured.

'He told me he's not touching a drop from now on.' Marcus bent his head close to Sarah's so she could hear him above the band. 'That's why he called this place the Manhattan. It's his own personal prohibition.'

'God knows I tried everything. You brought him back to life, Marcus.'

'Indeed, and my next project's working out very well.' Grasping the tips of her fingers, he pulled her hand towards him. 'She's already changing. More like the splendid woman my brother brought home all those years ago.'

'Oh, and what was I before you came along to save me? The dowager aunt?'

'Well . . .'

'Don't flatter yourself. You've done nothing, Marcus. Yes, perhaps I'm enjoying myself a little more, but that's my decision. My children have grown up, the hotel's fine. It's time I ventured out.'

'Just as I intended.'

'Will you stop it? In this day and age, a woman's perfectly capable of advancing herself without a man's support.'

'She said, drinking my champagne. Cheers.' He lifted his glass to hers.

'You don't just open a good wine and serve it,' Clive explained to Jim in between serving customers. 'It needs time to breathe. It's expensive.'

'Time to breathe,' Jim snorted contemptuously. 'What do you think this is, the Orient Express? They want it red and wet and on the table now.' Jim picked up the bottle he'd uncorked, wrapped a napkin around its neck and headed for the nearest table. Seeing Stephen watching them, Clive shrugged his shoulders.

'He'll learn,' Clive said philosophically as Stephen reached for a tray of glasses.

The Grand II: The Roaring Twenties

'Listen, Clive, it's up to you. This is just a suggestion, but if every night's like this, you could leave the Grand and work here instead. Full-time.'

'Full-time? I don't know. I don't just *work* at the Grand, sir, it's bed and board as well.'

'Yes, but with a good enough wage you could find rooms in town. 'I know we've had our . . .' Stephen hesitated, remembering one particularly bloody fight between them, a fight more over Kate than anything else. 'We've had our disagreements in the past, but this is my chance to make amends. Think about it. The offer's there.'

'I will, sir, thanks.' Taking the champagne he'd set in an ice bucket, Clive stepped out from behind the bar.

'What happened to Cassian?' Stephen asked, as Adele perched on a stool in front of him.

'Nothing,' Adele drawled in a jaded tone. 'I don't think anything's happened to Cassian, ever. Boring childhood, dull education, all the wit of an ox.' She glanced at the men sitting at the table behind her. 'There's always Graham Flately I suppose. He's demanding a night at the theatre, but I'm not sure I want to go with him. Flately, Adele Flately? When it comes down to it there's so few to choose from. Besides, everyone's asking about you. Jeanette Fisher and Helen Courtney are begging introductions.'

'Tell them I'm taken.'

'Oh.' Adele arched her eyebrows. 'Who's this? Do I know her?'

Stephen handed her a fresh drink. 'You'll be able to meet her soon. In fact, any day now.'

Kate leaned back against her pillow straining her eyes to see the black thread against the black stocking heel,

15

as she plied her darning needle by candlelight. The springs on the bed next to her creaked as Brenda slipped out. Standing next to Lynne for a moment to make sure she really was asleep, she grabbed her biscuit tin and darted back to bed.

'She'll murder us,' Kate whispered.

'She's all talk.' Brenda opened the tin and tossed a biscuit across to Kate. 'I met this bloke once – well he was a boy really. Turned out both his parents were teachers – that's posh down my neck of the woods. And I *danced* with him.'

'Oh, give it a rest.'

'I'm just saying. But he's that nice to you, Stephen Bannerman.'

Kate bit through the thread and laid the needle on the box beside her bed. 'All right, we're friends. Sort of. He talks to me once in a while, and that's all.'

'That's worse, that is. Most blokes don't want to talk: they're after something else. If he's happy talking, then he *really* likes you. And you've never kissed him, not ever?'

'See that empty bed there? There should be someone sleeping there, a girl called Monica Jones. But she's not, she's gone, and all because she reached too far. Do you honestly think I'd try the same thing?'

'No. Sorry, Kate.'

'Well think next time. Now get to sleep.' Laying the stocking next to the needle and thread, Kate blew out the candle.

'I said sorry.' Brenda's voice echoed, small and lost in the darkness.

'Thanks for the biscuit.'

'It's not me you should thank.' Brenda punched her pillow into a comfortable shape, and settled down. Kate turned her face to the wall, but she didn't close her eyes, not yet. The time she spent in her bed was too precious for sleep. It was the only time she could call her own. Her time for dreaming.

Stephen leaned forward on the bar and watched the singer. A tall, slim, highly desirable woman was crooning a soft, romantic love song that made him wish he was elsewhere, or, even better, that there was someone standing alongside him. A short, pretty someone.

He glanced at his sister's table. She was draped over yet another handsome lump. He knew the boy by sight, Lysander Pettet. His older brother, Michael, had been in his regiment. Killed on the Somme. Suddenly he felt a pang of envy for Lysander and all the boys of his generation. They'd be allowed to live through their boyhoods.

The song finished and a polite ripple of applause fluttered around the room. He eyed his uncle and his mother, waiting for their reaction. The singer walked to the edge of the small stage. She reached up, grasped her hair – and lifted it off her head.

The applause died in a collective gasp. Sarah was the first to laugh. The sound was infectious. Then she stood and clapped, and suddenly everyone was on their feet, shouting, stamping, clapping as the singer took his bows. Marcus raised his glass to Stephen.

'What's that about?' Clive asked Jim as he hauled a crate of beer in from the stockroom behind the bar.

'What do you think? Singer's a man.'

'I don't see what's so funny. It's disgusting.'

Jim's laughter joined the rest as Clive turned away in revulsion.

Ignoring John's suggestion that she sit down, Isobel

Crawford prowled round the Bannermans' private living room, inspecting every stick of furniture and every ornament.

'Very homely,' she declared, standing back to survey the general effect. 'I certainly know I'm in Manchester now. And this brother of yours, Mr Bannerman, this sudden member of my family, where is he?'

'He's invested in a club. Tonight's the opening, he's employed my son as—'

'Does he often leave his wife alone?' Isobel demanded.

'No, as I said, it's a special night . . .'

'Yes, he does it often. As often as he can,' Ruth contradicted.

Isobel seemed peculiarly delighted by Ruth's confirmation of Marcus's neglect. 'Splendid, excellent. I can't wait to meet him.'

Conscious of the sleepers behind the doors, Collins moved softly, quietly, along the first-floor corridor. Pausing outside the last room on the left before the fire escape, he tapped lightly. The door opened a fraction, and the beautifully preserved face of Esme Harkness peered out.

'Enter very quickly, and close the door behind you straight away.'

Bemused, but too professional to allow his curiosity to show, Collins did as she asked. As soon as he stepped inside he saw the problem. A pigeon was perched high on the corner of the curtain pole.

'I see.'

Esme pointed to the cage. 'I was going to say it flew in through the window, but I suppose this rather gives it away.'

The Grand II: The Roaring Twenties

'Most people keep parrots, Miss Harkness.'

'It's not mine. The things some men demand. I'm past surprises.'

'I'm sure it's none of my business.'

'A peck on the cheek, indeed,' she snorted. 'Perhaps his first experience was in Trafalgar Square. I've stopped asking.'

Collins suppressed a smile as he walked to the bathroom to fetch a chair to bring the pigeon down.

At two o'clock the Manhattan club was busier than it had been at midnight. Clive, Jim and Stephen were working flat out at the bar. The air was thick, turgid with the smell of alcohol, perfume, cigarette and cigar smoke.

Marcus paused on his way from the bar to talk to a thickset man who looked like a bruiser despite his immaculately tailored evening suit. Slipping his hand into his pocket, Marcus extracted a bundle of bank notes and passed them to the man, who slid them inside his coat in a single, swift, practised movement.

'Sorry about that,' Marcus apologised, as he rejoined Sarah at their table. 'A small matter of business.'

'Now you're back, sit down. You know what they say about a woman on her own in a nightclub.'

'It's said she's out whoring?'

Sarah glared at him, thunderstruck, but only for a moment. Fumbling blindly for her bag, she rose to her feet and went to the door. Marcus watched her go. He drained his glass before following her out into the street. It was quiet – discreet. He'd chosen the location for his club well.

'Sarah!' She kept on walking.

'I can find my own way home. Or perhaps I should

stop here, and ply my trade? What the hell was that remark supposed to mean?' she charged furiously as he caught up with her.

'You tell me. A year ago you couldn't bear to be in the same room as me. Now you're there, every time I turn around.'

'I *thought* we were friends.'

'You know that I want something very different, you *know* that, but there you are, at my side every day. The time has long since gone when I made all the running, Sarah, so tell me: what *are* you doing?'

'I made one mistake. I kissed you. And if I'm proving anything now, it's that I can spend time in your company, and not have that kiss mean anything.'

'And yet you will keep mentioning it.'

Seething, Sarah turned on her heel. Reaching for his cigar case, Marcus watched her go.

Collins looked at the pigeon tucked safely and securely in its cage. Raising the small glass of sherry Esme Harkness had poured him as a thank-you, he nodded and smiled.

'Your very good health, Mr Collins. I do appreciate it. So many people are quick to judge me. But not you.'

'A blind eye. It comes with the job.' His smile hardened. 'Sometimes I see too much. And say nothing. But I *should.* If I don't, I'm failing the job, it's worthless.'

'It's nothing I've done surely . . .?'

'It's not you, Miss Harkness.' Finishing the sherry, he rose to his feet. 'I should go. I'm on duty.' He went to the door. 'Six years ago my son was executed as a coward. I've spent the intervening years wondering how that could be. Now I know. I know where he got it from.'

He knew he'd upset Esme, but all he could see, all he could think of as he walked down the corridor, was Sarah's face as she'd looked at Marcus earlier that evening. It wasn't his place to judge Sarah, but he was desperately worried for John Bannerman. Worried to the point where the knowledge of what John's wife and brother were doing was destroying him.

Marcus glanced at his watch. Any minute now . . . Even as he looked up, the door to the club burst open and a posse of policemen flooded in. A burly sergeant stood his ground barking orders.

'Just stay where you are. Everyone please, stay where you are. Sorry, sir.' He blocked the path of an anxious-looking man heading towards him. 'No one's to leave.'

'Oh my God, we're being arrested.' Adele's face was bright with the thrill of unlooked-for excitement.

'My officers will need every name and address. Just sit down, thank you, sir.' The sergeant pushed an agitated customer back into his chair. 'If we could have some quiet. Could the manager please identify himself?'

Marcus pointed at Stephen. 'That's him.'

'It's a licensed club,' Stephen protested. 'I've got the papers. It's all above board . . .'

'That may be, sir, but we've had information about certain monies changing hands. Counterfeit notes.' He spun around as the man he'd spoken to earlier attempted to bypass him again. 'I said no one's leaving.'

'Can they do this, Marcus?' Stephen demanded.

Marcus nodded to a man in the crowd. 'That man there, Tom Baxter. Watch him.'

Katherine Hardy

A policeman approached Baxter and pushed him. Baxter pushed back before swinging his arm wide and punching the officer. Within seconds the club erupted. Bottles, glasses and drinks flew into the air as tables crashed on to their sides. Chairs were tossed overhead. The police sergeant ran forward shouting.

'What's he *doing*?' Stephen dived forward, intending to go to Baxter's aid.

Marcus yanked him back by the collar of his jacket. 'Earning a tenner, and if you think that's expensive, you should have seen what I paid the police.'

'You planned this?' Stephen questioned incredulously. 'Whatever for?'

'Headlines. When this hits the papers, you'll be packed out every night. Congratulations, Stephen, you've engineered a great success.'

Chapter Two

Lark Rothery clutched a small cardboard suitcase tightly to her chest, as she stood beside her mother in the cramped passageway below stairs in the Grand.

'She's got some liquorice water for her dinner,' her mother prattled to Mrs Harvey, who was even more sour-faced than usual. 'Now, once you've done, Lark, give the bottle to Mrs Harvey. There's a halfpenny back. And you write home every day – there's paper in your case. Don't go bothering Mrs Harvey – she's a busy woman.'

'Indeed I am, Mrs Rothery. Things to do.' The housekeeper ushered her closer to the door that opened into the yard.

'Make me proud.' Mrs Rothery shed a few tears as she kissed Lark's cheek. She took a last look at her daughter as Mrs Harvey opened the door.

Kate waited until the housekeeper turned her back. 'I'm Kate. You'll be working with me. What's your name again?'

'Lark Rothery.'

'How old are you?'

'Fourteen, miss.'

'From Moss Side, your mam said. That's not too bad, bus ride home on your day off.'

The minute Mrs Harvey finally succeeded in

sweeping Mrs Rothery out, she called to the girls.

'Kate, step back. Don't touch her,' she ordered abruptly. 'Lynne, get her coat off. Quick sharp. Polly, the bowl. Brenda, jug of water. Do it!' she screamed as they stared at her blankly.

The scream was the decisive factor. The girls burst into action.

'What have I done?' Lark asked, terrified by the bustle.

'Vermin. Head full of lice,' Mrs Harvey declared authoritatively.

Lynne threw Lark's jacket to the flagstoned floor. 'Oh bleeding hell. I'm touching her clothes.'

'Kate, my office,' Mrs Harvey commanded. 'Fetch the Red Precipitate.'

'I'm not dirty,' Lark protested, bursting into tears.

'It's no comment on your family, girl. Your mother is a good, clean woman, but I'm cleaner still. Now, breathe in.' Grabbing the bowl Brenda handed her, Mrs Harvey grabbed Lark's head and pushed it down as Brenda poured the water over her hair.

'And I don't have any say in this?' Marcus demanded as two porters under Mr Collins's supervision carried furniture out of the bedroom he shared with Ruth. He glared at John and Sarah, who were having trouble concealing their amusement.

'Pregnancy makes certain demands.' Isobel slipped a proprietary arm around Ruth's shoulders. 'One of those being separate bedrooms for husband and wife. We could have discussed this last night, but you were busy gallivanting.'

'There is not one valid medical reason—'

'Oh, they always think they know best.' Isobel crossed her arms as she surveyed Marcus. 'I've had three husbands, sir, and survived every one of them.'

'How did they die? Suicide?'

'There's a child on the way,' Isobel reminded Marcus sternly. 'It demands our vigilance. And the needs of a husband can be something of a threat. It's not talk for the servants. I'm sure you understand what I mean.' She stepped closer. 'If your appetite can't be curbed, then look elsewhere for the duration.'

'We'll leave you to it.' Not trusting herself to keep a straight face any longer, Sarah took John's arm and walked down the corridor.

'Now move along, Marcus.' Isobel pushed him from her path. 'You're in the way.'

Seething, Marcus left for the living room. Ruth followed, but only after receiving a nod from her grandmother.

'I refuse to be treated like this in my own home!' Marcus's face was livid in anger.

'What, bullied around? Told what to do, and what to say? It's my home, and I'm treated like that.' Ruth hesitated. 'But she's right, Marcus,' she ventured. 'She's always right. We should take care. Grandmother knows that better than anyone. She was there.'

'That won't happen again.'

'You can guarantee it?'

He stepped towards her, but she retreated, refusing to accept his comfort.

'Please, Marcus, she'll have to stay. Just until it's over.'

Marcus nodded. He knew when he was beaten. But he was determined that Isobel's victory – and visit – would be as short-lived as he could make them.

Kate hitched the coal bucket higher in her hand as she

stood at the corner of the corridor, watching Lark padding up and down.

'What's this? St Vitus' dance?'

Lark grinned, embarrassed at being caught out. 'Carpets!'

'Get going, you. Work to do. Room forty-nine.'

Lark sprang lightly, dancing one last jig on her way to the room where Lynne and Brenda were already hard at work.

'I go to bed with ten biscuits,' Lynne was saying, 'and wake up with eight. If it's not back to ten by dinner time, someone's having her windows pushed in.'

'What you telling me for, Lynne?' Brenda asked innocently.

'If I'm looking for someone who nicks biscuits, you're the right size.' She opened two canvas bags on the trolley as she turned impatiently to Lark. 'How many times have I told you? Sheets in there, pillow cases in there. If you're not careful you'll be out by Thursday.'

Brenda waited until Lynne went into the room next door, before consoling Lark. 'Lynne's wasted on peacetime. Would have made a great army sergeant. Don't worry, you just stick with me.'

Lark barely heard what she'd said. She was staring open-mouthed at an open jewellery box crammed with diamonds and pearls. 'They just leave that stuff out?'

'It should be in the hotel safe, but some guests have more money than sense. Roll up the sheets. Go on.' She followed Lynne, leaving Lark staring at the jewellery.

Kate crept up the back staircase to the Bannermans' private apartments. Setting the towels she was carrying on the hallstand, she checked her reflection in the mirror, bit her lips to redden them, and picked up the towels. Then she heard Stephen's voice echoing from the living room.

'There must have been a dozen policemen . . .'

'More like twenty,' Adele corrected, her voice high-pitched in excitement. 'They took all our names. They had vans and everything . . .'

'Oh my God,' John said in mock horror. 'And half the people there gave this place as their address. One night and you've ruined me. Ruined!'

Kate stepped back, but she could still see the images of John, Sarah, Adele, Marcus and Stephen reflected in the glass. She had no business to be on the top floor at that time of day, but she stayed.

'I'll lend you some money, Dad,' Stephen joked. 'The bar took three hundred quid, and that's with being closed down early. Keep on like this, we could open more places – the start of an Empire.'

'John, stop him,' Marcus ordered. 'He's out of control.'

'It's your doing,' John laughed.

Suddenly Kate realised that she had no place, not in the Bannermans' private quarters, and not in Stephen's life. Hugging the towels closer, she opened the service door.

The laughter from the living room reverberated in the darkened room Isobel had transformed into a sitting room for herself and her granddaughter.

'We could join them.' There was a pleading note in Ruth's voice as she peered through the gloom her grandmother insisted she live in for the sake of the child she was carrying.

'Do you trust me?' Isobel asked sharply.

'Of course I do.'

'Then you're a fool. You can only trust in God. And pray for his forgiveness. He knows what you've done.' Isobel took her granddaughter's small, cold hand into her own with a compassion that frightened Ruth more than any brutality could have done.

Adjusting the reading lamp at her elbow, Isobel returned to the book she was reading, leaving Ruth to her thoughts, and the silence.

'He's an excellent barman,' Stephen said forcefully as he and Marcus walked into the foyer.

'Clive *is* excellent – for the Grand,' Marcus qualified. 'But look at him. The only thing he's been taught is deference. The Manhattan needs someone to charm the customers, to captivate and fleece them. That boy's nothing but a copy of Mr Collins.'

'Then I'm sorry, but it's too late. I've already asked him. It's my club.'

'If you want to pay me back, then grow up, Stephen. The holiday came to an end last night. You want the staff to be your friends, then fine: stay in the Grand sitting on your father's lap, all cosy and safe. Otherwise treat your business with respect by acting like a businessman at all times. Lecture over.' He clapped his nephew soundly on the back. 'Good luck for tonight. No police, I promise.'

Marcus went into the bar. A crowd of fashionably dressed men and women called out to him, and he joined them, laughing, joking, very much the life and soul of the party. Stephen glanced uneasily at Clive. Businessman, his uncle had said. He had to be a businessman! Steeling himself, he headed out through the door.

* * *

The Grand II: The Roaring Twenties

John shifted uneasily in his chair as he and Sarah sat alone together in their living room. He'd been waiting for an opportunity to talk to her all day, but now it had actually arrived he felt ill at ease. It was ridiculous. He felt uncomfortable with his own wife.

'Martin Lyons came round,' he said at length. 'He's chairman of the Wainwright Committee. They're doing some good work, raising funds for the hospital. He thought I might like to join. He said they needed a treasurer.'

'Oh. Good idea,' Sarah said without enthusiasm.

'Mmm. Sounds it.'

His failure to read her sarcasm kindled her anger to the point of eruption. 'John, all you do is find yourself more and more work. We only get a few evenings off together as it is. If you're going to start joining civil committees—'

'All right, fine. They can find someone else.'

'No, that's not fair. If you want to do it, you should do it.'

'Sarah, if you'd rather I stayed here and paid you more attention, then I'm the first to agree. I've thought that countless times, but then I turn around, and you're not here. You're . . . busy.'

'Am I? Doing what?'

'I thought you'd like my having an interest outside the Grand, so you could have even *more* time to be busy.'

Furious, Sarah went on the attack. 'What am I supposed to do, John? Sit and wait until you're free? Perhaps we could draw up a timetable. One of your meticulous rotas?'

'Yes, let's do that!' he snapped.

'There you are, even more work for you. Perfect! Have we finished?'

'*I* have.'

'Good.' She left her chair and stalked out of the room. John sat back, wishing with all his heart that he knew how to touch her, just as he had been able to a few short months ago, before Marcus had moved into the hotel.

Sarah went where she always did when she quarrelled with John. Marcus was already waiting at the bar. He clicked his fingers and her favourite drink appeared. He smiled and she joined him, just as she'd done so many evenings before.

Mrs Harvey supervised impatiently as Lark polished the silverware. It took all her powers of forbearance not to snatch the rag from the girl's inexpert fingers and show her again how do it. Deliberately turning her back on the recruit, she watched Kate, who was washing out tea towels in the sink.

'The room list, Mrs Harvey.'

Stephen Bannerman was at her elbow.

'Very kind of you, sir,' she murmured, wondering why he was below stairs.

'They said something about a double booking.'

'Really, sir. If I had a penny . . .' Leaving the girls, she hurried off to the office to sort out the problem Stephen had invented on the spur of the moment.

Stepping behind Lark, Stephen looked to Kate, pointed at the ceiling and held up two fingers. She knew what that meant. The roof in two minutes. Nodding to show she'd understood, she wrung out the last of the towels and stacked it next to the others on the wooden draining board.

'Where do you think you're going?' Mrs Harvey shouted from the office as she stepped into the corridor.

'Just . . . upstairs,' Kate mumbled, panic-stricken at being caught out.

'In that apron?'

Kate looked down at her dirty apron, sighed and changed direction. Running down the corridor to the bedroom she shared with the others, she tore off the offending garment. Once inside, she pushed it into a bucket in the corner that held clothes soaking for the wash and rummaged through a pile of garments on a chair. The only clean apron was creased. Grabbing it, she darted back into the scullery.

'Kate?' Lark rested her chin on the pile of linen she was carrying. 'Mrs Harvey told me to put all this away. What goes on what shelf?'

'I'll tell you later.'

'But Mrs Harvey was shouting.'

Kate doubled back. 'Come on then, quick as you can. I can't spare you more than a couple of minutes.'

Five minutes later she finally reached the scullery. Having grabbed one of the irons resting on the hearth, she opened the hotplate and slammed it on the range. She was still tying the bow when she reached the service door at the end of the corridor.

'I thought you'd changed your mind,' Stephen said when she finally emerged on to the roof.

'Sorry, I had to stop and—' She suddenly realised that he wouldn't understand what she'd been through to steal a couple of minutes. How could he when his idea of work was managing a club for his uncle? 'It doesn't matter.' She smiled as she joined him close to the parapet. 'I'm here now.'

Half hoping to find Sarah, John stuck his head around the door of the living room to see Ruth sitting alone, lost deep in thought.

'Ah, wrong Mrs Bannerman.' Encouraged by her smile, he joined her. 'There's no one else around. The place is a ghost ship. Everything all right?'

She patted her burgeoning figure. 'Don't worry about this one. Children are like animals – they can survive anything.' She looked up at him. 'My mother died in childbirth. Died so that I might survive.'

'I didn't realise,' he murmured sympathetically.

'Not one of you knows anything about me. No one bothers to ask.'

'Marcus knows . . .?'

'Oh yes. That's why he pays for the best doctors. He's good with money.'

'But that was . . . what? Thirty years ago. They know so much more these days.'

'Quite the man of parts.' Isobel's strident voice filled the room as she brought a drink in for Ruth. 'Owner of this hotel with a doctorate of medicine to boot?'

'Just common sense, Mrs Crawford. There's little chance of Ruth being in the same danger.'

'I know how she thinks. I brought her up. Her father found so much business to occupy his time. It was understandable. He'd looked at his child, and she reminded him of that night. No matter, she had me. And I'm back at her side as that night comes round again. Full circle, Mr Bannerman.'

'Though a much happier occasion this time, God willing,' he said briskly, masking his uneasiness at Isobel's attitude beneath a veneer of confidence.

'Hotelier, doctor and now seer. God was willing to murder my daughter, sir. I pray he's done with this family, and smiles upon us now. But so few prayers are answered.' Handing Ruth the drink, she plumped up the cushions around her. 'She needs her sleep. Good night.'

'Good night.' John hesitated at the door. Isobel's back was turned to him, and Ruth gave him a pleading, disturbing look. She was asking for his help. He knew that much. What he didn't know was what he could do.

'Just when you are free in the evenings, I start work. And we're keeping the club open all night,' Stephen explained to Kate. 'Once the drinkers have moved on, the card sharks arrive.'

'Isn't that against the law?'

'Marcus pulled strings with the council.'

'Blimey, the circles you move in.'

'If we're closing at four, five in the morning, what time do you start work? Six? Let's say half past five, here? No one would see us.'

'Don't see the need, though. You've told me most of it.'

'I *haven't*. Not the important stuff. You *have* to see the club, Kate. And it's got rooms above. They're empty, haven't been used in years, but they could be cleaned up.'

'Oh, that's it. You want me cleaning?'

'No. They're perfect for someone to live in.'

'You moving out?'

'I could. *We* could.'

'Don't talk daft.'

'It's only impossible in *this* place. So, we leave. Start again. And you won't be lady of the manor. It's not that smart. It's just a club, but the life that goes with it, Kate, we could never find that here.'

She smiled, excited by the vista of opportunities he was opening up to her – but there was a part of her that couldn't believe what he was offering. No matter how much she wanted to.

'Listen, for all you know, I had me heart set on lady of the manor. Maybe it's not posh enough.'

'Then I'll make it posh.'

'You're all talk, aren't you? I'm not living with a bloke. Me mam would skin me.'

'Then marry me.'

Kate laughed nervously. 'You drinking again?'

'We could do anything. We could *be* anything. Outside the Grand. Completely different people.'

'I thought you liked me as I am.'

'There's always room for improvement.'

'You cheeky sod. You'll be late. Go on.'

'It sounds like I'm rushing things, but I've prepared all this. That's why I've been working so hard. This is what the club is for.' He glanced down at his wrist and realised his watch was still with Collins. 'Damn! What is the time? Look, tomorrow morning, half past five. Here?'

'All right, yes.'

He stared at her, knowing he should go, yet loath to leave her. Stepping forward, he finally kissed her, lightly, gently, and when she didn't object he gathered her into his arms and kissed her the way he'd wanted to for a long, long time.

'Harold, his name was,' Marcus continued, encouraged by Sarah's laughter. 'He became the best-known burglar in Manchester.'

'Somehow, Marcus, it doesn't surprise me. Even in school, you were consorting with criminals.'

'The story goes, I think it was 1910, there had been a burglary and the police came round, and asked his wife where he was. She said, "It's not him, he's in bed. He's done nothing wrong, why don't you leave him alone?" So they said, "Do you mind if we take a look?" When they went to the bedroom, there he was, lying there. They pulled the sheets back; he still had all his clothes on. Even his gloves.'

'You're making this up.'

'It's true.' Turning his back on Collins's disapproving face, he held his empty glass up to the barman.

Esme Harkness took the note from the duty clerk at the reception desk, read it and screwed it into a ball.

'It seems the gentleman has to cancel,' she complained to Mr Collins. 'If they only knew the effort I make for a night out. Still, the restaurant's waiting, and it's your night off. Yes, I know everything. You're not the only one to stand and watch.'

'Thank you, it's just not possible,' Collins apologised.

'Exactly, Mr Collins, that's the challenge.'

'Very kind of you, Miss Harkness. I'm sure you understand. I just can't.'

Shrugging her shoulders, she headed for the stairs.

Collins watched Marcus place his hand in the small of Sarah's back, as they left the bar for the restaurant.

'Miss Harkness?'

'Mr Collins?' She turned back from the stairs.

'Why not?' He dropped his voice to a whisper. 'I'll be changed in five minutes. It's best if we meet outside.'

Wondering what had caused his change of mind, Esme picked up her wrap; then she saw Marcus and Sarah through the open door of the dining room. And she understood.

Chapter Three

Jacob Collins scanned the restaurant, noticing the small things that might have escaped the attention of other diners. The cleanliness of the silverware, the degree of starch in the waiters' white cotton jackets, the freshness of the food . . . Miss Harkness certainly knew quality. He only wished he didn't have to pay for it.

'After all those years of service, your voice must carry some authority in the Grand. I've heard you bossing the staff around. You scare the life out of me, Mr Collins. So why can't you speak out about this problem, whatever it is?'

'The bearer of bad news. It's the messenger who gets put to the sword.'

'Very unlike you, to be so concerned with yourself. I'd hazard a guess that others might be at stake. Perhaps this problem of yours reaches the highest level of the Grand?'

'I really couldn't say.'

'You don't need to. Those who stand and watch . . .'

'Then, you might guess, the future of one man is at stake. One very good man.'

'Do you know this for a fact?'

'No . . . well . . . yes. I did once see the people concerned. Together. And even if nothing's happened since, then it will. I promise you that. I could speak up, I could . . .' His voice trailed in confusion. 'They walk past me with their smiles and their little looks, and it's beyond me. I don't understand any of it.'

'It's simple to understand. All the wrong people are with all the wrong people.'

Collins smiled wearily. 'Are they?'

'You know my advice. The single maxim of my job: keep the secrets and keep yourself safe. We're both servants. We should know our place.'

'But surely it's our duty to help?'

Esme sipped her wine and wondered just how far she could press her friendship with the concierge. Then she realised it wasn't just Collins she should be considering.

'The night before Monica's execution, I went to her cell. And I saw him. The man who paid for Monica's defence. That very good man.' She saw that Collins knew who that man was. 'I'd do anything to help John Bannerman, and because of that, I'm telling you now, stay quiet.' She pursed her lips in an attempt to keep emotion at bay. 'I tried to help Monica. Now I wish with all my heart I'd never spoken to her. Not once. I could have left her, an ordinary housemaid, happy in her ignorance. Today she's buried in prison grounds and I can't even visit her grave. All because I sat down with a young girl one day and imparted my wisdom. Don't interfere, Jacob, please.'

'Then I stand back? While he's made to look a fool?'

'He thinks she loves him, and that's enough. The illusion is enough.' She reached for his hand and squeezed it lightly. 'It's better than anything we've got, Jacob.'

Clive waited until Stephen was working alongside

him, before broaching the subject uppermost in his mind.

'So, I asked me dad, and he said, "You daft beggar, course you should." So yes, after thinking about it, sir, I'd like the job. Very much.'

'Right.' Looking around, Stephen saw that they were busy, but not so busy that he couldn't take five minutes to speak to Clive. 'Come into the office for a moment, would you please?' Closing the door, he faced the barman. 'There's been a mistake. I don't think it's right to take staff away from the Grand. Not this early. We've only just set up the club. So I'm asking Jim to run the bar. We'll review the situation in six months. See how it goes.'

'So you changed your mind but left me to think about it until now?'

'I've had a thousand things to do.'

'Of course you have,' Clive agreed coldly. 'It's all right, sir. Just a favour, wasn't it? And favours don't mean much, not to lads of my background.'

'You can still work here on your evenings off.'

'Oh yes, sir. I'll do that, sir. Anything to earn an extra penny off me masters. Excuse me, sir.'

Stephen stared at the papers on the desk as Clive left. It hadn't been that difficult to turn himself into a businessman. Not difficult at all.

Mrs Harvey stepped cautiously into the foyer. After checking that there were no guests around, she headed for the office. She'd just rammed the domestic receipts for the day on to the spike for John Bannerman's attention, when the front door opened. She stood in the darkness, staring in disbelief as Mr Collins escorted Esme Harkness inside.

Moving behind the office door, she eavesdropped

as they walked into the foyer.

'We should do this again,' Esme suggested lightly.

'Perhaps somewhere less expensive.'

'I did offer . . .'

'The times might be changing, but not that fast,' Mr Collins said firmly. 'And the things I told you, I trust . . .'

'You don't have to ask.'

Esme held out her hand. The concierge kissed it, before they went their separate ways, Collins to his room in the basement, Esme to her suite.

A prostitute! Mrs Harvey felt nauseated. A common prostitute. How could a man in Jacob Collins's position even think of being seen in her company?

Kate studied the narrow strip of window at ceiling level in the basement. A soft, grey light filtered through the darkness. The first tentative rays rested on the sleeping figure of Lark, before reaching Lynne and then Brenda. Holding her breath, she lifted her head from the pillow. She was aching from stale excitement and a sleepless night, and she found it an effort to drag herself out of bed. Gathering her uniform from the chair, she tiptoed to the door. She didn't dare to make a noise that would alert the girls, so she'd have to wash and change in the scullery, but it would be worth it. After all, hadn't he asked her to marry him?

She saw the time as she looked through the locked door of Mrs Harvey's office. Twenty to six. Horrified by the prospect of missing a second with Stephen, she turned on the tap and pulled off her nightdress.

The town clock was striking the quarter-hour as she ran on to the roof. It was empty. She still had time to tidy herself. She straightened her cap and apron and buttoned her cuffs. Then she went to the parapet and looked down. Below her, the rattle of a milk cart told her the city was beginning to wake up. Any minute now . . .

Stephen stared grimly at the mess in the Manhattan. Half-full glasses and empty bottles were strewn everywhere. Puddles of alcohol had set stickily, gluing overflowing ashtrays to the tables. He'd just shouted to Jim to get a move on and give him a hand to clear up when Marcus strolled in with three men in tow. Stephen recognised one as the police sergeant who'd raided the club.

'Still open?' Marcus whistled in surprise. 'What an investment. Stephen, we'll start with brandy, the select, and some coffee, soon as you can. This is the precise and best time for a game of poker. This lot's half asleep.'

'Don't bank on it.' The sergeant turned to Stephen. 'Hello, again.'

'Jim can serve you,' Stephen said. 'I'm just going.'

'No, Jim,' Marcus ordered. 'Run down Deansgate and get us some breakfast. Oh, and here it is.' Marcus produced a key, glancing at Stephen as he handed it to Jim. 'I told Jim he could have the rooms above this place. It will be good for security.'

'Breakfast coming up.' Jim ran out through the door.

'I hope the back room's cleared.'

'It is,' Stephen said sharply, angry that Marcus had put paid to his plans.

'Come on then, let's have some service.' Marcus snapped his fingers. Stephen read the clock. Quarter to six. He reached for the brandy bottle. There was no point in trying; he would never make it now anyway.

Kate waited on the roof until the town clock struck

the hour. Feeling sick and miserable to the pit of her stomach, she turned and retraced her steps down the servants' staircase to the basement. Back where she belonged.

'Marcus?' John had been talking to Collins in the reception area, but now he waylaid his brother as he walked into the hotel at nine, still in his evening dress. 'Mrs Crawford might be here to help Ruth, but she seems to be doing the opposite. Perhaps you could stop cavorting around Manchester for one night, and pay some attention to your wife.'

'That's rich, coming from you.' Brushing past his brother, Marcus headed for the stairs.

John grabbed his lapels. 'What exactly does that mean?'

'Do you mind?' Marcus pushed John's hand away. Seeing fury mirrored in his brother's eyes, he murmured, 'Nothing.'

John continued to stare. Marcus was the first to look away.

'I'll speak to Ruth. Thank you, John.'

Collins breathed again, grateful that this time at least, there would be no confrontation between the brothers. Then he caught sight of Mrs Harvey in the office, talking to Sarah.

Tired, dishevelled, feeling in desperate need of a bath and sleep, Stephen raced along the hotel corridors looking for the maids. Hearing voices, he slowed his step.

'It's true. Tell them, Brenda,' Lynne shouted as she heaved a pile of clean linen into a bedroom. 'She went to Mr Harbendale's tea dance. We should have fifteen of those towels. Count them again,' she ordered Lark, who was sorting through bath towels. 'And Mr Harbendale himself asked her for a spin.'

'He was being kind, that's all,' Brenda said, hoping for a contradiction.

'Kind or blind,' Lynne declared. 'One of the two. It's not real, that leg of his. It's tin. I ran me hand up it once.'

Disappointed that Kate wasn't with them, Stephen glanced at his wrist, before remembering that his watch was still with Collins. He headed for the stairs just as Kate left Esme Harkness's room.

'Kate,' Lark ventured shyly. 'I didn't like to ask Lynne. When the guest leaves out money, that's a tip, isn't it? But we don't take it, do we? We hand it in, and it's shared out at the end of the week, isn't it?'

'What are you asking me for, if you already know the answer?' Kate snapped irritably. 'Do us a favour and think for yourself. I'm not your mother. Now bag that lot. Hurry up.' Dumping the laundry on the trainee, she returned to Miss Harkness's room. Lark did as she'd been told, then sneaked into the room with the jewellery box. It was still on the dressing table. Only this time it was closed.

John and Sarah faced Mrs Harvey and Mr Collins across the office. The tension heightened as the concierge looked from the housekeeper to John.

'Personally, I have to say I've found Miss Harkness quite decent in her manner,' Mrs Harvey conceded. 'But that doesn't alter what she is. Let's say the word. A prostitute. And it would be a shame, a very great shame, Mr Collins, to have your good name attached to hers.'

'And this hotel is suddenly so large, you've forgotten where my room is, Mrs Harvey? You couldn't have a word with me in private?'

'Well, perhaps I should have, yes,' Mrs Harvey admitted hesitantly.

'All right.' John looked from the concierge to the housekeeper. 'Let's calm down. Mrs Harvey does have a point. You're the hall porter, Jacob, the most important man in this hotel. Out there, in public you *are* the Grand. And to be seen with Miss Harkness, well . . . if the invitation comes again, I think it's best to refuse.'

'Very good, sir.' Collins agreed coldly. 'It won't happen again. And I'm sorry if I've done anything to dishonour you.'

'Oh, I don't think it's gone that far.'

'Mrs Bannerman?' Collins looked to Sarah. 'What do you think of my actions?'

'It's something and nothing,' she said, trying to sound as though she didn't care either way. 'Let's not dwell on it.'

'But you think I did the wrong thing?'

'Now come on, it happened, it's over.' John rose to his feet. 'Let's get back to work.'

'Very good, sir.' Collins left for the foyer and his customary position.

'Thank you, sir. Sorry to cause such a fuss,' Mrs Harvey apologised as she went to the door.

John returned to work, but not Sarah. Sitting back in her chair, she watched Collins for a moment before picking up a stack of files and following him.

'Mr Collins?' conscious of the people around them, she kept her voice, low. 'I hope we don't—'

'I've known Marcus Bannerman far longer than you ma'am,' he interrupted bluntly. 'I know his strategies and his intentions all too well. You don't know what you're doing.'

'And I suggest, Mr Collins, that your head has been turned by a member of the opposite sex. Perhaps that's exciting. And perhaps you're seeing that excitement in others where it doesn't exist. I'm not doing anything. I *know* that. I know it for a fact. And I won't be *told* what to do, not by him, and certainly not by you.'

'You could find a better doctor, Marcus, someone less provincial,' Isobel criticised as he joined her and Ruth in the Reading Room for tea.

'Fine, just give me the name,' Marcus said agreeably.

'It will cost.'

'We can share the expense. Thank you.' He took the sugar bowl she handed him.

'Though the best doctor in the land can only pray for luck.'

'Then I'll pray,' he said. 'I think I remember how it's done.'

'I prayed before. It didn't work.'

'As it's a long time since he's heard from me, he might sit up and pay attention.'

'You seem to find this amusing,' Isobel remarked, lifting her teacup to her lips.

'You seem to find it terrifying. It's a pregnancy. The most natural thing in the world.'

'Not in the history of my family.'

'Well, Ruth's my family now.'

'God help her.' Isobel pushed her face close to Marcus's. 'I was in that room thirty years ago.'

'*So*?' he enquired caustically. 'You saw one disaster, just one, and it's blinded you—'

'Blind, am I? Blind to what she did? I saw it, better than anyone. The baby, they all said. Oh the *baby*. As though we should worship her as she clawed her way into the world, hands full of blood.'

'You're talking as though Ruth killed her mother.'

'I did.' Ruth spoke so quietly Marcus couldn't be sure he'd heard her correctly. Then he looked at Isobel and saw her eyes glittering.

'You've . . . I beg your pardon? Is this what you've told her, Isobel?'

'They wiped this one clean as they pulled the sheets over the victim. She'd done her job. There was a choice. At the vital moment, a choice, mother or child. But who made that choice? To whom did the doctor turn? The husband. The man who'd known my daughter a scant three years. If the choice had been *mine* . . .'

Marcus clenched and unclenched his fists. He had never wanted to punch a woman until now. But Ruth sat beside him, white-faced, trembling. He didn't dare risk upsetting her any more than she was already. Rising, he took hold of his wife gently by the arm.

'Ruth, with me. You're not listening to one more word of this. Come with me. Come with me right now. On your feet. *Come with me,*' he reiterated, raising his voice when he realised she wasn't listening to him.

She moved slowly, awkwardly, like a puppet with broken strings, as he helped her to the door.

'God almighty, Ruth, I'll do whatever you want,' he hissed as they reached the foyer. 'I'll send her away. Is that what you want? I'll get rid of her.'

'Don't, Marcus.' Ruth turned a tear-stained face to his. 'It was my fault. She saw it happen. She . . .' Slipping from his grasp she ran up the stairs. He stood and watched her go. Then he glanced back at Isobel, calmly sipping tea in the Reading Room as though nothing had happened. For the first time in his life, he felt utterly powerless. Beaten by one old woman.

Clive heard a noise as he walked past the storage room. Doubling back, he opened the door. Lark was sitting on the floor, sobbing as though the world was coming to an end.

'Oi.' He crouched down beside her. 'What you doing here, little one?'

Still crying she held out her hand.

Staring in horror at the sapphire and diamond brooch nestled in her pink palm, Clive leapt to his feet. Leaving Lark crouched on the floor he ran down to the scullery where Kate was scrubbing out a bucket.

'What the hell has happened to you?'

'You what?'

'Come and do your job.'

Mystified, she followed him to the storeroom where Lark was still sobbing and still clutching the brooch.

'Only gone and nicked it.'

'Oh my God!' Kate covered her mouth with her hands.

'Room forty-nine, the Dansons. They've gone to the races. They'll be out all day, so we can put it back.'

'I'm sorry,' Lark wailed.

Kate knelt beside her and took the brooch.

'I'll keep a lookout.' Clive half closed the door.

'Oh, sweetheart, what were you thinking?' Kate asked.

'I'm not a thief.'

'If you were, you'd be sacked. Come here, Lark Rothery.' Kate hugged the girl. 'You daft thing.'

'It was just sitting there. If me mother had this she could buy a house. It's not for me. Me mam was in the draw club at the corner shop, but the bloke ran off with every penny. And there's nothing left. She's got newspaper on the windows and everything. If she just had one piece of this, one tiny little piece.'

'But she can't,' Kate said gently.

'I know. Am I going to be arrested?'

'No, you're not, because they won't ever know. I won't report you. You know whose fault this is?'

'I'm sorry.' Lark began to sob again.

'It's mine. You're in my charge. I'm supposed to look after you, every hour of every day. So, I'm the stupid one.'

'Head in the clouds,' Clive said from the door, 'or did Stephen Bannerman need owt?'

Taking Clive's reprimand to heart, Kate hugged Lark again.

'I'm here now. Here to stay. Clouds are gone. Look, blown away, just you and me left. You're not the first girl to go wrong, sweetheart, but I'll look after you this time. I promise.'

Mr Collins knocked on Esme's door and waited. She opened it, and smiled.

'Come in.'

'I won't if you don't mind, Miss Harkness. John Bannerman has asked that we don't . . . associate. Perhaps he's right. A moment's madness.'

'I don't think so. Did you discuss anything else?'

'Not with him,' he said awkwardly. 'I can't.'

'Cowardice?'

'I'm sorry . . .'

'No, and now you know that men can be cowards through decency, and the best of intentions.' Hesitating, she broadened her smile. 'They actually saw us as a couple?' She laughed softly, making him laugh too. 'All the wrong people, Jacob.'

'Good day, Miss Harkness.'

'It's funny. I've devoted my life to gentlemen, when all the time the real gentlemen were serving my drinks and taking my messages. And I never even noticed.'

Marcus strode purposefully into Ruth's bedroom.

'We can stop this nonsense with the bedrooms. If Grendel's mother doesn't like it . . .' He fell silent as he noticed her dressing table. Ruth had laid out a glass of water and pills. More than he would have thought a single bottle could hold.

'I've often thought it would suit you,' Ruth murmured. 'Winning a child by losing a wife. We're the perfect couple.'

Sweeping his arm across the surface, he sent the pills scattering over the floor. He threw the glass against the wall. It shattered, shards and splinters bouncing back over the carpet towards their feet.

'Christ, but you're stupid,' he snapped.

'Stupid being here, with you. Every day of my life she told me that I'm only on this earth because I killed someone. I moved away as soon as I was old enough. But I found the same thing all over again.'

'A man who would keep on punishing you?'

'A husband. So I could change my name, so I could have a new name. But it *is* just a name.'

He tried to hold her, but she pulled back.

'If you *dare*. If you try to hurt him . . .' He touched her stomach tenderly. 'He's the most precious thing in my life.'

'Oh yes, not me, *this* thing. It will kill me. She said so.'

'Then she will never speak to you again.' There was a cold finality in his words that chilled even more than her grandmother's presence.

* * *

48

The Grand II: The Roaring Twenties

Marcus stood beside Collins in the foyer. Heaped at his feet were leather-bound trunks, hatboxes, and a jewellery case. Every time the door opened, he looked up. She appeared eventually but not until an hour after the shops had closed.

'Mrs Crawford.'

'Mr Bannerman.' She stared at the boxes as she returned his greeting. 'Those are my things.'

'You noticed?'

'And the meaning of this?'

'You're leaving.'

'Not possible, sir. If the troubles to come are as great as we fear . . .' Her eyes widened, as Marcus picked up the case closest to him and flung it across the foyer. It fell against the door, cracking the stained-glass panel. But the damage didn't stop him from reaching for another case and another and another . . .

'You're leaving and you're leaving *now*. You can go back to hell and sit with the corpse of your daughter, and don't you ever, *ever*, talk to my wife again for as long as you live.' Oblivious to the stares of staff and guests, he tossed the last suitcase towards her.

'I recognise you now, sir. Just the husband for her.'

'*Not one more word!*'

John and Sarah walked out of the office and surveyed the wreckage. Seizing the opportunity, Isobel looked to John.

'Mr Bannerman?' she whispered hoarsely.

John saw his brother, white-faced, shaking in rage and nodded briefly, 'Good day, Mrs Crawford.'

'Well, Marcus, I'll go,' Isobel said at last. 'Satisfied that you finally know your wife. That she was born in blood and darkness and she'll bring you down, sir. Nothing good can come of her or the pig in her belly . . .'

49

She didn't say another word. Striding towards her, Marcus slammed the back of his hand across her face.

'Marcus!' John shouted.

Isobel fell weakly against the wall, sobbing. Suddenly John saw her for what she was. A bitter, broken, feeble old woman. She looked mutely from him to Sarah, then she glanced at the stairs. Turning, John saw Ruth standing there.

Isobel backed towards the door and left. It was all Collins had been waiting for. Gesturing to the footman on duty, he pointed to the broken cases and mess of glass and clothes.

'Come on,' he ordered succinctly.

'Let's clean this up.' John said, stepping forward.

Sarah looked to Marcus. He was watching Ruth. The only thing left for her to do was help her husband.

Stephen wondered if he'd ever get used to working nights as he left his bed at dusk and wearily pulled on his dressing gown. A brisk knock was swiftly followed by Kate, carrying the inevitable bundle of towels.

'At last.' Stephen smiled. 'Don't mind me.'

'It's all right. I can't stop.'

'I'm sorry I didn't make it. I couldn't get away. Have you thought about what I said?'

'Oh that, yes. Nice little dream, then I woke up and there were floors that needed scrubbing. So it's back to normal.'

'But it's not. It can be different. I mean it – well, actually there's a problem with the rooms . . .'

'Here we go.'

'Just give me a few days . . .'

'Stephen, when you came back from the war, you were falling apart. It's all back together, now, and I'm that proud of you. You've turned into a proper toff. And I'm that busy. It's really wasting time, all this.'

'But last night . . .'

'Well, I kissed you, so what? Who wouldn't, handsome lad like you? I told the girls. They're all laughing, mad jealous they are. Had to take me chance – they were nagging. Once in a lifetime. Then it's back to normal.'

'Look if this is because I missed one meeting, I'm sorry. I did try . . .'

'I tried an' all, Stephen. You lot, you've no idea. We don't have watches down there, we don't have clocks. I was up all night listening for the town hall clock. I'm not doing that again.'

'Kate, I need . . . this. I need you. Maybe it looks like I'm having the time of my life – I *know* it looks like that, because I'm trying so bloody hard. But it's as thin as ice.'

'Clive said you weren't up to it.'

He finally rounded on her, matching her icy tone. 'What makes *him* so clever? He's just a barman.'

'It doesn't matter. Go back to the old ways, sloping about, drinking. Then you'll need me again. I quite liked all that charity work.'

'No, I won't need you for that.'

'Then you don't need me at all, sir. Excuse me, I have to go.'

Kate headed downstairs and sought sanctuary in her bedroom. Feeling more miserable than she would have thought possible, she wrenched the cap from her head and sat on the edge of her bed. But her peace was short-lived. The door burst open and Lynne, Brenda and Lark tumbled in.

'Mrs Harvey – do you know what she is?' Lynne asked Lark. 'She's a Red Indian.'

'Here, I nicked a scone, have it.' Brenda tossed it across to Lark.

'Red Indians, when they've got a prisoner, they don't tie them up with rope. They slit them open, pull their guts out and tie their guts around their ankles. That's true, that is.'

Hiding her tears, Kate laughed with the rest of the girls.

'Harvey would do the same to us,' Lynne declared with mock gravity, 'then fry the guts for dinner.'

Stephen walked down the stairs. Glancing into the bar and seeing it empty of customers – and, more important, family – he stepped inside. Clive was serving. Without looking at him, Stephen ordered whisky. Clive poured it without comment. Stephen picked up the glass and knocked the spirit back in one. His first drink in months, and it felt bloody marvellous.

Stephen picked up his coat and returned to the foyer.

'Sir?' Collins handed him his watch.

'Thank you.' He strapped it to his wrist. 'Everything back to normal, Jacob.' Pushing the doors open, he stepped out into the darkened street.

Chapter Four

The audience in the music hall was noisy and restless and the younger staff of the Grand, who'd commandeered the first two rows of the stalls, were making as much noise as the rest.

'New acts,' Lynne jeered. 'New acts my eye. I saw this lot at Easter. They were rubbish then. They drug them balancing dogs, I was told.'

'You liked that comedian.'

'Ah, but I wasn't laughing at him, Lark. I was laughing with him.'

'Wrong way round,' Kate corrected.

'All them cracks about Lloyd George. I hate it when they do politics.' Brenda wrinkled her nose to emphasise her irritation.

'We're better off at the picture house. I wanted to go to the picture house, but would you lot have it? No. And that chanteuse, Miss Lily Farris, star in Paris indeed? She's been no further than Sheffield. I know, me mam said.' Lynne rummaged in the depths of a bag of boiled sweets in search of sherbet lemons.

'Who's going to do it?' Kate asked Clive. 'You or me?'

'Do what?'

'Kill her.' Kate pointed at Lynne.

* * *

'I won't be late.' Sarah crossed the crowded foyer of the Grand, to reception where John was checking the room occupancy. Marcus and Ruth followed a few paces behind.

'It's becoming quite a regular event,' John commented, 'you and Marcus. I mean the club's opening night, that's expected, but it's been twice a week ever since.'

'I think Stephen needs our support. And Marcus can hardly take an expectant wife. Besides, it keeps Ruth happy if there's someone to keep an eye on him.' She cast an eye towards her brother-in-law. 'And you said today that you need to catch up on the paperwork.'

Deliberately avoiding her gaze, John pretended to study the register. 'I see. That's Stephen, Ruth, Marcus and me. It's for all our sakes. How very selfless.'

'I won't be late.' Marcus unconsciously echoed Sarah's words as he said goodbye to Ruth.

'Take as long as you like. We'll sit here and incubate. And that's the benefit of separate bedrooms. I don't have to be woken up by you smelling of cigarette smoke. Both of you,' she added as Sarah joined them.

'Sir,' Collins interrupted. 'The car's out front.'

Sarah and Marcus passed Esme Harkness. She watched them climb into the car before addressing the concierge.

'Mr Collins? Business as usual?'

He smiled grimly as he returned to his duties.

'You'll have to move on,' Jim warned the vagrant sheltering in the doorway of the Manhattan. He felt sorry for the man. Tramps of any age were pathetic, the ex-soldiers in their twenties the most pitiable, but he had only just got this job, and he couldn't afford to lose it out of misplaced sympathy for a down-and-out. 'We're opening. People will be arriving any minute.'

'I can help,' the man offered. 'Take their coats, anything. You don't have to pay me. I'll do it for tips.'

'Is there a problem?' Stephen stepped outside.

'It's all right, sir. Just a bit of trouble. I can handle it.'

Stephen stared at the itinerant. 'Reynolds . . . my God, William Reynolds?'

'Bannerman. You made it then.' Then he added, 'Obviously.'

'It's good to see you.' Stephen shook the man's hand. 'How are you?'

'Not so bad. Just on the way to the town hall for dinner with the mayor.'

Stephen laughed to hide his embarrassment. 'Yes, stupid question. Come through.'

'No, better get off, thanks all the same.'

'It's all right. I'm the manager. Jim, could you make some coffee? Unless you'd prefer something stronger, William?'

'I wouldn't mind a Scotch.'

'Two Scotches,' Stephen ordered Jim as he led the way to his office. 'It took a second to recognise you out of uniform.'

Jim shook his head as Stephen closed the door. Bloody bleeding hearts! Every demobbed soldier had worn one on his sleeve since the war. Bloody bleeding hearts!

'Ladies and gentlemen!' Harry Frindel's voice boomed through the auditorium, commanding attention from even the most disinterested of the audience.

Katherine Hardy

Kate stared at him, wondering how anyone so fat could fit in the master of ceremonies' box.

'John Jericho, the juggling jester, for your delight and delectation.' He waved his arm expansively at the stage behind him. 'I thank you for showing your appreciation. Now, ladies and gentlemen, there will commence an illuminating interval of twenty minutes. The bars are open at the back, with meat pies on sale in the foyer. Satisfy and satiate your stomachs for a simple sixpence. Thanking you . . .'

'Ooh, I'll have a pie,' Brenda cried.

'Owing to the vagaries of the railways,' Frindel boomed on, 'the Amazing Amarettes, the luscious lady log-jugglers from Leicester, won't be joining us. They are stuck in a siding outside Sandbach. So the second act will commence with the famous and fêted Harry's Half-Hour, presided over by my good self, Harry Frindel, you're hamiable host.'

'Oh, amateurs now,' Lynne bawled out at the top of her voice.

'Harry's Half-Hour hintroduces the men and maidens of Manchester – amateurs perhaps, but local lads and ladies with glamour and gold dust in their eyes. Tonight could see the birth of a new star in heaven. That's in twenty minutes, thank you very much indeed. Pies for sixpence, hot chicken for a shilling.'

'I should go up there and show them.' Lynne didn't bother to join in the trickle of applause that marked Harry's exit. 'I'm better than anything we've had so far.'

'Oh, and what's your act? Walk on stage and nag for twenty minutes?'

'I'll have you know I can sing, Kate Morris. You've heard my singing. It's better than Miss Lily Farris any day. If I was locked up in a box and dumped at the bottom of the Atlantic Ocean, I'd still sound better.'

The Grand II: The Roaring Twenties

'I liked her,' Lark murmured.

Kate left her seat. 'I've had enough of this. Clive, get the pies in. You' – she jerked her head at Lynne – 'get your coat.'

'What for?'

'Harry's Half-Hour. You're on. Think you can do better? Prove it.'

Marcus shrugged off his coat as he and Sarah walked into the Manhattan. Handing it to Jim, he nodded approvingly as he looked around. The place was already half full, two hours before he'd expected any real custom.

'Evening, sir.' Jim ran his hands lightly over the cashmere cloth.

'Where's Stephen?'

'He's busy right now, Mr Bannerman. Bottle of the usual?'

'At the table please, Jim.'

'Good evening, Mrs Bannerman. It's good to see you.' Jim took Sarah's wrap. 'You're becoming a bit of a regular.'

Sarah glared at him, but the look was lost. He was already on his way to the cloakroom.

'Must have been hard, in the trenches, or so everyone says. I tell them it's hard now.' William twirled his empty glass on Stephen's desk.

'Yes, they all say that. They don't know the half of it.'

'That time they broke through the lines . . .' William's eyes clouded as his mind retreated into that other, horror-struck world.

Stephen laughed. It was the only way he could cope with the memory.

'We bloody ran.' William's laughter joined Stephen's.

'Never run so fast in my life.'

'Everyone running.' William's laughter heightened to hysteria.

'Remember that bloke, shouting? What was his name, Wilson?'

'Tom Wilson.'

'Shouting Chocolate, my bloody chocolate!– They were slaughtering us, and he'd left his chocolate.' William sat back in his chair. 'They taught us to handle a gun, and that was it. Not much use in cities.'

'I suppose I was lucky.'

'Oh, right.' William looked around the office. 'This is luck, is it?'

'Yes. My uncle owns this place. He gave me a job.'

'That's not luck, Stephen. That's money.'

'Yes, but up until then I'd wasted months, not knowing what to do. I started drinking and then . . . You know what it's like. Just . . . lost.'

'So where did you live until this cropped up?'

'The Grand Hotel. My father owns it, it's the family home. I know.' He gave a deprecating smile. 'Heartbreaking, isn't it?'

'Don't apologise – if you've a good background and connections, use them. I would. In uniform we all looked the same. Couldn't see what your mates had waiting back home.'

'Stephen,' Marcus said, opening the door. 'Jim's running the place single-handed.' He looked at William. 'Who is this?'

'William Reynolds, Marcus Bannerman, my uncle. William and I served together.'

Marcus shook William's hand with the respect he accorded all ex-soldiers. But his respect didn't stop him from frowning at William's filthy clothes.

'It's a pleasure, but could you two swap tales of army life some other time?'

'No . . .' Stephen thought rapidly. 'I was . . . interviewing him. We need extra staff, Marcus, someone to bottle up, lend a hand. Will, you can start tonight.'

'Very well. On your head be it. If you could *both* get to work, please.'

'Stephen it's very kind,' William demurred. 'But look at the state of me for God's sake.'

'Jim's got the rooms above. You can have a bath. He's got a spare jacket. Why not?'

'If you're sure . . .' William looked doubtfully from Stephen to Marcus.

'Welcome aboard.' Stephen sealed his offer with a handshake.

Harry Frindel's office looked as though it hadn't been cleaned since the day the theatre had been built. The wall was covered with layer upon layer of theatrical posters and signed photographs of artistes, some well known, most not. The desk was an island of waste paper in a sea of discarded props. A pile of puppets flopped to the right of the door, and balancing precariously behind them was a three-foot, gold-painted hand with an open palm, a long pole jammed into the severed wrist.

'Enter,' Harry shouted in respond to a knock. Kate marched in, pulling Lynne behind her. 'Give us a minute.' He didn't even look up.

'That's handy,' Kate giggled as she pointed out the hand to Lynne.

Frindel smiled, pleased to have his treasure noticed. 'The hand of the heathen god.'

'Oh, aye?' Kate queried disbelievingly.

'Swansea Empire, 1885. The world premiere of *Thus Spake Zarathustra*. Miss Mary Malone in the role of hapless young virgin, tied to the altar by tribesmen from the Dark Continent, as sacrifice to the fiery, vengeful one. And the hand of the heathen god came on from the prompt side, to pluck the poor girl away to some foul nirvana. Operated by my good self, Harry Frindel esquire. First job in the theatre, never looked back since. Now, what's it to be? Chorus? Any experience?'

'We're here for Harry's Half-Hour.'

'You missed it. Come back next week.'

'Oh but Mr Frindel, *you'll* miss it, if you turn down the chance of seeing Miss Lynne Milligan on stage.'

'It's starting in five minutes. Get out.'

'She'll be snapped up,' Kate assured him solemnly. 'I'm warning you. Mr Joseph Cattering of the opera house, Streatham, has been begging, *begging* her to appear.'

'And how would you know Joe Cattering?'

'I stayed with him in the Grand Hotel,' Kate lied.

'I thought Joe was into boys.'

'I'm very boyish,' Kate retorted.

'What does she do?' He looked Lynne up and down with a lecherous eye.

'She's a lady log-juggler.'

'I can sing.' Lynne glared angrily at Kate.

'You've got cheek, I'll give you that. Well they're all rubbish, so you'll fit in. I'll put you on number six. Five minutes, not a second longer. There's no payment. If you're dying, I'll pull you off. If you're blue, I'll chuck you out. See the bandleader about sheet music, third door down, or more likely he's propping up the bar. Now stop wasting my time. Get out.'

'Thanks.' Kate backed towards the door pulling

Lynne with her. 'Thanks ever so much.'

'I'll kill you,' Lynne threatened as soon as **they** reached the corridor.

'I'll die laughing first,' Kate grinned.

William shifted crates and filled shelves behind the bar of the Manhattan, but, no matter how quickly he worked, it wasn't quick enough for Jim, who was rushed off his feet serving the customers up front.

'That's a little extra.' The club's most lavish spender, Thornton, slapped a note on the counter in front of Jim. 'It's to ensure good service. Should keep your family fed for another week, eh?' he smirked patronisingly.

Jim pocketed the money, then glared at William, who was staring at Thornton, or, to be more precise his bulging, open wallet.

'Must be difficult, William.'

'What?'

'Losing the use of your legs at your age. Those glasses aren't like pigeons – they don't bring themselves home.'

'You told me to wash these . . .'

'Wash them and collect those, and clear the tables. Move a bit faster can't you? My granddad's quicker on his feet, and he's dead.'

Stephen glanced at the two men as he went to Marcus's table. He'd no sooner reached it than there was an almighty crash behind the bar.

'Yes he's very good. I'm so impressed.'

'Give him time, Marcus.' Stephen smiled at his mother. 'Enjoying yourself?'

'Very much.'

'This has become your regular table.'

'Oh for God's sake, Stephen! I've spent twenty years

sitting inside the Grand every single night until I became part of the woodwork. Excuse me while I try something a little different. Do you find that so alarming? Or do you think I'm missing out on something utterly scintillating back home? Come on, Marcus. Let's dance.'

Bewildered by his mother's anger Stephen returned to the bar to help William clear up the mess of broken glass.

When the band stopped playing and couples separated to applaud the musicians, Marcus clung to Sarah's hand.

'Don't I get a reward?'

'Count yourself lucky I don't slap you across the face.' Sarah pulled her hand away. 'Your manners go back to Mr Darwin's apes. Swing down and haul the nearest female up a tree.'

'I see. Is that what you'd like?'

'You'd have a fight on your hands.'

'Better and better.'

'Oh shut up.' Sarah couldn't help laughing.

'I lost it,' Marcus confessed mockingly. 'All my appeal. This must be middle age. I can't steal a single kiss.'

'You certainly can't.'

'Not even if the situation demands it?'

'I can't imagine what situation that might be.'

'Neither can I.' He gave her a predatory smile. 'Yet.'

The clock ticked heavily into the silence in the Bannermans' living room as John pored over the account ledgers set on the table in front of him.

'Good night.' Ruth left her seat and went to the door.

'Good night, sleep well.' He gave her a smile, before

returning to the columns of figures. Running his finger down the list, he began to make notes.

Lynne broke into a cold sweat as she stood in the wings, watching, as a young boy with enough spots on his face for the entire adolescent population of Manchester collected a range of boos and hisses from the audience.

'Lost your friend?' Frindel appeared at her side.

'She's no friend of mine.'

'Limber up, girl, you're on next.'

'What's she singing?' Lark asked excitedly as Kate rejoined the others in the stalls.

'"After the Ball".'

'Bit mournful, isn't it?' Clive asked.

'It was the only one in the sheet music she knew.'

'You just watch. I bet she goes down a treat,' Fred enthused.

'Her and the *Titanic*, yeah,' Kate laughed.

'I think that meat pie was bad.' Brenda moaned.

They looked up as the boy took a last bow, desperately trying to pretend that heckling was a substitute for applause.

'Thank you, thank you, that was Whammy Wilfred, the wonder warbler from Wooton. Now, ladies and gentlemen, stay sedentary for sundry sensational singing skills, as I bring you the noxious new nightingale of the northwest.' He looked to the wings, where his scene dresser was pushing a terrified Lynne on stage.

'Introducing, the lovely, lovelorn larynx of little Lynne.'

Tears of laughter coursed down Clive's cheeks. 'What *is* she wearing?'

'They had this skip full of old clothes. It was that,

or the back end of a horse,' Kate gasped, in between howls of laughter.

'Hush,' Fred hissed, poised on the edge of his seat.

The band tuned up while Lynne stood centre stage, clearly petrified.

'Get on with it,' a heckler yelled down from the circle.

It was the spur Lynne needed to find her voice. She began to sing, softly, tentatively. Her voice carried, not loud enough for most of the audience, but to Kate's astonishment, it was actually all right.

'She's not bad,' Clive whispered.

'She's too quiet,' Kate contradicted.

'Come on love, show us your legs,' the heckler shouted from the gods.

Valiantly ignoring him, Lynne managed to miss only a word or two of the song.

'Clive, tell him.' Kate dug her elbow into the barman's ribs.

'It'll only make it worse.'

'Oh my God, this is all my fault.' Kate turned, hoping to stare the heckler into silence.

'My dog can sing better,' the man shouted.

'Oi,' Lynne quipped back. 'Leave your wife out of this.'

The audience cheered.

'Watch your lip you cheeky tart!'

Forgetting her song Lynne addressed the crowd. 'Expert in tarts is he? Only way he'd get a woman.' Encouraged by a few cheers and a smattering of applause, she continued. 'You watch your lip, old buster, or I'll be up there to smack you one.'

A cheer rocked the auditorium.

'I'd like to see you try,' came the angry reply from the circle.

'And I'd like to see you dead.' Lynne looked down at the band. 'Oh give up, you're wasting your strings.' She headed for the wings as the orchestra ground to a halt.

'Lynne, give us "I Don't Want to Play in Your Yard".'

'You what?'

'"I Don't Want to Play in Your Yard",' Fred repeated.

She looked down into the orchestra pit. 'Do you know it?'

'Get rid of her,' the heckler screamed.

'Shut your gob, or I'll see you outside, mate!' Fred threatened.

'Nice and fast,' Lynne directed the bandleader, 'give it a bit of oomph.'

Straightening her back, she stared out into the darkened theatre. 'Right, sing along. I'm not doing this on me own!' Lynne thumped out the lyrics. Within minutes she was waving her arms, dancing across the stage, carrying the entire audience with her.

Kate sat back in her seat shaking her head. 'I just don't believe it.'

Frindel was waiting when Lynne finally had to relinquish the spotlight to another amateur.

'If you come by tomorrow night, I might find you a little spot.'

'What, like a proper turn?' Lynne asked excitedly.

'No, covering the noise while we're shifting the scenery. Singsong out front. Keeping them happy.'

'Do I get paid?'

'That's your payment, out there, the applause of the great British public. That's better than any filthy lucre.'

'I thought so.' She tried to hide her disappointment.

'Good girl. That's what I like, good girls. Off you trot.' He patted her behind as she hurried off to the dressing rooms.

Marcus signalled to Stephen to get his coat as the last guests prepared to leave the club. Ignoring Jim berating William, Stephen returned from the cloakroom and crossed the floor to his uncle's table. Marcus shoved a bundle of notes in his hand.

'What's this for?'

'A little extra for that friend of yours. Then sack him, tonight.' Marcus returned to Sarah, leaving Stephen staring in exasperation.

Thornton was still at the bar, pulling notes from his wallet and counting them out to Jim, who had now finished his harangue against William, and had turned his attention to his customer.

'And another makes fifteen. Remember, just keep it coming the same tomorrow night, lad, and make sure it's the best.'

'Fetch you a taxi cab, sir?' Jim asked Thornton, as he pushed the notes into the till.

'Not at all. I need a breath of fresh air. Where's . . . what happened to that girl?'

'She went, sir. Two hours back.' Jim suppressed a smile.

'Did she? The bitch!'

'I'll open the door for you, sir.'

William had watched the money pass from Thornton to Jim with barely concealed fascination, and was only peripherally aware that someone was calling his name – not once, but three times.

'William!' It was Stephen. 'Will,' he said, breathlessly, pushing the money Marcus had given him into his friend's hand – 'that's for tonight. And' – he took a few notes from his own pocket – 'there's a bit extra. I'm sorry, I can't have you back. It's my uncle, he's the owner, he can't afford any more staff . . .'

William hardly heard a word of what Stephen was saying. Taking the money, he pushed it into his pocket.

'Don't worry about it.'

'If you're passing by in the daytime . . . I can ask around, about jobs . . .'

'Yeah, sure.' Taking off the jacket he'd borrowed from Jim, he threw it on the bar and headed for the door.

'Oh, thanks very much,' Stephen muttered sourly as he watched him go.

The street was dark. Above the blackened roofs on the skyline ahead, Thornton could just make out the glow of the lamps on the main thoroughfare, a good ten-minute walk away. Weaving his way unsteadily towards them, he began to sing tunelessly to himself.

Behind him, William stepped out of the club. It took a few seconds for his eyes to adjust to the gloom. Then he saw the bulky silhouette moving ahead. Sticking close to the shadows, he put his head down and ran.

'It's the same in the capital, sir.' Jim turned half a dozen chairs, seat down, on to a table. 'There's dozens of them sitting around Leicester Square. And I'm sorry and all that, but cry your eyes out for one ex-soldier and you'll be sobbing like a girl, all day long.'

Not trusting himself to remain in the club with Jim and keep his temper, Stephen grabbed his coat. 'Thanks, Jim. That's good to know.'

'You off? There's tons that needs doing . . .'

'Oh, now, Jim, don't make me cry.' Stephen strode purposefully towards the door.

William Reynolds's chance came when Thornton turned into a narrow alleyway sandwiched between two warehouse walls. He watched Thornton lean against a wall and mop his forehead, and decided that all that champagne must be disagreeing with him now that he was in the cold night air. Creeping closer, William pulled a gun from his pocket, then pounced.

Gripping Thornton's neck in a stranglehold, he jabbed the barrel into his back.

'Give me your money.'

'Don't . . .' Thornton squealed. 'Don't . . .'

'Give it!'

Thornton scrabbled for his wallet. As he pulled it out of his coat pocket, he jabbed his elbow backward, into Reynolds's stomach. The two men fell, grappling to the floor.

Stephen heard the noise as he stood outside the Manhattan enjoying the cool night air. It was a sound that had no place in the quiet streets of Manchester. He spun in the direction of the shot and started running.

William heard his gun fall to the floor, but he didn't reach for it. Staggering back, he slumped against the wall. There was a sharp pain below his ribs. He touched the site, and felt hot, sticky blood pumping from his body.

Thornton's face loomed white in the darkness. He remained only as long as it took to scoop his wallet from the pavement, then he headed for the main road, screaming, 'Police . . . police . . .'

The Grand II: The Roaring Twenties

Stephen charged down the alley. He heard footsteps running away, but he stopped dead when he saw the body lying at his feet.

'Reynolds?'

'Help me. Stephen. Please, help me?'

Chapter Five

Stephen dropped his keys as he tried to unlock the door of the Grand. Bowed beneath the weight of William's body, he spent a few panic-stricken seconds searching for them, finally breathing a sigh of relief when he succeeded in lurching inside.

'It's all right,' he mumbled, not believing it, as William groaned and fell to the floor. Leaving him, he ran to reception and glanced along the rows of keys hanging on the board. He grabbed one at random. Then he reached for the register and flicked through the pages, checking to make sure that the room really was empty.

Running back to William, he lifted him by his shoulders.

'It's all right. It's all right, it really is,' he repeated unconvincingly, as he half carried, half dragged him to the lift. Jumping at every creaking board, cough and whisper that came from behind the closed doors of the guest rooms, he finally reached room eleven. Propping William against the wall, he opened the door, pushed William inside and dragged him to the bed.

'It's all right. We'll get you patched up, then we can have you out first thing, before anyone wakes. Get you out of the city . . .'

'Shot me,' William rambled. 'The bastard shot me.'

'Christ, Will, you were trying to rob him. If you were that desperate, you should have said . . .'

'Shot me!' William struggled to focus on Stephen.

Stephen gently prised away the jacket he had bundled and pressed against William's wound. It was soaked in blood, ruined. He only hoped his mother wouldn't notice its disappearance. Tossing it aside, he dived out of the room and back down the stairs to the foyer. Even in the half-light, he could see the bloodstains where William had fallen.

Kate heard footsteps. Instantly on the alert, she sat up in bed.

'What the hell's that?' Fumbling in the dark, she lit the candle and looked around. Lark and Brenda were asleep, but Lynne was sitting up, hugging her knees.

'Get some kip,' Kate snapped crossly.

'They loved me, Kate. They were clapping. All of 'em. Like thunder.'

'It's like that book, *Doctor Frankenstein*. I've built me own living monster. And it sings.' Listening hard for a moment and hearing nothing more, Kate settled back on her pillows and closed her eyes.

Stephen barged around the downstairs area, realising that, although he'd lived in the Grand all his life, he knew virtually nothing about the layout below stairs beyond the main corridors. As if to taunt him with the fact, a pile of crates loomed before him, which he blundered into, sending some of them crashing to the floor. He stood a while, hoping the sound hadn't woken anybody. Then he heard the drip of water, so knew he couldn't be far from the sink. He brushed against a light switch and flicked it on. A bucket with a rag balanced on the handle stood in the corner of the scullery. Stephen hauled it to the tap and filled it with water.

Running carefully so as not to slop the water, he made his way back to the foyer and started scrubbing.

Jim pulled his shirt closer to his shivering body as he peered out of the door of the Manhattan.

'Mr Thornton identified him as one of your staff.' The policeman took a pencil and notebook from his pocket.

'Look, officer, I don't know a thing. He only worked here tonight. You want to find him, you talk to the manager. They were old pals. Stephen Bannerman, Grand Hotel, he's your man.'

'It's all right, Will, you're in the Grand.' Stephen ran his hand over William's forehead. His skin was hot, clammy to the touch.

'Don't be stupid, Bannerman . . .' William tried to sit up, but sank back on the pillows. Clutching his abdomen, he looked down at his hand. It was covered in blood.

'Oh God! Oh Jesus!'

'I'll get something. Just don't make a sound while I'm gone, please.' Closing the door behind him, Stephen headed back to the staff quarters. He decided to risk a light, and opened door after door of the row of cupboards that lined the servants' hall. None held bottles, only stacks of neatly folded linen. Forgetting to be quiet, he cursed angrily, as he slammed them shut.

'Wish they'd shut up,' Fred mumbled from the depths of his bed.

'I dunno, some people treat this place like a hotel,' Clive countered caustically. 'They spoiling your dreams?'

'How do you mean?' Fred asked warily.

'Little Lynne?'

'Get off!'

'I've seen you watching her. Nothing little about that gob of hers. She can be heard on the moon.'

Fred pulled his pillow over his head, annoyed that Clive had struck so close to the truth.

Collins stood in the doorway, watching, as Stephen searched frantically through the kitchen drawers.

'Sorry.' Stephen blanched, as he caught sight of the concierge in his pyjamas. 'Did I wake you?'

'No,' Collins answered drily. 'As you can see' – he tied the belt on his dressing gown – 'I'm always up and about at this hour. Can I help you?'

'I brought a couple of friends back from the club. One of them dropped a wine glass. Graham, that's my friend, he's cut his hand, that's all. It's not much. I thought I'd find some Lysol in here, or . . .'

Collins took a bunch of keys from the pocket of his robe. 'In the office. I think Mrs Harvey needs the odd sip when she's had a busy day.'

Stephen followed him up the corridor; he waited while Collins unlocked the door, went to the desk and opened a drawer.

'There you go. That should do.' Collins handed him a packet of gauze, a bottle of Lysol and some ointment. 'I could call the doctor, if it's bad . . .'

'No, really. It's a fuss over nothing.'

A bell sounded in the distance.

'It's all happening tonight.' Leaving Stephen, Collins went to answer the door.

Katherine Hardy

*   *   *

To Jacob Collins's surprise, two policemen were already standing inside the reception area.

'Jacob, nice uniform.' The older of the two grinned at the sight of the usually immaculately turned-out concierge in his dressing gown.

'Thank you for noticing.'

'I rang the bell, but someone left the door unlocked. You'll be murdered in your beds.'

'Is that all you wanted? It's gone three o'clock.'

'No, Mr Stephen Bannerman, if you please.'

Stephen soaked a wad of gauze in Lysol and pressed it against the wound. William's face contorted in pain.

'Hold it there, William,' Stephen whispered urgently. 'There's someone at the door. I have to see who it is. I'll be back as soon as I can.' He rushed into the bathroom, grabbed a towel and wiped the blood off his hands. 'Two minutes,' he promised, as he darted out of the door.

'He's not in his room,' Collins announced as he returned to the foyer. 'He's drinking with his friends somewhere.'

The lift opened and Stephen stepped out.

'Hello, something the matter?' he enquired as innocently as he dared.

'Mr Bannerman, I'm Sergeant Roberts.' The officer studied him with a professional eye. 'If I could ask you a few questions. Apparently, a member of your staff was involved in an assault earlier tonight.'

'Is Jim all right?'

'No, that would be James Craig. We've spoken to him. He named the man as Mr William Reynolds. He's wanted as the assailant, sir, not the victim.'

'Really? I don't think so. Mind you, I hardly know him . . .' His voice trailed as Collins switched on the lights. He glanced from the door to the lift, looking for traces of blood. When he saw none, he couldn't resist examining his shirtfront.

'We'd like to talk to Mr Reynolds, and what's more, we believe he might be in urgent need of medical assistance. Do you know his address, sir?'

Stephen thought rapidly. Perhaps now was the time to tell the truth. It would come as a relief . . . Then John walked down the stairs in his dressing gown.

'Good evening, or good morning, gentlemen.'

'Sorry to wake you, sir,' the sergeant apologised.

'What's going on?'

'It's nothing, Dad. Just someone at the club,' Stephen broke in. He looked to the policemen. 'I'm sorry, I don't know his address. I'm not sure he's got one, to be honest.'

'Perhaps we'd better go into the office,' John suggested.

William opened his eyes to unfamiliar surroundings, then pain jolted him back to remembrance. He reached for the headboard on the bed. Using it to lever himself up, he eased himself tentatively, and painfully, out of the bed and placed both feet on the floor. He tried to make it to the door, but before he reached it, the floor rose to meet him in sickening, undulating waves. His cry of pain was lost in blackness. A deep soft, wonderfully comforting blackness.

'So this Mr Thornton?' Stephen asked the Sergeant. 'Where is he now?'

'At the station, sir.'

'No doubt he'll be facing charges?'

'What for?'

'I thought you said he shot Reynolds?'

'We've found the gun. It's a service revolver. It belonged to your friend, sir. Mr Thornton's lucky to be alive.' The sergeant continued to watch Stephen as he rose to his feet. 'Reynolds could still be on the streets. It's a warren down by Salter's Road. We'll keep looking. Thanks for your time.' He nodded to Collins, who was waiting by the door to see them out. 'Sorry to wake, you, Jacob.'

'You didn't. Mind yourselves there. The step is wet.'

'Right you are. Goodnight. If we get any news, we'll be in touch.'

John shook his head at Stephen. 'Jacob, goodnight. And thank you.'

Stephen hung back until his father was out of earshot. He'd heard the concierge's remark about the newly washed step.

'Well,' he said, smiling nervously, 'I suppose it's time we went to bed too.'

'What about your friends, sir? They weren't upstairs earlier when I was looking for you. Are they still here?'

'No, I showed them out of the side entrance. They're gone. Good night, Jacob.'

'If you don't mind my asking, where were you? I tried the Lancaster Suite and the family floor, but no sign – only I'll have to lock up, sir.'

'In a guest room,' Stephen divulged awkwardly. 'I've locked it.'

'Which room was that, sir?' Collins pressed. 'Best get it tidied in the morning before your father finds out.'

'No need. One of them is staying, one of my friends.'

'Is it in the book?'

'I'll sign him in tomorrow.'

'I'll do it now, sir. What room?'

'Can't remember.'

'Never mind, I'll check the keys.'

'It's . . . eleven. Mr Sullivan. Actually, he's had a bit too much to drink. If you could tell the maids to leave the room alone. Let him sleep.'

'Very good, sir.'

As Stephen climbed the stairs, he knew that Collins hadn't believed one single word of his story.

Something heavy was lying behind the door of room eleven. Even after he'd unlocked the door, Stephen had difficulty pushing it open. Setting his shoulder against it, he heaved with all the strength he could muster, and finally managed to open it wide enough to step inside.

'It was your gun, William,' he muttered furiously as he hauled him back on to the bed.

'The bastard turned it back on me,' William mumbled through his pain.

'Jesus, William, you were trying to rob him. I could understand that he wouldn't miss the money. But this? If I'd known it was your gun . . .'

'What? You'd have left me there?'

'Yes!' Stephen asserted savagely.

For a few seconds the only sound that punctuated the silence was the rasping of William's breathing.

'And there's me saying I'm good with a gun. I didn't even get the sod's wallet.'

Stephen smiled despite himself, then he stared in horror as the door handle moved. They both watched transfixed as it turned. Collins stood in the doorway.

'I'm sorry, sir. I'll have to call the police.'

Stephen stepped past him and closed the door.

'It's my fault, Jacob. I gave him the job. I *put* him in there, in front of all that money. If it wasn't for me, he wouldn't be like this.'

'If nothing else, sir, he needs help.'

'He's right, Stephen.'

'You're in no state to move.' Stephen looked at Collins, begging, pleading for understanding. 'I couldn't just leave him there, bleeding, lying in the dirt. You've no idea how many times I've run past men in his condition and carried on running. I tried not to look. But you could hear them. I couldn't let it happen again, Jacob. Six months we spent together. I just couldn't walk on.' He looked at William in despair, 'Oh God, we can't move him. And they can't find him here.'

'No, sir,' Collins agreed bitterly. 'Quite a little trap. And thank you so much for including me.'

'Exactly what sort of club is he running? John asked Sarah angrily as he paced around their bedroom.

'It doesn't sound like the club's at fault, John,' she answered from their bed. 'Stephen met this man in the army.'

'A police raid. Now this? Perhaps that's considered to be exciting in this day and age. No wonder you like it so much.'

'And in your view of the world, a woman's allowed out twice a year, is that right? Birthdays and Christmas.'

'No,' John asserted abruptly.

The silence grew, blinding, intense, around them.

'I won't go again, if that's what you want.'

'Oh thank you. Then what do I become? A man who forbids his wife to go out?'

'That's what you're doing.'

'And who put me in this position?'

'I'm owed some time. We both are. That time you're supposed to have when your children grow up and you can be with each other. We didn't have that. We were cheated. We were almost there, then Stephen went to war. So we sat here and worried instead. And then it was the Grand reopening. I didn't even have time to celebrate his return. I was cheated again. Well, that time is mine now, and if I have to take it on my own, then I will.'

He didn't know what hurt more, her icy determination or lack of apology.

'All right, tomorrow night. I don't know . . . the picture house, a restaurant, anything? You and me?'

'Marcus will be at the club. Who's going to run this place?'

'The offer's there. You decide.'

'Fine, tomorrow night.'

'Good.' John opened the curtains and stared down into the darkened street. Anything was better than looking at the dead, cold expression in Sarah's eyes.

'He probably didn't mean it,' Lynne said as she helped Kate to polish the newly washed ashtrays. 'If I turn up he won't even know who I am.'

'He will. He thought you were good. And even Lillie Langtry had to start somewhere, and she ended up sleeping with the king. Lark?' Kate gave her trainee a warning look. 'Don't you go repeating that.'

'Do you really think I was that good?'

'Lynne!' Kate dropped her polishing cloth and turned to face her. 'You know full well I can't stand the sound of your voice. I put you on that stage so you'd look a fool. And even I have to admit, you were good. In fact, since you've forced it out of me, you were great. You'd be mad, turning down a chance like this.'

'I'd better dig out a proper frock. I'll sing "Kitten of the Keys". They'll love that.'

'You're being very nice to her,' Brenda commented curiously as Lynne pushed her trolley down the corridor.

'Well, she's got talent.'

'And of course, if she's a big success, she'll be leaving the Grand.'

'That as well,' Kate agreed.

'It's remarkable, truly remarkable,' Marcus said to Stephen as he sat back to allow the maid to set the chafing dishes on the family breakfast table. 'Your father stays in the Grand all night, doesn't go near the Manhattan, yet he's able to furnish me with a complete account of events at the club last night. *My* club.'

'I'm sorry, you were asleep.'

'And what an account! It's bad enough you employ some itinerant. But no! That's not that end of it! He only attacks a customer with a gun! In the street.'

'I'm really sorry.'

'You'll be more than bloody sorry. I should sack you on the spot.'

Appalled at the way Marcus was speaking to her son, Sarah instinctively moved closer to John, taking his hand under cover of the tablecloth.

'Look, I gave him the job in good faith. How was I to know—'

'You're in charge, Stephen. You're responsible. Act like it for once.'

The Grand II: The Roaring Twenties

'Marcus,' John interposed coolly. 'The board of this hotel allowed you to pursue your interests at the Manhattan with one proviso. That it never interfered with the running of the Grand. Right now, it's interfering, very much indeed.'

'He's your son.'

'And he was very stupid, but he's apologised. If you lowered your voice, you might have heard him.'

Disconcerted by John's quiet authority, Marcus looked again to Stephen.

'I want a full explanation.'

'Later,' said John. 'Myself, I'd like another cup of tea.' He raised his cup to Sarah.

'Absolutely.' Sarah picked up the teapot.

'Sorry,' Stephen muttered before backing out through the door.

'It was simply the best idea,' Ruth sang out brightly. 'All of us living together.' She handed a plate to Marcus. 'Toast?'

Stephen found the maids hard at work on the first-floor corridor.

'Kate, have you got those instructions? Room eleven, leave it alone.'

'Yes.' She lifted her list. 'It's written down. What is it? A friend of yours?'

'Just leave him. It's a simple enough instruction.' He regretted his brusqueness as soon as he'd spoken. Kate was the one person who might have understood why he'd helped William, and the one person he didn't dare implicate in the whole bloody mess. 'He's . . .'

'What?' Kate asked, sensing that something was wrong.

'It doesn't matter.'

'What though?'

'Stop bothering me. That's what you said, and that's what I'm doing. It's your decision.'

'We can still talk.'

'It's a good decision, Kate. You should stay well away from me. Keep yourself safe. Just get back to work,' he muttered irritably, 'since you love your precious job so much.'

Kate had heard the sharp edge of Stephen's tongue before, and knew that he rarely meant what he said when he was in a mood. What concerned her was what had happened to upset him.

'I thought you said he was nice.' Lark returned to the trolley to fetch more linen.

'He is,' Kate said firmly, watching him walk away.

Stephen continued along the corridor. After looking back to make sure none of the maids were watching, he pulled the key of room eleven from his pocket and opened the door. Collins was already there, monitoring the wide-eyed, white, shivering figure hunched beneath the bedclothes.

'Oh Jesus!' Stephen exclaimed when he realised William was delirious. 'What are we going to do?'

'I'm sorry to disturb you, Miss Harkness.'

Esme opened her door wider. 'This is an unexpected pleasure, Mr Collins. Please, come in.'

Collins waited until she'd closed the door behind him.

'I need to find a doctor, Miss Harkness. One who won't ask questions.'

'Shame on you, Mr Collins,' she countered playfully. 'Is that how you think of me? As a woman who consorts with criminals?' Her smile faded, as she realised that whatever was troubling him was serious.

'What is it? What's wrong?'

'I really can't say, Miss Harkness. But you were the only person I could think of.'

'Is it one of the maids?'

'If you've heard of anyone, a doctor or nurse . . .'

'I don't know. I can ask among the local girls, but I'm not sure you should be involved in something so dangerous. Jacob, whatever it is, I won't be shocked. I'm sure I've heard worse. Tell me.'

'I can't.' He reached for her hand. 'Please, trust me. But it's urgent.'

'Give me an hour. I'll do what I can.'

Mrs Harvey stepped into the centre of the kitchen. Clapping her hands, she shouted,

'Right, pay attention, all of you, and pass it on. There's a function in the Lancaster Suite. The League of Women, now, they will insist on radical ideas. They want female staff serving, no men allowed, so you're all on extra duties. But don't go listening to their fancy notions – they're half Bolshevik in my opinion, not that my opinion counts these days. So all of you on the third shift, you're moving to fourth, waitress uniforms. Make sure they're clean.'

'Is that tonight?' Kate asked.

'Yes, it's tonight, Kate.' As Mrs Harvey hurried to the office Kate looked at Lynne.

She dropped the mop she was holding. 'Bugger!'

Esme entered the foyer with a short, square man who had the red face and bleary-eyed look of a habitual drinker.

'Mr Collins?' She waylaid the concierge at the reception desk. 'I'd like to introduce Dr Samuel Grady.'

'Thank you, Miss Harkness.' Collins walked out from behind the desk and waited for Esme to leave.

'What is it, then?' Grady queried bluntly. 'And don't give me the story, just tell me what needs doing.'

'Yes, sir.' Collins bowed to Esme. 'Miss Harkness, I'm sorry.'

'Jacob, Dr Grady has certain charges. If you need money, you only have to ask.'

'I won't, miss. But thank you very much.'

'Very well.' Esme went to the lift. The concierge waited until the doors closed.

'If you'll come this way, Dr Grady.' Collins led the way up the stairs.

Stephen raced down the corridor, carrying a suit, shirt and tie. Only just remembering to look around to check the corridor was empty, he burst into room eleven.

Grady was sitting on the bed taking William's pulse. Collins had heaped the clothes the doctor had cut away on the bathroom floor. Stephen noticed that his friend was still shivering, but his colour was stronger and he seemed more conscious of his surroundings than he had been half an hour before.

'I got you this.' Stephen held up the suit, then dropped it on to a chair and scooped up the dirty clothes. 'I'll get rid of these.'

'In the pocket.' William pointed at his soiled trousers. 'My wages.'

Stephen fished around and drew out a bundle of notes. He handed them over.

'I suppose you've earned this.'

'Excuse me,' Dr Grady interrupted. 'You don't imagine he's going anywhere?'

The Grand II: The Roaring Twenties

'There's a boarding house. They'll take me in,' William volunteered. 'It's off the Oxford road. They don't ask questions, take in all sorts . . .'

Ignoring William, Grady addressed Collins. 'I've patched him up best I can, but I wouldn't move him.'

'But the fever's gone?' Stephen looked to Grady for confirmation.

'The quinine should control it, but there's no guarantee. Blood poisoning's more dangerous than the wound if you're not careful.' He gathered his instruments together. 'I've left you some laudanum. Give him one draught every six hours. If you need more it will cost double.'

Stephen took the doctor to one side. 'He can't stay here.'

'Oh, this is not good enough? A bed at the Grand?' He stopped at the door. 'Do you know, I couldn't tell you the times I've walked past this place. I'd look up. Fine establishment, I'd think, that's the life, you'd want for nothing.' He laughed coldly. 'And look at you. I've done my bit. The rest is your problem.'

Chapter Six

Kate and Lynne stood side by side, like two recalcitrant children, in front of Mrs Harvey's desk.

'I spoke to Hetty,' Kate ventured hesitantly. 'She can swap with Lynne. She doesn't mind.'

'I've got to go, Mrs Harvey,' Lynne blurted out. 'It's me big chance . . .'

'It's her family.' Kate lied quickly, kicking Lynne with the heel of her shoe. Unlike Lynne, she knew Mrs Harvey would be more sympathetic to family commitments than a theatrical break. 'They're having a get-together . . .'

'It's big, Mrs Harvey,' Lynne interrupted recklessly. 'It's important. More important than anything here. I'm on stage, at the Alhambra. Me!'

Mrs Harvey laughed. Her laugh took on a mocking tone as she looked up and saw the earnest expression on Lynne's face. 'Are you? Are you indeed? Well upon my soul.'

'You see? I have to go.'

Mrs Harvey shook her head as she carried on laughing. 'You don't need an audience, Lynne, you've amused me enough. I've never heard the like. You'll work here tonight. You'll work and work and work.' She suddenly stopped laughing. 'Now get out. Waitress uniforms by seven o'clock.'

The Grand II: The Roaring Twenties

Kate looked anxiously at the defiant set to Lynne's mouth as they went to the door.

'If I could just have the night off, Marcus.' Stephen followed his uncle down the stairs into the foyer. 'I've one or two problems . . .'

'By all means.' Marcus knew that Sarah was standing behind the reception desk, listening to every word they were saying. 'And when you turn up tomorrow, you'll find your replacement in charge.'

'I'm owed one night. I'm taking it.'

'Keys.' Marcus snapped his fingers as he held out his hand.

'What?'

'Thanks for all you've done. Good luck in the future.'

Furious, Stephen pulled the club's keys from his pocket and threw them at his uncle, before storming back up the stairs. Marcus held them up to ensure Sarah saw them, before thrusting them into his own pocket.

Mrs Harvey strolled up and down the line of maids in waitress uniforms, inspecting their shoes, their stockings, the starch in their caps and aprons – and all the while she was as conscious as they were of Lynne Milligan's absence.

'Now I'm serious. Some of these ladies may be titled, but their ideas are halfway to communism, and that's one little spark of modern life I'll not have spread amongst my staff . . .' Footsteps rang along the back corridor. Knowing who it was the maids shuffled uneasily, not daring to turn around. Mrs Harvey glared as Lynne reached the back door. Lynne returned her stare, opened the door and walked out, quite deliberately closing it behind her. 'Well, that's a bed spare. I'll advertise in the morning,' the housekeeper announced decisively. 'Susan, Janey Birdsall, Kate, you're at table. Alice, Polly, Brenda you're in charge of the wine. Wait until I give you the nod. Pauline, Lucy, Esther . . .' As she continued to bark orders, a sick feeling of foreboding rose from the pit of Kate's stomach. Lynne wasn't the first maid to go her own way, but the last had been hanged. Why hadn't Lynne remembered that?

'I wasn't sacked.' Stephen smiled valiantly at his mother, desperately trying to pretend that everything was fine. 'It was a resignation. Good thing, too – the club was wearing me out. I haven't slept all night. This should make life a bit easier from now on, so don't worry about me. I've got to go . . .'

'Stephen, please. How can I not worry?' Sarah asked. 'Look at you, you're falling apart. Sit down. For God's sake, just tell me what's happened?'

'Got someone waiting, honestly. Friend of mine . . .' He ran out of his bedroom towards the lifts that led to the lower floors. Sarah almost went after him, then she remembered. He was a man, not a boy. And no man wanted his mother interfering in his life.

Frindel proudly unrolled the poster in front of Lynne. In the tiniest of boxes in the bottom left-hand corner was a notice so small as to be almost illegible: LIVERPOOL'S LITTLE LYNNE

'I'm not from Liverpool.'

'It sounds better. It's all in the phrasing.'

'Mr Frindel,' Lynne said awkwardly, embarrassed at having to ask, 'I don't suppose, I mean I'm not pushing, but there's no chance this could be permanent is there? With a bit of payment? Not much. I don't mind. I'll do the sweeping up after and everything.'

Dropping the poster, he put his arm around her shoulders. 'Don't talk money, it demeans you. You're an artiste. You're above such worldly matters. Your talent is your fortune – ten bob a week?' She nodded bleakly, she'd hoped for more. 'Done?'

'Yes,' she agreed reluctantly.

'It's the first time in my life that I've seen it. Raw talent, and it blazes out of you, Lynne. It's like staring into the sun.' He moved closer. She could smell the fish and chips he'd had for tea on his breath. 'You are what we call in the profession a born natural.'

'No, me mam had a terrible time. I was three weeks late.'

Carried away by his own rhetoric, he gave a virtuoso performance. 'And you feel it, don't you? The bond between us?'

'I do,' she conceded, wondering if it was too early to ask when she'd see her ten shillings. 'I can feel it now.'

'Take to the boards, Lynne. Blind them with sunlight. And then supper. You and me. Fine wines, perhaps a little tête-à-tête?'

'I'll drink anything, me.'

Cupping her face, he stroked his thumb across her lower lip. 'Lynne, little Lynne.' Suddenly businesslike, he left his desk. 'You've got ten minutes. If they start heckling, don't get ribald. There's nothing worse than smut from a woman. Off you dash.'

'Thank you, sir.'

'*A bientôt.*'

'Me too.' She stood in the passageway. Then she heard it echoing from the auditorium. Applause.

Taking a deep breath, she began to run. It was Showtime . . .

'I'm needed on duty, sir,' Collins whispered as Stephen walked into room eleven. 'If he's no better in the morning, we'll have to consult a proper doctor. No matter what the consequences.'

'Yes. And that's *my* duty. You won't be involved. I'm so sorry I made you part of this.'

'Well, that will teach me.' Collins went to the door. 'I'll have to stop being so bloody clever.'

'What about your job?' William asked as Collins left.

'Sod it. I got the sack, and deserved it. You get some sleep.' Stumbling into the chair beside the bed, Stephen closed his eyes, and William realised his friend was as exhausted as he was.

Ruth sat in the corner of the Bannermans' private living room and watched John and Sarah. Both of them were dressed for a night out, but Ruth knew as well as Sarah that John would be staying.

'I've got to go,' John,' Sarah explained quickly, not allowing him to get a word in. 'It's for Stephen. Just think what he was like a year ago. He survived the war only to find he had nothing left. The club isn't just a job. It's his entire future. If he loses that, John, then I'm scared. Scared of what he'll do to himself. Someone's got to talk to Marcus.'

'Then I'll come with you,' John broke in impatiently.

'It'll be the same old argument with the same two brothers. Just like this morning, both of you locking horns. He'd fire Stephen just to spite you.'

'And he'll listen to you?'

'Oh, I think so,' Ruth interrupted from the sofa.

John hesitated, but only for a fraction of a second.

'I'll cancel the reservations.'

'We could go later,' Sarah suggested.

'No, another night perhaps.' Pulling a chair out from the table, John sat down.

'It's so difficult, keeping track of the days with every evening looking the same,' Ruth commented as Sarah left.

Stephen was slumped forward in the chair, his breath locked into the soft, even rhythm of heavy sleep. William watched him as he fought to control his pain. Gritting his teeth, he moved slowly, carefully, and grabbed a glass phial of laudanum. He sank back, clutching it to his chest. Still watching Stephen, he snapped the glass top and poured the contents down his throat.

He didn't have to wait long for the drug to take effect. As soon as he thought himself strong enough he sat up. But then he gasped as a jolt of agonising pain shot through his body, causing him to fall back on to the bed. Stephen slept on, oblivious of the efforts he was making. William reached out and scrabbled for another phial. His hand shook, and they scattered, rolling over the floor beneath the bed.

He summoned every ounce of remaining strength, and swung his legs to the floor. Falling forward, he wrapped his fingers around a phial, which he clutched carefully as he put one shaking foot in front of the other and rose to his feet. Two steps, that was all, two steps and he'd be at the other side of the room where Stephen's suit was hanging on the wardrobe door, waiting. His ticket out of the Grand Hotel and Stephen's life. Just two steps, but they were the

longest he had ever made. He reached for the clothes
and flung them back on the bed. Then he cracked the
second phial.

'What the hell are you doing?' Disorientated, his
limbs sluggish from sleep, Stephen stumbled clumsily from the chair to help him.

'I'm all right. Help me . . .'

Stephen lowered him on to the bed. The drugs were
working too well. William's limbs felt strange, un-
naturally heavy.

'Are you trying to make yourself worse?'

'Getting out,' William whispered huskily. 'Doing
you a favour.'

'You've got nowhere to go.'

'I just need to get out through the door. First policeman I find, I'm done.' He laughed mirthlessly. 'Funny
isn't it? People have ignored me for the past couple of
years. Walked past me in the street as if I wasn't there.
Now I'm a wanted man.'

'But you'll go to prison.'

'So? And that's your fault? Don't you think I'm a
little bit to blame? You're an idiot, do you know that?'
he said fondly. 'Always the same. Cares of the world
on your shoulders. We used to laugh at you.'

'Oh, great.'

'About last night. Don't make me out the poor old
soldier. I was just doing what I *always* did, even as a
kid. Bit of stealing, picking pockets, begging free
meals off the parish. The army was a godsend. Food
and clothes, and your mates, told what to do every
day. I loved it. I really did. How about that? I was
happy when I was killing.' He looked Stephen
intently in the eye. 'There's you, losing your job, and
that bloke Collins risking everything he's got, for me.
I've helped no one in my whole life. I'd have shot

Thornton. I'd have shot him if I could. I don't deserve to be helped. I'm going to prison and that's my own fault. Let me do this please.'

'Will, I'm sorry.'

'Maybe you were right. You're lucky – only your worst bit of luck was me walking in through the door. So, it's time I walked out. Give us a hand? One last favour.'

Stephen helped him up. 'Don't forget this, Will.' He held out his wages.

'Keep it. Pay for the room. I won't need it where I'm going.'

'I can't let you go like this,' Stephen remonstrated as William staggered to the door.

'You can't be seen with me. Not by anyone. From now on, you're nothing to do with me. We're not soldiers now, we're not equals. Get back to your life and forget you ever knew me.' William turned the doorknob. 'And that's just as it should be. Like the war never happened. Go on ahead. I'll make it down on my own.'

Stephen offered his hand. 'Goodbye, Reynolds.' He opened the door and walked away.

The fixed expression on William's face dissolved as he leaned against the wall. Gulping air into his lungs, he gripped the doorpost and followed Stephen out into the corridor.

Lynne was in her element. All arguments and ultimatums from Mrs Harvey forgotten, she stood, centre stage in the Alhambra, leading the singsong, the music from the band and voices of the audience holding sway in her head as the clamour crashed, deafening, through the auditorium. She turned and saw Frindel watching her from the wings, then someone shouted for an encore, and she thought no more about Frindel – or where she was going to sleep that night. The here and now was too important – and magical – to worry about the future.

'Mrs Harvey,' Kate entreated. 'You know how stubborn she can get . . .'

'The answer's the same as it was ten minutes ago, Kate, and half an hour before that. No!' Mrs Harvey emphasised the finality of her decision by slamming a pile of papers on to her desk.

'It's my fault. I led her on . . .'

'No!'

'If you'd just talk to her . . .'

'No! She's never fitted in. I only gave her the job because I was in service with her mother. Now I'm drawing up an advertisement for one chambermaid, and I can very easily make it two, if you don't get back to work, quick sharp.' The housekeeper started scribbling as though they hadn't even spoken.

Fred knocked on the dressing room door and pushed it open. Lynne was standing in front of a greasepaint-smeared mirror, anxiously checking that the rouge she'd applied to her cheeks and lips hadn't smudged.

'You're not from Liverpool,' Fred commented.

'It's all in the phrasing. How did you get in? This is artistes only.'

'I said I was Miss Milligan's chauffeur.'

'You might be soon. They loved me.'

'Lynne, I can sneak you back into the Grand. We'll wait until Mrs Harvey's turned her back. She'll have calmed down by tomorrow morning.'

'Oh, Frederick, there's no need. I'm off to supper with Mr Frindel, wine and everything.'

The Grand II: The Roaring Twenties

'Just you and him?'

'You should hear him. He says I'm like a sunny day. He can see what I've got more than Harvey ever did. Mustn't keep him waiting. Tell the housekeeper I'll send for my things.' She smiled brightly as she skipped past him. Crestfallen, he watched her go, wishing he'd never heard 'I Don't Want to Play in Your Yard'.

Lynne ran along the corridor to Frindel's office. Hearing voices, she slowed her steps.

'First time in my life I've seen it. Raw talent, shining out of you, Dilys. It's like staring into the sun, blinding. You feel it, don't you? The bond between us?'

Lynne stole to the door and pushed it open. Frindel was standing with his back to her, but she could see that he was unbuckling his trousers. A girl was lying on his desk, her skirt hoisted to her waist. It took only a moment for Lynne to register that she was crying.

'You could knock,' he grumbled as Lynne stormed in.

She grabbed the girl. 'You! Get out! Go back to your mother and tell her what you've been doing! For shame! Go on, run, or I'll boot you all the way home!' Shoving her out of the room, she turned to Frindel. 'And you!'

'For God's sake, can't you wait your turn?'

Lynne grabbed the nearest thing – it happened to be the golden hand. Holding it in both hands, she jabbed it towards his crotch.

'Now Lynne. Little Lynne . . .'

'Mr Frindel, the hand of the heathen god.' Advancing, she stabbed it into his soft, pudgy flesh.

*   *   *

Mrs Harvey was leaving the office when the back door opened. She'd checked the curfew roster and, knowing that all the staff were in, except one, she waited. Lynne took one look at Mrs Harvey and did the only thing she knew would elicit sympathy. She burst into tears.

'Not all it's cracked up to be?' Mrs Harvey asked as Lynne sank down on to a chair.

'Horrible,' Lynne sobbed.

Mrs Harvey went to her. 'I could have told you if you'd only come and asked,' she murmured as she stroked her hair away from her face. 'But you never do. It's best forgotten, just this once. We'll say no more. What in the world made you think you could be an actress?'

'Dunno.' Lynne saw Kate hanging back out of Mrs Harvey's sight. Sobbing all the louder, she gave her fellow maid a broad wink. 'I dunno, Mrs Harvey.'

Sarah danced with Marcus in the hot, smoky, perfumed atmosphere of the Manhattan. For once, he wasn't trying to hold her close. But she knew that nothing had changed between them. He still wanted her. And she was prepared to use that desire, or anything else that would get the keys to the Manhattan back to Stephen.

When the dance ended, Marcus went to the office. She followed. He closed the door, and when he turned to face her, he had the keys to the club in his hand. She kissed him as she took them from his fingers. A wild passionate kiss that was as different from the first kiss they'd shared as frost from fire. She'd won. She left with the keys. But the passion she'd engendered terrified her. If John should ever find out . . .

Stephen waited impatiently in the foyer. Every time

the lift clanged open, he and Collins looked up expectantly. Finally, they were rewarded. William Reynolds stepped out, blinking against the light and noise.

Stephen could see that Reynolds's pain was excruciating, almost unbearable; the only wonder was no one else noticed it, as he limped unsteadily to the door. William looked back just once, then the door closed on him and he was gone. Weak with relief, Stephen nodded to the concierge before heading upstairs – to sleep.

Kate and Lynne were opening the curtains in the public areas, ready for the new day ahead, when Fred found them. Looking over his shoulder to check that Mr Collins was nowhere in sight, he handed Lynne a rolled-up poster.

'Souvenir,' he whispered.

'I'm not from Liverpool, mind,' Lynne said, and gave him a smile as she took it from him.

Clive whistled, setting the other boys off catcalling and clapping.

'Sweethearts!' Kate looked from Lynne to Fred and tapped her head in dismay. 'Fred Willets, you want locking up.'

'Stephen?' Sarah called, as he crossed the foyer. She held up her hand, dangling the keys.

He dropped a kiss on her cheek as he took them from her. She hugged him, and, after a moment's hesitation, he returned her embrace.

A frown creased John's forehead as he watched from the office. His expression hardened, as he wondered just what Sarah had done to get the keys back from Marcus.

* * *

Outside the hotel, the pace of life quickened as the morning wore on. Milk and delivery carts gave way to chauffeur-driven cars. The newsboys offered their wares to well-dressed men and women heading for the shops. Few spared a second glance for the forlorn figure huddled in the doorway of the boarded-up shop. One or two wondered where he had got the good suit he was wearing, but no one bothered to read the scrawl on the cardboard propped at his side. After all, the message was all too familiar.

Ex-soldier. Please help

But then, the figure wouldn't have known if they had stopped. His sightless eyes continued to stare down at the pavement as his body grew colder, and colder. As cold as the paving he was lying on.

Chapter Seven

'You left a bit in the bottom, like I told you?' Kate asked Lark as the trainee charged headlong into the scullery carrying half a dozen, ostensibly empty, bottles of wine.

'Yes.' Lark ranged the bottles carefully alongside the others that the staff on clearing duty had brought downstairs.

'Château Ancoats is that. Best there is.' Kate eyed the labels and chose one. Holding the bottle to the light to check exactly how much was left in it, she put it to her lips.

'Did you see that bloke up there?' Lynne ran in with a tray full of dirty plates and glasses. 'The one near the bar. He's got a twitch. Looks like a rabbit. He smells an' all.' She looked meaningfully at Kate. 'That's perfume, that is.'

'You couldn't smell a dead cat, amount you've supped.' Brenda dumped her tray on the table and reached for two bottles. She handed one to Lynne as Kate picked up another.

'I want those canapés up there in two minutes,' Mrs Harvey shouted down the corridor.

The girls hastily hid the bottles in their skirts.

'It's all right, she's gone back up.' Fred stacked another pile of bottles with an inch of wine left in the bottom alongside the others.

'Canapés?' Lark had obviously never heard the word before.

Lynne took one from a tray and handed it to her. 'Frog food,' she scorned derisively, as Lark sniffed it.

'Hey, Lynne? Look what one of them Aussies gave me?' Pulling a cricket ball from his pocket, Fred showed it to her. 'And he reckons he can get me a ticket for Saturday.'

'Get those canapés upstairs. Now! And you' – Mrs Harvey pointed a condemnatory finger at Lark as she appeared in the doorway – 'there's plates and glasses to be cleared upstairs.' Unnerved at being singled out, Lark pushed the canapé she'd been examining into her mouth.

Lynne picked up a tray as the housekeeper turned to her. 'I were just on my way, Mrs Harvey.'

'Me an' all.' Kate added, as she and Brenda handed their empty bottles to Fred, and grabbed a couple of trays.

Fred smiled weakly as Mrs Harvey glared at the cricket ball he was still holding.

'Watch your backside,' Brenda warned Lark as they made their way upstairs. 'Once they've had a few, their hands are everywhere.'

'Is that wishful thinking?' Lifting her tray to shoulder height, Kate moved into the crowd.

Lark hung back, awed by the sight of the Grand in all its glittering glory. The Lancaster Suite was crowded with elegantly dressed and bejewelled guests. A string quartet set on a dais at the far end of the room played baroque music softly, taking care to keep the sound below the level needed for conversation. Red and white banners had been hung on the ceiling: MANCHESTER LIBERAL ASSOCIATION and GOOD LUCK ARTHUR.

Esme Harkness was at the centre of a throng of men, beautifully dressed and completely at ease, charming everyone around her.

'You must feel very proud, Mr Shaw,' she congratulated.

'On the contrary, I feel quite humble that so many people have come here tonight.'

'It's a mark of their respect.'

'You're very kind, Miss Harkness.' A man beckoned him closer to the dais. 'Would you excuse me?'

'Of course.'

Arthur Shaw bowed and left. Esme stopped a waiter, and took another glass of champagne. Seeing John Bannerman's daughter, Adele, hovering on the fringes of the crowd, Esme joined her.

'You know, my dear, you shouldn't really be here.'

'Why not?'

'You're so young. And you look so lovely, you put the rest of us to shame.'

Adele smiled gratefully. 'I thought I might meet some dashing young politician.'

'In my experience, those words seldom go together. Politicians are born aged.'

Adele laughed as the maids passed by with more canapés and champagne.

'Like a rabbit I'm telling you,' Lynne muttered beneath her breath to Kate, as they moved through the crowd.

'Do frogs really eat this stuff?' Lark asked Brenda as she loaded discarded glasses on to her tray.

'Don't be daft.' Brenda saw the relief on Lark's face and decided to have some fun. 'It's made from frogs.'

Katherine Hardy

'Ugh!' Lark charged back down the stairs.

'You've done me proud tonight, John,' Arthur Shaw said gratefully.

'No more than you deserve, Arthur. Ten years as treasurer is quite a stint. You remember Arthur, darling?' John asked Sarah.

'Of course.'

'Lovelier than ever.' Arthur took Sarah's hand and kissed it. 'You're a lucky fellow, John.'

'That's what I keep telling him,' Sarah agreed humourlessly.

'Well?' Lynne demanded of Kate. 'Did you get a whiff of him?'

'It's his wife, stupid.' Kate frowned as Lark rushed past. 'What's up with her?'

After checking that no one was watching her, Brenda popped a canapé into her mouth. 'No idea.'

Ruth searched frantically through a chest of drawers in her bedroom. As she pushed aside papers, writing sets and discarded pens with ink stained nibs, she grew increasingly desperate. Her face darkened as a perfunctory knock on the door announced the unexpected entry of her husband.

'How many times, have I told you, Marcus? Don't just walk in here.'

'I'm about to go.'

'Fascinating.' She turned back to the drawer and carried on rummaging.

'I thought . . . if you needed anything sending up . . .'

'No,' she broke in abruptly.

'What are you looking for?'

'My book. I put it down somewhere. You haven't

seen it?'

'What would I want with some trashy romance?'

'You tell me. You seem determined to have one.'

Ignoring the gibe, Marcus slipped his cigarette case into his pocket. 'Enjoy your evening.'

'I'm having an early night. Don't bother calling in when you get back.'

As Marcus left, Ruth found what she was looking for. A small bottle of pills. Fighting a surge of pain, she tipped three into her hand and swallowed them.

'Are you still on for the pictures tomorrow, Lynne?' Fred asked as they cleared the mess of bottles, glasses and plates from the kitchen below stairs.

'Who's in it?'

'Some bloke called Rudolph Valentino.'

'There were a photo of him in the paper,' Brenda announced, swaying on her feet as the wine she'd downed began to take effect. 'He were right broody.'

'I thought you're coming with me tomorrow night, Lynne,' Kate reproached.

'Oh, aye, I'm not missing that.'

'What?' Fred asked.

'S-E-X.' Lynne spelled it out slowly with a sideways look at Kate.

'It's not just about that,' Kate countered.

'You're what?' Fred's jaw dropped open.

'We're going to a lecture.' Kate pulled a piece of paper from her apron pocket; it was a handbill. Brenda grabbed it before she could hand it to Fred.

'What every working woman should know . . . about intimate relations with men.' Brenda paused, shocked rigid. 'You mucky so and so's.'

'Can I come?'

'Women only, Fred,' Lynne smirked. 'But I'll tell

you all about it. I might pick up a few tips.'

'It's about meeting the right bloke. Getting married, and all that stuff. What's up with you?' Kate asked as Lark walked in looking green.

'I've been proper poorly. It were that frog I ate.'

'You daft ha'p'orth,' Brenda laughed as she searched through the bottles for one that still held wine. 'I meant it were French. It's horse.'

Lark dashed to the sink, as Mrs Harvey loomed, large and furious in the doorway. As Fred jumped from the bin he'd been sitting on, he accidentally dropped his cricket ball on a tray of glasses, smashing half a dozen.

'What on earth?'

Fred dived towards the cellar. The maids scattered. A piece of paper fluttered to the floor, and Mrs Harvey bent to pick it up.

Dressed in a loose-fitting coat and cloche hat that covered most of her face, Ruth crept stealthily along the upstairs corridor. Anxious not to be seen, she stepped back into an alcove as a door opened and someone stepped out. She waited until the guest moved on, clinging to the wall for support as yet another pain racked her body.

The string quartet packed up their instruments and moved aside to make way for Arthur Shaw. Bored by the proceedings, Sarah left John and his friends, and moved to the door. Her face lit up when she saw Marcus. He crossed over to her.

'Has Lloyd George arrived yet?'

'I thought he spent his evenings engaged in more intimate pursuits.'

'Sensible fellow.' Marcus glanced over at John.

'Shouldn't you be over there?'

'I suppose I could go and tell them to vote Conservative.'

'I thought I might have missed the speeches.'

'And I hoped there wouldn't be any,' Sarah sighed.

'You play the part so beautifully.'

'I've had a lot of practice. I suppose you're having one glass and clearing off?'

'Come with me?'

'Don't tempt me.'

'You only have to say the word.' He looked into Sarah's eyes and realised she was close to doing just that. Reluctantly, they both turned their attention to Arthur Shaw.

Behind them, the front doors opened, and a stylishly dressed young woman walked in and made her way to reception. She smiled as she skirted the back of the crowd, passing Kate, who was still clearing plates and glasses.

'Christina Lloyd-Price to see Stephen Bannerman.'

Kate stopped and stared as the footman manning reception picked up the internal telephone. Seconds later Stephen came rushing down the stairs.

'Christina!' Oblivious to the presence of the maid, he kissed her cheek.

'Of course, the association is going to need a new treasurer,' Arthur Shaw's voice boomed through the Lancaster suite. 'And as far as I'm concerned, there's only one man for the job. John Bannerman.'

Stunned, and gratified by the compliment, John found himself the centre of a group of congratulatory party officials.

'Now that's something to look forward to,' Marcus observed caustically.

Horrified by the prospect of her husband becoming immersed in local politics, Sarah forced her way through the crowd.

'Surely, you're not going to accept?' she whispered urgently, as she drew him aside.

'Why on earth not?'

'Think what it would mean. You already complain about not having enough time.'

'It could be a tremendous opportunity, Sarah. At the very least, it will be good for business. Who knows where it might lead?'

'I don't want to spend time with these people. I'm not prepared to get involved. You know my political views.'

'I think you're getting things out of proportion.'

'At least let's discuss it properly before you commit yourself.'

'John.' Arthur slapped John on the back as he joined them. 'Everyone's asking for you.'

Some distance away, at the foot of the stairs, Ruth watched the proceedings, waiting for her moment. When everyone's attention was focused on John and Arthur standing side by side on the platform, she slipped quietly out through the front doors.

'Mr Collins?' Mrs Harvey accosted the concierge as he walked into the staff kitchen. Thrusting the handbill at him, she stood back expectantly, waiting for his reaction.

'What's this?'

'I found it earlier. One of the girls must have dropped it.'

'I'm on my way to the cellar.' He held up the keys. 'There's a gentleman asking for Château Lafite. Clive's got his hands full . . .'

'Read it, Mr Collins,' she ordered imperiously.

' "A short film about intimate relations with men. Followed by a lecture on the same subject".' He shrugged his shoulders.

'It's not right, Mr Collins.'

'Perhaps they're trying to stop girls getting into trouble.'

'Such matters should not be discussed in public. It will put ideas into their heads.'

'I think the ideas are already there.'

'What would Mr Harvey say if I went to something like that?'

'Indeed.' Collins had difficulty hiding his amusement at the notion. Handing her back the handbill, he continued his way to the cellar.

'You'd rather go to a lecture than the flicks with me?' Fred caught Lynne's hand, and pulled her into a secluded corner behind the service lift.

'It were Kate's idea.'

'You don't have to go. Nobody's forcing you.'

'I want to.' She tossed her head coquettishly. 'I want to better myself.'

'You don't have to go to a lecture to learn about the birds and the bees.'

'How else am I going to find out?'

'Like this.' Fred kissed her. To his utter amazement, she kissed him back.

'Call yourself an expert?' she baited when they broke for air.

'I'm short of practice. Then again, perhaps I should ask someone else to share my banquette . . .'

'Suit yourself.'

'They reckon in America this Rudolph Valentino is as big as Charlie Chaplin.'

'I don't believe that.'

'Not much of a name for a start, is it?'

'Neither is Fred Willets.'

'But you don't have to pay tuppence to see me on a screen, do you? You can have the real thing for free.' He kissed her again.

'I've had my tonsils out already, you know.' She pushed him away.

'I bet it weren't as much fun as this.'

'Give over.' Lynne fought him off. 'I'm trying to get my breath back.'

'I suppose we'd better get back upstairs.'

'Yes.' But instead of making a move, she looked into his eyes, daring him to kiss her again.

'You're supposed to find power attractive,' Marcus commented to Sarah as they watched John receiving yet more congratulations.

'Who says I don't?' She realised Marcus was looking at John. 'And you, of course, have no power over women?'

'Not over the woman who matters.' He glanced back at his brother. 'Things just seem to fall into John's lap. I have to fight for everything.'

'Do you remember really wanting something when you were a child? And as soon as you got it, losing interest?'

'Father used to tell us that Christmas Day was an anticlimax. All the pleasure was in the build-up. Not for me. I used to love ripping the paper off my presents. Particularly those I didn't expect.'

'And what little homilies will you pass on to your child?'

'I'll tell him to go to bed early. Not to drink.' He laughed at the sceptical expression on her face, then fell serious. 'I want to be a good father. It's Ruth I'm concerned about.'

'That's a first.'

'I mean it. I have no idea what kind of mother she's going to be. And that worries me.'

Sarah suddenly realised that Marcus was as vulnerable as everyone else. 'You married her to have children. That's what she's doing.'

'I married her to spite you,' he admitted with startling honesty.

Sarah bit her lip, touched by what he had told her, but before she could respond, John and Arthur interrupted them.

'Sarah, we're invited to a meeting tomorrow night.'

'What?'

'It's quite an honour. You'll enjoy it.'

'I couldn't think of a better man to take over from me,' said Arthur. 'You must be very proud.'

'Oh yes.' Sarah couldn't resist pricking Arthur's ego. 'Not that I'd vote Liberal myself.'

'I'm going to die. I know it,' Ruth insisted as she followed the midwife into her living room. 'I'm going to die.'

Margaret Newman took a steadying breath. She'd witnessed Ruth Bannerman's hysterics before, but they'd never been quite as bad as this. She resorted to the blunt, common-sense, reassuring tactics that she used on all her patients.

'Calm yourself, Mrs Bannerman. Tell me exactly what seems to be the problem.'

'I told you. I'm going to die.' Ruth's voice rose precariously.

'Let me take your coat, then we can talk about this properly.'

'It's going to happen. Just like before.'

'What is?'

'I'm going to die. Like my mother.'

'That is no way to talk,' Margaret said firmly.

'Why won't you listen?' Ruth stared intently at the midwife. 'Listen to me,' she repeated urgently. 'There's something wrong with the baby and I'm going to die. Help me.'

'Of course I'll help you. But I don't think there's any point in getting yourself all worked up. You were fine when I saw you last week.'

'Do something. Just shut up, and do something . . .'

'I'll examine you . . .'

'Yes . . . Yes. Just do it . . .'

'. . . but getting yourself into this state isn't doing your baby any good. Now, take a deep breath . . .'

'Just get on with it.'

'Can I come? To that film?' Lark asked as she and Kate tackled the debris in the Lancaster Suite.

'I don't know. You're a bit young. Has anyone ever told you anything about babies? Where they come from?'

'Me gran says the coal man brings them. She says he's brought five down our road. But I reckon there must be more to it than that.'

'There is. When a man and a woman . . .' Kate faltered, realising this was neither the time nor place to instruct her trainee on the facts of life. 'Perhaps you better had come.'

'Want a hand, Kate?' Clive left the bar to help her with a heavy tray. He looked over to where Fred and Lynne were laughing in a corner. 'They think they're invisible.'

'They'll need to be, if Harvey turns up.'

The Grand II: The Roaring Twenties

'Hey, Kate?' Lynne slurred as she stumbled across the room. 'Guess what I saw earlier. Stephen Bannerman with that new lass of his. That's twice this week. It must be serious.'

Concerned for Kate, Clive turned on Lynne. 'I'm surprised you can see anything, the state you're in.'

'Sorry, vicar.' Still laughing Lynne went back to Fred.

'It's all right, Clive.'

'There's a good film at the Gaumont, Kate. We could—'

'Honest, Clive, it's all right.'

Clive finally picked up the tray, knowing it was anything but.

The Manhattan club was packed when Stephen walked through the doors with Christina. The cloak-room girl smiled as she greeted Stephen, and took their coats. A waiter walked over.

'Your table is ready, Mr Bannerman.'

'What do you think?' Stephen asked, shouting to make himself heard above the noise of the band.

'I think it's marvellous,' Christina enthused.

'Everything all right, Jim?' Stephen enquired as they passed the bar.

'Yes, sir. Oh, there was a call from the wine merchant . . .'

'I'll ring him back tomorrow. Jim, this is Miss Lloyd-Price.' He turned to Christina. 'Jim runs the bar.'

'Pleased to meet you. Not a face I'll forget, sir. Champagne, is it?'

'Great,' Christina enthused.

'Good idea, Jim.'

'I can't believe you manage this place,' Christina

said as the waiter led them to their table.

'Why not?'

'I suppose it's because I've never met a nightclub manager before. You're not what I imagined.'

'I didn't exactly plan it.'

'And this is it?'

'What?'

'The rest of your life?'

'God, I don't know. I don't even know what I'll be doing next year, do you?'

'I'm giving it some serious thought,' she mused as Jim laid a silver champagne bucket on their table.

Ruth lay back and stared at the ceiling in Margaret's bedroom. It wavered in hot circles of pain that seared her eyes and scalded her abdomen.

'I can't lose this baby. I mustn't,' she pleaded.

'Lie still.' Margaret pulled back the sheet. 'Then I can take a proper look at you.'

'Will my baby survive?'

'It may not come to that.'

'Tell me?'

'At six months . . . no . . . it wouldn't,' Margaret admitted reluctantly. She pressed down lightly on Ruth's abdomen, replaced the sheet and went to the door.

'Where are you going?'

'To send for a doctor. I'll only be a minute.'

'No!' Ruth screamed. 'No doctor.' She fought back the wave of pain. 'You can't call a doctor. He'd tell my husband. My husband mustn't know.'

'Mrs Bannerman, please . . .'

'I said no!' Ruth's words ended in a moan of pure agony that left the midwife no choice. Turning back to the bed, she gripped Ruth's hand.

The Grand II: The Roaring Twenties

* * *

'You should get to bed, before you cause any more trouble,' Marcus suggested to Sarah, as John and Esme stood in the foyer shaking hands with the departing guests.

'I'm being the dutiful wife. Saying farewell to my guests.' She smiled insincerely as she waved off a group of elderly female fundraisers.

'Have you made your peace with John yet?'

'What do you think?'

'I have a poker game waiting. Behave.' He kissed her cheek before leaving.

'Miss Harkness.' Arthur Shaw clung to Esme's hand longer than was strictly necessary. 'You've been a most charming companion.'

'Thank you, Mr Shaw.'

'Would you allow me to buy you dinner tomorrow?'

'Mr Shaw, I should point out that you're not the only one who's retired.'

'You misjudge me. I simply want to take you for dinner and a glass of champagne.'

'In that case, I'd be delighted.'

'You do me a great honour.' He gave her a small, formal bow. Esme turned to find Sarah standing behind her.

'Exciting times ahead, Mrs Bannerman.'

'Yes, and your diary must be full after tonight.'

'I beg your pardon?'

'I'm sorry, Miss Harkness.' John glared at Sarah. 'I think my wife must be unwell.' Steering Sarah into a secluded corner, he finally erupted. 'Esme Harkness has brought more credit to the Grand tonight than you have. She made an effort to be civil.'

'There was no effort required. She's slept with most

113

of them.' John paled, and she realised she'd gone too far. 'I'm sorry. I really don't know what's got into me. That was unforgivable. I'm tired,' she explained lamely, looking for excuses. 'I need a few early nights.'

'For goodness' sake, Sarah . . .'

'I know.'

'What is it?'

'I've been feeling . . . I don't know . . . I've been feeling . . . strange. I can't explain.'

'Are you ill?'

'No . . . I don't know.' She knew she was being irrational, but she simply couldn't tolerate John's concern on top of everything else.

'We need a break. Let's go away. Next weekend? The Lake District? What do you say?'

'We'll see,' she replied noncommittally.

'What could be better?'

'Let's talk about it in the morning.'

'All right.' He knew as well as she did that they wouldn't be going anywhere. 'I'd better get back to our guests.'

'You're not bad, do you know that?' Christina complimented Stephen as the dance ended and they applauded the band.

'What you mean?' he asked warily.

'The dancing. You didn't kick me once.'

'I don't get much practice. Too busy.'

'When I first saw you I thought you looked terribly serious.'

'It was a very boring party.'

'Until I walked in?' she asked, blatantly fishing for compliments.

'Of course. Mind you, I did worry about the company you were keeping.'

'What you mean?'

'That awful man. You were laughing at all his jokes.'

'I wasn't.' She punched him playfully.

'Ouch! What are you doing tomorrow? We could have lunch if you're free.'

'I'd like that. How about your hotel? You could show me around.'

'It's not terribly exciting.'

'You take it for granted. It's all new to me.'

'Fine. Come tomorrow.'

'All right. Now I really must be going.'

'Already?'

'It's not long until tomorrow.'

'There was nothing I could do.' Margaret took a clean towel and covered the tiny body lying in the sluice dish. Reaching out, she touched Ruth's hand – but Ruth snatched it away and turned her face to the wall.

'It should have been me that died. I was sure it would be me.'

'Because of your mother? You shouldn't think like that.'

'I'm never going to be able to have children, am I?'

'I'm not a doctor. I can't answer that.'

'How soon can I get pregnant again?'

'After what's happened tonight, it's hard to say.'

'You don't have to pretend. I know it's not going to happen. I didn't want a baby. It was for Marcus. It's all he wants.'

'You need to rest,' Margaret murmured, not knowing how to comfort her.

'He won't want me any more. Was it a boy?' she asked suddenly.

'No.'

'He wants a boy.' Ruth sat up slowly, painfully. 'You must tell no one about what's happened here tonight.'

'You should spend the night in hospital.'

'I want you to continue your visits to the Grand.'

'What?' Margaret stared at her blankly.

'Once every two weeks, as usual.'

'Mrs Bannerman, you've lost your baby,' she explained patiently.

'You'll be well paid. Just name your price. All you have to do is visit.'

Margaret sighed. 'All right.'

'And I need to use the telephone. I have arrangements to make.'

Ruth slipped as easily into the Grand as she'd left. Walking slowly to hide her pain, she passed the porters who were straightening the furniture after the party, and stepped into the lift.

The top-floor corridor that housed the family apartments was in darkness apart from a single sidelight burning in the living room. Ruth took off her coat and threw it on to the sofa before going to the sideboard, reaching for the Scotch, and filling a glass.

'Couldn't you sleep either?'

She turned in alarm. 'My God.'

'I'm sorry, I didn't mean to startle you.' John joined her at the sideboard. As he poured himself a drink, Ruth edged into the shadows. 'I remember when Sarah was pregnant. She found it hard to sleep.' He downed his whisky in a single mouthful. 'It was a long time ago.' He reached for the bottle and refilled his glass. 'She's a bit weary at the moment. Gets ground down by the routine of running this place. I thought I'd take her away for a holiday. I can't remember when we last had a break. It will do us good.'

John's self-delusion coupled with her pain was too much for Ruth.

'You could take her twice round the world and it wouldn't change a thing.'

'We've been married for a long time. There are bound to be ups and downs.'

'She's forgotten you exist. Book a week in the South of France, then ask her who'd she'd like to spend it with.' Taking her glass, Ruth walked away leaving John to face the plain, unvarnished truth.

Chapter Eight

Racked by pain that made even the smallest movement sheer agony, Ruth picked up her cosmetics bag and hairbrush and pushed them into a small travelling case.

'Who is it?' she called in answer to a knock on the door.

'There's a taxicab downstairs for you,' Marcus said in surprise as he walked in.

'Right.' Closing her bag, she straightened her back.

'Where are you going?'

'London, it's just my routine check-up.'

'But you were there last week.'

'He had to change the date,' she lied quickly. 'You chose him. He's the best there is.'

'Why don't you take Adele with you?'

'What on earth for?'

'It's a long way to travel and you're six months pregnant. She'd love it. She's been talking for ages about a shopping trip.'

'I'm going for our baby, Marcus. And that's all I want to think about. I'm in a hurry.' She pushed past, before he could say another word.

'Good morning, Ruth,' Sarah called from the dining room where she was breakfasting alone.

'Good morning,' Ruth replied tersely.

'Are you all right?'

'I'm pregnant.'

'I've been meaning to come and see you.'

'Why?'

'I just wanted to say if there's anything I can do to help . . .' Sarah's voice trailed guiltily. 'After all, I know what you're going through.'

'I don't think so.'

'Well, if there is anything I can do . . .'

'You're a bit late, Sarah. You should be having this baby. Marcus would love that, wouldn't he? Excuse me, I've a taxicab waiting.'

'Kate?' Adele walked in as the maids were bagging dirty linen, ready for the laundry. Leaving the others, Kate walked over to her.

'Miss Bannerman?'

'I wonder if you could iron this dress for me.'

'I don't know, miss. I suppose I could.'

'Only I'm going out for lunch. And I'm hopeless at it.' Seeing that Kate wasn't prepared to object, Adele showed her the dress. 'You'll have to be very careful with the collar. It's silk. It cost a fortune,' she prattled on, oblivious to her father standing behind her. 'Oh, and the skirt's pleated.'

'The maids aren't employed as your personal slaves, Adele.'

'I know that.' She blushed, as she turned to her father.

'I think you'll find ironing is a very useful skill to acquire.'

'I'll probably ruin the collar.' Irritated that he'd caught her out, she ran back up the stairs.

'You must not let her take advantage of you, Kate,' John advised.

Katherine Hardy

'Thank you, Mr Bannerman.' Kate watched him walk into Mrs Harvey's office. 'I wonder what Harvey wants with him?' she said thoughtfully as she watched Lark's feeble attempts to unblock a sink full of greasy water. 'You'll never shift anything like that.' She grabbed the plunger and wielded it herself. 'I'm not doing it for you.' She handed it back. 'Looks like Harvey's having a right go at Mr Bannerman.'

'There was a wedding down our way last Saturday,' Lark chattered as she put more effort into operating the plunger. 'One of the bridesmaids got killed.'

'How?' Kate asked absently, still watching John Bannerman and Mrs Harvey.

'The lass that were getting wed stuffed her mouth full of confetti. Choked her.' Giving the plunger an extra vigorous swing, Lark sent greasy water cascading all over the kitchen.

'You clumsy beggar!' Kate shouted, as she dived for cover.

'Are we showing a profit? Sarah asked as she walked into the office to find Marcus sitting there, alone.

'There're a few bills waiting to be settled.'

'Some people are like that. They leave things late.'

'There are only so many reminders that one can issue,' he said, standing up and closing the door. He turned to her, reached up and stroked the side of her face, and for once she offered no resistance.

'It's sponsored by the government, but that doesn't make it right,' Mrs Harvey pronounced angrily. 'You've seen those women behind the Opera House, the same as I have. I don't want any of my girls ending up there.'

'No . . . of course. Neither do I.'

The Grand II: The Roaring Twenties

'Perhaps you should be present when I tell them.'

'I really don't think that's necessary,' John demurred. 'But you must do what you think is best.'

Mrs Harvey waited until he left, before going through to the kitchen. Clapping her hands to gain the maids' attention, she shouted, 'Stop what you're doing and listen to me.' As they gathered around her, she flourished the small handbill. 'Some of you are thinking of going to a so-called lecture tonight.' Taking the paper in both hands, she tore it to shreds. 'I'm not having you filling your heads with filth. You're not to go. Any of you.'

'What's wrong with trying to educate ourselves?' Kate asked.

'It only takes one mistake to ruin your life. There's precious little mercy shown to a woman who's strayed. I wouldn't wish that on any of you.'

'I bet she's never seen Mr Harvey with his drawers off, never mind anybody else,' Brenda muttered acidly as the housekeeper walked away.

'I don't see how she can stop us going,' Kate countered mutinously.

'We'll just go. And see how she likes that,' Lynne added.

'Whatever you do, you should stick together,' Fred advised.

Kate piled the linen she was holding on to Lark. 'I'm going to see Mr Bannerman.'

'Shall we come with you, Kate?' Lynne shouted. But it was too late. Kate was already in the service lift.

'He's not going to support her against Harvey,' Brenda predicted.

'He'll probably sack her,' Lynne concurred.

'Then you all walk out,' Clive said firmly.

* * *

Katherine Hardy

Kate knocked at the open door of the study. Seeing Marcus and not John, she backed away.

'Sorry, sir, I was looking for Mr Bannerman.'

'You've found him.'

'No . . . I meant . . .'

'I know what you meant. What's the problem? Well, come on?'

Cornered, Kate reluctantly proceeded, convinced Marcus would be unsympathetic.

'There's this lecture, by the government, about relationships with men, having kids and all that. Mrs Harvey won't let us go, and it's not fair. Why shouldn't we?' she questioned, carried away by her indignation at the housekeeper's meddling. 'There's one of the maids, she's fourteen years old. She thinks the coal man brings babies. She'll end up having a kid that nobody wants. It happens all the time where I come from. And it's wrong. We want to go, and Mrs Harvey's got no right to stop us.' She hesitated, realising just who she was talking to. 'I'm sorry . . .'

'Don't apologise, just leave it with me.'

Stephen stopped Kate at the corner of the corridor. 'I wanted to tell you myself . . .'

'I could bring up some sandwiches the next time Miss Lloyd-Price comes round. Get Clive to dig up a nice bottle of wine for you.'

'If you like,' he answered evenly, too ashamed to rise to her sarcasm.

Too angry to say another word, Kate ran back to the servants' quarters, the only place she was beginning to feel she would ever belong.

'Is that everyone, Mrs Harvey?' Marcus asked as the maids assembled in the downstairs area.

'It's not a good time.' Intimidated by Marcus's glare, she looked to the staff. 'There's one or two still to come. Hurry up, Kate,' she shouted impatiently as Kate rounded the corner.

Marcus turned to the maids. 'I understand there's an educational lecture taking place this evening. And that some of you wish to attend—'

'I've dealt with that,' Mrs Harvey interrupted.

'I don't think so.' He glanced at Sarah, who walked in and stood behind the housekeeper. 'Those of you who want to go are free to do so.'

The maids stared at him incredulously.

Outraged, Mrs Harvey erupted, 'I'm sorry, Mr Bannerman, but I've expressly forbidden it. Have you any idea what this lecture is about?'

'Yes I have. And in fact, I think you should all go. Ignorance is the enemy of progress.' He continued to stare at the housekeeper. 'We have evidence of that wherever we look.'

'I've already spoken to Mr Bannerman.' Seeing Sarah, Mrs Harvey appealed to her. 'Mrs Bannerman . . .'

'I'm sorry, Mrs Harvey, but I happen to think they should go.'

'I'll speak to my brother.' Marcus addressed the girls. 'I'll arrange for transport to pick you up from the rear entrance at seven thirty sharp. And it will bring you straight back.' He smiled coldly at the housekeeper. 'Mrs Harvey, you may dismiss the staff.'

Ruth inspected the dark, dingy, furnished rooms Douglas Curzon had rented at her instigation. A friend had given her his name and told her that he'd been a medical practitioner until his name had been struck off the register. She hated doing business with

123

anyone of his reputation, but she knew of no one else who could offer the services Curzon could.

'Here we are.' He opened a door and walked across a room scarcely larger than a cupboard to another door. 'Bit of a bathroom. You're lucky, not many have bathrooms. Kitchen down the hall. Five guineas a month. Pay for your own gas and electricity.'

'Very well.'

'Telephone's extra. Will you want a telephone?'

'Yes, it's essential.'

'Right, a month in advance. Cash.'

Ruth reached for her purse. 'And you've arranged for me to see some women?'

'You didn't give me much notice.' Taking the money, he pushed it into his pocket. 'I've got four for you this afternoon.' He moved to the door. 'Make yourself at home.'

Ruth looked at the grim surroundings and shivered.

John shook Christina's hand. 'I'm pleased to meet you,' he muttered absently.

'Mother,' Stephen said as Sarah walked into the living room, 'this is Christina.'

'How do you do?' Sarah glanced uneasily at John as she shook Christina's hand. 'I'm afraid Stephen's told us hardly anything about you.'

'He doesn't know much. I think it's a good idea to have a few secrets, don't you?'

'Stephen did say something about a print works,' Sarah murmured, unnerved by John's preoccupation.

'Daddy's business. Terribly dull.'

'Christina was a nurse in the war,' Stephen announced proudly as they all sat down.

'Weren't you rather young?'

'I lied about my age, Mrs Bannerman.' Christina

enjoyed the shocked expressions on John's and Sarah's faces. 'What's a lie if it gets you what you want?'

'And is that what you want to do? Be a nurse?'

'God, no. I wouldn't mind being a doctor.'

'Isn't that a bit ambitious?' Sarah asked.

'Yes. I've been in touch with Oxford.'

'You never said,' Stephen interposed.

'They've deigned to let women take degrees now. I expect I'll have to wear a suit and smoke cigars. I'd like to find something I really want to do. I think that's important, don't you, Mrs Bannerman? Does Stephen inherit his business acumen from you, Mr Bannerman?' Christina addressed John, without giving Sarah an opportunity to answer.

'I'm sorry?' John apologised, his mind clearly elsewhere.

'He showed me the Manhattan. It seems to be a great success.'

'Don't sound so surprised.' Stephen remonstrated.

'Marcus,' Sarah called as he passed the door. 'Do join us. Come and meet Christina.'

'How do you do?' Marcus said breezily as he entered the room and shook Christina's hand. 'You're a friend of Stephen's?'

'And full of dangerous ideas,' Sarah said as she moved to make room for Marcus to sit beside her on the sofa.

'I like the sound of that.'

'Marcus is my uncle,' said Stephen. 'He owns the Manhattan.'

'So it's the sins of the uncle,' Christina smiled.

'I'm sorry?'

'Christina's amazed it's still standing with me in charge,' Stephen joked.

Marcus looked at John, sensing his exclusion. 'All Stephen's virtues stem from John. He has achieved things I never could.'

Reading something Marcus hadn't intended in the comment, John left his chair. 'If you'll excuse me, Christina.'

'Shall we go in for lunch?' Sarah suggested, concealing her disquiet as John left them.

'Yes, thank you.'

'Are you going to join us, Marcus?' Sarah looked to her brother-in-law.

'Why not?'

'We are honoured.'

'He's a very elusive figure is Marcus,' Stephen said as he offered Christina his arm. 'We don't know where he is half the time.'

'We wouldn't want to,' Sarah observed drily.

'I'm sure Christina knows what it's like having a busy social calendar. Church fêtes to attend. Charity luncheons . . .'

Christina's laughter joined Sarah's and Stephen's as they walked towards the lift.

John heard them in the study. Without realising what he was doing, he crumpled the bills he was holding into a tight ball.

Ruth sat opposite Curzon, watching as he lit a cigarette.

'I want to get it over with. I have to go back tonight.'

'You'll have to stay here. Catch a train in the morning.'

'My husband's expecting me.'

'Doesn't he know you're here?' When Ruth didn't answer, he raised his eyebrows. 'Well, well. What's all that about? Come in,' he called out in answer to a knock at the door.

A slatternly woman walked through the door. Ruth recoiled in disgust. She clearly hadn't washed in days.

'I know she doesn't look much,' Curzon said as he drew heavily on his cigarette. 'But she's reliable enough, is Rose. I've sold three of hers. Never had a complaint.'

'Who's the father?' Ruth asked.

'She's not sure. She never is. But in her case that's not a problem. She hates blacks.'

Fighting her initial impression, Ruth forced herself to look at the woman.

'No,' she refused abruptly. 'I don't think so.'

'Why not?' Rose demanded belligerently.

'Ask her to go,' Ruth ordered Curzon.

Curzon nodded impatiently at Rose.

'What about my money?' Rose whined.

'You get your money when I find a buyer. You know that.'

'I'll get rid of it.'

'No, you won't,' Curzon contradicted. 'Get out.' He turned to Ruth as Rose closed the door. 'You can't afford to be choosy.'

'She wasn't right. None of them has been right so far.'

'You're not going to get a debutante. This is a business for these women. If you're not careful you'll be going home empty-handed. Then what are you going to do?'

Chapter Nine

'It's been lovely meeting you.' Sarah shook Christina's hand.

'Yes, you must come and see us again,' Marcus added warmly.

Christina sank back on the sofa as they closed the door behind them. 'They like me.' Looking at Stephen, she patted the seat next to her.

'How can you be so sure?'

'I have that effect on people.'

'They'll ask me about you later.'

'What will you tell them?'

'I haven't the faintest idea. Oxford was a bit of a surprise. Is that what you want to do?'

'I don't know. I might. Do you think women should stay at home and tend to men's needs?'

'How should I know?' He moved closer to her.

'I can do that as well,' she smiled, inviting him to kiss her.

Ruth studied the pale, thin woman standing in the doorway. She looked sick, undernourished, but, for all of the obvious signs of poverty, there was a quiet dignity in her posture.

Curzon read from a list as he lit another cigarette. 'Edith West, twenty-five, lives in Millwall with her mother and four brothers—'

'And my two little ones,' Edith interrupted.

'They're like bloody rabbits,' Curzon condemned scathingly. 'Father, Michael Norris, sailor, white. Currently God knows where. She's clean. Stupid but clean.'

'Please, sit down.' Ruth indicated a chair, but Edith remained standing. 'What can you tell me about yourself? Why should I choose you?'

Edith shrugged her shoulders, unsure how to respond to the question.

'There's no point talking to them, Mrs Bannerman. They don't have brains. If they did, they wouldn't be here.'

'I need the money,' Edith snapped defiantly. 'I can barely feed the two I have already.'

'It's money. It's always money.'

'I want my baby to have a decent life. I can't give him that.'

'Him? You said him?' Ruth broke in eagerly.

'My mum says it's sitting like a boy.'

'What does his father look like?'

'He's quite tall,' Edith said slowly. 'He's got dark hair, a nice smile.'

'His eyes?' Ruth prompted.

'Brown.'

Ruth turned to Curzon. 'This is the one.'

'You're paying.'

'She knows—' She looked at Edith 'You do know you've got to live here?'

'Will I be able to see my little ones?'

'I need to know where you are. That you're all right. You mustn't do anything that jeopardises the baby. Do you understand?'

'I wouldn't.'

Katherine Hardy

'Don't worry about money. You'll have everything you need.'

Edith finally sat down; stunned, sick to the pit of her stomach, she could barely believe what had just happened.

Kate sat back on her heels and stared at the mess on her uniform. Both her dress and apron were filthy. She hated scrubbing floors.

'There's towels needed upstairs,' Mrs Harvey ordered abruptly from the doorway.

'You told me to do this. I'm filthy.'

'Then you'll have to get changed.' The housekeeper stared down at her. 'Are you going to refuse my instructions?'

'You'd like that, wouldn't you?' Kate retorted, allowing her temper to get the better of her.

'It was you, wasn't it? Went running off to Mr Bannerman?'

'You wouldn't listen to me.'

'Don't be in such a rush to know everything,' the housekeeper advised, softening her voice. 'Hold on to what's left of your innocence.'

'Don't you ever look out of the window and wonder?'

'That's foolish talk.'

'The only thing that reminds you that you're alive is being nasty to us.'

Kate saw the housekeeper cringe. 'Mrs Harvey . . .' she began tentatively, regretting her insensitivity.

'Towels, room fifteen, room twenty-two,' Mrs Harvey barked, retreating back into her shell. 'And Stephen Bannerman,' she added cruelly.

'What was it like when you gave birth?' Ruth asked

The Grand II: The Roaring Twenties

Edith.

'What do you mean?'

'When your first child was born? How did it feel?'

'I hope you don't mind me asking. But can't you have babies of your own?'

'We're trying, but it hasn't happened yet. Tell me.'

'I had a terrible time carrying him. I was sick mostly.'

'That's not what I meant.'

'But when he was born . . .' A smile lit Edith's thin careworn face.

'Yes?' Ruth pressed impatiently.

'He was making a terrible noise. Soon as he came out. He was all squashed up. But he was the most beautiful thing I'd ever seen.' She faltered for a moment, looked at Ruth and saw the eagerness on her face. 'He wanted feeding, so I just . . . did it. It's like nothing else. You will look after my baby, won't you?' she pleaded, looking for reassurance.

'Good evening, my dear. You look wonderful,' Arthur Shaw complimented as Esme walked down the stairs of the Grand into the foyer.

'Thank you.'

As they turned to leave, John left reception with a sheet of late bookings. 'Arthur.' John shook his hand. 'Miss Harkness.'

'I hope all goes well tonight,' said Arthur. 'I've had a word in the appropriate ears. If Sarah could be there . . .' he added tactfully. 'It does help.'

'I know, and thank you, Arthur.'

'I shall need some sort of padding,' Ruth informed Curzon as she gathered her things together.

'Normally I'd say stay indoors, and if you have to go

out wear a big coat.'

'Can you do it?' she asked impatiently.

'I can do anything if you pay me enough.'

'I'll need it very soon.'

'I should have known when you turned up on your own. I usually meet the husband.'

'The padding?' she reminded sternly.

'Does he know you've lost it? Is he out of the country?'

'That's none of your business.'

'It's such a comedown, isn't it? Having to do business with a man like me. Where do you think I came from?'

'Get out,' Ruth ordered fiercely.

Curzon threw the keys on the table. 'Don't forget to lock up.'

As the door closed behind him, Ruth picked up a chair and threw it to the floor. Using every ounce of strength she could muster, she continued to smash it until it was no more than a bundle of matchwood. Only then did she allow herself to cry for the child she had carried for so long and would never know.

'Are my seams straight?' Brenda asked Lynne, lifting her skirt.

'Stockings? Where do you think we're going?' Lynne joined the queue of maids waiting by the back door. 'Hurry up, Kate.'

'I know I'm late.' Suddenly realising she was the only maid still in uniform, Kate dashed towards the door, bumping into John Bannerman.

'Kate?' John frowned at the assembled maids, as he folded the list of late bookings he'd brought down for Mrs Harvey. 'Where's everybody going?'

'We're going to a lecture. Excuse me, sir.' The rest

of the maids fell silent, as she darted off down the corridor.

'Mrs Harvey,' John called as he went to the office and handed the list to the housekeeper. 'What's going on?'

'Didn't your brother tell you, sir?' she enquired coldly.

'What do you think they'll tell them? At this lecture?' Fred handed over the bottle of beer he was sharing with Clive, and lit a cigarette.

'I don't know. What is there to say?'

'Right. I mean you either know it, or you don't.'

'Yeah.' Clive took a swig from the bottle.

'They don't have lectures for blokes, do they?'

'No,' Clive replied thoughtfully, holding the stub of his cigarette between his fingers and drawing on it.

'Have you ever been with a lass? You know . . . all the way?

'Have you?'

'Course I have. I mean not a lot. And I'm not one of those blokes who goes on about it. Well, I mean I do. When I've got to. You know, in the pub.'

'What were it like?'

'What?'

'When you did it?'

'You know . . . you know what it's like.'

'Yeah, course,' Clive lied, handing the beer back to Fred.

Arthur leaned close to Esme across their table in the Manhattan.

'Another time I'd like to take you to a little place in Didsbury. It only opened recently.'

'French cuisine?'

'Do you know it?'

'Only by report.'

'It's charming.'

'I'll look forward to it. I'm very fond of Manchester, Mr Shaw, but decent restaurants are hard to find.'

Arthur raised his glass. 'Here's to an enjoyable quest.' He blanched as Esme touched her glass to his. 'Excuse me, a business associate.' He left the table and hurried over to the door, where a group of men were handing their coats into the cloakroom. Seeing Esme watching him, he turned his back to her.

'What the hell do you think you're doing?' John raged at Sarah as he entered their living room.

'What?' she looked up from her book.

'Mrs Harvey told the maids they were not to go to the lecture. I gave her my full support. And you went against my decision.'

'I think you were wrong.'

'You defied me. In public.'

'I used my own judgment.'

'But Mrs Harvey is in charge of the staff. And she didn't think it was appropriate for them to go.'

'So, Mrs Harvey's your moral guide now, is she?'

'Don't be ridiculous.'

'I'll tell you what's ridiculous, John. Foolish girls stumbling into pregnancy because they don't know any better.'

'You're missing the point, Sarah.'

'I don't think so.'

'You sided with my brother against me. In front of the staff. You betrayed me.'

'By doing what I felt was right?'

'We should stand together, side by side. That's what people expect.' He watched as she went to the sideboard. 'You haven't time for a drink. We're due at the Liberal Association.'

'*You* might be.'

'I want you there. With me. I insist on it.'

'I beg your pardon?' Sarah demanded, outraged

'I have a right to expect your loyalty and your support.'

'And I have a right to my own opinions.'

'Do you imagine my mother would have hesitated for one second if my father had said what I just have?'

'Your father was a bully. I despised him.'

'He achieved things. He made his mark. And my mother stood by his side without question and without reservation.'

'Then she was a fool,' snapped Sarah.

'I want you to do something for *me*. What's so unreasonable about that? You've got everything you want. I've never denied you anything, and this is what you give me in return. Are you so selfish that you can't see beyond your own petty self-interest?' He glared at her and she stared back, her eyes, cold, frosty. 'I want you with me tonight. You *will* come with me, Sarah.' He raised his voice to her for the first time in their married life. 'You *will* come.'

Slowly, deliberately, Sarah reached for the brandy. She poured herself a drink and lifted the glass to her lips. Clenching his fists, John turned and stormed out through the door.

'Miss Harkness,' Stephen led Christina to the table where Esme Harkness, was sitting alone. 'May I introduce Christina Lloyd-Price?'

'Pleased to meet you. Do join me.'

'Miss Harkness is a resident of the Grand,' Stephen explained.

'Really? I think it's wonderful.'

'I showed Christina around today.'

'I see.'

'Christina's a . . . friend of mine. A good friend,' Stephen added.

'I can see that,' Miss Harkness smiled, noticing that they couldn't stop looking at each other.

'You're not waiting for someone?' Christina asked.

'I was expecting a gentleman, but I think I've made a mistake.'

'You got the wrong date?'

'It's easily done.' She glanced across at a neighbouring table where Arthur Shaw was telling a ribald joke.

Marcus was using the telephone in the office when John ran down the stairs and out through the front door. Marcus had caught only a glimpse of his brother's face, but it had been enough to gauge his mood. Having cut his conversation short, he headed for the lift.

Sarah was alone in the living room. Seeing Marcus, she poured another drink. As she handed it to him their fingers touched. Setting the drinks aside, he cupped her face in his hands and kissed her. When she returned his embrace, he broke free and stared at her. Then he left.

Marcus cursed under his breath when he saw Collins manning the reception desk. Then one of the Australian cricketers demanded the concierge's attention.

'Excuse me.'

'Yes, sir.' Collins glanced at Marcus as he spoke to the guest.

'We need you to recommend a decent boozer.'

'Certainly, sir. I think you'll enjoy the King's Head. Turn left out of the hotel. Two hundred yards down the road. You can't miss it.'

'Thanks a lot. Let's go,' the cricketer shouted to the noisy crowd waiting behind him.

When Collins looked back, Marcus was already halfway up the stairs. He glanced at the board. There was a key missing. Room thirty-two. Setting his jaw, he directed a waiting party of guests towards the dining room.

'If you put your fingers like this' – Fred laid his index finger along the seam of his cricket ball – 'that Aussie reckons it'll turn a mile.'

'Let's have a go.' As Clive reached for the ball, the maids trailed into the back yard.

'Come on then. Tell us all about it?' Fred urged Lynne.

'Get lost!'

'What?'

'I said get lost. Are you deaf?' she walked away.

'What did I say?' Fred asked innocently.

'It was horrible.' Kate sank down on the step beside the boys. 'All they did was frighten us. They told us that if we went with lads, we'd be no better than prostitutes. That we'd catch syphilis.'

'They talked about that?' Clive was aghast at the thought.

'The things they said and showed us . . .' Kate closed her eyes recalling images she wished she hadn't seen. 'They were disgusting. That's not why I went.'

'They had no right to frighten you,' Fred said angrily.

'They lied to us. They bloody lied to us. It doesn't

have to be like that. Not if you love somebody.' She saw Clive looking at her, but much as she wanted him to agree with her, he remained silent.

As Christina left Esme's table to join Stephen, Esme picked up her handbag, and signalled to the cloak-room girl to bring her wrap. Then she walked over to Vincent Markham's table, where Arthur Shaw was still holding court.

'Mr Shaw? When you invited me out this evening, I had my doubts as to your motives, and despite your public standing, I had limited expectations of the occasion. But I did not imagine common courtesy to be beyond you.' Making a small bow, she acknowledged Arthur's companions.

'Mr Markham, do you still enjoy the Norfolk Broads?' Holding her head high, she walked out through the door.

After half an hour of searching, Fred found Lynne huddled in a corner in the pantry.

'Lynne . . .'

'Go away.'

'Kate told us. What they said.' Seeing a tear on her cheek, he drew closer. 'They shouldn't have done that.'

'Get your hands off,' she cried as he tried to hold her.

'It's not going to happen to you.'

'It might have happened already for all we know. I must have been bloody mad.' She pushed his hand away.

'You've only ever been with me, haven't you?'

'Course I bloody have, and I wish I bloody hadn't. I should have listened to my mum. She always told me to drink nowt stronger than tea, and keep my knees together. What's up with you?' she asked, when Fred smiled.

'Nothing. I was just thinking about last night.'

'I wish it never happened.'

'We didn't do anything wrong.'

'If you tell anybody, I'll kill you.'

'I won't.' Braving her anger, he put his arm around her. Lynne rested her head on his shoulder. It actually felt good to accept his comfort.

'We don't have long.' Marcus stroked Sarah's hair as she snuggled down in the bed beside him.

'What have we done?'

'What we've wanted to do for a long time,' he suggested.

'I know. But it won't happen again. It can't.' She leaned across and kissed him as he swung his legs out of the bed.

John walked into the living room, laid his gloves on the sideboard and looked around. There were two full glasses of brandy on the table. He checked his bedroom, then went downstairs.

'Have you seen my wife, Jacob?' he asked Collins, who was still manning reception.

'No, sir.'

'She didn't go out?'

'I really have no idea, sir.' John pulled the ledger towards him. 'I've checked the bookings, sir. It's all in order,' Collins protested as John ran his finger down the list. 'How was your meeting, sir?'

'It went very well, thank you, Jacob.' John looked up at the keys. 'I thought you said you'd checked the book.'

'I have, sir.'

'We don't have a booking for room thirty-two.'

'No, sir.'

'Then where's the key?'

'I've no idea, sir.'

'I can trust you, Jacob? If someone was using a room without registering, you'd know about it.'

'That's right.'

John headed for the stairs as Ruth walked in.

Sick with apprehension, Collins greeted her. 'Good evening, Mrs Bannerman.'

Ignoring the concierge, she followed John up the stairs.

Marcus pulled on his jacket. Straightening his tie, he kissed Sarah one last time before leaving the room. Looking neither left nor right, he walked quickly down the corridor – which was why he didn't see John standing in the window alcove.

Stepping into the lift, he immediately hit the button for the top floor – and his wife's bedroom. Less than a minute later, he knocked on the door, and waited for her to call 'Come in' before opening it.

The sight of Ruth lying, spent and exhausted on the bed, pricked his conscience.

'How are you feeling?' he asked solicitously. 'You must be tired?'

'I'm fine,' she replied unconvincingly.

He sat on the bed next to her. 'I've made some plans for the nursery. You can see them tomorrow and let me know what you think.' Ruth looked away. 'I want us to agree on what we want. It's something we can do together.' Rising to his feet, he kissed her gently on the forehead. She didn't even look up as he walked away.

The Grand II: The Roaring Twenties

* * *

John had to wait another half-hour before the door of room thirty-two opened a second time. Smoothing the skirt of her dress, Sarah hurried away.

He pushed the door of the room open. The sheets on the bed were flung back, rumpled. A bottle of wine and two glasses stood on the bedside cabinet. He picked up the bottle. It was empty. He touched the bottom sheet. It was still warm. He lifted it to his face. It smelled of perfume – Sarah's.

Only then did he allow the tears that burnt at the back of his eyes to fall.

He slammed the door behind him, sank his face in his hands and cried, knowing that no matter what happened now, he had lost everything he had valued in life. And there was no way of winning it back. Not the way it had been.

Chapter Ten

John prepared for bed that night, but he remained in his dressing room. He couldn't bring himself to lie next to Sarah. He simply couldn't. Hunched in his dressing gown, he wandered to the window and opened the curtains to look down on the sleeping city, occasionally glancing through the door to the bedroom where Sarah seemed to be sleeping peacefully. When he couldn't stand his resentment or thoughts a moment longer, he stepped out into the corridor.

He had only to close his eyes to see and hear them. Those two small boys that had been him and Marcus. Boisterous, warring, screaming, always fighting . . .

'Bang! Bang! You're dead!' Had that been him, or Marcus?

And then the blow that was a fraction too hard. The tears that invariably ended their games and the mocking laughter of the victor. Him? Or Marcus?

He stepped into the darkened living room and saw a woman standing in front of the fireplace, young, breathtakingly beautiful. She smiled, and held out the baby in her arms.

'I thought, Catherine. Catherine Mary Bannerman.'

John stepped forward and she faded. Right place, wrong time. He'd never be able to reach that other, younger Sarah again, not now. She'd gone. Faded into his brother's arms – and his bed.

Thrust rudely from sleep by a banging on her door, Esme Harkness reached for her robe. She opened her door, surprised to see John Bannerman standing in the corridor, wild-eyed, dishevelled.

'Are you alone?'

She opened the door wider to show him that she was, and to invite him in.

'A small matter of business, Miss Harkness,' he said thickly. 'Strictly business. I'd like you to find me a girl. That's your profession, isn't it?' he questioned in response to the blank expression on her face. 'I want a girl.'

'What sort of a girl?' she asked coolly.

'I don't know, a girl,' he repeated dully.

'Blonde, brunette . . .?'

'Blonde.'

'Age? In her twenties, thirties?'

'Twenties, young,' he said decisively.

'With their own accommodation, or can she visit you here?'

'Here. Definitely in the Grand.'

'If you want quality, that's three guineas.'

'Fine.'

'Of course I'll do no such thing.'

'Am I not good enough?'

'I'd say the opposite, Mr Bannerman.' She hesitated. 'It's not my concern, but if there's a problem in your marriage—'

'That's what you're here for isn't it? You and your kind. If there's a problem, the men come to you and the marriage keeps going, the world keeps turning. Thanks to the whores . . .' Realising how insensitive that sounded, he stopped himself from saying more by walking away.

Esme watched him go, genuinely concerned for one of the few good men she had met in her life.

Holding the candle above her head, Kate clutched the edges of the shawl she'd flung over her nightdress, and peered cautiously into the kitchen.

'Lynne?' she whispered anxiously. 'Lynne?'

Lynne popped her head around the door of the pantry, her hair wild and her dressing gown open. 'I'm here, Kate.'

'You've been gone ages. I thought you were sick.'

'No, not me. I'm just . . . tidying up.'

'It must be two o'clock. What's there to tidy?'

Fred wrapped his arm around Lynne's shoulders as he looked out. 'Me,' he smirked.

'Shurrup, you.' Lynne slapped him.

'I'm going,' Kate smiled. 'I'm going.'

As Fred grabbed Lynne and pulled her back into the cupboard, their laughter echoed eerily around the deserted kitchen.

'We draw up a contract with the Midland Hotel,' Marcus said as he laid the papers on the office desk in front of John and Sarah. 'If we're full one week, we pass surplus guests on to them, and vice versa. It should profit both of us.'

'It makes sense, John,' Sarah persuaded. 'The two hotels working together instead of being at war.'

'Good.' John rose to his feet. 'It seems you're both decided, fine. Well done.'

'Where are you going?' Sarah asked.

'Out.'

'Of course, if it was *his* idea, we'd be celebrating

now.' Marcus thrust the papers into an envelope as John walked out of the front door.

Sarah handed him a folder. 'You might take time to read this. The MacMillan banking house, they've got a good reputation and they're looking to expand . . .'

'Why are you showing me this?'

'We could approach them to buy out your share in the Grand.'

'So you want rid of me?'

'It was my invitation that brought you to the Grand. I asked you in and it worked. You got what you wanted. So, this is my next decision. It's time for you to move on, Marcus.'

'Mr Collins, sir?' The porter on reception duty called the concierge to the desk.

Jacob turned to see a man he'd hoped never to see again, walking through the front doors. David Jeffries handed his case to a porter, only too aware that the entire duty staff of doormen and bellboys were staring at him.

'Mr Jeffries, you weren't expected,' Jacob Collins said coldly.

'I telephoned last night.'

Collins checked with the receptionist. 'I've not seen a booking. Is that true?'

'Adam was on duty last night, sir. He's new, he wouldn't know the name.'

Collins went to the office and rapped on the glass. 'Mr Bannerman?'

Marcus looked up from his paperwork. Seeing Jeffries, he walked out into the foyer.

'Look,' Jeffries pleaded. 'Just give me the key. I'll keep out of your way. Let's get this over and done with.'

'Send him away, Collins,' Marcus commanded, without looking at Jeffries. 'Get rid of him.'

Jeffries took a deep breath, hating every minute of the scene he'd caused.

'If that's your position Mr Bannerman, I'll have no choice but to instruct my father's solicitor.'

Marcus finally looked at him. 'In here,' he ordered, opening the office door.

Clive slammed down the crate of empties he'd been carrying out of the bar and walked down the corridor that led below stairs. He was almost running by the time he reached the maids' workstation.

'David bloody Jeffries just walked in, proud as you like,' he told Brenda. 'Where's Kate?' Horror-struck, Brenda gaped gormlessly at him. 'Kate?' he repeated.

'Back door.'

'Kate, got a minute?' Clive pushed his way through the throng of maids, emptying rubbish from their trolleys.

'Yeah, sure, some time next year.'

'Clive Evans, we're that busy you can chat in your dinnertime,' Mrs Harvey said crossly. 'Go on. Off with you.'

'You should all know. Mr Jeffries, Mr David Jeffries, he's come back.' He looked at Kate. 'Sorry.'

The maid stood in silence for a moment while the news sank in. Then she picked up the brush and pan from her trolley and started cleaning them.

'Who's Mr Jeffries?' Lark asked in a small voice.

'He's a guest,' Mrs Harvey answered. 'Remember that, please, all of you. He's one of the guests.'

'You've made your point,' Marcus shouted angrily. 'You came back in February, and we suffered that, on condition that it happened once and once only.'

'It's one night,' Jeffries explained. 'There's an emergency at the Manchester office, an insurance claim. I have to put things right, then I'll be gone, I promise. I didn't want to stay here. My father insisted.'

'Then this is absolutely the last time. Mr Collins, give him a room. And, Jeffries, you stay in that room. You don't use the restaurant or the bar, and you don't ever talk to any of my staff. Understood?'

Jeffries nodded agreement and went. Marcus waved out the concierge, unable to face the disgust mirrored on his face.

Jeffries took the key the receptionist handed him and ran across the foyer to the lift.

'Hold that,' he called, and stepped in, alongside Esme Harkness. Bowing politely, he murmured, 'Excuse me.'

Collins called out to the liftboy. 'Alfred?' but he was too late. Alfred slammed the door and sent the lift to the second floor. He turned to the concierge.

'Yes, sir?'

Having no other choice, Jacob Collins headed for the stairs.

Esme stared straight ahead. Anything other than look at Jeffries. A few seconds later they stopped at the first floor.

'Good day.' Jeffries left the cage.

Esme didn't acknowledge him. She waited until he disappeared into room thirty-five before going to her own room and slamming the door soundly behind her.

Trembling, she gripped the edge of the table in an attempt to compose herself.

'Who is it?' she called out, ridiculously frightened by a knock on her door.

'Miss Harkness, are you all right?'

Pulling herself together, she opened the door. The concierge stood there, panting, out of breath having run up the flight of stairs.

'I'm so sorry. None of us knew.'

'No matter. I've been expecting it. He would always come back.' She stepped back, inviting him into the room. 'He doesn't know me. We never met. Isn't that funny? I saw him in court from the public gallery. I was a face in the crowd. The crowd baying for her blood . . .'

'It's for one night.'

'Blood will out, Mr Collins. His punishment will find him. Be certain of that.'

The glitter and glitz of the Manhattan appeared cheap and tawdry in the afternoon sunlight as John stood before the bar, while Stephen, shirtsleeves rolled to his elbows, shifted crates of empties.

'It's a bit last minute,' Stephen apologised, 'and I know it's boring, but Christina's parents want to meet you. So, I thought, dinner, tonight. Jim can run this place for a few hours. Mum says it's all right. Do you want a drink?'

'No, I was just . . . passing. That's the entire family I suppose? Marcus as well?'

'If he wants to come, but it's you they want to meet.'

'He's been very good to you, Marcus,' John continued, 'giving you all this.'

'I won't get rich on these wages.'

'Oh, you'll succeed. You're just like him, in all sorts of ways. Sharp in business. Popular, especially with women.'

Puzzled by his father's mood, Stephen shoved the last crate towards the storeroom. 'There, come on.

One drink.'

'You're so very like Marcus. It must be in the blood . . . I should go. Sorry, I'm in the way.'

'What about tonight?' Stephen asked.

'I'll be there, dependable as ever.'

Stephen looked after his father as he went to the door. He was in such a strange mood. Then he looked at everything that needed to be done if he was going to take most of the night off, and set to work.

'You see these advertisements in the posh papers,' Lynne confided archly to Fred as they sat on her bed in the room she shared with Kate and Lark. 'Butler and cook, married couple preferred.'

'Who's that, then? You and me?'

'I'm just saying.'

'Blimey, Lynne, that's a bit previous.'

'Don't get your hopes up. There's plenty chasing me, Frederick Willets. Though you did say . . .'

'Say what?'

'You love me.'

'Well, yeah . . .'

'I knew it!' She thumped his shoulder – hard. 'Lying through your teeth! You're all the same: bit of turmoil in your trousers, and out pop the words, love, love, love. It's like them whatchamacallits. Pavlova's dogs.'

'It's just, it's all a bit fast, that's all. I didn't plan this to happen . . .'

'What do you mean, plan it? Who the heck plans it? Monday, get me hair cut; Tuesday, visit Mother; Wednesday, fall in love. You're mad, you are. And don't go thinking I'm in love with you, sunshine.'

'Are you though?'

'None of your business.'

'You might be, though?' He smiled.

'I might be many things. I might be the Queen of Sheba.'

'Maybe I meant it. But only if you meant it too.'

'If you're lucky. And lucky means, say, they had another war, and all the men in the whole wide world got killed, except for you, because you were stuck in a cupboard – then, maybe . . . perhaps . . . you might stand a chance. Now shut your face and give us a kiss.'

As his lips touched hers, they were interrupted by a hammering on the door.

'Staff meeting, all of you, right now,' Mrs Harvey called sharply.

'Hide!' Lynne pushed Fred off the bed. He dived under it as she went to the door.

Lynne leaned out to see Mrs Harvey walking along the corridor knocking on all the doors.

'Staff meeting!' the housekeeper repeated.

'What's it about?'

'Not like you, Lynne Milligan, to be behind with the gossip. Hurry up and you'll find out. That's you as well, Fred,' she called back as she walked on.

Sarah, Marcus and Mrs Harvey stood in front of the assembled staff. Marcus nodded and Sarah stepped forward.

'Now, some of you are new, and I'd rather you heard the facts from us instead of rumours. Last October a member of staff in this hotel, a housemaid by the name of Monica Jones, was in the company of Mr Jeffries . . .'

'She wasn't staff, she'd resigned. She wasn't in my charge,' Mrs Harvey broke in, looking to absolve herself of any blame.

'Accepted, yes,' Sarah agreed. 'Monica was in the company of three men, Mr Jeffries, Mr Armitage and a Mr Tyler . . .'

'They raped her.'

'Kate, please . . .' Mrs Harvey admonished.

'I think we should all be allowed to speak,' Marcus interrupted.

'The three of them, they raped her,' Kate reiterated loudly.

Sarah hesitated, knowing that to agree with Kate would make her a party to slander. 'Monica retaliated against one of those men, Mr Jackson Tyler,' she continued, choosing her words carefully. 'She killed him and for that crime, Monica Jones was hanged. But in court, the two surviving men maintained that Monica was in the bedroom of her own free will. That she was being paid. The court of law believed those men. No charges were brought against them. As a result we're stuck with David Jeffries as a paying guest whether we like it or not.'

'It's your hotel. You can chuck him out.'

'The law's on his side, Kate,' Sarah explained. 'Mr Jeffries' father has taken legal action against anyone slandering his son's name. The Piccadilly club tried to withdraw Jeffries' membership, and his father sued them and won. They had to pay a thousand pounds in damages. The Grand couldn't afford that.'

'It all comes down to money in the end.'

'Yes it does, Kate,' Marcus agreed pragmatically. 'If we were fined, we'd have to pay for it by losing staff. Half of you would get the sack.'

'It's the second time he's come back,' Sarah pointed out. 'We coped before, we'll cope again. None of the maids will have to go near him. Mrs Harvey will clean his room.'

'Wouldn't touch her, would he?' Lynne muttered to Brenda.

'But Mrs Harvey goes home every night,' Clive complained, 'and last time he was calling down for all sorts. He wanted suits laying out, meals in his room, and Mr Collins is busy half the time. I had to go up there.'

'Tell you what, I can do that,' Fred offered.

'You will not!' Lynne exclaimed.

'I wasn't here. I don't know him—'

'You can button it, you can—'

'Lynne! We're not in the monkey house, thank you very much,' Mrs Harvey reprimanded.

'It's a very good idea, thank you, Frederick,' Sarah accepted quietly.

'Traitor!' Lynne whispered.

'I know this is difficult,' Sarah said finally. 'So I'd like to thank you, very much indeed. Now, that man's wasted enough of our time. Back to work.'

Muttering mutinously, the staff began to move away. Marcus put his arm around Sarah's waist and led her back upstairs. Until in the end only Kate was left. Bitter, angry and tearful.

'The truth is rather more complicated. Isn't it always?' John asked Collins as he sat back in his chair in the office and poured himself a glass of whisky. 'Jeffries' father owns Imperial Shipping. All their clients stay at the Grand, a special deal arranged by Marcus. All neatly sewn up, thanks to my brother. Marcus can say the right thing, then do the opposite, and, of course, then he has to go further. Money isn't enough. Profit isn't enough, no. He has to find something far more exciting. Sleeping with my wife. That's about as exciting as you can get, don't you think?' As he looked at

Collins he realised it was the first time he'd actually admitted Sarah's infidelity to anyone. 'How long have you known, Jacob?'

'Mr Bannerman, I'm sorry, I really couldn't say . . .'

'How long have you known about this?' he repeated.

'I don't know, sir. I first saw . . . an indication on the wedding day. Your brother's wedding.'

'Eight months?' John smiled briskly as he rose to his feet. 'Well, you needn't worry about Mr Jeffries. You needn't worry about a single thing, not any more. You're sacked. You'll get paid off – money for a good retirement. Marcus can pay.'

'Mr Bannerman—'

'I said you're sacked.' John's pent-up emotions finally burst to the surface. 'Eight months and you said nothing! Get out! Get out of my sight!'

Concerned only for John, Collins walked away. The staff in the foyer stared towards the office, but John remained oblivious. He reached for the whisky, and poured himself another glass.

For once, the maids worked in silence in the downstairs service corridor. After replenishing their trolleys, Lynne, Brenda and Lark set off for the guest bedrooms. Kate took a pile of clean linen just up from the laundry, and went to the cupboard. Sorting through, she piled like on like, sheets on sheets, pillow cases on pillow cases . . .

'You're Kate. Kate Morris?'

Whirling around, she saw David Jeffries in the doorway. She wanted to scream but the sound died in her throat.

'You gave evidence, you were her friend, you were kind to her that night. I just wanted to—'

'Leave me alone.' Her voice was hoarse, barely audible.

'Look, it's all right, you're perfectly safe. I don't mean to—'

'You're not allowed in here, it's private, it's staff. Get out!'

He held out his hand and offered her a roll of bank-notes. 'It's money, that's all. It's for Monica, her family. The court paid me damages, her family should have some . . .'

The air – thick, red – seemed to close in on her. Jeffries' face loomed, leering, terrifying, above her own. She could feel his breath, hot, scalding, on her cheeks, just the way Monica must have done. Losing all control, she went wild. She dropped the linen and flew towards him, hitting, kicking, crying. She wanted to hurt him – the way he had hurt Monica.

'It's for her!' he pleaded. 'Her family! I'm trying to help, can't you see that?'

He fell back as she pushed him aside and ran down the corridor, crying, screaming, totally distraught. Wanting someone, anyone, but most of all, Monica.

Collins knew John Bannerman too well to begin packing. He sat in his room and waited for the knock that he knew would come.

'Jacob?' John walked in. 'I didn't mean . . .'

'No, sir.' He rose to his feet.

'I keep thinking, What have I done wrong? All the time hoping that the answer is nothing. Done nothing wrong. I could cope with that. Being a martyr, but I'm not. What have I done wrong? Jacob, it's such a list. Such a long, long, list.' He finally broke down. As his sobs heightened into hysteria, Jacob stepped forward. He wanted to help, but nothing could change the situation between them. John was the master, he the servant. That was the way it had always been, and always would be.

Chapter Eleven

Lynne pulled her stool closer to the fire, and whispered as her fellow maids gathered closer.

'. . . and Monica's screams echoed through the building, up and down the stairwells. But there was no escape from that terrible lust. They locked the door and had their wicked way . . . twice.'

Brenda tapped her tea mug on the table. The entire group sat up straight, sipping their tea in an exemplary, ladylike manner. Mrs Harvey gave them a highly suspicious look as she walked past.

'And none could save sweet Monica Jones,' Lynne continued as soon as the housekeeper was out of earshot. 'I was tucked up in me bed, dreaming soft dreams, while me best friend was plundered—'

'Excuse me,' Brenda broke in. 'You hated her.'

'You can hate your friends, Brenda Potter. Believe me.' Lynne turned back to the girls. 'They say on a dark night you can still hear those screams. She's trapped in everlasting torment, locked within room thirty-five for all eternity.'

Lark stared wide-eyed, open-mouthed, taking in every word.

Fred checked the room number, thirty-five, knocked on the door and carried in the dinner tray.

'Down there,' Jeffries ordered sharply.

'Anything else, sir?' Fred asked, as he laid the tray on the table.

'Sir?' Jeffries mocked. 'It's a long time since anyone in the Grand Hotel called me that.'

'Just asking? Anything you need, sir?'

'Yes, have a good look round, tell them all about me. Very clever putting me in this room. Oh, yes. I've got work to do. I'm a busy man. How am I supposed to sleep in this godforsaken room?'

'Sorry, sir. It's not up to me.'

'Go on, bugger off.' He stopped Fred at the door. 'And you can tell them I didn't *ask* to be here. I'd sooner sleep on the streets. But my father has to rub it in.'

'It's nothing to do with me, sir. I'm new, only been here two months. I didn't even know her. For what it's worth, sir, we don't all judge you.'

'Well, then, you should,' Jeffries bit back acidly.

'You're not the first man . . . look, I had a bit of trouble meself, a while back with a girl. It can happen so easy. I know that. I had to move on and I ended up here.'

'What sort of trouble?' Jeffries' curiosity overrode his angry mood.

'With a girl. I did nothing wrong, it was all her fault. Anyway, just to say, sir, you're not the only one.' He smiled conspiratorially as he opened the door. 'Better be off. And, sir. That's just between you and me. I've got to work with these people. They might not like it.'

'Of course,' David Jeffries agreed, pleased at the confidence.

Stephen walked into the family living room to see Kate laying the dining table with the best china and cutlery.

'Excellent, well done, Kate. You've got the forks the wrong way round.'

'Where?'

'No, you haven't.' When she turned her back on him and continued to work, he apologised. 'All right, it wasn't funny.'

'You don't even know, do you?'

'What?'

'Another world, you. David Jeffries is back.'

'In the hotel?'

'No, in me mother's pantry.' She turned a strained, tear-stained face to his. 'He talked to me. He was that close. I keep seeing his face, I can't stand it. Me head's in bits . . .'

'Come here, sit down.' He settled her on the sofa.

'That's what she must have seen. His face, up close.'

'Kate, take a holiday, just until he's gone. I'll clear it with Dad. For once, I wish I was running the Grand. I'd throw him out.'

Kate smiled through her tears. 'I'd like to see that. Stephen Bannerman's Grand Hotel. Free drinks and gambling on every floor.'

They both laughed, then Stephen rose quickly to his feet as Christina walked in. Embarrassed, Kate dried her eyes and returned to the table.

'I'm the advance party,' Christina announced. 'My parents arrive in ten minutes, so you'd better man the barricades.'

'Christina Lloyd-Price, Kate Morris. Kate is one of the maids,' Stephen explained.

'Thank God for that. For a moment, I thought it was fancy dress.' Seeing that Kate was upset, she retreated. 'I'll come back.'

'No, I'm done.' Kate picked up the empty cutlery tray. 'Nice to meet you, miss.' She bobbed a curtsy as she left.

'You look beautiful,' Stephen complimented.

'Really? I can wear a maid's uniform if you'd prefer.'

'Now you're talking.' He smiled as he kissed her.

John replaced his clothes brush on his dresser.

'They'll be here any minute.' He barely glanced at Sarah as she emerged from her dressing room. 'I'll head down.'

'How do I look?'

'Good. Lovely. Everything would appear to be fine.' He walked out of their bedroom, leaving Sarah with the uncomfortable impression that something was very wrong.

'Go on, tell me,' Lynne nagged Fred as they sat in the kitchen. 'Did Jeffries have his meal in front of you? What was he like? Dribble, down his chin? Ooh, he makes me shiver.'

'Lynne, maybe he's not that bad.'

'Not that bad? Not that bad!'

'Bit louder,' he suggested caustically. 'There's an old woman in Wrexham didn't catch that. Look,' he sighed, 'he's not . . . I don't know . . . he's an ordinary bloke. Come here.' He pulled her closer, intending to give her a cuddle.

'Poor little Fred,' she teased.

'Yeah, yeah.' He kissed her, gently at first, then, when he realised they were alone, his hands wandered over the bodice of her dress.

'Now steady . . .'

'Let's go to your room.'

'Cheeky beggar.'

'Just to talk?'

'Oh aye. No chance, Fred Willets.'

'Sod off, then.'

'I will an' all.' She flounced away, but she paused at the door, watching, as he left the stool he'd been sitting on, to kick the coal bucket.

'Fred,' she called back. 'I'll see you later?'

He nodded grimly as he walked away, leaving her wondering if she'd carried her teasing too far.

Fred retreated to the bedroom he shared with Clive to find his roommate reading his private papers and laughing.

'What are you doing with those?' Fred demanded, angrily seizing the letters.

'I was looking for matches, that's all. Not bad references. "I can attest Frederick Willets has the most pleasing disposition . . ." All right, calm down. You never said you worked at the Savoy. That's posh.'

'Well, it never cropped up.'

'What d'you want to leave a job like that for? Me dad's brother worked there. Loved it. That old bloke, Macready – did you get on with him?'

'Dunno, there was lots of staff.'

'Fred, he's the hall porter.' He smiled slyly as he flicked the papers. 'You made these up.'

'You calling me a liar?'

'All right. Keep your lid on. It's nice to know that you can forge me a late-night pass when I need one.'

Fred tore the papers in half as Clive strolled, whistling, out of the door.

Collins drew Esme Harkness aside as she walked into the foyer.

'I'm afraid it's happened. That problem we discussed. John Bannerman, he knows.' He glanced anxiously at his employer, who was greeting his guests some distance away.

'Yes, he came to my room last night.'

'What for?'

Esme ignored the question. 'The last time Jeffries stayed here, he didn't go back to London: he travelled on to Scotland. Is that right?'

'I believe so,' Collins answered, mystified by her train of thought.

'Why?'

'They own a house somewhere on the west coast. A hunting lodge. The Jeffries use it as a holiday retreat.'

'Thank you.' She walked away, as John Bannerman continued to greet his guests.

'And my sister-in-law, Ruth Bannerman.' John smiled disarmingly at Christina's parents. 'It does get confusing, all these Bannermans. It's quite easy to end up with the wrong wife sometimes.' He looked at Ruth. 'Eric Lloyd-Price, Eliza Lloyd-Price.'

'Delighted,' Eric enthused. Noticing her apparent pregnancy, he beamed. 'Heavens, dear lady, when is the happy day?'

'I wish I knew,' she replied coolly, 'but the baby is due in three months, if that's what you mean.'

'Ye-es . . .' His laughter broke the word into two, reminding John of a donkey braying.

'Now come on through.' The perfect host, John led them towards the bar. 'I thought we could have some champagne in here, before we go upstairs.'

'Lead on, delighted, yum, yum,' Christina's father enthused.

'Just the one glass, Father,' Christina warned.

Sarah hung back with Marcus as everyone else filed into the bar.

'That husband of yours.' Marcus frowned. 'Have

you been putting something in his tea?'
    'Have you said anything? If you've told him—'
    'About what?' He lowered his voice.
    'I think he knows.'

Lark crept along the lower guest corridor into the service room. Stacking the box of soaps Mrs Harvey had given her beneath the others, she jumped as a door closed somewhere behind her. She peeped out through the door and, seeing only the empty corridor, she closed and locked the service room. Room thirty-five loomed between her and the staff lift. As she recalled Lynne's tales, the number burned, searing into her mind. She had to pass it. There was no other way. She could be dismissed for using the main stairs or guest lift.

She forced herself forward, her blood running colder with every step. A breeze blew chill on her face, a window flew open, a net curtain billowed wide in front of her. Screaming, she ran for her life, not stopping until she reached her bedroom.

'She was there – Monica,' she gabbled breathlessly to Lynne and Brenda. 'Just like you said. Her spirit walking the earth, trapped in torment for all infinity.'

'I know just how she feels,' Kate said hollowly from the corner where she'd hoped to find privacy.

'And there was this smell. This perfume . . .'

'Monica had perfume,' Brenda confided, egging Lark on. 'Miss Harkness gave it to her.'

'It was violets. The smell of violets.'

'She had mimosa . . .'

'That was it, Brenda,' Lark broke in swiftly, contradicting herself. 'Mimosa.'

'You've had a visitation, Lark,' Lynne declared solemnly. 'She's calling to her friends. She wants us to lay her soul to rest and set her free.'

'Lynne, stop tormenting her, it's not funny,' Kate said irritably.

'We'll have to exorcise Monica, tonight, all of us,' Lynne continued, ignoring Kate. She lowered her voice. 'There's an allotted time for the banishing of the undead.'

'When's that?' Lark asked.

'Ten o'clock. As soon as Mrs Harvey's gone home.'

'The wine you ordered, sir.' Fred carried a tray that held a bottle and a glass into room thirty-five.

Jeffries looked at the bottle. 'Same old trick. Send him the dregs.'

'Right then, sir . . .'

'Hold on, I don't even know your name.'

'Frederick Willets, sir.'

'Well, Frederick. I'd like to thank you, for what you said earlier.'

'It's not to be repeated, sir.'

'No, but it's some consolation. If you don't mind my asking, what did happen?'

'The usual. Girl saying no when she meant yes. How the hell are we supposed to know? I mean, I'm sorry, but they put it out, don't they? Then start screaming, first time we make a move.'

'Did it come to court?'

'Nah, I scarpered. Been paying for it ever since, though. I was a mechanic, had a good wage, loved it. But word got around. I had to go. Everyone staring. Changed me name and everything – but that's to go no further. They'd sack me. I'm Frederick Willets in the Grand. No one knows different.'

'Then Frederick it is.'

'Make it Fred, sir. Frederick sounds daft. I could

have picked better.'

Jeffries looked at the wine. 'You're welcome to find another glass.'

'I won't, thanks. It's rubbish, that.'

'Why drink inferior wine when there's taverns by the dozen in this city. I'm tired of being a prisoner, Fred. You could join me.'

'Well, I'm finished for the night. Thanks all the same, sir, you don't want to bother with me.'

'I'd appreciate it. After all, fellow travellers. And if you've the time, I'd like someone in this hotel to hear what really happened.'

'You don't need to tell me, sir. She got what she deserved. You see those women, out there on the streets, asking for it. Yeah, let's go out,' he smiled suggestively. 'Five minutes, sir, on the steps.'

'Excellent, excellent. Full as an egg,' Eric complimented, as the waiters carried the empty dinner plates out through the door of the Bannermans' living room. 'I have to say, John, Eliza and I have dined in your restaurant a number of times.' He leaned towards his wife. 'You found the duck rather fatty, didn't you, Eliza?'

'I did not,' she demurred.

'Yes, you did.' He dug John in the ribs. 'Save the good stuff for your own table, eh? Quite right.'

'Christina's told us you own a printworks, Mr Lloyd-Price.' Marcus changed the subject.

'That's right, just outside Oldham.'

'And what do you print?'

'Bibles.'

'I see.'

'Don't worry, I'm not about to sell my wares over the dinner table. Well not until dessert.' His donkey-braying laugh echoed around the table.

'My sisters and I are a great disappointment,' Christina revealed. 'He wanted a son to inherit the family concern. That's what he said, isn't it, Mother?'

'He did not.'

'It's our lot in life, Christina,' Adele commiserated. 'Daughters are second best.'

'We were blessed with two daughters,' John mused. 'The firstborn, Catherine, died twenty years ago.'

'A tragedy.' Eric's face folded into suitably woeful lines. 'Yes indeed. I was one of six children, there's only three of us left . . .'

'I don't suppose your marriage is ever quite the same once that happens.' John finally looked at Sarah.

'I don't think I've ever been inside a printworks,' declared Marcus, now more anxious to change the topic of conversation than ever. He glanced anxiously at Ruth. 'I wouldn't mind looking round . . .'

'Delighted.' Eric clapped him soundly on the back.

'Well have you, or haven't you?' John asked Marcus irritably.

'I'm sorry?' His brother looked at him blankly.

'You don't *think* you've been round a printer's. You must know. Or are you telling our guest it's a thoroughly forgettable experience? My brother's not quite himself tonight, Eric. As a rule, he knows his mind. Knows what he wants, and takes it.'

'John, I think you might call down for dessert,' Sarah suggested uneasily.

'No,' Ruth countered, 'not yet. We're fine as we are.'

'I've seen it, the printer's,' Stephen explained. 'It's a huge building, and the smell of ammonia is overwhelming. They use it in the machines . . .'

'So, it's not as much fun as owning a hotel?' John asked.

'Not as much work, I'd say.' Eric laughed again, much to his daughter's annoyance. 'It's a labyrinth, this place. Eliza, she said watch out for minotaurs, didn't you?'

'I did not.'

'Yes, labyrinth,' said John. 'That's a good word. A labyrinth. And it's murder keeping track of everything that goes on here. So many bedrooms, with so many keys. And so many people ready to take advantage of that. When we were children, Marcus and I used to run around this place, hiding in different rooms. We'd be soldiers quelling mutinies on the frontiers of India. Serving in the war between China and Japan. Fighting for gold in the Transvaal, all before your time, Sarah. But they're still going on, those games.' He smiled at the assembled company. 'You've stopped drinking. Come on.' He lifted a bottle. 'There's plenty more, and I don't think any of us will have an early night.'

Sarah laid her hand over her glass, paling as her suspicions hardened into certainty.

Steeling herself, Esme knocked on the door of room thirty-five. When there was no reply, she pulled a fine, steel blade from her purse. Inserting it in the keyhole, she skilfully manipulated it. Seconds later the lock turned.

She slipped inside and leaned against the door, flicked on the light and looked around. It was the first time she had been in the room. Staring hard at the bed, she fancied she could see Monica lying there, broken, bloody, used. And abused.

Shutting out the image from her mind, she looked at the desk. Jeffries had spread out his papers on it. She started searching through them.

The Grand II: The Roaring Twenties

* * *

'So, what do we do?' Lark whispered fearfully to Lynne as they stole along the upstairs corridor with Brenda.

'What do you mean, what do we do?'

'To exorcise her. To release her from eternal torment and set her spirit free?'

Lynne looked to Brenda, hoping she would come up with a suggestion. When none was forthcoming, she said, 'We say the Lord's Prayer.'

'I don't know the Lord's Prayer.'

'Everyone knows the Lord's Prayer, Brenda,' Lynne sneered.

'I only know it when lots of people are saying it.'

'Make it up then,' Lynne said impatiently. 'Come on.' She pushed them down the corridor until they stood outside room thirty-five.

'I want to go back to bed.'

'You were chosen, by Monica, Lark,' Lynne reminded. 'It's your solemn task.'

'Course, if you think about it,' Brenda said dreamily, 'she didn't die here. She died in prison when they hanged her. So what's she doing back here?'

'Well, if you were dead and you had to walk the earth for all eternity, where would you rather be? Prison or a luxury hotel?' Lynne asked practically. 'Now stop your noise. Ready?' She took a deep breath. 'Our father . . . Is this going to be just me, or what?' she questioned angrily when the others didn't join in.

'Me mam says this is blasphemy.'

'It's the opposite of blasphemy, Lark. It's . . . well whatever the opposite of blasphemy is. Now, ready? After the count of three. All of us mind, got that? Or it won't work. Right! One, two three . . .'

On the count of three, the door flew open and a

woman's silhouette towered above them. All three girls screamed as they ran full pelt down the corridor.

Esme Harkness stepped out, clutching an address book. For all their noise, she barely noticed the girls as she returned to her own room.

'Splendid night, splendid,' Eric blustered, laughing again to hide his embarrassment at the peculiar atmosphere that had plagued the dinner. 'You'll have to visit our humble abode. Enjoyed yourself, didn't you, Eliza?'

'Yes. Yes I did.'

'I need to pop into the club. Just for an hour,' Stephen apologised.

'Both of you?' Eric looked to Christina.

'Yes, both of us.' Christina lifted her eyebrows. 'That's if you think he's safe with me.' She led her parents and Stephen to the door.

'Thank you again,' Eric enthused. 'Good night.'

John turned to Adele as they finally left. 'Go with Stephen,' he suggested. 'I don't mind. Enjoy yourself.'

'Dad! Stephen and Christina don't want me. Honestly, sometimes you don't think.'

'Then go to bed. Good night.' He kissed her on the forehead.

Knowing she'd been dismissed, Adele walked up the stairs. 'Good night,' she called back to her mother, Ruth and Marcus.

'I thought it went terribly well . . .' Marcus began.

Seeing Adele move out of earshot, John swung round and punched his brother squarely in the face. Marcus made no attempt to defend himself. He reeled back, taking a second punch on the jaw.

'Mr Bannerman, sir.' Collins ran across from the front desk.

The Grand II: The Roaring Twenties

John stepped back, straightened his jacket, then, thinking better of his forbearance, punched Marcus again.

'John, stop it. *Stop it!*' Sarah cried as Marcus fell to the floor.

John stood over his brother, wanting, daring him to defend himself, but Marcus made no move. It was the final straw that drove John over the edge. Stepping back, he kicked him.

'John!'

Grabbing Sarah's arm, he dragged her up the stairs. Ruth stood over her husband, smiled, then walked away, leaving him lying on the floor.

Chapter Twelve

'It was once.' Sarah faced John in their bedroom. 'I swear to you on my life, it only happened once.'

'Oh well, then. Fuss over nothing.'

'He'd smile that smile. Circling round me, whispering. He had the space and the time. You gave him that. You were never here; you were in the same building, the same office, the same bed. But over and over again, it was the Grand. The bloody Grand . . .'

'Don't! I know the list.'

'It was driving you mad, this place. I watched it happen. You'd care so much for the staff and the guests and Stephen. Even little Monica. Driving you mad. Maybe I wanted that. To mean as much. Equal status, an equal for once . . . *He* put me on the board of this hotel, not you. And every time I turned around, he was there. He listened to me, John. And then . . . maybe it was spite. Or some power of my own. But he was there, your brother. A version of you. And then once, just one night, I was angry, and one thing led to another and—'

'One thing led to another? Explain that. Tell me all those things I did wrong. How exactly? Tell me: how exactly did all those things lead to that other? How did they lead to sex? How did they lead to intercourse with my brother?' He stared contemptuously at her.

'Tell me that, for God's sake. Tell me, please, because I don't know . . .' He broke off, remembering something Collins had said. 'If it only happened once, then tell me: what happened on his wedding day?' As he looked at her, he saw the fear in her eyes.

'Nothing.'

'What happened?' he repeated sternly.

'It was . . . it was nothing. It was a mistake, it was . . . This is Jacob Collins, isn't it?' she asked angrily. 'What's he said?'

'And long before that – Marcus has been whispering for years. All our married life. He was in church, at the altar, my best man. Tell me: Stephen, Adele and Catherine – who is their father?'

'You are. Oh my God, they're yours, John, I swear it,' she exclaimed, horrified that he could even think anything else. 'They're yours.'

He continued to stare at her, wanting to believe her.

'Then tell me: how could you do this to my children?' He watched the tears fall from her eyes. For the first time in his life he was unmoved by the sight of her crying. 'And isn't it ridiculous? It feels like I still love you. What good is that? Now I love something dirty. Come here. Sarah?' he called her name softly.

Slowly, fearfully, she went to him. He kissed her, then pushed her away.

'You taste of him.'

Breaking free, she ran out of the room. He took hold of the door and swung it viciously shut behind her.

Adele heard the door slam and flinched. She continued to sit up in bed, shaking, crying, wishing she hadn't heard every word.

Sarah stood in the corridor, fighting for breath. She

looked around; even her surroundings seemed unfamiliar. Not knowing where else to go, she walked towards the glass-panelled door that led into the hotel, and slammed it behind her.

Ruth heard the slam in her bedroom, where she was quietly sewing her padding. Her needle moved rhythmically in and out of the wadding, as she sat back, smiled coldly, and absorbed the pain Marcus had caused.

The foyer was in darkness when Sarah walked down the stairs, the front doors locked for the night. She looked around, starting nervously when she saw someone in the Reading Room.

'Sorry.' She looked at Esme Harkness. 'Are you waiting for someone?'

'Not at all. Good night.' Esme smiled maliciously. 'I gather I missed the entertainment.'

'It was nothing.'

'I know what it was, Mrs Bannerman.'

'It's always our fault in the end. No matter what happens, we get the blame.'

'If you're looking for comradeship, then I'm sorry. You've always looked down on me, Sarah, but I know the rules. You had not the first idea.'

Esme's footsteps echoed over the marble floor, then stopped. Sarah looked up to see John standing on the stairs. Marcus stepped out of the darkened office. Miss Harkness moved on as they confronted one another.

'It was Harkness!' Lynne laughed as she bounced on her bed in her nightdress. 'Old bloody Harkness, the grey lady of the Grand Hotel.' Brenda's and Lark's laughter joined hers while Kate scowled in her corner. 'Harkness in Jeffries' room. How much do you think he paid her? Tuppence?'

'It's nice to know that when I'm dead and gone, you'll be here, laughing your heads off.' Kate walked out.

'That's you, that is,' Brenda accused Lynne.

'Got a face on her like a lemonade maker. I was only having a laugh. Monica knew that. Must have done. Did the same to Fred tonight. Got him in a tizz. I just open me gob . . . just when he said he loved me too,' she added with a sly glance at the other two.

'He did not!' Brenda gasped.

'He did an' all.'

'That makes you engaged. Oh my Lord!'

'Beat that, Brenda Potter,' Lynne crowed.

'Oi, you lot,' Clive shouted from his bedroom. 'Bunch of bloody fishwives! Keep it down!'

'What you going to do?' Lynne called back. 'Make me?'

'Is that an invitation?'

'I'm taken, Clive Jenkins, you mucky pup.'

'I'm not,' Brenda chimed in hopefully.

Kate heard them and smiled, as she sat alone in the scullery, munching a couple of chocolates she'd taken from Stephen's room.

Jeffries carried the whiskies he'd bought at the bar of the seedy, canalside pub over to the table where Fred was sitting.

'Everyone thinks we got off scot-free, but we're still paying,' he explained defensively. 'Look at Armitage? He's living proof of that. That's the third man in the room. Sacked from his job, parents threw him out, never saved a penny, that lad. Ended up in prison, for

173

fraud. Got his punishment in the end.'

'And it was her fault?'

'No, no, I don't think so . . .'

'But it was,' Fred suggested. 'I've got this girl, now, Lynne, back at the Grand. Says one thing, means another. What we're asking, it's only natural, isn't it?'

'I'm not proud. Can't believe what I did, I was drunk . . . and . . . her face. Pretty little face . . .' A tear fell from his eye as the drink made him maudlin.

'She was willing. And it must have made it easier, three of you. Saves time: you don't have to listen to all the chat, women wittering on. All that bloody courtship, no, it took three of you to get what you wanted. I can see that. Good for you. Two's enough.' He looked meaningfully at Jeffries. 'You and me, how about it? You can get girls down the canal at this time of night. Reckon I've waited long enough. You've got money?'

Jeffries squirmed uneasily as he reached for his whisky. 'Time I went back. Fred . . . I . . . I haven't actually . . . I've not been with a girl since that night.'

'We could just take a look. It's not far.'

'I'd rather not.'

'Then she's beaten you, that Jones girl?' Jeffries nodded agreement. 'It's not fair, sir. We deserve better. You should just see them. Flouting their wares, begging for it. Come on, take a look?' he coaxed persuasively.

'Well. No harm in looking . . .'

'Told you, you can't harm girls like that. And all girls are like that. It doesn't matter if they have posh accents and everything. They're all the same underneath. All on heat. Come on.' He rose to his feet and finished his drink. 'Quick look.'

'If it isn't far, then . . .'

The Grand II: The Roaring Twenties

'They're not ladies, mind,' Fred grinned. 'Rough old pieces, all of them, but that's better. Won't scream and shout if they get a good slapping.' Putting his arm around Jeffries' shoulders, he led him off into the night.

John sat on the foot of the stairs and looked up at his brother and Sarah, who were standing in the foyer, as far apart as space would allow.

'Five hours until the Grand wakes up. It never stops.'

'John, tell me what you want,' Marcus urged.

'You can leave us alone. It's between husband and wife.'

'We're a partnership. All three. And this is business. Decisions have to be made; this place won't wait for us to weep and wail.'

'Do you want her?'

'I'm not a piece of property to be passed around . . .' Sarah began indignantly.

'Are you not?' John looked at her.

'I'll go. If this is all to become my fault, I'll go. I can manage without you; it's time I did.'

'John, what do you want?' Marcus reiterated.

'All I ever wanted was this place.'

'Not your wife?' Sarah asked bitterly.

'This place *was* you. I thought I'd die an old man here, with my family around me, like Father. Now it's . . . infected. Not just that one bedroom, but every single room. All these months, the two of you dancing around each other, whispering. If I could go, if I could just turn my back, and . . .' He looked up at his brother in despair. 'You could have it. If you had the money. It's nothing now, it's contaminated. But there's the staff, so many staff . . . if I pulled out . . .' He laughed

175

harshly. 'But look at us. We're trapped.'

'I've got the money.'

John understood Marcus immediately. Appalled, Sarah backed away from both of them.

'But you gave us your entire savings . . .' She faltered.

'I've always had the money. I could have the contracts drawn up by nine o'clock tomorrow.'

'You don't care about the Grand . . .'

'I was never allowed to, Sarah. It was my brother's inheritance. I was given nothing. Father dictated that it could never be mine except in the most remarkable circumstances.'

'Did you . . .' John almost choked on the words. 'Did you plan this?'

Marcus smiled cynically. 'Who could plan something on such a scale?'

Finally realising she'd been used, Sarah strode furiously towards Marcus and slapped him hard, across the bruises John had already inflicted, then ran up the stairs.

John gave his brother a look of pure loathing, before going after her.

Marcus returned to the office. Without bothering to switch on the light, he sat down. Hearing a movement behind him, he turned to see Collins standing in the entrance to the side corridor.

'Is that what it was?' the concierge asked, dropping his professional subservience. 'All to gain the hotel? Nothing to do with Sarah Bannerman?'

'Perhaps,' Marcus replied flatly, 'or perhaps I told them that, so that they could live with each other.'

'You've destroyed any chances of that.'

'Really? John Bannerman? You know him that well, Jacob?' he murmured despondently. 'She hit me.'

'Oh, my every sympathy, I'll call a nurse.'

'You don't understand. She hit me. As if there's some passion. As if she was stupid enough to love a man like me. A woman in that predicament, she'd need to be saved, and he's a saviour, my brother. I'll tell you what they're doing right now, Jacob. She's in tears, and he's comforting her. He can't think of himself for long, no matter how hard he tries. She's lost, she's drowning, and there he is. To rescue her. He's a good man,' he mouthed the word as if it were an insult. 'He's the best of men. What it must be like to care so much.' He poured two whiskies and pushed one towards Collins. 'When we were children going to church on Sunday, Father would march us along. His little soldiers. And the sermon would say to love another is to see the face of God. All I could ever see was bricks and mortar. If they go, no doubt you'll go with them, Jacob. Unless you want to stay . . .'

'With you in charge?' Jacob rejected the whisky Marcus had poured him. 'Not in a thousand years.'

The smell of the canal wafted strong in the foggy, night air – a stench ripe with the mixed odours of rotting vegetables, caulked rope and sewage from the old cottages along the bank.

'Come on, it's just over here.' Ignoring the mist, Fred sauntered over a bridge.

'Best not,' Jeffries said, suddenly fearful. 'I've had a bit too much to drink. I'll head off. Which way is it?'

'What's this, sir?' Fred taunted. 'Streak of yellow down your back?'

'Oh, Fred, you know me all too well.' Jeffries leaned weakly on the parapet wall.

'It's Robert,' Fred said softly. 'I haven't used that name for months now. Two months, since I came to the Grand. Good name, good family name, Robert Jones. Of course, I can't use it now – everyone knows the Jones family. Them with a daughter, the whore, the girl they hanged. See, there *was* a girl. I *did* have to move on – all because of my sister.'

Jeffries backed away, but Fred was quicker. He pulled a knife and pressed it against Jeffries' windpipe.

'You don't know,' Fred muttered. 'You can't imagine the shame. We moved house, but it followed us. Everyone knows. The shame . . . the shame . . . my mother and the laughing. The filthy pub songs with her name in the middle. Monica . . . Monica . . .'

'I'm sorry,' Jeffries gibbered. 'I'm so sorry.'

'You are, aren't you?' Fred hated himself for pitying the man. 'You really are. I thought, he'll come back – came back February, he'll come back again. All I have to do is wait. And then you came. I spent months imagining David Jeffries, but you weren't him. I tried hard, but you wouldn't be him. You had to be sorry, didn't you? So bloody sorry. Couldn't make it easy for me, could you? She was seventeen . . .'

'They'll find you,' Jeffries warned. 'All that shame, all over again. Think of your family. I won't tell. It was all my fault; I've said that from the start, haven't I? Don't, please . . .'

'You brought this on yourself, you deserve it.'

'Yes. You're not a murderer, I am.'

The confession drained Fred. Bringing the knife down, he released Jeffries. Too scared, too guilty to run, Jeffries stepped back and froze.

Fred glared at him for a moment, then walked away.

'I'm sorry,' Jeffries called after him. 'She was a lovely girl.'

Fred stopped. A terrible fury gathered inside him.

The Grand II: The Roaring Twenties

He tried to subdue it but it was too strong. In two steps, he was at Jeffries' side, knife at the ready. Plunging it between Jeffries' ribs, he registered the soft, pliable feel of his flesh, the terror on his face as his blood drained out, drenching the stonework. Hauling up the body, Fred pushed him over the parapet into the water. He heard the splash as he ran off into the darkness.

Pulling her dressing gown close, Kate walked along the guest corridor towards room thirty-five. All she could think of was Lynne's stories. She *knew* they were nonsense, but that didn't stop her heart from beating at twice the normal rate as she stole closer to the door. A breeze fluttered through her hair. She spun around, saw the curtains billowing wide at the bottom of the corridor, called, 'Monica?'

But there was no one there.

'A lovely girl,' Fred said contemptuously. 'He knew nothing about her. Cheeky little kid, Monica. Always giving lip. Job at the Grand, that was it, she was posh, wouldn't let us near. For shame. No wonder Lynne hated her, but she was my sister.'

'She was my friend, and I loved her,' Esme said gently.

Fred grimaced as he put down the glass of wine she'd given him. 'They open the lock gates before dawn. He'll wash away. A kid fell in there last year. It was two weeks before they found her, miles away.'

'The letters are written, with his signature. To the Grand saying he's moved on, and to send his cases to the house in Scotland. Letters to the office, Manchester and London, his father. Enough confusion before he's missed.'

'She's still doing it now – Monica,' Fred muttered darkly. 'Spoiling things. I was starting to like it here, got me girl downstairs. Didn't plan that.' He smiled as he recalled Lynne's words: 'Who the heck plans it?'

'You could stay. If questions are asked, I can help . . .'

'What sort of a woman are you? I'm soaked in blood. You think I can just carry on? I couldn't do that to Lynne. She wants a proper man, a good man.' He laughed bleakly. 'I tried to tell her goodbye. She thought I was trying it on. Funny really. I'll leave a note, say I've moved on. Job or something. They don't notice lads like me. We come and go.'

Esme took a thick envelope from the table next to her and handed it to him.

'That night, before the police came, Monica was looking for me. She wanted money, to escape, but I wasn't there. I wasn't there for her.'

Collins stood in the corridor of the downstairs area watching the porters and maids preparing for the day ahead. One of the younger maids ran past in her night-dress, her hair in rags, to her shame and the accom-paniment of jeers and catcalls from the boys. He turned away, knowing he had a decision to make.

'I'm clobbered, me,' Lynne complained as she pulled out her trolley. 'That's your doing, Brenda Potter, gassing all night. I'm asking Mrs Harvey for married quarters.'

'Here, Lynne,' Lark called. 'There's a letter for you on the notice board.'

'Love letter,' Brenda smirked knowingly.

'Nothing for you,' Lynne crowed. She opened the envelope and began to read. The staff moved around her, chatting, laughing. She drew back and read the note again . . . and again . . . not wanting to believe a word of it.

'Mrs Harvey . . .' Collins walked into room thirty-five where the housekeeper was packing Mr Jeffries' clothes into his cases.

'He's a fine one,' she complained. 'Mr Jeffries' cases to Strathclyde indeed! Who pays the carriage? Not my budget . . .'

'Mrs Harvey, we need staff on the Bannermans' floor. Emergency duties.'

'What is it now?'

'Sylvie, quick as you can.'

After he left she picked up the tray that held the remnants of Jeffries' evening meal. Tartare sauce had congealed over the fish and mashed potatoes. It already smelled high. She scooped the food on top of the clothes in his case before slamming the lid shut and locking it.

'We'll go out the side entrance. There's enough talk around the hotel as it is.' John glanced around the bedroom. Their cases were packed, locked and corded, waiting by the door. Their personal possessions had been pushed into a packing case. Already the room had taken on the impersonal air of quarters waiting for new tenants.

'If they're talking, then I want it said that I left this place as your wife. Let them all see it,' Sarah pleaded. 'No matter what's ahead of us, that's how I want to be seen. Because that's the only thing that's important to me now.'

Collins stood in the foyer presiding over chaos, as he

directed porters and luggage to their correct destina-
tions. 'That one goes to the car. Put this one over there
with the rest – they'll be sent on. And that. No, that's
Mr Jeffries' – take it to the taxicab at the end of the
street . . .'

Stephen rushed after Adele, who was running
down the stairs. 'It's impossible. I can't go. Christina's
here, and the club. I've got to stay . . .'

'I've got no choice. I'm part of their baggage.'

He laid a restraining hand on her arm. 'What the
hell is going on?'

'What did they tell you?'

'Just . . . they'd planned it, moving on one day. Dad
said he was *bored*, for God's sake. That he wanted to
start again.'

'Then that's what they're doing.' Unable to look
him in the eye, she walked on.

John walked briskly up to the concierge.

'I was at school with him, Adrian Beckett. He's out
of town for the season so we'll rent his house until we
find something permanent. Rather pleasant, Knights-
bridge.'

Collins nodded, as John saw Marcus and the notary
waiting by the office. John went to them, as Christina
walked through the door.

'I got your message, Stephen. What on earth—'

To her surprise, he kissed her in front of everyone.

'But who's to sign the dockets?' Mrs Harvey asked
Jacob Collins frantically. 'And the invoices. Who's to
give approval . . .?'

'Marcus Bannerman,' Collins informed her coldly.
'From now on, Marcus Bannerman is in charge of the
Grand Hotel.'

* * *

The Grand II: The Roaring Twenties

John signed the papers Marcus had prepared. He thanked the notary who'd been called in to witness the signatures and headed for the door.

'John . . .'

Ignoring his brother, John paused in the doorway and stared into the foyer. He had only to close his eyes to see those two small boys playing. Both aggressive. The games that always ended in tears. Striding forward, he blinked and realised Stephen was waiting for him.

'Son.' He hugged him. 'Visit!' he ordered.

'I will,' Stephen promised

'Christina, watch him, make sure he behaves.'

'I'd imagine you'd want to leave,' Marcus said as Ruth approached him.

'Freedom?' She patted the front of her dress. 'We're rather tied together, don't you think?'

'Plenty of money in my pocket, a fortune,' John confided to Jacob. 'Enough for staff quarters wherever we end up. You'd be welcome.'

'Thank you, sir, but you don't want me,' Jacob answered, knowing that, if he went with John, it would only be a reminder of things best forgotten. 'Besides, all those lads downstairs, all those girls, who's to protect them in the new regime? I'm needed here.'

'Just be careful. Marcus doesn't play fair.'

'Oh, I've learned one or two tricks over the years. It's about time I used them. Let battle begin, sir.'

'It's John.' He shook the concierge's hand.

Kate looked through the glass panel of the staff corridor into the foyer.

'We're not allowed,' Lark whispered from behind her.

Kate pushed her way through, swinging the door back on Lark, shutting her out. She looked around, taking in the scene as Sarah embraced Stephen.

'Sarah,' John prompted from the door.

'Coming.' She looked at her husband and daughter waiting for her, then she looked at Marcus. She joined John and Adele.

'Excuse me, sir.' Kate fought her way forward. 'Excuse me, sir, Mrs Bannerman . . .'

The door swung back behind them.

'Let's see them off.' Stephen led Christina out through the door.

The chaos subsided as people moved out of the foyer. Collins looked to Marcus.

'Mr Bannerman?' Marcus turned and met Collins's condemnatory gaze. 'Was it worth it?'

Chapter Thirteen

'But what does it mean, sir?' Clive hovered in the doorway of the concierge's room.

Collins stared at his reflection in the mirror as he applied his clothes brush to his jacket. 'For the last time, Clive. Every receipt, every invoice, every docket goes to Marcus Bannerman. He is the sole owner of the Grand. If you don't like it, tell him and see what good it does you.'

'But what does it mean, sir?' Clive reiterated irritatingly.

'It means he's in charge.'

'What does that mean for us?'

Collins's exasperation subsided when he saw the confusion on Clive's face. 'God only knows. Just keep your head down. Do the job and don't give him a chance to find fault. Stay calm, and maybe we can keep the Grand as it was. The same goes for all of you. Spread the word.'

'Yes, sir.'

Collins frowned. 'If you really want to help, do that for me, Clive. Just stop the gossip. Keep the lid on the girls, for their own sakes.'

'Course I will, sir.'

'Hey that's my apron.' Brenda snatched it from

Katherine Hardy

Lynne's hand as she went to the washstand. Emptying a jug of cold water into the china bowl, she picked her soap and flannel out of the row ranged on the marble slab, and started to wash.

'That Spanish bloke, Chico Venezuela, the one at the grocer's,' Kate said as she pulled on her stocking and studied the back of her leg, checking that the darn in her heel wouldn't be seen above her shoes. 'Well, he told me he'd heard on good authority that Marcus Bannerman wants to turn this place into a casino.'

'Big Lucy told me he's sold the Grand to the army,' Lark informed them solemnly as she waited her turn at the washstand. 'There'll be two hundred soldiers barracked above our heads.'

'Here, it's all yours, Lark.' Brenda emptied her water into the slop pail, wiped out the bowl with a cloth, and pushed her soap and flannel behind the others. 'What happens to us now? That's what I'd like to know.'

'Out!' Kate declared flatly as she tied on her apron. 'I give him two days. Then all of us will be out on our ears. Hurry up, Lark.'

'I am. Mind you, he was nice to us, Mr Bannerman, that while back.'

'Nice? Nice like a wolf's nice,' Kate warned, 'all big teeth and smiling. Then he bites. I'm telling you, it was John Bannerman who looked after us. Without him, we're nothing, just slabs of meat. I'm for breakfast, who's coming?'

'You see?' Brenda picked up the butter dish and sniffed the contents, as she and Kate climbed on to the bench set in front of the massive, scrub-down table in the staff kitchen. 'Yesterday it was butter. Today it's margarine.'

The Grand II: The Roaring Twenties

'They should tell us what's happening.' Kate tore her bread roll apart. 'I know he's in charge of the Grand, but I'd like to know *how come.* You finally made it then?' She made room for Lark on the bench.

Lark leaned towards Kate, Brenda and Lynne. 'I was told by me other sister, the one's that's walking out with this bloke who knows this other bloke . . . and he's gardener for the Bannermans' accountant . . . well he said . . .' She eyed the maids sitting on the other side of the table and dropped her voice to a whisper. 'He said Marcus Bannerman slept with John Bannerman's wife.'

Kate glanced at Lynne and Brenda. All three burst out laughing. 'Blimey, Lark, I've heard some stories, but that's ridiculous.'

'Clive?' Brenda waved him over as he emerged from Mr Collins's room. 'What did he say?'

'Come on,' Kate urged, 'if anyone knows, it's Mr Collins. Out with it.'

Clive leaned over her shoulders. 'I'm not supposed to say.'

'Go on,' Kate coaxed.

'Well . . .' Grim-faced, he looked around the table. 'Suppose you've got a right to know. They're pulling it down, the entire hotel. Covering it with tarmac, building an aerodrome. Planes flying in from London and Paris, right into the heart of Manchester.'

'Never!' Brenda gasped.

Clive winked at Kate.

'Clive!' Kate pushed him away.

'Your faces,' he chortled.

Marcus spread his newspaper over the table. 'Now there's a way of saving money.' He smiled at Ruth as he realised that this was the first time they had breakfasted alone together since their honeymoon.

'What?' For once, she actually returned his smile.

'The things they print. Apparently, if you have eight thousand letters that need posting, it's cheaper to post them in France. It saves thirty-two pounds.'

'But then there's the cost of travelling to France. That will eat into the profit.'

'We could go. Paris? Shopping? You'd like that?'

'In this condition? Sailing the English Channel?'

'When he's born. We could go as a family.'

'Yes, I'd really like that.'

Stephen blundered in, bleary eyed, unwashed, unshaven, his dressing gown flapping open over his pyjamas. 'God, it was madness in the Manhattan last night. There wasn't room to breathe.' He grabbed a piece of toast as he dropped on to his customary chair.

'Stephen, I think you could dress before coming to table. I'm not sure my wife wants to see you in that state.'

Stephen looked up in surprise. 'It never bothered you before.'

'It does now.'

'Do you mind?' Stephen asked Ruth.

She turned to Marcus, deferring to his judgment.

'Right, sorry . . .' Embarrassed, Stephen retreated to his bedroom.

Marcus passed his teacup to Ruth. 'I told you, I had no intention of adopting him.'

Clive took the new handyman, Bob Jessop, through the downstairs workstations, reciting the names of the areas as they passed through them,

'Linen cupboards, butler's pantry – we store the cutlery and silver in there – passage to cellars . . .'

'I heard,' Brenda's voice rang out above those of the

other maids, who were busy filling the beeswax jars on their trolleys, 'that when Marcus Bannerman was running the theatres, he used to call in the chorus girls and measure their waists. If they were too fat, he'd sack them.'

Lynne flung her jar to the floor, where it crunched into a blob of molten wax and broken glass. 'Can't just one of you shut up? Who cares if they chuck us out? This stinking place . . .'

'Oi!' Bob stared at the mess she'd made. 'I'll have to sweep that up.'

'And you . . .' Lynne glared at him. 'He runs off, and you're taken on. I look at you, I'm looking at him . . .' Her bottom lip trembled as tears poured down her cheeks. She fled in the direction of the bedrooms. Kate nodded and Brenda went after her.

'Who ran off?' Bob asked in bewilderment.

'Fred Willets, her boyfriend.' Kate took a shovelful of sand from the bucket and sprinkled it over the mess. 'He just upped and disappeared overnight.'

'Aye, it were shocking.' Clive nodded. 'Lynne having a boyfriend I mean.'

Kate chucked a wet cloth at him. 'Here, you can show Bob how to clear up.'

'Orchestra on the *Titanic*,' Collins said as he heaped the ledgers into a pile on Mrs Harvey's desk.

'What was it the captain said?' she asked, adding to the mountain of account books.

' "Be British", Mrs Harvey. "Be British". Now if we start on the offensive, that's the trick. There, that's all the paperwork requiring the management's approval by the end of the day.'

'Those are the tax accounts – we don't touch those until next April.'

Katherine Hardy

'I wonder if Mr Bannerman knows that.' Collins smiled archly as he carried them through the door.

'They need to be checked and signed, sir. By six o'clock today.' Collins dropped the pile of paperwork on to the desk in the main office.

'Don't be ridiculous.' Marcus reached for his jacket. 'I'll get them done by the end of the week.'

'Ah, if only, sir. You see, if the invoices aren't processed, the suppliers can't be paid, and if they're not paid, they'll complain to the bank, and you don't want the bank breathing down your neck, sir. Not at the very start of your new empire. On top of that, there's the rotas for approval, and the menu to be confirmed, and something of a mystery in the foyer. A trunk has just come in by carrier. I can't make out the name on the paper . . .'

'I do not bother with trunks!' Marcus broke in indignantly.

'There might be something in the Despatched and Consigned Book, sir. Your brother used to keep it in very good order.' The concierge opened the door wider, so Marcus could precede him into the foyer.

A porter was standing guard over an enormous steamer trunk. Marcus recognised its quality.

'Maybe it should have gone to the Midland.' He tried to decipher a monogram set below a coat of arms dominated by a double-headed eagle. 'Can you make that out, Collins?'

The concierge crouched down and studied the letters. 'If only they'd favour block capitals, sir.'

'Deal with it,' Marcus ordered abruptly.

'Certainly, sir. I did think to help you with the paperwork, but chasing this up could take all day. Very sorry, sir.'

The Grand II: The Roaring Twenties

Well aware that Collins was being deliberately difficult, Marcus retreated to the office. As he closed the door, a woman walked into the foyer. Every man in the vicinity turned his head and stared. Young, and extremely beautiful, she was dressed in the height of a European fashion that had reached Manchester only on the pages of the best illustrated papers. Collins recognised her furs as sable, her jewels as diamonds, her shoes and handbag as bespoke, and her clothes as French designer, and very, very expensive. He glanced at the porter, who'd lifted the trunk on to a trolley.

'Mystery solved.'

He smiled as he approached her. 'Can I help you, ma'am?'

She beamed at the concierge as if he were an old family retainer. 'This needs a stitch,' she purred in a heavily accented, seductive voice as she handed him a monogrammed umbrella. 'Could it be attended to?'

'There should be no difficulty, ma'am.'

'Give it to somebody who uses a needle, not a pitchfork. Have my things arrived?'

'A steamer trunk, ma'am. Per White Star Line?'

'Two . . .'

'One has arrived, ma'am.'

'Do you think it safe to assume that accommodation has been arranged?' she sighed.

'I'm sure Mr Bannerman will attend to it, ma'am.'

'Then tell me where I can find some tea, and send him to me.'

'Through this way, ma'am.' He signalled a porter to accompany her into the Reading Room.

'Thank you.' She gave Collins another smile, one that made him feel as though he were the only man in the world.

* * *

Marcus felt like strangling Collins for running to him with every petty problem and arrival. Then he walked into the Reading Room and saw the owner of the trunk talking to a waiter, and fell victim to an instant and overwhelming attack of lust.

'Good afternoon, ma'am. Can I be of assistance to you?'

'You are the manager?'

'For the moment, ma'am. For my sins.' He stared blatantly. He had never seen such blue eyes, such flawless skin.

'Which are no doubt, many?' she suggested coolly.

'Alas!' Marcus smiled deprecatingly.

'My accommodation should have been arranged by the White Star Line.'

'They've made no bookings.'

'And forwarded only one trunk. It's . . .' She threw her hands in the air, a gesture that few women could make without appearing pretentious. 'I must have somewhere to lay my head. A suite if you have it.'

'Certainly we have a suite.'

'It may be your practice to pass on the names of guests . . . of a certain standing to the local papers.'

'Some wish it, Madame.' He used the French pronunciation of the word. Given her accent, it seemed appropriate.

'I do not. Most emphatically, not.' Marcus nodded agreement. 'The hotel can supply a lady's maid? At least a girl with some intelligence?'

'But Mr Collins, they aren't lady's maids. They're not trained.' Mrs Harvey stood beside the concierge and surveyed her staff as the girls sorted through the laundry.

'Mr Bannerman insists.'

'You see? It's not yet ten o'clock and he's already asking the impossible. Well, there's only one girl with a grain of sense. Kate Morris, over here, quick sharp.'

Madame moved gracefully around her suite, removing items from her trunk with deft, sure movements, arranging her silver-framed photographs on the desk, her gold and enamelled perfume bottles on the dressing table, her manicure set and toilet bags in the bathroom. For her jewellery cases, she decided on a side table, but before placing them there, she opened the largest box, lifted the tray and checked the small, pearl-handled lady's revolver hidden beneath it.

'Who is it?' she called, lifting the gun in response to a knock at the door.

'Management sent me up, ma'am. They said it was urgent.'

Reassured by the young girl's voice, she dropped the gun back into its compartment.

'Come in.'

Kate opened the door, feeling awkward and peculiar in the black serge skirt and white blouse Mrs Harvey had insisted she wear as a lady's maid's uniform.

'What do they call you?'

'Kate, miss,' she answered nervously.

'Madame.' The guest stressed the word in French fashion.

'Madam,' Kate failed to follow her intonation.

'Ma-*dame*,' the woman repeated slowly. 'And you are a lady's maid?'

Deciding honesty was the only policy, Kate replied, 'No, not really, Ma-*dame*.'

'Then I will tell you everything you must do. I do

not expect to tell you anything twice.'

Brenda carried a tray past the laundry area and found Lynne sitting in the middle of a stack of sheets crying her eyes out.

'Grab a shovel and wipe your face, Harvey's about,' she whispered.

Sniffing valiantly, Lynne sat up and tried to look busy.

'What are you snivelling for?' The housekeeper thrust the new guest's umbrella at Lynne.

'Stuff got in me eyes, Mrs Harvey.'

'Wipe them, and put a stitch in that.'

'Yes, Mrs Harvey.' Lynne took the umbrella.

'Broken heart, is it? Or worse?'

'Worse,' Lynne mumbled.

'If there's no brat on your hip this twelvemonth, well and good.'

'Won't be!'

'Can this really be our Lynne, as tells everyone what for?' To Lynne's amazement, the housekeeper handed over her own handkerchief.

'Thank you.'

'Thought you'd got to womanhood when you started the monthlies, didn't you? Well you didn't. This is the full and glorious state of womanhood, this, and its name is disappointment. I want that,' she said as she pointed at the handkerchief Lynne had used to mop her tears, 'back washed and ironed. As soon as you like, and with the parasol.'

Incensed and frustrated at being called out of the office to deal with the problems of a male guest who couldn't speak a word of English, Marcus turned in desperation to Esme Harkness.

The Grand II: The Roaring Twenties

'Miss Harkness, how is your French? This gentleman has some difficulty.'

'*Bonjour, M'sieur . . .*'

Marcus heaved a sigh of relief as Esme went into full flow. Turning back to the office and the pile of paperwork, he was accosted by Madame.

'Mr Bannerman? I am expecting something by post. Would you make sure it is brought immediately?'

'I will make a point of bringing it myself, Madame.'

'That might be convenient. I may need a witness for signing a document.' Overhearing Esme speaking to the Frenchman, she joined in their conversation. For the first time in his life, Marcus wished he'd taken the time and trouble to study the language.

'Your relationship with M'sieur has improved, Mr Bannerman,' Madame informed him as he hesitated at the office door. 'Your bill is ten times less than he thought.'

'Your help is appreciated, Madame.'

'No one has introduced us.' Madame offered Esme her hand as the Frenchman finally paid his bill. 'I am Euphrasine De Bourg D'Oisans.'

'Esme Harkness.'

'Perhaps you would care to join me this evening? I am in need of a companion.'

'I'd be delighted.'

Marcus eyed the women as they walked towards the dining room. Both beautiful, both elegant, and one so much younger than the other. He looked up to see his wife watching him from the stairs. She turned away, as though she knew exactly what he'd been thinking about Madame – and wishing for.

'Christina,' Stephen called, leaving the bar as she walked into the foyer. 'I booked that restaurant on

Oxford Road.'

'Fine.' She kissed his cheek. 'But I thought you wanted to lunch here.'

'I'd rather get out.' He looked around reception. 'I was born in this place, now I feel like one of the guests.'

'"And",' Kate mimicked Madame's accent as she related details of her new job to her roommates, '"nothing is put away before you go over buttons, seams and hems. And where attention is needed, ply your needle accordingly! Dressing for dinner is no time to find a dropping hem."'

'Oh God forbid!' Brenda exclaimed theatrically.

'And then she says, "And when I retire you will be here to undress me."'

'Undress her!' Lark gaped.

'So, I said, "undress you, Madame? Why? Are you usually dead drunk by then?"'

'You never! You didn't!'

'I was tempted.'

'You'd have been put out in the street.'

'Look on the bright side, Brenda: at least I could get a job as a lady's maid, now.'

'Always you, innit?' Lynne griped. 'Mrs Harvey's blue-eyed.'

'It's all just skivvying.'

'All the same, we never had jobs like that before.' Brenda spooned an extra lump of sugar into her tea. 'Maybe it's not that bad with Marcus Bannerman in charge.'

'Give him time,' Kate muttered as she checked the clock to see how many minutes were left of her break.

Madame surveyed the Manhattan Club as she and

Esme took their seats at the table the waiter had shown them to.

'I am a permanent guest at the Grand,' Esme explained.

'A lady of means and independence then? Forgive me, that was very rude.'

'Not at all, I am proud to be independent.'

'We seem to have much in common. My parents believed that wealth was ordained by nature.' Madame shrugged her beautiful and naked shoulders. 'But the world has changed. Money must be made to work.'

'Does one not leave that to bankers?'

'Leave your servants to run your house in their own interests and they will rob you blind,' Madame warned. 'And bankers are very greedy servants. I make my own investments.'

'I can only wonder in what line.'

'What I know about. Clothes. Manchester knows about cloth. Do you speak Italian?'

'But of course.'

'That is wonderful. You see, Milan also comes into my calculations. Manchester, Milan and Manhattan.'

'Manhattan!' Esme repeated in surprise.

'It's where the money is. They want English cloth and European style. And they can pay. Have you ever thought of going into business?'

'I have never frowned on the idea.'

'I will need someone in Manchester. Your languages would be useful.'

'The little I know is more suited to the bedroom than the boardroom, Madame.' Esme looked into the younger woman's eyes, to see if she was shocked by the revelation.

'If I understand business correctly, Esme. That is no

handicap.'

'Can't you leave the club for one night, Marcus?' Ruth enquired testily. 'I thought we could have supper. Just the two of us.'

'I'm busier than ever, running this place single-handed. In future, if you're making plans you'll have to give me notice in advance.'

'I'll make an appointment,' she snapped caustically.

'Mr Collins,' Marcus called, accosting the concierge as he stepped out of the lift. 'I've finished that paperwork.'

'Really, sir? All of it?'

'Even the accounts that aren't due until next April. Thank you for that. It gave me the chance to review the entire financial plan, and I've found one or two savings.' He handed the concierge a sheet of paper. 'I'm sure I can leave it in your capable hands. I want it implemented by the end of the week.'

'I don't see the harm in it,' Christina protested to Stephen as he escorted her away from the dance floor in the Manhattan. 'Of course, I wrote to your parents. I consider them my friends.'

'What did you say?'

'Just that it would be nice to see them if ever we're in London.'

'And I don't see why we should make the effort. It's their business to come back to Manchester. If they can't be bothered—'

'Stephen, you have to go and see them. Aren't you in the least bit curious?'

'About what?' he asked, angry at her interfering.

'Why they left.'

'They told us. A new start, a new life. And if that involves leaving their son behind, then never mind.'

'Talk to them. There must be more to it than that.'

'Christina, can't you just leave it? They've gone. They wanted to go. Now can we stop talking about them.' He snapped his fingers to attract the attention of a waiter.

'It's not Paris, I know,' Esme apologised to Madame, 'but it is as close as we come to Montmartre.'

'In Montmartre, you might meet anyone. Here, it seems, one meets the manager of one's hotel.'

'A little more than the manager,' Esme revealed as Marcus crossed the floor, greeting guests at every table. 'I believe he now owns it outright.'

'He's behaving as though he owns this place as well.'

'He does.'

'Now I am impressed.' She smiled as Marcus reached their table.

'Madame, Miss Harkness. What a pleasure to see you here. May I send champagne?'

'So kind,' Madame murmured, 'but we have already called a taxicab.'

'It can be sent back into the night.'

'I have matters to attend to, Mr Bannerman. But I am sure Esme will be pleased to take champagne with you.'

'I could not possibly allow you to go back alone . . .'

'Nonsense, Esme. I have crossed oceans alone.'

'I would very much appreciate your company, Miss Harkness.' Marcus took a seat at their table, just as Jim approached and bowed.

'Madame,' said the barman, 'your taxicab's arrived.'

'Thank you.'

'I can't—'

'You have been such good company, that I have neglected things I must do. Tomorrow we will stay up and gossip all night.' She embraced Esme before turning to Marcus. 'Goodnight, Mr Bannerman. My coat?' she prompted Jim.

'Interesting lady,' Marcus observed, watching her leave.

'With interesting ideas,' Esme concurred.

'Like?'

'A business on both sides of the Atlantic. Her name on the products, herself as the figurehead.'

'And what line would all this be in?'

'Fashion and all things deluxe.'

'And behind the scenes, who's the partner? The businessman?'

'Why would she need one?'

'She hasn't got one?' Marcus mused as the champagne arrived. 'Now she really *is* an interesting lady. Extraordinary flair for business, the French.'

'She's not French. She's Russian.'

'She sounded French to me when she was gibbering away this morning.'

'French was always the language of the Russian court. Didn't you know?'

'No wonder there was a revolution.'

'Most of her family were killed. She lost everything. Every rouble. From what I can gather, there's some property in France, which is why she's adopted her grandmother's name. A wise precaution given those who'd see her survival as something of a threat.'

'Miss Harkness, I think you should forego any more alcohol if you're believing stories like that.'

'We're very safe and cosy in the confines of Manchester. But out there, Marcus, whole countries are burning. The Great War's finished, but it's left a thousand fires in its wake. We'd rather look away. They're only foreigners, after all. But if one refugee has escaped to our society, we can't shrug and deny these things are happening.'

Jacob Collins waited until Mrs Harvey had finished work for the day, before showing her the note Marcus Bannerman had given him.

'He can't do this,' she protested indignantly.

'Oh, but he can,' Collins contradicted.

'I'd say the opposite. I'd say we are short of staff, run off our feet, not this.' She tapped the paper in disgust.

'The instructions are clear enough. We've got to lose four members of staff by the end of the week. That's four of them out on the streets.'

Kate heard the last part of Mr Collins's sentence and stole back into the linen cupboard where she'd been sorting dusters.

'Which ones?' Mrs Harvey demanded. 'Who's supposed to go?'

'He's left the choice to us, Sylvie. Very clever, so we get all the blame.'

Chapter Fourteen

Marcus glanced at his wristwatch as he tapped Madame's door.

'Who is it?' she called as she transferred her gun from her purse to her jewellery case.

'Marcus Bannerman, Madame.'

'One moment.' She replaced the gun in her purse before unlocking the door.

'I think you were expecting this.' He handed her a large manila envelope.

'The post arrives at midnight in Manchester? How efficient.'

'Someone put it aside. I noticed it in reception when I returned from the club. If any of my staff have caused you a problem, they will be dismissed.'

'Do you always flirt with guests, Mr Bannerman?' she enquired bluntly.

'No, but in exceptional circumstances, I feel no effort should be spared.'

'It is you who should be dismissed – as unfit to manage a hotel.'

'Unfortunately there is no one to dismiss me. I own the hotel.' Marcus stepped into her room.

'You have enjoyed much success, I imagine with . . . women?'

'One or two have been pleased by my attentions,' he

conceded drily.

'Ah, but have they been satisfied by them?' She laughed, when she realised she had succeeded in disconcerting him. 'Women for the most part have not very high expectations. A lady, on the other hand, might be more demanding.'

'A matter of rising to the occasion, should one have dealings with a lady.'

There was a knock on the door and Kate walked in with Madame's dress swathed in tissue paper. Flustered at the sight of Marcus, in Madame's rooms, she backed out.

'Sorry, sir, Madame. I'll come back?'

'Don't go away, I want to undress.'

'I trust Kate here meets your standards, Madame?' Marcus asked.

'She does.'

'Doing me best, sir,' Kate muttered, keeping her head down. 'I wouldn't like to put a foot wrong. Not these days.'

'Good night, Mr Bannerman. I'll call you tomorrow, should I feel the need to do so.' Madame lifted the envelope. 'About this I mean.'

'At any time.' Marcus bowed and left, closing the door behind him.

'See the door is locked – and the window,' Madame ordered Kate.

'The window is closed, Madame.'

'I said locked.'

'Yes, Madame.' Kate went to the French windows that opened on to the balcony and slid the bolts home.

'What's to be done?' Jacob Collins asked Mrs Harvey as they shared a bottle of wine in her office. Her coat had been replaced on the hook behind the door, all thoughts forgotten of going home on time for once. 'How do we decide? Two of the lads, two of the girls?'

'On what basis? Last in, first out? That's Lark Rothery and Jenny Tate. Fine workers those two. There is another option, Jacob?' She refilled both their glasses.

'What's that?'

'Put ourselves on the list. I've heard talk the Wainwright trust is opening a small hotel, out in Didsbury. Fifteen rooms, tiny place, handful of staff, but they'll need a housekeeper and hall porter. We're a good team, Jacob.'

'I suppose we are.'

'Not much work. It would be like an early retirement, for both of us.'

'We're a bit young for that, Sylvie.'

'And too old for this,' she said determinedly, looking down at Marcus's sheet of paper.

'And your ambition?' Madame asked as she rested her tiny foot on Kate's lap, so the maid could lace her boot.

'Ambition? Haven't got any ambitions, Madame.'

'Do you have dreams?'

'Can't afford dreams.'

'Do you have no imagination?' Madame persisted.

'What good would it do me?'

'The answer lies in your imagination.'

'Which I haven't got. So that's lucky.' Kate finished lacing the boot, and went to the window, opening it wide to the fresh morning air.

'Is it lucky?'

'No use imagining things if you can't make them happen, is there?'

Madame reached for her sable wrap, and draped it around Kate's neck.

'And so you tell lies?'

'I don't tell lies.'

'That you have no dream? No dreams beyond changing bed linen and fetching towels and emptying slops? No? No dreams?' She pressed the soft, sensuous fur against Kate's cheek.

'I had a friend once, she had dreams of being a lady. They did her no good at all.'

'No imagination, you said! I'm not asking you to be a lady,' Madame laughed. 'Quite the opposite. I'll need a lady's maid, travelling with me at all times. It's the same old servitude, I'm afraid. But, Kate, the horizons would be so much wider.'

'I'm sorry, sir.' Collins was polite, but terse. 'I'm not at liberty to discuss the guests or who might, or might not, be in residence.'

The man opened his hand, revealing the corner of a pound note.

'I'm not at liberty, sir,' Collins reiterated firmly.

'Maybe that's not your currency,' the stranger suggested. 'It's only to keep me one step ahead of the other press boys. You slip me a list of the toffs that are stopping. Ladies, beautiful for preference. Always a few column inches in them, you see – and something in it for you.'

'I'm sorry, sir, I have things to attend to.' Collins looked up as a carrier's boy appeared in the foyer, wheeling a trunk that he recognised. It was identical to the one that had been taken up to Madame's suite.

'Mrs Harvey?' Lark popped her head around the door of the housekeeper's office. 'I've got the order for the laundry. Should I pass it on, or do you have to sign it first?'

'No, pass it on. I thought Janey Birdsall was doing that.'

'It's not her fault. I offered. You know what it's like when you're the new girl: you have to do that bit extra. I don't mind. Anyway, laundry, sorry to keep you.'

Mrs Harvey stared at the piece of paper Jacob Collins had left on her desk and damned Marcus Bannerman, wishing he could know, just for one moment, what it was like to live with the threat of losing both job and the roof over his head.

'It is only when one takes a stranger to see the town that one realises just how little of it there is to see,' Esme apologised as she accompanied Madame into her suite.

'I think there is rather too much. They should remove a hundred acres or so in the middle.' Madame unpinned her hat and set it on the dressing table.

'To do what?'

'Without thinking at all, what is the most fashionable address?'

'Park Avenue.'

'Until this city has a park – or at least a boulevard – it will have no such thing as a fashionable address, and so can never be fashionable.' She reached into her jewellery box. 'Does it even have a reliable jeweller?'

'A good enough jeweller. I know him.'

'Could he do something with this?' She held up a tiny pendant.

'Oh, that is exquisite.'

Madame lifted it to her ear. 'The other was turned into ready money to pay for certain travel arrangements.'

'A crime to separate them,' Esme cried feelingly.

The Grand II: The Roaring Twenties

'The man who made the bargain wanted the pair. We cheated each other.'

'Could you not get it back?'

'He's either dead or in Siberia. It could be put on a clasp – or chain. See what your friend can do.'

'You would entrust this to me?' Esme asked in amazement.

'Why not?' Madame dropped it into her hand. 'At least until I have an urgent call for ready money. One warning, Esme. I trust your jeweller is discreet. Once the origin of this artefact is known, it could attract certain . . . interested parties. People I would rather knew nothing of my whereabouts.'

'I guarantee it,' Esme promised solemnly.

'Thank God for a friendly face,' Stephen said feelingly as he walked into the Bannermans' living room to find Kate wielding a duster. 'It's so strange walking through the foyer and seeing Marcus in the office on his own. Even this floor, Ruth presiding over everything. It feels wrong.'

'Oh, and I'm here, same as ever, good old Kate. Well not for much longer, with your uncle running the shop.'

'What do you mean?'

'I've been offered a job. Lady's maid, travelling all over.'

'You're not taking it?'

'Stephen, the Grand Hotel has been famous for years, and do you know why? Because we've been treated with respect, all of us. Your dad knew the difference between servants and staff. Now that's gone. Like you said, it's all changed. So what's to stop me going?' Giving the table a final wipe, she picked up her tray of cleaning materials and walked out, leaving

Stephen with the impression that the last piece of his life had just fallen away.

'I could make savings in the hotel budget – anything,' Mrs Harvey suggested to Ruth. 'But I need every single member of staff. We can't lose one, let alone four. I just thought, if you could have a word with your husband—'

'About the hotel?' Ruth interrupted.

'Yes.'

'Why would I do that?'

'Well, begging your pardon, ma'am. But in the past I could always come to Mrs Bannerman for help.'

'Mrs Sarah Bannerman? Do the same now, by all means; off you go, catch the train to London. I've got her address somewhere. Take your time, take as long as you like, so long as you stop bothering me with your sheer bloody domesticity.'

'Thank you, ma'am.' Mrs Harvey pursed her lips sourly. 'That makes everything absolutely clear.'

Dressed for the Manhattan, Marcus stopped to speak to the concierge on his way out.

'Goodnight, Collins. I trust by morning you'll have a certain list ready for me?'

'Message for you on the desk, sir,' Collins answered evasively. He watched Marcus pick it up. 'The lady called down not long ago, sir. Something about signing documents.'

'Cancel the car.' Screwing up the note, Marcus tossed it into a bin before running back up the stairs.

'Look at me, I'm Madame Milligan,' Lynne squealed as she swept across the maids' tiny bedroom in one of Madame's frocks.

'Lynne, take it off.' Kate's concern for the dress didn't stop her from laughing. 'She only wants it pressing, she'll kill us.'

'You look really snooty, you do,' Lark complimented.

'If I could only go out in this. I'd just . . .' Lynne giggled as she caught sight of herself in the plain, deal mirror screwed to the wall. 'I'd feel everybody was looking at me.'

'That's what they pay the money for.'

'You aren't half lucky, Kate,' Lynne said enviously.

'She likes me. She's asked if I want to go with her when she leaves.'

'Have you said yes?' Lark's eyes widened in alarm at the thought of losing her mentor.

'No. But I haven't said no neither.'

'Take it,' Brenda urged. 'While you've the chance!'

'What about me mam and dad?'

'You can send them what you send them now.'

'She goes abroad. On the Continent and everywhere.'

'I'd go like a shot,' Lynne broke in.

'Don't know about going abroad, though. You can't even eat the bread. It's that hard it makes your mouth bleed! It really does. Our Tom was in France.'

'That was the war, Brenda,' Lynne scoffed.

'Madame's just back from New York. She's taken an apartment there,' Kate revealed.

'America!' Lark exclaimed.

Lynne's eyes narrowed in jealousy. Gripping the neckline of the dress, she pulled at the bodice. 'If I just tore this up now. If I just did that! Be no America. Be no lady's maiding for our Katy . . . I'd give anything . . .'

'Come on, Lynne, take it off,' Kate persuaded gently.

Katherine Hardy

*   *   *

Marcus knocked on the door of Madame's room twice before trying the handle. It opened at his touch. He stepped inside. The air was filled with a heady, seductive perfume. A record was playing on the gramophone. A soft, romantic piece that he recognised.

'The papers I want you to sign are on the dressing table,' Madame called from the bathroom.

Marcus went to the gramophone, stopped the record, turned it over and started the turntable again. Taking his fountain pen from his inside pocket, he reached for the papers.

'Ah, Mr Collins.' Ruth cleared a space on her bedside table so the concierge could set down the tray of tea he'd brought up for her. 'If my husband comes back at a decent hour, could you tell him that I'd like to see him? He needs to be told that I can't have the housekeeper barging into my room on the slightest whim.'

'I'm sorry, ma'am,' Collins said, but sounded far from apologetic. 'I don't believe he actually left the building.'

'Really? Where is he?'

'He went to one of the guest rooms. To be precise, the room of Madame Euphrasine De Bourg D'Oisans. Room eighty-seven.'

'Thank you,' she snapped, dismissing him with a wave of her hand.

'Always glad to be of assistance, ma'am.'

'All done.' The breath caught in Marcus's throat as Madame emerged from the bathroom. She was dressed in an embroidered silk kimono, and her blonde hair tumbled loose around her shoulders. She looked sensuous, and extremely desirable. 'I'm sure you'd like to check the documents, personally,' he murmured hoarsely.

'They can wait until morning.' Pulling the silk cord that fastened the kimono, she opened it, allowing it to slide from her shoulders to the floor. For the first time in his life, Marcus felt overwhelmed by a woman as she stepped towards him, kissed him, and opened the buttons on his fly.

'When you suggested coming back here when you closed the club, I must admit I expected more than this.' Christina picked up her handbag and left the sofa in the Bannermans' private living room. 'I'd find more exciting company in a religious order. I should go.'

'May as well,' Stephen agreed gloomily as he gazed into his whisky glass. 'They all go in the end.'

'Oh for God's sake. Although,' she smiled wickedly, 'if it gets you out of this mood, I could always stay.'

Stephen left his seat. 'Yes, if you want. I'm sorry, I'm so sorry. I don't know why you put up with me. There's bound to be a guest room free.'

'I didn't mean a guest room.'

'Oh . . . Are you sure? I mean only if you want to . . .'

'As you insist on saying, your parents are gone. It's not quite the family home any more. You can do what you like.' She held out her hand. He took it and led her out of the room, down the corridor to his bedroom. Opening the door, he stepped inside. She followed.

'Talk to me,' Madame demanded as she rolled on top of Marcus in the bed. Straddling his body with her own, she pulled at the hairs on his chest with her long, manicured nails.

Katherine Hardy

Marcus ran his fingers through her hair, and down over her shoulders to her breasts. Fingering her nipples, he murmured, 'What do you want to hear? Love? Or filth?'

'All three.'

'Three?'

'Love, filth and . . . money!'

'Ahh . . . that works for you too . . .'

Outside Madame's room, the corridor was silent. Only the soft glow of a cigarette as it arced from the hand to the mouth of the stranger who had spoken to Collins in the foyer, punctuated the darkness. He listened to the unmistakable sounds of sex emanating from Madame's bedroom, and smiled.

And, as he listened, his smile grew darker.

Chapter Fifteen

'You tell her, it looked better on our Lynne,' Brenda called from the room next door to Madame's, as Kate arrived with her new mistress's dress, freshly pressed and checked for loose stitches.

Kate knocked and opened the door. 'It's Kate, Madame.' She laid the dress carefully over a chair, then went to the window to open the curtains. 'Madame?'

She paled when she saw Madame's bare feet sticking through the bars of the brass bedstead, her ankles tied by the sash of her kimono. 'Madame . . .' Summoning all her courage, Kate lifted the pillow that covered the woman's head.

Marcus stood in the doorway of Madame's room watching a detective dust the bedstead for finger-prints, while the officer in charge of the case, Detective Inspector Brattan, peered into Madame's empty jewel cases.

'Must we have a constable at the door of the hotel?' Marcus complained. 'I'm thinking of the other guests.'

'Until we've done what we have to, Mr Banner-man,' the inspector drawled in a tired voice, 'I'll need to fingerprint everyone from the hotel who has been in this room. If you could provide somewhere – just so we can eliminate them?'

Marcus nodded. 'How?' he asked in a strained voice.

'Suffocated, sir, with one of your pillows.'

'She can't be . . .'

'I'm so sorry, Miss Harkness.' The concierge took Esme Harkness's hand and led her towards the Reading Room.

'They always start with us, don't they?' Clive said testily as the staff formed a queue in front of the table in the downstairs kitchen.

'Just do as they say, Clive,' Mrs Harvey warned, as a uniformed constable pressed Lynne's inkstained fingers one by one on to his record pad.

'There are plenty of guests up there, going to and fro. The murderer could be halfway to London by now. But no, more likely one of us, isn't it? One of the workers.'

Mrs Harvey poured a cup of tea from the pot that was warming on the stove, and carried it across to Kate, who was crouched in the alcove rubbing fingerprint powder off her hands.

'One day,' the housekeeper muttered under her breath. 'One day he's been in charge. One day and it comes to this.'

Jacob Collins faced the CID inspector in the foyer.

'The man wanted to know if there were any lady VIPs in residence. He hinted he was a press man, which I believed.'

'Can you describe him?' Brattan asked.

'Five foot eight. Sandy haired, plenty of it. Waved in the front and not by nature. Pale, a bit like a man who's had jaundice.'

'You're naturally observant,' the inspector allowed grudgingly as he scribbled in his notebook.

'I'm *un*naturally observant, sir. It's why I'm good at my job.'

'Anything else?' Brattan asked in a friendlier tone.

'His shoes. A cut above the man himself, sir. Bespoke, a pair of Lobb's, sir. Definitely.'

'You'd know?'

'Guests leave their shoes out, sir, and overnight a lad polishes them. I can tell a Lobb shoe at half a mile. I used to be the lad.'

'Tell us what size they were, can you?' he chaffed.

'He'd be a size eight, sir.'

'Size bloody eight,' Brattan muttered in disbelief. 'What size am I?'

Collins glanced down at the inspector's shoes. 'You'd be a ten, sir.'

'I'm chucking my job in. Ah, Mr Bannerman.' He approached Marcus as he walked downstairs.

'I heard that you wanted to see me, Inspector?'

Brattan checked Marcus's hands. They were clean, with no trace of ink.

'Hardly necessary, I think . . .' Marcus said hopefully, but DI Brattan's expression told him there would be no exceptions.

Brattan unfolded a scrunched piece of paper. 'Mr Collins retrieved this from the bin, sir. Apparently, the lady requested your presence last night. And Mr Collins confirmed that you went up there last night.'

'Thank you, Mr Collins.' Marcus glared at the concierge.

'Not at all, sir,' Collins replied as he went to the desk.

* * *

'You don't think . . . Jacob? Dear God in heaven!' Mrs Harvey slumped on to a chair in her office as the concierge closed the door behind them. 'By all the saints. I mean, Jacob, I'm the last to sing Mr Bannerman's praises, but to think the man's capable of murder? Surely not!'

'I wouldn't have thought so. Even I wouldn't think that. But then again, I know him better than you do.'

'In what way?'

'Suffice to say, Marcus Bannerman had a brother. More than forty years they grew up together, and Marcus betrayed that brother. He lied to him, cheated on him, cast him aside like dirt. You tell me. A man like that. What would he do to a woman he's known for only one night?'

'So you see, Ruth, there will be fingerprints.' Marcus scoured the remains of the ink from his fingers with his handkerchief. 'The police will know I was there. So, they will ask where I was at certain times.'

'And where were you – at certain times?' She plumped up the cushion on the sofa behind her.

'Not murdering anybody. That's what matters. We don't have to advertise our . . . troubles to the world. Just say I was with you.'

'When?'

'Last night.'

'When last night?'

'Any time that matters. Any time they ask about.'

'Marcus, what have you done?'

'Nothing!' he insisted vehemently.

'You were in that room! With her,' she retorted furiously. 'Now give me one good reason why I should say otherwise.'

'Ruth . . . please . . .'

The Grand II: The Roaring Twenties

* * *

'Inspector,' Esme said, buttonholing the officer as he crossed the foyer.

'Ma'am.' He tipped his hat politely.

'The lady who was . . .' Her voice trembled as she struggled to regain control of herself. 'What arrangements have been made for the funeral?'

'I doubt if there will be much of a funeral, madam. There's nobody even claiming the body.'

'So what would . . .?'

'Doctors have to learn, don't they?'

'You've not been candid with me, sir,' Brattan accused, as Marcus invited the police officer into his private living room. Ruth offered him a chair, but he remained standing.

'No,' Marcus admitted. 'I should have been.'

'Would you prefer to talk at the station?'

'I didn't kill her.'

'You'll have to do better than that to convince a jury, sir. Your fingerprints were all over the bed.'

'I visited the room briefly,' Marcus admitted. 'To sign the documents. Then I came straight up here. Spent the evening with my wife.'

'Is that so, Mrs Bannerman?'

'I was in my bedroom. We have separate rooms. If my husband was on this floor, I didn't see him. He certainly wasn't with me.'

'Inspector, we've had a small argument this morning. My wife might be misleading you, a little mischief . . .'

'You can rot in hell,' Ruth interrupted vehemently. 'Or rot in Strangeways.'

'I think the courts can decide that, Mrs Bannerman. Although one option doesn't exclude the other. Now, if you don't mind, sir, I think it's time we went over this little story of yours, right from the start. Don't suppose there's any chance you could send down for a cup of tea?'

Hearing the request Collins moved away from the door where he had been eavesdropping. He took the lift to the foyer and went to the office, and, picking up the telephone, clicked for the operator.

'A London number, please. St James's I believe. The company name is Lobb's. Lobb's bespoke shoe-makers.'

'Perhaps you should leave us, Mrs Bannerman,' Brattan suggested tactfully. 'There might be some details of last night's activities a lady shouldn't hear.'

'I'm staying, thank you.' She settled back into the sofa.

'Ruth,' Marcus pleaded, 'for God's sake, do as he says.'

'Carry on.' Ignoring Marcus, she looked to Brattan.

'If you insist, ma'am. Now, Mr Bannerman, did you get a bit carried away, sir? If you'll pardon the phrase, ma'am, something in your loveplay, maybe?'

'For God's sake . . .' Marcus paced restlessly around the room.

'There's them that believe a touch of suffocation brings it on strong. Or so I've heard. Was that—'

'She was asleep when I left.'

'Which was?'

'About five.'

Brattan made a note in his book. 'Stamina!' He glanced up. 'Perhaps you thought she was asleep, when in fact—'

'Oh, I suffocated the woman, but it somehow escaped my attention at the time? Please, I've told you

218

the . . . relationship was spontaneous. I'd actually gone there on a matter of business.'

'Talked about money in bed, did you, sir?'

'As it happens.'

'Very often it's the last thing discussed before somebody gets murdered, sir. That and sex. You've managed both.'

The enormity of the accusation suddenly hit Marcus. 'In the name of God, why would I have killed her?'

'I'll wait for the why, sir. But I'll tell you *how*. Begging your pardon, ma'am. You suffocated her with the pillow. You crushed the pillow on to her face with the weight of your body and you held on to the uprights of the bedhead, to force your weight down. Fingerprints as tidy as I've ever seen, sir.'

'I don't follow. Wouldn't you just hold the pillow and push it down on someone's face? If you were—'

'I know that's how they always do it in *Othello* at the repertory, sir. And very easy it looks. But you and me, sir, we know they need more in the way of pinning down, don't we? A lot more. And the breath driving out of them with a bit of weight held on them? Stay like that a long time, did you? To make sure of it? Begging your pardon, ma'am.'

Collins set the telephone receiver on the stand, then clicked for the operator again.

'Yes, could you put me through? The head office of the White Star Line, please. As quick as you can, thank you.'

'Wait a minute,' Marcus argued as he ran the events of the previous night through his mind. 'If I were forcing myself down on her, then my right hand would be gripping this post, and my left . . . this.' He closed his hands into fists as though he were gripping the bed-head. 'If I were face down, forcing my weight down on the pillow . . . Do you see?' Irritated by the blank expression on the inspector's face, he blurted out, 'Can you tell the difference between a right-hand print and a left?'

'Certainly we can.'

'Then you'll find my hands were on the wrong bed-post for your theory.' Brattan held out his hands. 'No one suffocates a victim with their shoulder blades, Inspector.'

'And what were you doing at the time?' He stared quizzically at Marcus. 'You mean . . . the woman was on top? Begging your pardon, ma'am. Is that a typical position, sir?'

'Not that I know of,' Ruth snapped icily, finally walking out.

Closeting herself into her bedroom, she stared at herself in the mirror, hating the bulge that distended her clothes, the lie that had trapped her, tied her to a man she despised. Her hatred and loathing for Marcus began to build until she felt she was the one being suffocated. She plucked at the front of her dress, her fingers working in a frenzy of destruction. She shredded her frock, then after the cloth gave way, tore at the padding beneath. She dug her fingers in, ripping out lumps of cotton wool, grinding them to powder, all the while disgusted that she had allowed herself to become part of the life of a man like Marcus Bannerman.

'Start looking for the man Collins saw in the foyer,' Marcus insisted. 'I didn't kill her!'

'Ah, Mr Size Eight with the striking resemblance to

a red herring. Then there's the red herring of the missing jewellery, isn't there, sir? To make it look like a thief's business.'

'I've told you what happened, and that's the truth. I swear it.'

'And what exactly have you told me, sir? What exactly? Let's see. A full and frank confession that you engaged in a highly unusual sexual collusion with a woman you'd known for all of ten minutes. Perhaps I've got a bit lost, sir, but tell me: is that supposed to prove your innocence?'

Mrs Harvey glanced at Jacob Collins as she pushed the day's receipts on to the spike in the office.

'Everything all right, Jacob?' she asked, concerned by the preoccupied look on his face.

'Funny thing. I've prayed for that man to be brought down. And here we are. The answer to my prayers. But if he's arrested what happens to the Grand?'

'Gone! Never mind the list of four: every one of us is out of a job. I've not been idle, Jacob. The address of that hotel in Didsbury, I've found it. All we can do is save ourselves. God help the others.'

'But it's not about him. Regardless of what he deserves, a woman's dead. A lady. That can't go unpunished.' He finally left his seat.

'Where are you going?'

'To do my duty. Much as it pains me.'

Brattan lay, stretched out on the bed in the room that had been Madame's until that morning. Reaching up, he gripped the posts. Marcus glared at the three grinning, uniformed constables who were watching the inspector's performance with more amusement than interest.

'Inspector,' he remonstrated, 'is there need—'

'Just checking, sir.' He turned his head and looked behind him. 'I see. Yes, it makes sense.'

'I think, Inspector, that you're wasting my time.'

'Is that so, sir?' The inspector left the bed. 'Very sorry. Very sorry indeed. Let's see if I can't hurry things along.' He fell serious. 'Marcus Bannerman, I'm arresting you for the murder of the woman known as Euphrasine De Bourg D'Oisans at the Grand Hotel on the twenty-seventh of this month. Anything you say may be used in evidence at your trial . . .'

Marcus stared in disbelief as a constable stepped forward and clipped handcuffs on to his wrists.

'Excuse me, sir.' Collins rapped on the door.

'Come to enjoy the spectacle?'

'It's the inspector I need, Mr Bannerman.' He looked at Brattan. 'The gentleman I described in the foyer . . . I should point out that Madame's trunk arrived when he was there. If he recognised the monogram, he'll have known she was a guest . . .'

'I don't think this mysterious gentleman need concern me,' Brattan broke in cuttingly.

'His name is Mr Saxon.'

'How do you know that?'

'The shoes, sir. Lobb's shoes. A bespoke shoe always goes back to its last for repairs, so I made enquiries. For a size eight in oxblood leather. Lobb's were able to supply me with two names. One of them a Mr Saxon. The second was the headmaster of Eton. I didn't think it relevant.'

'Collins, what is the point of this?' Marcus enquired testily.

'If you'll let me finish, sir . . . I then telephoned the White Star Line. It turns out, on the trip over, Madame booked two cabins with a connecting door. The other cabin for one Mr Saxon.'

'The same man?' the inspector asked.

'That's up to you, sir. I'm not the detective. Though it does seem to be stretching the laws of coincidence. On further enquiry, Mr Saxon's luggage is in storage at Southampton awaiting collection. It's possible he's making his way there right now. I'd suggest it might be wise if the police are waiting for his arrival.'

'Bloody hell!' Brattan exclaimed.

The inspector walked into the foyer of the Grand, bright and early the next morning. Seeing Collins, he smiled broadly.

'There's a job waiting for you, Mr Collins, if ever you need one.'

'I might well do,' the concierge muttered, glancing at Marcus as he emerged from the office.

'That's Mr Saxon in custody,' Brattan told him. 'Turns out he's quite a regular on the White Star Line. And thought by the company to be plying his trade.'

'Which would be?' Marcus asked.

'Finding a mark with money and getting them into phoney businesses. A conman. There were two of them that worked it. The partner was a woman. Very classy and a looker.'

'Then she was a fake.' Marcus failed to keep the disappointment from his voice.

'For my money she cut him out and ditched him, and he didn't take to it.'

'He wasn't so willing to, er . . .' – Collins winked at the inspector – 'let the lady get on top of him, you think?'

Humiliated, Marcus returned to the office as Collins and Brattan exchanged smiles.

* * *

'That needs catching up.' Kate fingered the hem of one of Madame's dresses, as she folded it ready to pack into one of the trunks that Lark and Lynne had opened and set out on the floor of room eighty-seven.

'Don't be daft. What about this?' Lynne held up the sable wrap Madame had shown to Kate.

'Are you taking all day?' Mrs Harvey scolded as she walked into the room.

'Done, Mrs Harvey.' Kate closed the lids. 'Apart from these.' She held up the furs. 'They shouldn't go in. They need storing.'

'Don't gawp,' Mrs Harvey barked at the porters hovering in the doorway. 'Just pick those up' – she pointed to the trunks – 'and get them downstairs. Bring those furs down, Kate. It will all need sealing and signing for.'

'That's your fancy lady's maiding gone,' Lynne sympathised as Kate looked around the room one last time.

'You'll have to stay here with us in the same old job,' Lark said shyly.

'If the same old job still exists,' Kate said as she followed them out.

Marcus waited until the inspector left before speaking to the concierge.

'Jacob, I suppose I should make it clear how grateful I am . . .'

'It wasn't a personal favour, sir,' Collins cut in. 'More the injustice that concerned me. When the day of your downfall comes, Mr Bannerman, I'm sure it will be deserved.'

'I won't disappoint.'

'Oh and, sir?' Collins called after him as he went to the office. 'There is a way of showing your gratitude.

The list of four staff, sir, the jobs to be lost?'

Marcus nodded as Jacob tore the list in half.

'It is not the business of the hotel to arrange a hearse and plumed horses for unclaimed guests,' Marcus told Esme as they shared a bottle of wine at the bar of the Manhattan.

'Unless something is done, her body may' – she shuddered at the thought – 'be used for teaching purposes.'

'Some women have that calling.'

'She was a lady.'

'You heard what she was. A convincing fake. Like the name she used.'

'She was in danger. She used a . . . *nom de guerre*. But I spoke to her intimately, Marcus. And I know what she was.'

'I had dealings with her of some intimacy myself, and you are the only woman I know to whom I might say that she had an appetite that would astonish a whore.'

'That is entirely characteristic of the aristocracy. And, yes, perhaps she had been reduced to living on her wits. Fleeing from a revolution, you might have to.'

'My heart bleeds.'

'If she had a criminal partner, it was because she was preyed on. And she left him, obviously to set herself up again in a legitimate business.'

'Yes, she wanted to set herself up in a business. And mine would have done! I was the mark, the lamb to the slaughter. And I might have been just that.' He gazed blindly into the distance, remembering. 'She was that good.'

'I haven't ruled out that she was killed by

Bolsheviks and all of this is a cover-up,' Esme conjectured.

'Bolshevik assassins rubbing out Romanoffs in British hotels? And the authorities here just invent a story to cover it up?'

'That is exactly what they would do.'

'Believe it if you want.'

'Excuse me.' Esme left him for a middle-aged man who was standing in the doorway. 'Mr Bunner, you got my message?'

Marcus finished his drink and set his glass on the bar.

'Another, sir?' Jim asked.

'No, I don't think so. I'm calling it a night.'

'Not like you, sir, this early. Back home to the missus?'

'I think it's about time I was, yes.'

He glanced back at Esme and her guest, who were taking a table, as he went to the door.

'I'd value your opinion, Mr Bunner.' She handed him the pendant Madame had given her.

'Where did you get this?'

'It was a gift.'

Taking an eyeglass from his pocket, he examined it closely. 'Do you have the companions?'

'No, just that.'

'There would be a pair with a necklace.'

'And is it the real thing?'

'Fabergé, St Petersburg. A piece of a vanished world, Miss Harkness.'

'The vulgar question?'

'Sell it in America, that's where the money is.'

'And we are talking of?'

'Out of my league. But plenty. Wait until Mrs

Vanderbilt is in a mood to buy Fabergé. You'll find out what it's worth.'

'Fabergé, and the real thing,' she mused. 'Put it on a very simple chain for me. I shall wear it to a funeral.'

Chapter Sixteen

'I want that cutlery done again.'

'I've done it once. It's clean, Mrs Harvey.' Kate glanced uneasily at Clive as he walked through the work area to the back door.

'Not my sort of clean. It's been in and out of the mouths of God knows who. They've got smallpox in Nottingham. I want extra vigilance . . .'

The porters stacking crates in the cellar nodded sympathetically as Clive passed them.

'I'll be back by six o'clock, Mrs Harvey.' Clive opened the door.

'Take your time. And you lot' – she turned from Clive to the maids – 'at the double! If you got paid for standing about gawping, you'd be rich as kings, the lot of you.'

It was good to be out of doors on a fine autumn morning. There was a freshness in the air, despite the heavy traffic of carts and motor cars. Leaving the main thoroughfare, Clive negotiated the network of streets and alleyways that marked the end of the public face of Manchester, and the beginning of the slums. As the streets grew narrower and meaner, so the buildings grew taller. He stopped outside a grim, grey tenement block. Drawing the last taste of nicotine from the dog end in his mouth, he dropped it to the ground. He took a final deep breath of clean air and walked through a door that was hanging on a single broken hinge, and into a dingy hallway that stank of fish and urine.

Two small children were sitting on the concrete stairs that led to the third floor, clinging to one another as angry sounds escalated behind them.

'What's he done this time? Spent the housekeeping?' Clive tickled the small girl under the chin, lifting her head, and saw a purple bruise covering her eye. 'Who did that, your dad?'

She looked away sullenly. Fishing a set of keys from his pocket, he opened the first door he came to. He'd done it so many times before, only now – now – he stared at the boxes, the layers of dust on the floor where the heavier pieces of furniture had been, the smudges that outlined where the two photographs had hung on the wall. One of his mother in her Sunday best and one of him in his army uniform. Silence closed around him, dense, nauseating . . .

'It's only me,' he answered to a shout.

'And I was expecting the Crown Prince of Japan.'

He pushed aside the curtain and went into the living room. His father was sitting in the easy chair. The rug had been beaten and brushed, the hearth swept and cleaned, the tablecloth shaken. No need for a man to live like a pig just because there wasn't a woman in the house, or so his father always said.

'The Crown Prince is outside with his entourage, Dad. I told him to wait.'

'Did I tell you? Stan Oxley, he met him once. Don't stand there like an idiot, put the kettle on. He shook his hand. The Crown Prince . . . what's his name? Hirohito. Stan Oxley shook his hand.'

Katherine Hardy

'Don't be so daft.' Clive filled the kettle at the sink in the corner and fiddled with the gas cooker standing next to it. 'The Crown Prince of Japan didn't travel halfway across the world to meet Stan Oxley.' Giving up on the cooker, he kicked it. 'This bloody thing.'

'I'm telling you, they took the royal party to Vicker's Electrical. They showed His Highness round the canteen. God knows why, maybe they don't have canteens in the Far East – well anyway the bell goes off, and it's dinnertime, and half the workforce comes pouring in, and there he is! A Japanese royal prince standing by the meat pies.'

'He never was.'

'Stan said he's not yellow, that's not true, they're not yellow at all, just a bit off colour, like he'd been sick. And you?' He glowered at his son. 'I've heard all about you. No, don't tell me a thing – I have to be told down the pub.'

'Heard what?' Clive asked apprehensively.

'Bloody Bill Craven's wife, she passed it on. Told me last night. She went to the Grand for some do, Red Cross or something. Free sandwiches and a cup of tea. Nice for her. You've never invited *me* over the door.'

'What did she say?'

'You. Posh uniform and everything, like you're in charge. I had to lie through my teeth. Said I knew all about it. What is it, then? Promotion?'

'Yes.'

'And about time. More money?'

'Bit more, yes.'

'Lovely, more money for me. So, what's the job?'

'Hall porter. Deputy to Mr Collins.'

'There, now, didn't I tell you?' He rose clumsily from his chair, his limbs stiff and awkward with arthritis. 'I can hear this with a cup of tea in my hand, or with a pint in the Rose and Crown.'

'It's out of hours.'

'Jack Latham's open all afternoon, so long as you keep the noise down.'

'No, Dad, please, sit down a minute.'

'I won't send you back drunk. Have a pint of pop . . .'

'Dad, sit down.' Clive spoke more sharply than he'd intended. 'I don't want it said in the pub, and there's a lot that needs saying.' Picking up the wooden chair set in front of the kitchen table, he swung it opposite his father's chair. Then he sat down. 'It's not the job. There's lots of things. It's all – well it started with the job. But then perhaps it really started years back. I dunno when it started. Maybe it did start with the job.'

'What's wrong?' The look of concern. That caring look of concern. The one he remembered from his childhood. He turned away unable to face it.

'I'm saying, if you'll shut up. I thought if I said it in the right order, I could make sense of it. So, I got the job right, and Mr Collins, he's dead nice about it, gets me measured up, new uniform and all that. And it's an extra ten shillings a week. I'm thinking, This is it. I'm laughing. And you know what Mr Collins is: he has this proper bloody meeting, like the town crier. All the staff are there. Every last one, Mr Collins and Mrs Harvey standing in front of them, and me next to them in me new uniform, and he says, "So from now on, Walter, you'll be running the bar. Clive's going to be rather busy. Very busy indeed. Not that I'm retiring, mind – I'll be keeping an eye on the lot of you – but if I'm not around, Clive's in charge. Got that? Needless to say, in all matters concerning the hotel, you will treat him with respect, and address him as Mr Evans." Course, they all burst out laughing, and

Katherine Hardy

Lynne Milligan, she's one of the maids, she said, "I can't do that." "You can and you will," Mr Collins ordered. So I asked, "Do they have to, sir?"'

Clive paused for breath, studying his father's face for reaction.

'"Yes, they do," says Mr Collins. And he looked at the lot of them and said, "That's starting from today, and just because he's your friend don't go looking for favours. Now back to work, but before you do, one more thing. I think you might give Mr Evans your congratulations." And there was me, standing there while they all clapped. All of them, and I could see most of them were that pleased for me. And afterwards I saw Kate. By herself in the corridor. No one else about. That's why she did it. "Excuse me, Mr Evans, sir." And I looked round at her. "Just wanted to say, sir, something very important." And she kissed me. "Well done. It's brilliant."' Clive paused again, smiling at the recollection. 'I said, "Bet you don't do that to Mr Collins." "Maybe I do, for all you know." And she gave me a right cheeky smile before running off. So I shouted, "Don't run!" And she turns and says, "Sorry, sir." I knew she was taking the mick, but underneath it, she was pleased. And so was I. Mr Collins's deputy, in charge. At last, I was someone.'

'This Kate, that's the Morris girl?'

'Yeah.'

'You've not got her pregnant?'

Clive burst out laughing. 'No, it's not that. Oh my God, it's not that! Oh bloody hell, no.'

'What is it then?'

'This guest arrives, see. It was this guest. And I was good at the job, right, I was that good. Mr Collins, he's glad of the time off. He's not happy with Marcus Bannerman in charge. And there's this woman, Rosie

Skinner – she does the sewing and stuff. She pops in twice a week. Well, they got talking – we were all in the foyer, me, Bob, Mr Collins dressed for his afternoon off, and this Rosie walks in. She must be in her thirties, but she's a smart woman. Really smart. And Mr Collins was talking about what he was going to do. He says, "I thought I might take myself to the football. It's a big match . . ." And she interrupts: "Shame on you. The Royal Exchange is going to be the centrepiece of the town. It has to be seen. You might be a Geordie, but I think you can show a little Manchester pride." And it's all banter, but you can still see she really likes him, and he says, "It's not finished until the autumn. They said in the paper . . ." "And I've heard the King himself is going to open it. But they've got this area roped off, so you can see inside. It's completely beautiful. Now I insist, Mr Collins, I'm taking you right this second." "Well, I don't suppose I've got any choice by the sound of it." And she comes back with, "No, you haven't." That's when Bob and I start laughing, and Mr Collins gets angry. "Something funny?" he asks us. "No, sir, not at all, sir." And when they've gone, Bob says, "Lucky beggar. She must be ten years younger than him. All that sewing. She's good with her hands. He can inspect her stitches." But that's Bob for you, always has to push everything that bit too far. So, they started walking out, from that day on. Good for him. Never seen Mr Collins with a lady friend before. And then I had to go and spoil it.'

'All right then.' His father reached for his pipe. 'Don't tell me you made her pregnant.'

'So he's happy, old Collins,' Clive continued as if he hadn't spoken. 'More work he gives me, more time he's got for Rosie Skinner. And he taught me the lot. Sat for hours in his room, going over the paperwork.

He tells me everything about, "The receipts, the weekly accounts, the monthly accounts, the yearly accounts. Got that?" "Yes, sir." "But the paperwork, Clive, that's not half the job. It's my solemn duty to warn you. There's a baptism of fire yet to come." And he makes a face. "Mrs Harvey."

'So, he takes me off to Mrs Harvey's room for the weekly meeting, and there she is, all smiles, not a bit like the Mrs Harvey I know. The one that makes the maids' lives hell. "Sit yourself down, Clive. I said this to Mr Collins when I first became housekeeper, and I'll say the same to you now. It's like a ship, the Grand Hotel, an ocean liner, the finest you could build. And down here, we're the men in the boiler room stoking the engine, keeping a steady flame in the roughest of seas. And no one knows. We're invisible." And while she's yacking she gets out a bottle of sherry and three glasses, and then she turns to me and asks, "Sherry?"

'You could have blown me over, but I'm not going to turn down the chance of a free drink. "Yeah, thanks," I says. "It's our little treat, once a week," she says. "The engines need oiling, never forget that." So she pours out the sherry, three glasses, then she warns, "Just the one." Just the one!' Clive grinned at his father. 'Just the one bottle! Two hours later she doesn't know what she's saying or who she's saying it to. "Russia, they've got corpses in the street, there's cholera, smallpox, all sorts. Did you read today's paper? Anthrax! Anthrax in the British Isles! Just look at Sheffield. Riots in the street. Here in the Grand Hotel, we're the last bastion of civilisation."

'Half an hour later, we're still there, and she's moved on to the gin. "I don't just employ those girls: it's an act of charity. Me and Mr Harvey, charitable souls, both. Last Christmas, we had that frost. I went home early, and there he was, bless him. Had this girl in the front room, fifteen she must have been. Pretty little thing. But the clothes! Falling off her, they were. And I said, 'What's this?' And he said, 'Sylvie, what are you doing home?' Then he says she's a poor waif and stray, and he found her freezing in a shop doorway, brought her home for a bit of Christian succour. That man's a saint."'

'Mad old bugger!' his father grinned.

'And Mr Collins, he puts up with that every week!'

'I knew her when she was Sylvie Webber, lived on North Terrace. She moved the other side of town when she married Jack Harvey. They thought they were posh. Wanted a garden for the kid.'

'She's not got kids.'

'Did have. Little girl, I think. I don't know – lost track of them.'

'There's no kids, now.'

'Something happened, flu or something, accident perhaps, I can't remember.'

'She's never said.'

'Did you ever stop and ask?' He took a long pull at his pipe. 'Always had an eye for the ladies, Jack Harvey. Your mother wouldn't sit next to him. She used to say, "He's got that look, like a man's been hungry for a month, and he's staring at raw meat."'

'Then he arrives, this guest,' Clive continued. 'Walks into reception, and Mr Collins knows him at once. Been waiting for him. Young, good-looking, not that it will do the girls any good, still in his twenties, sharp dresser, theatrical. You know what I mean? Successful with the kind of success that brings money, and lots of it. "Villiers, Mr Sean Villiers," he announces. "I made the booking last week. You should have confirmation in writing." "Indeed, sir."

And there's Mr Collins treating him as if he was royalty. "Welcome to the Grand. You're in room twenty-nine. I hope it is to your liking. It has a very good view of the square. My name is Mr Collins, this is my assistant, Mr Evans. If ever you need anything, one of us will be on duty. Now, can we show you upstairs?"

'So this chap says, "To be honest, I'd rather find the bar. You can take the luggage." "Certainly, sir. The bar is over there. Your key, sir." "Thank you, Mr Collins – and what was it?" "Evans, sir," I said. But I didn't know. Not then. "Mr Evans." And then this Villiers, he orders the porters to take his luggage to his room and disappears into the bar. "Long-term potential, this one," Mr Collins confided in me. "Good for business. Theatrical manager. He's often in Manchester. Up until now he's stayed at the Midland. I've talked his office into giving us a go, so keep him happy. I'd better tell Mr Bannerman he's arrived."

'And that's when I noticed that he keeps looking at me. Villiers. Whenever he sees me, in the foyer, he gives me that bloody look. And I try to look away. Find things to do that don't need doing, like talking to the duty receptionist. "Right, Mr Villiers, you got the letter?" "It's in the file." "Right, good." And the duty man knows, and I know I didn't need to say that. But it's anything other than look at Villiers.

'And then there's the girls, the maids. They always know. Know everything, that lot, more than they should. And they were waiting for me when I went down for my supper after I finished me shift for the night. "You, Mr Evans, sir." That's Lynne Milligan, taking the mick. "You can do something about room twenty-nine, you can. It's that bloke, Mr Villiers. You're in charge Clive, it's not decent." "What's he

236

done?" Lark asked. She's new, a kid really, barely fourteen. "He's nice, he left us half a crown." "He's a bit . . ." Lynne looked over her shoulder – she knows she'll be for it if Mrs Harvey catches her talking about guests. "He's a bit so." "A bit so what?" That Brenda Potter never was very bright. "A bit so," Lynne repeated. "He never is." Kate's not much of one for gossip, but even she gets interested at that point. "He is an' all." "A bit so what, Lynne?" Brenda kept on. And then Lynne came right out with it. "He's an Oscar." "Lark, go to bed," Kate ordered. "Aww." "She should be told, she's cleaning his sheets. He likes men. In bed. Big Lucy knows this girl at the Midland who cleaned his room there. He's a pervert and that's a fact." "Don't be ridiculous, Lynne." That's Brenda again. "They only have those in London." "He's *from* London." "Oh my God!" "Told you!" And there's Lynne looking all triumphant at the lot of us. "He's not coming near me," Bob shouted. "I think you're safe, Bob." Kate tried to make a joke of it, as if anyone could laugh about something like that. "We're sweeping up after criminals." "And what if he is, Lynne? We had this bloke. Must have been seventy-odd, lived two doors down from us, and he was . . . well he was a bit musical. Sam Allan, that was his name. And he was lovely, never did any harm." But then that's Kate for you: always looking for the good in everyone.

"'In the war, right, the Germans had this little black book . . .'" "Oh, here we go, Brenda Potter's war." Lynne never lets Brenda get a word in edgewise. "It's true, this secret book with the names of forty-seven thousand perverts in the capital. MPs and ministers and all sorts, women as well. A list of the damned it was." "Villiers top of the list, I bet." And Lynne was only half joking. "It's official, Clive, this is my official complaint, and you're an official personage."

'So, I said, "Fair enough. We shouldn't have to put up with that." "Oh, Clive, it's only gossip."

'Kate was looking out for me, same as she always does but of course, I didn't listen to her. I think, I'm in charge and that's not right, so I go to Mr Collins in his room, and I tell him. "I mean, sir, he's breaking the law. If he was a bank robber, or a thief, we wouldn't have him . . ." And all he can say is, "Clive, it's none of our business, understood? You're in a new job now. You can sit and chat with your friends, that's fine, but the gossip goes no further. It stops the moment you set foot upstairs. You'll treat Mr Villiers like any other guest." "But if it's true—" "I'm sure it is, but it doesn't make him a monster." "You can't approve, sir?" "No I don't. But it's sad, more than anything. They've got the right idea abroad, where is it? Antwerp I think, somewhere outside Antwerp." "What's that, sir?" "You should read the papers, Clive. You need a view of the whole world in this job. It's some colony, near Antwerp. They've rounded up all the weak-minded, the idiots and the feeble, and men like Mr Villiers. They've all been shipped off to this colony, out of the way. It's a proper community with shops and houses." "Good idea. We should do the same," I told him, and he says, "We could use the Isle of Man, but failing that, Clive, we're stuck with them. And as staff we keep our personal opinions to ourselves."

'Then he gives me a bill. "That's unpaid. I've chased him up twice. You can have a go." As if unpaid bills matter more than the law.'

'Did he have a go?' Clive's father frowned. 'He did, didn't he, Villiers? Fair do's, he would, fine-looking lad like you. I'd like to have seen that! You're in the front line now, hall porter, fair game . . .'

'I'm not the hall porter any more. I lost the job.'

'Because of that bloke?'

'I should get back.'

'But what happened?'

'Told you, had the job, lost it. End of story. Extra ten shillings a week. I was going to give it to you to get that cooker mended.'

'You can't get up to go now. Sit yourself down. You're not leaving me with half a story.'

'I'm late as it is.'

'Sit down. Clive, lad, I won't be shocked. I've heard it all, me.'

'All right, I lost the job because of Mr Villiers.'

'Because he had a go? That's not your fault.'

'It was.'

'Bloody cheek. I've seen that Jacob Collins down the pub. I'll have a word. It's not fair, you getting the blame.'

'Dad, give us a listen. In the end, it was nothing to do with Villiers. Do you see, it wasn't him? That's what I'm saying.'

Frightened of what about he was to hear, the old man left his chair. Lumbering slowly, he rummaged in the rickety sideboard. 'Sod the tea. I've got some beers tucked away somewhere.'

Chapter Seventeen

Gripping the bottle of beer his father had given him firmly in his hand, Clive continued.

'So, we made a good team, old Collins and me. It's not like we're friends though; I mean it's work. We just talked about work, nothing else. Not one for talking me.'

'Except today,' his father interrupted drily.

'Even way back in the war, when his son was killed. Do you remember that? I went to see him. I was still in uniform. Didn't know if I'd see another leave after that one. None of us did. So, I went to his room in the Grand. The door was open and I looked in. Mr Collins was sitting there alone. I mean, there was me in the army and everyone knew about Peter. Killed in action, they said. Of course, we know different now. I liked Peter. He was a laugh. Good mates, me and Peter. I should have gone in – should have said – I don't know, but I didn't. I just walked away. Mr Collins didn't even know I was there. But then, a man wants to be left alone at a time like that. Then, the war's over, Peter's dead and buried. And I suppose I became that bit special to Mr Collins after that.'

'You were telling me about this Villiers.'

'Yeah, well, all the time there he was, walking in and out of the Grand. Just smiling. All the time that bloody smile. Just Villiers was bad enough. Then it was the two of them. Him and Miss Harkness. They met in the foyer on my shift. And the talk. You wouldn't believe half the things she says. And in public too.'

Clive attempted Esme Harkness's tones: "Mr Villiers, now there's one man I can guarantee hasn't come calling for me." "Oh my God! Esme Harkness. Haven't they buried you yet? I'm sure they did. I sent flowers." Then he kissed her. All over her he was. They're like two women who aren't really fond of one another but put on a show every time they meet. "Didn't you know?" she asks him. "The Grand's my new home now. It's rather appropriate. Slightly faded but battling on." "You, living in the provinces?" Villiers can even shriek like a woman. "Did they run you out of London in the end?" "That's quite a story, Sean, and not one for public consumption. Suffice to say, I rocked the Church of England to its foundations, and the rest I'm saving for my memoirs." "I'd pay good money to read them." "It's written in blood."

'And that's when it started. The whispering and the giggling. You'd think the two of them were lovers, and always those sly little glances in my direction, both of them, looking, always looking. Obviously talking about me. It even carried on in the Manhattan. I still do the odd night there when they're short-staffed. I couldn't escape them. And I wanted to ask, I wanted to know. What the hell was so bloody funny that they had to laugh every time they looked at me? That look, like they could see right through me. Like they knew.'

'What's there to know?'

'Kate told me. Kate of all people, just when I was having a last cigarette before bed. There was just the two of us in the staff kitchen. There often is, last thing

at night. And she asks, "Is it true what Bob says?"
"What?" I wasn't even listening to her, not properly.
That's why I was so gobsmacked by what followed.
"The Snake Pit, heard of that?" "Dunno, what is it?"
"It's this café down by the canal, and it stays open all
night. And five in the morning, all these lads go there,
lads from the market and the factories and that, and
they go there and they hang around, and *then*. Honest,
Bob Jessop told me this. These other men turn up, like
lords and posh people, all of them with money; they
wander in and . . . take their pick, from the lads. Give
them five quid and off you go. Like picking a side of
beef for your Sunday dinner. In the middle of
Manchester!"

'I was bloody furious. "What the hell's Bob Jessop
doing, talking about things like that?" "It's just a
story." "It's filthy, telling you. Telling a girl."

'And all she could do was laugh. "Oh shut up," she
says. "I lost me blushes a long time back working in
this place." "Well it's dirty. You shouldn't. And I'm
telling Bob an' all. I'm in charge now, and I'm not
having it."

'And still she didn't take me seriously. All I got was
a "Yes, sir, sorry, sir." And then I had to go and ask,
didn't I? "Where's it supposed to be, this café?" "By
the canal, behind Piccadilly." So like an idiot, I go
down there to see if she's right. Not in it, of course. I
hung back on the corner, waiting, having a smoke.
Then I see him with two other men. Bloody Villiers.
And what does he say? "Well, Mr Evans." Like he
expected to find me there. And all I can is stammer is,
"Sir." Like an idiot. "Rather late to be out and about.
Or rather early, take your pick. I gather there's a café
in this direction. If you'd care to join us . . ."

'I pushed past him and ran. I could hear him, laughing all the way, right up until I reached the back door of the Grand. He wasn't there, but I could still hear him. The bastard!'

'So why did you go there?' Clive's father asked.

'Where?'

'This Snake Pit thing. Why did you go?'

'I dunno . . . Then it all starts happening. I'm downstairs, helping with the crates. I'm still one of the lads. I've got me posh job, but I'm still mucking in, same as ever, good old Clive. Then Mrs Harvey walks in and claps her hands like she always does, as if we're a bloody load of chickens who'll come running every time she chooses to feed us the odd titbit. "Bit of hush there, Lark. I've a special announcement. Good news for all of us." And Mr Collins walks in behind her. "Mrs Harvey, I don't think Mr Bannerman wants this too formal . . ." "It's a wonderful day." And then I see Stephen Bannerman standing behind her. "And a very kind gesture, sir. It should come from you. Pay attention now, all of you."

'Stephen Bannerman steps forward, bold as brass, after all the times he's chatted to Kate Morris – and more – and not a word to her first, mind. Not that he could look her, or any of us, in the eye. "Right, I'm not one for speeches, but you've all met . . . well, you might have seen, my . . . lady friend, Miss Christina Lloyd-Price, and well . . . we're engaged. As from last night."

'Most of the staff are like sheep. Mrs Harvey, she starts clapping, so the rest of them follow. And Kate, she's clapping louder than any of them, as if she doesn't care about Stephen Bannerman, though we both know different, and all he can say is, "Bit out of the blue, I know. I thought I could tell you individually." "That's not all, is it, sir?" Mrs Harvey prompts.

Katherine Hardy

"No. I'm taking Christina down to London tomorrow, to see my parents. So before the off, well, we should celebrate. My father used to say you're all family. So there's a bit of a . . . party, I suppose, tonight upstairs on the family floor. You're all invited." "You're still on duty, mind," Mrs Harvey warned. Has to spoil everything, that woman. "So, you'll have to go up in split shifts. Now let's show our appreciation in typical Grand style."

'And while they're all clapping, Kate sneaked off. I saw her, and I couldn't let her go, not by herself. I found her in the scullery, tidying up. That girl never stops. "Doesn't waste time, does he?" I says to her. "Not the sort of bloke to be on his own for long," she says. "And she's nice; she's good for him. He could have done much worse." Meaning herself, as if anyone could do worse than Kate. But that's Kate for you. Always nice. So bloody nice, even when she's the one being hurt.

'And that's the night he comes in. Villiers. I'm just finishing me shift. He's been out somewhere, drinking by the look of him. And he's there. So he asks for his key and I hand it over. And he holds it up. "Room twenty-nine," he says slowly, as if I didn't know. "Yes, sir," I say. "Twenty-nine." And he repeats it over and over again, until I feel like a bloody parrot saying, sir . . . sir . . . sir . . . Then he asks, "Ever been there?" "Suppose so, sir. I've been in all the rooms sometime or other." "So, you know where it is?" "Of course I do, sir." "Well I'm going to bed. Room twenty-nine."

'And then there's that look, that bloody look, just like he gave me by the Snake Pit. So, I take Kate upstairs to Mr Bannerman and Miss Lloyd-Price's engagement party. And the room's full of staff and food and wine. The cheap stuff, mind. And there's a gramophone. It's not the Manhattan, but at least they tried. And Christina, that's Mr Bannerman's fiancée, she meets us by the door. "Help yourselves. I don't suppose I need to show you around, you know this place better than I do." "Oh yes, miss," says Kate and gives this wicked smile. "The things we could tell you."And I think, Good for Kate; didn't know she had it in her. "Well, make yourself at home," Miss Christina says. "Will you be living here, miss? When you're wed?" Kate asks her. "I'm not sure. We haven't talked about it."

'And that's when she gives it away. We can see she hasn't thought about her and Stephen. Not really. "Early days, miss." Kate and I go to the buffet. And Lynne's there, sitting on the family sofa with a plate piled high. "Hey, a bit posh this," she says. "I'm like a dog on a cushion."

'And Brenda's being silly like she always is. "Listen, I saw them chucking this cheese out last week. It's all leftovers. Isn't it your bedtime, Lark?" "I can stay up, Mrs Harvey gave me permission. To celebrate the happy couple." "Listen, titch, I've been in love, it never lasts. Grab the food while you can, that's my motto." Lynne hasn't been the same since Fred Willets walked out on the Grand and her.

'I get Kate and meself some food, and we talk. It's the first time I've been in the family rooms. But not her. She knows every inch of the Grand. Family bits as well as public. "See that corner over there?" she asks me. "I never clean that corner. It doesn't get sunlight so no one's ever seen. It's my own little piece of upstairs." "How long's it been, those two?" I asked. "A couple of months?" "You know what Lynne says," she says. "It's his mum and dad: they up and disappear, so look what he does. Starts a family of his own. Quite clever that, for Lynne," says Kate. "That Christina, though, she must know what she's doing." "Hope so," I told her. "Thing is, he sweeps you along, you can't get a word in edgeways. Good luck to her."

'And we both turn to see him – Stephen – knocking back drinks too fast, just like he used to in the old days when he first came home from the army. Drinking and laughing too loud. You know what I mean? And still Kate feels sorry for him. "Mr Collins says he wasn't like that before the war. It changed him." Then she dug her elbow in my ribs. "You went through it though, and you're all right." "Am I?" And I'm wondering as I ask her. "Course you are. Nothing puts you down for long." "Both of us fine and dandy." "I am." She hands me a canapé. "Try this, it's veal," she says.

'"What's so fine about us, though?" I asked. "You've got no one. Can't think the last time I had a lady friend." "Bob Jessop says you're the best in town at chatting up barmaids. He said he's taking notes." But what does Bob Jessop know about me?

'Then Lynne barged between us, slopping her drink and dropping sandwiches off the side of her plate. "Oh my God! Have you seen—" And in walks Mr Collins with Rosie clinging to his arm. He stopped to introduce her to Stephen Bannerman and Christina, and Mrs Harvey's so angry she's fit to burst. "Partners! Did anyone say partners? Was there any invitation for Mr Harvey? Not that I'm complaining, no!"

'And Lynne's still gabbing, never can keep her mouth shut that one. "Big Lucy was in the west corridor at midnight, and who's walking out quiet as a mouse? Only Rosie Skinner, that's who, and what's down in the west corridor? Mr Collins's room, the dirty dog." "Evening, Mr Collins, Miss Skinner," I say loudly to let Lynne know they're behind us. "Evening, Clive." Mr Collins smiled at me as if we were equals. "Have a word with the management. They've palmed us off with the Spanish wine. We're the ones who carry it to the cellars. We're the first to know it's cheap." "Tastes all right to me, sir," says Kate. "That's because it's free, Kate. Cheers, all. Now, can't stay long. I don't get out of this place from one month to the next, then I'm double booked on the one night." "You will have parties at the drop of a hat." Rosie smiled at me. "My sister's in town, and if she doesn't meet Jacob, my life won't be worth living." "She younger than you, your sister?" Lynne pipes up. "She is, yes. Why d'you ask, Lynne?" "Best be careful. He likes them young."

'Course, Lynne wouldn't have said that, if she hadn't been drinking. But Mr Collins, he's that angry. Still Kate gets in before him. "Lynne!" "Thank you, Milligan." Mr Collins has this look in his eye and we all know that Lynne will be sorry for what she said. "Just saying." "We'd better be off, Jacob." Rosie took his arm as if they were already married. "We've obviously caused quite a stir." So Mr Collins warns us, he says, "No more to drink now." But he was looking at Lynne. "Oh and, Lynne?" says Rosie. She'd stopped at the door. "Bit of sauce on your mouth." "Where?" Lynne wiped her lips. "Permanently." "What's that mean, then?" "It means Rosie Skinner's one up on you, Lynne," Kate said. "And you keep it shut, she's nice."

'Then Mrs Bannerman joins us. Now that's a royal visit. Gracing us with her presence. She's not seen these days. She's expecting. Locked herself away like she's carrying the crown jewels. But that one night, she had to pick that night. Her husband, Marcus Bannerman, it's as much as he can do to nod his head to her, then she sails around the room, saying one or two words to everyone, not that they want to hear them.

"'It's a boy.' That's Brenda Potter studying Mrs Bannerman's bump. "You can tell by the way it's sitting. Or is it the other way round? High on the hips — is that a boy or a girl?" "Me mam was a midwife," Kate says. "She saw Mrs Bannerman in town the other day. Said it didn't look right at all." "Well, Kate, right or not, God help any kid born into that family," says Lynne. "Why do you say that, Lynne?" Lark asked. "You'd want for nothing." "They keep disappearing, the Bannermans. You turn around and half of them's gone." She put on a bright false smile as Mrs Bannerman reached us. "Evening," she said. And Mrs Bannerman, she says, "Good evening." "Lovely party, Mrs Bannerman." That's Kate again, more manners than the rest of them put together, and that's including the nobs. "Very kind of you." "Nothing to do with me, I'm not his mother. So, are you enjoying yourselves?" "Yes, ma'am," we bleat like sheep. "Good."

'Then I open my big fat mouth and say, "Nice to see you looking so well, ma'am." "Thank you. I'm not staying." Then she stared at me and said, "I've seen you. Change of uniform. Is that a new job?" "Yes, ma'am. Deputy hall porter." "We're that proud of him, ma'am," Kate told her. "Good. Congratulations. A welcome change I suppose, it must be rather boring, stuck behind that bar all night." "Well, not really, but yes, ma'am."

'And then it came. "Do you know, it's ridiculous, but I've completely forgotten. What was your name again?" That's what she said, "What was your name again?" All the times I've served her, and she says, "What was your name again?" I've bowed and scraped, and fetched her all sorts, and I'm nothing to her. I'm a uniform. That's what did it. She's the one that did it.

'All around me, it's carrying on, everyone's chatting, and there's all this music and no one saw me. Who'd notice me? They're all having a fine old time. There's Marcus with his wife – at least she's there for him, even if they don't want one another – and Stephen kissing Christina on the cheek, and Kate goes over and right in front of Christina, she kisses him too and Christina doesn't even mind. And it's like they've got people. Special people. And I've got no one. And I can hear Villiers in my head, over and over again, saying, "Room twenty-nine, room twenty-nine, room twenty-nine" . . . And it's driving me crazy.

'So, I left. Walked down the corridor. Took the staff lift. But I didn't go down to the basement. I stopped on the second floor. The guest floor. The corridor was empty. Well, it would be, wouldn't it? That time of night. But even then, I didn't go there. I lit a cigarette, smoked it. Shouldn't have. Mr Collins and Mrs Harvey, they would have had a fit if they'd seen staff smoking in a guest corridor, but I didn't care. Didn't give a damn. I didn't even finish it.'

Unable to face his father, he sank his face into his hands. 'I couldn't. I threw it down right there on the carpet and trod on it. Then I went to room twenty-nine. And I knocked the door. Do you understand? I went to him. I was the one who knocked. And I went inside.'

Chapter Eighteen

'They've got jobs at the gas works,' his father said abruptly. 'Ted Sharples, he knows the foreman. He can get you in. Good job. Pay's not bad.'

'I'm not finished.'

'Proper job. They're a good lot, they go down the Rose and Crown, nice lads. It's the place you're in, the Grand, the high and mighty Grand Hotel. Too much time and too much money. The folk staying there, they're just playing. You're getting out. It's that place, it's changed you.'

'It's not the Grand.'

'What is it, then? Because it's not you.' Clive reeled as his father cuffed his ear. 'Filling your head with ideas. I'm not having it . . .' He cuffed him again. 'Coming here and telling me this. Do you think I want to hear this? What have I done, eh? Must have done something wrong, you turning up here with your filth and your dirt . . .'

'Get off me . . .' For the first time in his life, Clive pushed his father away. He glared at the old man, furious that he had dared to hit him as if he were still a child.

'You can go, Clive. You can get out. You've told me. Happy now?'

'Do you think I'm happy?'

'That's what it's all about. The world these days, kids making themselves happy, sod the rules, sod the law. Jeff Tate, he told me, he was down by the tracks last week. Saw these boys, ten years old, throwing stones at the trains. Could have killed someone. You tell me, where's the fun in that?'

'The things that happened that night, not one of them made me happy, dad.' Clive sat back on the chair and stared into space. 'I went downstairs afterwards. Wanted to wash. Felt . . . I dunno . . . filthy . . . dirty . . . Then the girls came trooping in. The maids from the party, and Lynne was talking, saying, "Lloyd-Price? What sort of a name is that? If she's Welsh, she doesn't look Welsh." And Lark asked her, "What does Welsh look like?" "Short and hairy, Lark." "She's got a slight moustache if you look close."

'"Is the party finished then, Brenda?" I asked. I just wanted them to go, wanted a bit of piece and quiet. And I can't get that. Not sharing a room with Bob Jessop. "They've all swanned off, the Bannermans. Gone to the Manhattan. Cocktails and dancing and fah fah fah. Don't have the likes of us there."

'Lynne was dancing round the room. Well gone. Must have drunk the best part of a bottle of wine upstairs. Kate, she'd had a drink or two like the others. They didn't notice, but she did. "You all right, Clive?" she asks me. "Shouldn't stop." That's what I said, although I'd wanted to be by meself two minutes before. "I'm not sitting on me own, not tonight. It's our night, special night, party shouldn't stop because the Bannermans have gone."

'Brenda's boiling the kettle and she shouts, "How many for tea?" "I'll have one." Anything going, Lynne's there. And then I said, "Mr Collins is out. I'm the hall porter, I'm in charge, so we're carrying on, right here." But Kate said, "Clive, we had a laugh, it's finished." Should have listened to Kate. But I wasn't thinking straight. Hadn't been all night, I suppose. "Who's for a party? Right now?" I asked 'em. "Fine by me." Lynne, that was. She cheered, and Lark came up to me asking if she could stay, and I told her she could, that we'd have a party, all of us. Then I went to the bar. The only one who tried to stop me was Kate. Always Kate.

'I took bottles, as many as I could cram into crates, and not just beer. Wine, brandy, whisky, whatever came to hand, and all the time Kate kept following me. "What are you doing? They'll be livid! Clive, just slow down. What is it? What's wrong? What happened?"

'Course, I wouldn't listen, just kept pushing those bottles into boxes. And you should have seen them when I went back. They were like locusts. Not all of them, but most, and Lynne was in the front, grabbing the biggest bottle. Champagne, and the best. "Oh, champagne, look at me, I'm doing a Monica." "Blimey, the best beer!" That was Bob Jessop. "Clive, you're a champion." And what did I say? "Drink up, there's plenty more."

'Brenda knew there was going to be trouble. She went to Kate and offered to take Lark to bed. Not that the kid wanted to go. "But Mr Evans said—" "Never mind Mr Evans." Brenda dragged her off. Some of the others were just watching, so I picked up the bottles and went around the room giving them out. "Have it. Go on, have it. Compliments of the house. Here you go . . ."

'And Kate got angrier and angrier. "Clive, for God's sake, stop it! They'll get in trouble, *you'll* get in trouble . . ." "So? What does it matter?" "They'll have your job." "Does it matter, Kate? Does it matter to you?" "Of course, it does. Now come on, tidy this stuff away. They'll never know . . ." "But why does it matter? Is it me?" I had to know. Had to know how much she cared. "You care. About me, don't you?" I asked her. "Yeah . . ." "*Why*?" I couldn't understand it. Why would anyone care about me? "You're me friend." "But we walked out together, didn't we? Just a couple of times, but we did. You liked me then, didn't you?" "That was ages back. Clive, what is it? One minute you're standing there, at the party, then you're gone, and look at you now . . ." "You and me, we could try again, we could, though. Just say yes, go on, say yes, for me, Kate, say you will."

'Before she could answer, Mr Collins came in with Rosie. "What the bloody hell is going on here?" he shouted, and everyone shut up. Could have heard a pin drop. "I want an explanation. Did Mr Bannerman give his permission? What is this?" So, I owned up. "I did it, sir." "And what's that?" He looked at all the booze. "Who's supposed to be paying for that?" "You can join us, sir, and Miss Skinner. You're both welcome. Celebration."

'But he took no notice. "You lot, clear this away. Mr Evans, I'd like a word in private."

'I wouldn't go with him. "We're allowed that, sir. Celebration. It's good news, sir. Sorry for the trouble, but it's really good news. Because it's me and Kate, sir. I'm asking her hand in marriage, if she'll have me. We're together, sir. Me and Kate." "Since when?" Bloody Lynne again. And Kate standing there with that look on her face. As if I'd tried to make a fool of her in front of everyone. Kate, the last person I wanted to hurt was her . . . but I did. Then she ran out of the room. I tried to go after her, but Mr Collins stopped me. "Clive! Just stay where you are!"

'And Rosie stepped in, tried to make things better, but all she did was make everything worse. "Now, Jacob, it's a few drinks that have got out of hand. We'll clear up . . ." And old Collins got on his high horse. "I think it best you leave, I'll see you tomorrow." Then Rosie says, "And I won't have tempers. It's not the end of the world. We'll look back at this and laugh." "Miss Skinner," Collins says, "this is hotel business. Could you please go."

'And she was fit to cry, just like Kate, and all because of me. I couldn't stand it. I just ran. I had to find Kate . . . and there she was, crying her eyes out in her bedroom. It was so bad even Brenda and Lark had gone. Left her to it, I suppose, when they realised there was nothing they could do. And then she turned on me.

'"Is that what I am? One big joke? I have to spend all night watching Stephen Bannerman, and it's fine, it's really fine, but it's *not*. And then you. How could you do that? I was *shamed*. Do you think it's funny? Is that what you do, you and the lads, talk about me and laugh? Like she can't have him upstairs, she'll have anyone. Because she's second-hand?"

'I tried to tell her but she didn't understand. "I meant it, Kate. We'd be good." "We had a drink, twice, we went out for a drink." "But you know. You're always spending time with me, and talking and laughing because you *know*." "Know what?" "That I'm . . . safe." "What do you mean?" "You could make do. With me, and still love him. I don't care. You can't love me, no one could. But I'd love you. You're not second best, you're the best thing I could ever have." "Clive what the heck is going on?"

'And then Mr Collins walks in. "Excuse me, Kate,

Clive a word?" "Can't you leave him, sir," Kate pleaded. "Give us a minute?" "No. Right now. Clive!"

'I hadn't listened to anyone all night, so why should I listen to Mr Collins then? I just carried on talking. Trying to make them understand.

'"There's one bloke," I said. "I almost told him. In the army. Two years we served together, every single day. And I loved him. Don't you see, Kate?" I looked at her, willing her to realise what I was really saying, but she just looked blankly back. "I loved him." "Course you did, you were mates." "I never said, but he loved me."

'She sat next to me on the bed. Held my hand. "What is it? Has something happened to him?" "He married. Got a wife and kids. Lives somewhere in London. He got it right. He found a girl, why can't I?" "Don't be daft, you will." "But I loved him."

'I told her again and she still couldn't see it. "What's wrong with that?" she said. "That's the army. You went through a war together. Thank God he was there."

'Then I saw Mr Collins. And I knew he understood what I was getting at. Understood only too well. He tried to back out. "We can sort this out in the morning, it's been a long night." Only Kate wanted to finish it there and then. "Oh but sir, let him . . ." "Get to bed, Kate. Clive, back to your room."

'And by then, I was so damned tired. I got up to go. But Kate wouldn't leave it. "I'm sorry, sir, but I don't understand. Clive, you've not said. What's wrong with you?"

'And I couldn't look her in the eye, and Mr Collins, he just wanted to sweep it under the carpet like it never happened. "Best left, Kate," he told her. "Now stop your questions. Good night."

'We never did talk, me and Collins. He couldn't look at me the same. Not after that.'

'Come on then, if I've got to hear it all, who's the lad? The soldier?'

'Doesn't matter, Dad.'

'Who is he?'

'Doesn't matter . . .'

'Thomas, that's the bloke you keep talking about. Thomas something. Was that him? Jesus, what's happening out there? The world's full of them.'

'I paid for the booze out me wages, and went back to the job. And Mr Villiers, he was still going to and fro – but it was easy, not looking. It's funny: you pretend it didn't happen. And it's like it didn't. Easy. Just hand over his key when he asks, don't look. Just serve. Easy. And Kate. Most girls wouldn't look at a fellow again after what I did. But not her. She's the best. She really is. Carried on as if nothing had happened. Still me best mate. Then it came. Mr Villiers' last night in town. He's been doing some play, it's a big success, and they're all in the bar, him and his mates, and Miss Harkness. She's old, but you wouldn't think it the way she dresses. She's still a looker. And he likes her. He really does.

'"Here she is, guest of honour! Esme, you look stunning." "I think so, Mr Villiers." Then she looks in the bar. "What's this, a meeting of the forty-seven thousand? Surely you've worked your way through the list by now?" "Just a couple to go."

'And she stops on her way to the bar. "Good evening, Mr Evans." "I'll say this much for her, at least she knows our names. Not like Mrs Bannerman. Shame you can't join us." "No, miss." I can't stop looking at what's happening in the bar, but I keep thinking it's fine. And it was – then. I knew he'd be gone the next morning. If he came back to Manchester, I could send him to the Midland. I'm in charge. I can make sure I don't see him again. But there's this *boy*. And he's so handsome. You've never seen the like. And Villiers can't stop touching him. That's no surprise. I'm nowt special, not like that boy. And the next thing you know it's all breaking up. Half of them go off to some club, but not Villiers. He stays with this boy, and Miss Harkness, right up until the bar closes. Then Miss Harkness comes to me. And I'm on duty; I can't say a wrong word.

'"Mr Evans?" It's always the women in the end, always the bloody women. "I wonder, I'm invited out to Cheshire tomorrow for lunch. Rather dull people, but the chef's a genius. Could you arrange a car?" "Of course I can, miss." "Thank you, shall we say twelve o'clock?" "Right you are, miss."

'But she couldn't leave it at that, could she? "Staying on duty?" "Yes, miss, until midnight." "I see." Then she leans forward and whispers. "Word to the wise. I wouldn't go to room twenty-nine tonight. Three's a crowd."

'He's only gone and told her, hasn't he? Bloody told her! And I'm standing there watching while he takes this lad into the lift. And Miss Harkness gives me a wink. "Good night," she says.

'Villiers looks right at me as the grille shuts on the lift and he goes up with the lad. She knew. Esme Harkness knew. Once in me life. One mistake. And he tells. And I'm like, I'm sort of working. And he's up there, with the boy, and I keep going, doing me job, clearing up – and all the time I'm thinking, Who else has he told, the bastard? Who's he told? I'm working in this place, it's me life, the Grand Hotel, and he's told them.

'That's when it all happens. Something breaks. All I can think of is Villiers in room twenty-nine with that boy. The same room as me, and him, and him telling everyone about us. Ruining me life. So I go up there. In the lift, the guest lift. Walk along the guest corridor and knock on his door. And I knock and knock and knock, but he doesn't bloody answer, so then I start kicking. And I kick until I break the door down.

'And the lad's lying in bed, terrified. And there's Villiers putting his dressing gown on as if nothing's wrong, as if nothing ever happened between us. And Mr Bannerman comes. Mr Marcus Bannerman. And I tell him, "We should call the police, sir."

'And he stands there in his evening suit, the one he wears to the Manhattan. "Police? What the hell do you mean? Police?" "We should call the police, sir. It's against the law, sir. They broke the law."

'And Marcus Bannerman can see the boy. He's grabbed his clothes, pulled on his trousers and he's sneaking out the door. But he can see that he was in bed with Villiers. But Marcus Bannerman grabs me. Me!

'"Mr Villiers is a guest! In my hotel! Get out of my sight, you stupid, bloody peasant." He pushes me away, then goes to Villiers. "I'm so sorry. I can't apologise enough. There won't be any police, of course there won't, and there's no charge for the room . . ." "What about him?" And Villiers points at me. "He's sacked." "Look, there's no need for that . . ." Him. Bloody Villiers standing up for me.

'And then there's Mr Collins. "Clive, what were you doing?" And I told him. "They broke the law, sir." "Come on, lad. All right, you've told me. About your friend in the army. And never mind that, I don't want to know, but if you're the same as . . ." ' – and he looked at Villiers – "then how can you?" "That's my business, sir," I told him. "It's mine!" he says. "I gave you the job, have you forgotten that? And I'll get the blame, just you wait. But don't think of me, oh no, not once."

'And he looked so sad . . . so disappointed. That was the worst. "Clive, I trusted you. I expected so much better."

'And then I said it. The worse thing I could. "I'm sorry, sir. I am sorry, but I'm not your son." I wish I hadn't said that. And even then, he stands up for me with Mr Bannerman. "I accept it was a mistake, sir, but the mistake was mine. He's a good lad."

'"Oh," says Mr Bannerman, "and what's your definition of a good lad? Tell you what, Jack the Ripper, he could still be alive, bring him in as doorman. Sack the chef, employ the Kaiser. That boy is out!" "Please, sir, I've not asked you a favour, not once in my life . . ."

'And Kate comes. She's heard the rumpus. Who hasn't in the hotel? And she just sits next to me outside the office and takes my hand. I look at her and she says, "I heard." "Everyone's talking about me?" "They're worried, Clive."

'All that shouting, but there she is, and it's so simple – she just says, "I just wish you'd say. You and your tempers and everything. What's changed?" And I repeat, "What's changed?" like a parrot. A bloody parrot. And I tell her, "Nothing. Nothing's changed. Look at me, have I changed? I'm still the same."

'And I go into the bar to prove it. And she comes running after me. And Mr Bannerman, he follows and shouts, "I'm not finished with you." And it's there, it's all still there like when I was working the bar. Mr Collins says, "Clive, for heaven's sake." But I have to make them understand: the only thing that changed was me, and that wasn't right. Lads, like me, we find our place and we stick to it. I tried different, tried it all. But that's where I should be. Standing behind the bar. I'm a barman, the best. I'm good at one thing and that's it. And I tell them. I show them, I don't even have to look.

'"Top shelf, first left, White Horse Old Blend, first right, Turnbull's Favourite Club Whisky, second left, Old Boys Scotch, second right, Martell Cognac, third left, Lemon Hart Rum, third right, Seager's Dry London Gin, fourth left, Geneva Black Prime, fourth right, Green Ginger Wine . . ." And I carry on telling them everything that's there. I don't have to look at a thing. Not one single bottle. Even under the bar, I tell them what's there and where it is, Guinness and bitter and mild, two crates of soda, one crate of lemonade, one bottle of disinfectant . . . And then I beg: "Please, Mr Bannerman, I'll stay here. Please. Let me stay."

'Mr Bannerman and Mr Collins, they just look at me and go. But not Kate. She stays and asks, "Top shelf, second right?" And I tell her cognac. And we both laugh and I know it's going to be all right – with her at least.

'And it is. So it's back to the old job. Like it never happened. Leaving Mr Collins without his deputy, and he's back to working all hours. It's a madhouse, that place, takes up all your time. No wonder he wanted help. Rosie Skinner kept calling, but he didn't have the time, so that all came to an end. No rows, no shouting, just drifted away. Now she brings in the sewing twice a week, and all they say is, "Mr Collins." "Miss Skinner."

'Villiers went. He won't be back. I saw him the morning – the morning after it happened. There I was, back behind the bar. And there he was talking to Miss Harkness in the foyer. He gave her a note. She walked in and handed it to me, said, "From Mr Villiers," as if I didn't know. "I am sorry if it was anything I said. It seems to be my speciality, causing damage where none's intended."

'I never opened it. Chucked it in the bin. Didn't want to read anything he'd written. Not to me.

'So, that's how I can tell you, Dad. Because he's gone. Because it won't happen again. I won't meet anyone like him ever again in me whole life. And there might be others, those lads in the Snake Pit, and those toffs with their clubs in London, but they're not me. There's no one like me. There's no forty-seven thousand. I'm the only one.'

'But there's the two of us, isn't there? Two of us have got to live with this, because you've told me. You can go back to your fancy hotel, and I've got to sit here. That's all I do, sit here, all day long, and I'll always know. That me son's a . . . no son at all.'

'Sorry.'

'Why did you tell me. Clive? I didn't have to know. What would your mother have said?'

'Don't.'

'But how . . .? How did you end up like this? You were a kid, you were fine, you were running about, you were . . . Remember that time you got lost down Maccateer Street. I was up searching till midnight. We did it proper. Brought you up. Proud of you. Where's it *from*?'

'I don't know. It's just here.' Clive stabbed his finger into his chest. 'I dunno. If I knew, I'd cut it out. It's me, and it's not. It's . . . I don't want it. It doesn't stop. It's like it's twisting, and I hate it, Dad. It's so strong.'

'There must be doctors . . .'

Katherine Hardy

'I'm not telling anyone else.'

'Then why did you say it to me? All the beer in the city can't blot this out. Mind you, I could try. There was this bloke once, Alan Wells, worked at the brewery. Fell into the vat, drowned in beer. Come the funeral, his coffin starts fizzing. He'd fermented or something. Just a story. Probably not true, anyway.'

'I had to tell you. Because it's what's inside me – it's dirty and it's wrong, but it's not going away. And imagine there's this world. Not a perfect world, just different. Where you could know all this, don't have to like it, can hate it, same as me. But you could know. And still love me. Could you do that, Dad? Because that's what I've come for. Could you?'

'Yes.'

His father spoke so softly, Clive wondered if he'd imagined the answer he wanted so much to hear. Then a knock at the door shattered the moment. He opened it to see Mrs Harvey carrying a covered basket.

'Not interrupting?'

'No, what's the time? Is it gone six?'

'Don't worry about that, the Grand can cope without you for one afternoon. I can come back.'

'No, sorry, come in.'

'Just thought I'd lend a hand. You said the new tenants move in next week. Best to leave the place spick and span. Speaks well of the family.' She uncovered her basket to reveal coils of wire wool, bottles of bleach and disinfectant.

'There's no need, Mrs Harvey.'

'No, but I want to. Nice to see the church so full.'

'Yeah.'

'I knew your father, way back. We used to live on this side of town.'

'He said.'

The Grand II: The Roaring Twenties

'Really? What did he say?'

'Nothing, just that.'

'You should have told us, Clive. All those . . . troubles . . . If you'd said your father was ill . . .'

'Yeah, never been a great one for talking, me.'

'Now, I can manage. Don't you worry. Those walls could do with a scrub. Too many cigarettes. Kettle on, I think.'

'Can't, the cooker's broken. I told him I'd fix it, but I never found the time.' He took a deep breath, swallowing the emotion building in his throat. 'Sorry.'

'Do you know, I sit there watching you lot, and half those lads don't go home one year to the next. Not you though, Clive. Once, twice a week, off you'd trot. Just as it should be.'

'Used to sit here, talking about football and that. Him and his stories. Just been thinking this afternoon. All sorts of things I never said.'

'Well, that's always the way.'

'Can't tell him now.'

'Some things are best not said. There's too much talking in the world, and too much thinking. In my day you kept it private, and it was a lot simpler, believe me. Anyway, work to be done. Those boxes staying or going?'

'Going.'

'You stack them, I'll start in here. We'll be done in no time. Back home for supper.'

Chapter Nineteen

Ruth rolled on her stockings. After checking that the seams were straight, she clipped the welts into her suspenders, then reached for the padded corset that was now as tightly packed as the satin gussets would allow. Full term! She felt as though she had been waiting for the birth of this child for ever. As she buckled the final strap, someone knocked on the door. She glanced up, checking that she'd turned the key in the lock, although she already knew full well that she had. Reassured, she ignored the next knock, hoping whoever it was would go away.

'Ruth! For God's sake, if you can hear me open the door or I'll break it down.'

'Coming, Marcus.' She slipped on her robe, taking care to cover every inch of the padding. Unlocking the door, she stepped back as he walked into the room.

'Are you crazy? If you go into labour with the door locked . . .'

'I was getting changed,' she explained briefly, picking up her hairbrush from the dressing table.

'You are not to lock the door. Understand?'

'Fine. I'll undress in the foyer.'

'I don't want to argue with you. Not now. I want the baby to be born safe and well, that's all.'

'So do I.'

'How are you feeling?' He moved towards her, intending to caress her, but she retreated, slamming her back into the wall.

'Stop touching me, Marcus. You're always touching me.'

'I'm sorry. I just wish something would start happening.'

'It's only a week late. That's not unusual with first babies.'

'But what if there's a problem? I think you should see a doctor . . .'

'What for? There's no need. I've got Mrs Newman.'

'She's only a midwife. Where's the harm in getting a qualified medical opinion?'

'I don't want a doctor. I've already seen a Harley Street specialist. It's out of the question.'

'All right, I have to go to the club. If things start happening, ring me.' He finally went to the door. Ruth slammed it shut behind him. She waited until the lift door closed, then, softly, quietly, she turned the key.

'Right!' Kate climbed on to the bench, laid a pack of cards on the table where the staff ate their meals and looked around at the other maids. 'Snap it is. You sure you're not playing, Brenda?'

'After all the bleaching Mrs Harvey's had me doing today, me hands need waxing.' She carried on rubbing the white stick over her fingers. 'I'll have a game later.'

Kate dealt out the cards. After half a dozen uneventful rounds, Lynne began yawning.

'This is a great game, I'll be asleep in a minute. You done something to these cards, Kate?'

'Snap!' Both girls cried simultaneously.

'It was me,' claimed Kate.

'No, I was first,' Lynne contended.

'What do you reckon, Clive?' Kate asked, when she saw him standing behind her.

'You, Kate. You were too busy yacking, Lynne, as usual.'

As Kate took the cards and shuffled them to the bottom of her pile, Mrs Harvey emerged from her office.

'Right, you lot, it's back to work, I'm afraid.'

'But we've finished for tonight,' Lark protested.

'That trade union delegation. They've arrived. Ten of them. I've got jobs for all of you. So come along, move yourselves.'

'Me as well, Mrs Harvey?'

'Yes, Lark, you and all. If it was up to me, I wouldn't have them in the place. They're probably all communists.'

'But I'm off in ten minutes,' Lark persisted. 'I'm going home. It's our Michael's birthday.'

'And I'm supposed to be getting Mr Harvey's supper. I'm sorry. But there's nobody else.' She handed Kate a list. 'There's fires to light, baths to run, beds to air, and when you've done that, back here. They might want dinner in their rooms.' Mrs Harvey returned to her office.

Seeing tears in Lark's eyes, Kate followed her as she ran down to their bedroom. She found her sitting on her bed, clutching a painted lead soldier.

'Is that for your Michael?' Kate asked gently, sitting next to her.

'I saved up for it. My mum was going to wait until I got there, so I could help him to blow the candles out.'

'It's a lovely present.'

'What's he going to think when I don't turn up? He's only seven.'

'Kate, get a move on,' Lynne shouted down the

corridor.

'I'll start on room forty-six.' Kate left the bed and went to the door. 'You come up when you're ready.'

Marcus surveyed the Manhattan as he walked in. The place was crowded, all three barmen busy. By the look of things the club was making more money than even he'd hoped it would.

'Large Scotch, Jim,' he ordered as he went to the bar. He made a face as he sipped it. 'This isn't our usual brand, is it?'

'No, I was offered a good deal.' Stephen frowned at a group of women who'd commandeered the table closest to the band. They were expensively but provocatively dressed, clearly advertising their profession to potential customers.

'Cancel it, it's rubbish,' Marcus commanded.

Stephen jumped from his stool as one of the women crashed drunkenly into the table, sending bottles and glasses flying.

'That's it. I've had enough. Jim, get those whores to leave.'

'Just a minute, Jim.' Marcus held out his hand. 'Let me see their tab. Three guineas, and it's still early. Do they pay?'

'Yes, sir.'

'What kind of manager are you, Stephen? Throwing money away.'

'It used to be one or two. And they were discreet. Now they come in droves and they've got no idea how to behave.' The end of his sentence was drowned out by a burst of raucous laughter and more crashing glass.

'If they don't come here, they'll go somewhere else. I'd regard that as a missed opportunity.'

'Marcus, we're supposed to be running a nightclub, not a brothel.'

'Why do you think people come here? They want excitement, danger – and sex. We should give them what they want.'

'And to hell with our reputation?'

'What we need to do is take control, say who can work here and who can't. We'll make a lot of money – good whisky, good whores, what's the difference?'

Esme returned the menu to the waiter. 'I'll have the consommé, and the salmon. Thank you.'

'Excuse me, Miss Harkness.' Collins nodded to the waiter, who left the bar for the dining room. 'I'm sorry to interrupt, but there's a gentleman to see you.'

'Really? I wasn't expecting one of my regular dining companions.'

'I don't think I've seen him before. Very distinguished.'

'How intriguing. What's his name?'

'Mr Edward Lawrence.'

The smile froze on Esme Harkness's lips as the blood drained from her face.

'Miss Harkness . . .'

'I can't see him. Please, tell him to go away, Jacob. I can't see him.'

'Very good, Miss Harkness.' Collins glanced anxiously at her as he returned to the foyer. 'I'm sorry, Mr Lawrence, but Miss Harkness is unable to see you.'

'I see. Does she have company for dinner?' He looked away, embarrassed when the concierge ignored his question. 'She did remember my name?'

'Yes, sir.'

'Very well, I understand.'

Esme caught sight of him leaving in the mirror

above the bar. She leaned back, terrified that he would see her.

'Miss Harkness?' The waiter stood helplessly before her as she stared blindly at him. 'Miss Harkness?'

'Yes.' Seeing the front door close, she turned to the boy.

'Your table is ready. If you'd like to come through to the dining room.'

'I've changed my mind. I won't be having dinner.'

'Very good, Miss Harkness.'

Rising from her seat Esme went to the bar. 'Clive, a bottle of champagne, please. Non-vintage, the stuff you use for weddings and funerals.'

'I wish I could take a photograph of you, right this moment.' Stephen pulled Christina closer as they danced to a slow, romantic number, in the Manhattan.

Christina pulled a face. 'Too late, the moment's gone.'

'You should do that on our wedding day. For the proud parents.'

'I might, but nothing I do shocks them any more.' She lifted her eyebrows. 'Even marrying you, the racy nightclub manager.'

'I see, you're backing out now?'

'No chance of that. You're the man I want. In fact, I think we should marry as soon as we can.'

'Really?'

'Why wait? What's the point?'

'All right.' He returned her kiss. 'Why not?' he re-iterated headily when she finally released him.

'Here you are, Mr Bannerman.' Jim set a glass of whisky on the table in front of Marcus. 'It's the good stuff.'

Seeing his preoccupation, he ventured, 'Is there a problem, sir? If it's about the whisky, I can explain . . .'

'Bad whisky can be replaced. It's simple. My wife's logic, on the other hand, is beyond comprehension.'

'I'm sure you'll work it out, sir.'

'So am I,' Marcus said shortly.

Clive kept half an eye on Esme Harkness as he ran the bar. It was more crowded than usual between the regulars and the trade union delegates, but unusually for Esme, who was normally the life and soul of every party, she sank deeper and deeper into a silence that appeared to border on depression.

'Drink up, Billy, it's my round,' Maurice Lamb, instantly recognisable as a trade union delegate by his cheap suit, demanded of Billy Hooper, who was as badly dressed.

'Give us a chance,' Billy complained.

'How about you?' Maurice asked Clive. 'Would you like one?'

'No thank you, sir.'

'We'll have less of that.'

'What?' Clive asked.

'Sir! I'm a working man, same as you.'

'Force of habit. It goes with the job.'

'Not with me, it doesn't. Maurice Lamb.' He offered Clive his hand.

'Clive Evans.' Clive shook it. 'So, what are these talks about?'

'Longer hours, less money.'

'Again,' Billy chipped in, finally finishing his drink.

'They'll try all sorts of tricks. But our lads won't back down. Right, two more brown ales it is.'

'I'll have to fetch some more. There's not usually

much call for it.'

'It's not my normal drink, you understand. I fancied a change from the pink gin, you know how it is?' Maurice joked in a posh accent.

As Clive headed for the cellar, Miss Harkness called him back.

'Another.' She set the empty champagne bottle on the bar.

'Is everything all right, Miss Harkness?'

'Another bottle please, Clive.'

Kate and Lynne hauled coal buckets past the kitchen as Lark scuttled in with a tray of dirty plates. Clive noticed her tearful expression as he unlocked the cellar door.

'You all right, little one?'

'Mind your back, you lot!' Brenda shouted, staggering unsteadily across the kitchen beneath the weight of a huge cauldron.

Lark turned. The pan went flying, splashing hot water over her.

'You stupid—'

'My hand!'

'All right, Brenda, it wasn't her fault.' Kate dropped her coal bucket and ran to help.

'Whose fault was it, then?' Brenda demanded indignantly.

Clive saw tears starting in Lark's eye. He put the empty crate he was carrying on the table and grabbed her hand. 'Come here, quick.' Scooping a fingerful of butter from the dish on the table, he rubbed it gently into the reddened area on her hand. 'This will stop it hurting.'

'What's going on?'

'It was an accident, Mrs Harvey,' Kate explained as

the housekeeper left her office.

'It weren't my fault,' Brenda protested defensively.

'Get that water mopped up, Brenda, before someone breaks their neck. And you.' She looked at Lark. 'We'd better get you bandaged up. Clive, bring her in here.'

'You tell him.' Christina nudged Stephen as he carried a bottle of champagne and three glasses towards Marcus, who was standing, lost in thought at the bar of the Manhattan.

'No, you tell him.'

'He's your uncle. He might not approve.'

'I'm pouring the champagne. Go on, you know he likes you.'

Christina turned to Marcus. 'As senior member of Stephen's family, I know you take your responsibilities very seriously. So, we thought we ought to tell you that we've decided to name the day. Get married as soon as possible, and we'd like you to celebrate with us.'

'Isn't that wonderful?' Stephen handed Marcus a glass of champagne.

'That's great,' Marcus murmured absently. 'I hope you'll be very happy.' He tipped his glass to Christina. 'To your future.'

'The future.' Christina stared deep into Stephen's eyes.

'You'll have to excuse me.' Marcus set his glass on the bar. 'I have an urgent call to make. Thanks for the champagne.' Going into the office, he closed the door, opened his pocketbook and picked up the telephone.

'Sorry, love,' Billy Hooper apologised as he accidentally brushed against Esme, who was sitting at the bar with the remains of her second bottle of champagne.

'That's enough for me.' Maurice Lamb handed Clive his empty glass. 'I want a clear head in the morning.'

'So, you think we've got a chance?'

'Course we have, Billy. What they want to do, it's wrong, just remember that. We should be given a decent wage for the work we do, and we keep telling them that until they're sick of hearing it.'

'Excuse me, Miss Harkness,' Mr Collins said as he walked through from the foyer. 'Mr Lawrence sent this.' He handed her a slim, black, leather jewellery box. She opened it and stared down at a finely wrought gold necklace. Finally, the tears she'd held in check all evening began to fall.

'Would you please take me to my room, Mr Collins?'

'Of course. And Mr Lawrence asked if you would like to join him for coffee tomorrow, Miss Harkness. The lad's waiting for a reply.'

'Yes. Tell him yes.'

'Right, Lark Rothery.' Mrs Harvey tucked the blankets firmly around the girl, and smoothed the pillowcase. 'Get yourself a good night's sleep. You'll feel better in the morning.'

She picked up a maid's cap that had fallen to the floor, but when she looked up she saw that Lark had buried her head beneath the bedclothes. She knew the girl was close to tears, but there was nothing she could do. Homesickness was the one problem the maids had to come to terms with themselves.

Collins watched Esme anxiously as she refilled her glass with champagne.

'You've nothing to be ashamed of, Miss Harkness,' he insisted, disturbed by her mood.

'The girl he fell in love with. She would have been ashamed. I haven't seen Edward for nearly forty years. When I saw him, I could see her too. I wasn't for sale then. A young, innocent girl with dreams of a good life. A family, respectability.'

'You've always been proud of who you are. No one has the right to take that away from you.'

'I can still be innocent, Jacob. Ribbons in the hair, frilly white dress. It costs a little extra. Alleyways, against walls . . . that's how I started. Squirming, trembling. Give me the money . . . give me the money.'

'Esme, don't do this.'

'Respectability! You have no idea. I don't feel proud, Jacob. Edward knew who I was. Who I *was*. If he looks at me now . . . Maybe he knows. What if he knows and he's come for sex? He's come to see the whore.'

'If this is how Mr Lawrence makes you feel, he had no right coming here.'

She picked up the necklace. 'He bought me this when I was twenty-one. Maybe he wants me to wear it tomorrow.'

'You've had a lot to drink. Why don't you call it a night? Get some sleep.'

'People think we only sell our body. We sell it all.' Taking the bottle, Esme tipped it up over her glass. It was empty. 'I can sleep now.' She curled on to the bed, her eyes closing the moment her head hit the pillow.

Collins slid off her shoes and folded a blanket over her. Taking an extra rug from the top of the wardrobe, he wrapped it around his shoulders, and settled down in her chair for the night.

Marcus knocked on Ruth's bedroom door. When he

got no reply, he tried the handle. The door was open. He walked in to find her sitting in a chair, reading a book.

'What do you want?' she asked without looking up.

'Has Dr Lewis arrived yet?'

'What? I told you I didn't want to see a doctor. What the hell do you think you're doing? You had no right to do that.'

'I had every right. I need to know the baby is safe. And I'm worried about you. You're going to have a full examination. I'll go downstairs and wait for him.' He went to the door, and hesitated. Looking back at Ruth, he deliberately removed the key from the lock and slipped it into his pocket.

'Dr Lewis.' Marcus shook the man's hand as he walked into the foyer. 'It is good of you to come at such short notice.'

'Not at all.'

'I suggest we go straight up.'

Ruth shrank back into the shadows of the study as she heard the lift doors opening lower down the corridor.

'Ruth?' as Marcus's voice echoed towards her she pulled her hat over her head and buttoned her coat. 'Please, go into the living room, Dr Lewis. I'll be with you in a moment.' He walked down the corridor opening doors. As he returned to the living room, Ruth picked up her bag and hurried towards the service lift. She pushed between the trolleys and laundry baskets, entered the cage and pressed the button for the basement.

When the lift reached the staff quarters, Ruth opened the door just wide enough to slide out. She hid under the stairs. As soon as Mrs Harvey was safely ensconced in her office and the last of the maids headed upstairs with trays, she slipped quietly out through the back door.

'She was here a minute ago, Dr Lewis,' Marcus apologised. 'I'll ring reception. Someone must know where she is.'

It was the doctor who noticed the envelope on the mantelpiece. He handed it to Marcus before he had a chance to pick up the telephone.

Chapter Twenty

Stephen pulled back the curtains in the living room and turned to see Marcus sitting in an armchair, still dressed in the suit he had worn to the Manhattan.

'Marcus, what are you doing? Have you been here all night?'

Leaving the chair, Marcus handed Stephen Ruth's note. 'She says, and I quote, "I need rest and I need quiet. If our child is born safely, you will hear from me immediately. If not, I'll save you the trouble of getting rid of me."' His face contorted in rage. 'How dare she?'

'What does she mean? "Save you the trouble of getting rid of me"?'

'I have no idea. I thought it was one of her games. She's made her point. I thought she'd be back by now.'

'What are you going to do?'

'Find her.' Marcus walked determinedly to the door.

Ruth burst into the rooms she'd rented in London, confronting Edith, who was sitting reading a copy of *People's Friend*.

'I want my baby,' she screamed at Edith, terrifying her. 'Is something wrong? Is it dead? Well is it?' she repeated hysterically. 'Tell me?'

'No!' leaving the chair, Edith backed towards the bedroom.

'It should have happened by now. Why is it late? Why? It is dead, isn't it?'

'It isn't late. My baby isn't late.'

'What did you say? You told me it was due at the same time as mine.'

'I said it was about the same time.'

'You mean you don't know?' Ruth grabbed her shoulders and shook her violently. 'What do you mean, you don't know? You must know.'

'I don't know when it happened. Not exactly. He was home on shore leave for three weeks. We hadn't seen each other for months. I didn't know what bloody day of the week it was. You know what it's like.'

'How much longer?'

'It could be two weeks.'

'Two weeks! Have you any idea? I haven't got two *days*. I need it now. What the hell am I supposed to do?' Her anger dissipated as she sank down on to a chair. 'What am I going to do?'

Kate walked into her bedroom. She tugged at the blanket Lark had cocooned herself in and pulled the pillow from under her head. When she finally succeeded in freeing the blanket, she saw that her trainee was still clutching the soldier she'd bought for her brother.

'Put that toy down and get up. I told you before, Lark, you can't stay here all day.'

'I don't care.' Curling into a ball, Lark opened her eyes and stared up at Kate defiantly. 'I don't want to get up. I want to go home.'

'You can't. Mrs Harvey's asking for you. You can

see Michael on your next day off.'

'It's not just Michael. It's my mum and dad. Everybody. I never see them. And when I do, my mum's that busy. It's like I don't belong there any more.'

'Of course, you do,' Kate reassured patiently. 'But it's different now. I remember when I left home. I hated it. I was that miserable I ran away, so they sacked me. Imagine having to tell that to your mam and dad. It does get better, you get used to it.'

'I wish my mum was here now.' Scrabbling for the sheet that had fallen to the floor, she turned away from Kate and hid beneath it.

'All right,' Kate conceded, 'I'll tell Mrs Harvey you're poorly. But you know what she's like. You won't get away with it for long.'

'Good morning, Miss Harkness.' Collins opened the curtains in Esme's room. 'I wondered if you were feeling any better.'

'I would have felt a lot worse without you, Jacob,' she murmured as she opened her eyes to the morning light. 'It was good of you to stay.'

'You'd had a shock. Would you like any breakfast?'

'I wouldn't mind some coffee.'

'Very good, miss. Would like me to cancel the arrangement with Mr Lawrence?'

'No, Jacob.'

'Are you sure it's a good idea to see him, after the way he upset you?'

'I have to see him.' Her eyes were wild, fearful. 'I don't want to, but I have to. Can you understand that?'

'She wants her baby now, and it's impossible. Tell her, Dr Curzon,' Edith pleaded. 'She'll have to wait.'

'Shut up.' He looked at Ruth.

'She lied to me. She could have another two weeks to go. I can't wait that long.'

'You could always tell your husband.'

'Don't be ridiculous. We have a business arrangement.'

'Childbirth is an imprecise science. As I'm sure you know. We're dealing with the beasts of the field.'

'Would her baby survive if it was born now?'

'There's no reason why it shouldn't, Mrs Bannerman.'

'I want you to induce it.'

'It will cost you.'

Edith backed towards the door. 'Oh no . . . What are you going to do to me?'

'I don't care about the money,' Ruth said flatly.

'You're not doing it . . .'

Ruth shouted at Edith, 'I've paid for that baby and I need it now.'

Curzon barred Edith's way as she attempted to open the door. Turning the key in the lock, he faced her.

'I've paid for that child,' Ruth reiterated fiercely, 'And I need it now.'

'No. Not like that. You can't . . .'

'The child's not yours, Edith,' Curzon reminded. 'You took the money.'

'It needs to be as quickly as possible,' Ruth pressed. 'Can you arrange it?'

'I'll do it myself. I'm very good. When I was in practice, it would have cost you three guineas just to talk to me.'

Edith screamed and lashed out. 'It's not natural. You'll kill my baby. I won't let you do it. I thought you were a doctor. It's a baby's life.'

Curzon grabbed her wrists and squeezed them

together, forcing her to her knees.

'Can we please just get on with it?' Ruth demanded.

'This is the most recent one I have, Mr Lambert.' Marcus handed the private detective a photograph of Ruth.

'And you've no idea where she is?'

'If I knew that, I wouldn't have hired you. You come highly recommended. I expect results.'

'You'll get them. What about her family? Friends?'

'There's a grandmother. She wouldn't go there.'

'I'd still like her address.' He saw Marcus hesitate. 'We know what we're doing.'

'All right, but she won't be there.'

'And there's no one else?'

'No, not that I can think of.'

'I've started with less, Mr Bannerman. But she's a good-looking woman and she's pregnant. I have three lads working for me. They'll check the nursing homes and hospitals in the Manchester area. If she's not there, we'll check with the rail and bus companies. We'll find her, Mr Bannerman. We never fail.'

'Lark's still in bed, Clive,' Kate confided as he hauled a crate along the corridor.

'Fourteen years old and she's on strike.'

'Good job Mrs Harvey's busy.' Kate looked through the office window as they passed.

'Have you heard about Mrs Bannerman?' Brenda asked from the table where she was folding napkins with the other maids.

'She ran away, last night,' Lynne revealed, upstaging Brenda.

'In her condition? She's having a baby any minute.'

'Her and Marcus Bannerman were heard screaming

at each other last night,' Lynne continued, as Marcus walked down the stairs behind her.

'Well I won't miss her,' Clive said as he dropped his crate at the cellar door. 'She gives me the creeps.'

'Maybe he hit her,' Lynne suggested. 'He looks the type, I've always thought that.' Realising that everyone else had fallen silent, she looked around and saw that they were staring at something behind her. She turned to see Marcus. He glared at her, before going to the office.

'Does anyone want a kitten?' Lynne asked as soon as he was out of earshot. 'I've just had half a dozen.'

'Miss Harkness is expecting me,' Edward Lawrence announced to Collins as he entered the foyer.

'Yes, sir.' Collins beckoned to the receptionist. 'Would you let Miss Harkness know Mr Lawrence is here to see her. Perhaps you'd like to wait in the Reading Room, sir?'

'Thank you.'

'Jacob?' Marcus called from the office. 'If a Mr Lambert should get in touch, you are to contact me immediately. Do you understand?'

'Yes Mr Bannerman.'

'It's of the utmost importance.'

Collins looked back to see Esme walking down the stairs. 'Mr Lawrence is in the Reading Room, Miss Harkness.' He gave her an encouraging smile.

'Thank you, Jacob. How do I look?'

'You look lovely, Miss Harkness.'

'Thank you.'

'Miss Harkness,' Marcus called, stopping her. 'I've been meaning to have a word. I have a business proposition that might appeal to you.'

'Now?'

'It will only take a minute. Girls have started coming into my club. Whoring. It's inevitable, I accept that, but it's chaotic. It needs organising, putting on a sound business footing.'

'And you'd like me to do it?'

'Who better? It would be extremely profitable.'

'I'm sorry, Marcus. I couldn't possibly. Not at the moment. You'll have to find someone else.' She walked into the Reading Room and stood by the door.

'Esme.' Edward left his seat and came to meet her. 'You got the necklace?'

She opened her handbag and removed the box. 'I never thought I'd see it again after I lost it in Brighton.'

'I found it after you'd left. I meant to give it back. But it was all I had left of you.'

'It was a long time ago.'

'I remember every minute of every day. We must have been mad, going in the autumn. It did nothing but rain. Not that it matters. If you knew how often I've thought about that weekend. The last time I felt truly alive.'

'I find that hard to believe.' She found it impossible to return his smile.

'I can understand that. You must think I'm crazy coming to see you after all this time. But I had to come. I had to see you.'

'It was good of you to return the necklace. But I've managed to live all these years without it.'

'I wanted to come before. But it would have been too painful to see you. I was married. I had a family. My wife died six months ago.'

'I'm sorry.'

'It was a marriage like any other,' he dismissed casually. 'You never married?'

Katherine Hardy

'No.'

'Seeing you again, I didn't know what to expect. I didn't know how I'd feel. You were the first woman I truly loved. And I've never forgotten you, or the love we shared. And here, now, nothing has changed. I feel now what I felt then. I've come to make amends Esme.' He took her hand and held it between his own. 'I want to marry you. Please, Esme, be my wife.'

'Marry you?' Her eyes widened in disbelief.

'You would make me very happy.'

'Edward, it's been forty years.'

'Then say nothing. At least don't say no. Please, think about it. I'll come back this afternoon.'

Curzon checked the equipment he'd laid out on the table. 'Castor oil, quinine, I think that's everything.'

'You can keep your money,' Edith cried in desperation. 'I don't want it. I've changed my mind.'

'It's too late. You've taken half of it.'

'I'll give you another five guineas . . . ten,' Ruth offered.

'I can't refuse that. You know I can't!'

'It's time we got started.' Curzon opened the bottle of castor oil. Pushing Edith into a corner, he wrapped his arm around her neck, tilted her head back and began to pour.

'Yes, Lark?' Mrs Harvey looked up as the girl knocked on her office door. 'What do you want?'

'I . . .'

'Well, don't just stand there.'

'I want to go home.'

'Well, yes, we'd all like to go home, but we've got work to do.'

'I want to go home. To see my mum and dad, and

tell Michael why I missed his party.'

'Don't be silly. Who's going to do your work? Those girls out there? There's no one to cover for you. It can't be done. You've been a bit poorly that's all. You'll soon feel better.' The housekeeper picked up the roster from her desk. 'Look, you're off next Wednesday, you can go home then. Now go on. Back to work.' Mrs Harvey returned to her paperwork.

Lark left the office and went to the maids' station where the girls were polishing silver.

'Feel free to join us,' Lynne invited caustically.

'I want to ask you something.'

'You take the knife in one hand and the cloth in the other,' Lynne held up the cloth.

'Mrs Harvey says if you do my work, I can go home. I'd do it for you. If you asked me.'

'We've been working every hour God sends. Or haven't you noticed?'

'Course not, she's been in bed,' Brenda griped.

'Hang on, think about it,' Clive interrupted. 'You'll only have to do a bit extra.'

'Nobody's ever done anything like that for me.'

'Perhaps they would, Lynne, if you started helping each other,' Clive suggested.

'I don't mind,' said Kate. 'I've got nothing better to do.'

'Creep,' Brenda snapped.

'She wants to see her brother,' Kate insisted. 'Give him his birthday present. You know how upset she was.'

'It makes sense to me,' offered Clive.

'And me, Clive,' said Kate.

Lynne picked up another knife. 'I must want my bloody head examining.'

'Does that mean I can go?' Lark asked excitedly.

Clive nodded and winked at her.

Mr Collins tapped on Esme Harkness's door. 'How did it go?'

'You're not going to believe this, Jacob. Mr Lawrence has asked me to marry him.'

'What?'

'It was a shock for me, too.'

'I don't understand. I mean you said you knew him. You were in love with him, but it was such a long time ago.'

'Yes, it was, and I realise how absurd it must seem.'

'Yet he comes back after all this time?'

'I worked for his family as a housemaid. When we were lovers, we kept it a secret. For over a year. We wanted to get married. We were going to run away together, but his family found out. The night before we were going to leave, he came to see me to say he couldn't go through with it.'

'I'm sorry.'

'He says he loves me. He's always loved me. And I've never felt for any man what I felt for Edward.'

'I see.'

'You know what my life has been like, Jacob. I've had other proposals. From satisfied customers. They wanted me on a kind of permanent hire. But I don't think Edward knows what I am. He can't, surely. He wouldn't ask me if he knew.'

'Perhaps he doesn't know now . . .'

'Does he *have* to know?' she cut in eagerly. 'If I marry him, we can begin our own life. Away from here. Pick up from where we left off. That's what he wants. Why shouldn't it happen?'

'If you think he can make you happy, then find out. See if he can.'

The Grand II: The Roaring Twenties

'I don't know if I dare. Can I do it?'

Collins believed she was deluding herself, but he couldn't demolish the dream world she was building. It would hurt her, possibly even more than she could bear.

'This book is a disgrace,' Marcus raged at the receptionist. 'What does that say? It doesn't make sense.'

'I hadn't finished,' Tom mumbled apologetically. 'It's—'

'I'm not interested. Just sort it out.'

'Yes, sir.'

Marcus looked up to see Lambert, the private detective, walking through the door. 'Well?'

'Your wife's in London. She went on the overnight train. Took a taxicab to Hampstead.'

'The address?'

'She didn't give one. She got out at the Highgate end of the Heath. My lads are making further enquiries. I should have more information for you soon.'

'Good. As soon as you get it . . .'

'I'll be in touch.'

The laundry lists fell, neglected, on to the staff table as Mrs Harvey stopped to stare at Lark dressed in her best coat and hat.

'I was looking for you, Mrs Harvey. I wanted to tell you I'm going now.'

'Going where?'

'Home. I did what you said. I asked the others to cover for me.'

'And they agreed?'

'Yes. So can I go now?'

'Well, yes,' Mrs Harvey agreed, not knowing what else to say. 'I suppose you can.'

'Bye.' Lark walked out through the door.

Esme sat in the bar toying with her sherry. It was packed with the usual lunchtime customers, most of them businessmen, but they weren't just the hotel's customers: a substantial number were also hers. And Edward . . .

'Excuse me, Miss Harkness,' Mr Collins interrupted. 'There's a gentleman to see you.'

'Edward?'

'No, Miss Harkness. One of your . . . companions. He says he has an appointment.'

'I'd completely forgotten. Get rid of him, please. Whatever it takes.'

'Leave it to me, Miss Harkness.'

'Esme?'

It was Edward's voice. Esme left her seat. 'Edward, you're early.'

'I thought I was late,' he stammered, almost but not quite as nervous as she was. 'Shall we have tea?'

'Yes, why not?' She sank back into her seat.

'Tea for two, please,' Edward asked Collins. 'I must say,' he complimented as Collins returned to the foyer, 'it's a beautiful hotel.'

'Yes.'

'A perfect setting for you.' Encouraged by her smile, he continued. 'To be honest, I've been on tenterhooks all day.'

'Really?' Esme's blood ran cold as one of her 'companions', as Collins had euphemistically termed them, greeted her. She acknowledged his presence with a reserved nod of the head, hoping Edward hadn't seen him.

'I couldn't concentrate. I ended up digging the garden, and I employ a gardener.'

'You'll be cooking before you know it.' She looked into his eyes and knew there was no way she could begin living a lie, not now, at her time of life. 'I wanted to marry you, all those years ago, Edward. It was my dream, my ambition. But it wasn't to be. My life changed after that in a way I never expected. We have to make the best of things, don't we? And it changes us. We can't stay the same. I'm not the young girl you knew then.' She forced herself to meet his gaze. 'You had your inheritance, and I don't blame you for that. And I had to survive. I found a way of earning money that changed me . . . irrevocably.'

'I know what happened to you, Esme. I've known for a long time.'

Humiliated, feeling that he'd forced her to confess to something he already knew, she rushed out of the door.

It took a moment for Edward to regain his composure after the suddenness of Esme's departure, but when he reached the foyer he was just in time to see the lift door closing. He went swiftly to the stairs and ran up to the first floor.

'Forgive me, Esme,' he pleaded as he caught up with her outside her room. 'I thought you were going to turn me down. I would have told you before that I knew. But I didn't know how to begin. It doesn't matter. I don't care what you've been.'

She touched the necklace she was wearing. 'Is this the going rate for marriage?'

'It's the most precious thing I've ever known.'

'It would have been more honest to have offered me money.' Tearing it from her neck, she threw it to the floor.

'I wanted to ask for your hand. If you knew how many times I've rehearsed that moment . . .'

'And I no doubt, said yes? I've played the blushing bride many times, Edward. It costs a little extra.'

'Don't!'

'It's the laundry. White stains so easily, you see.'

'Stop it, please!'

'I could tell you far worse.'

'Stop it!'

'What do you think my life has been, Edward?' she asked, suddenly wanting to hurt him as much as he had hurt her. 'Do you imagine I've been able to preserve Brighton in aspic? Used it to cheer myself up when things at the office were a little dull? I can't forget what I am. I only wish I could.'

'I loved you then. I still love you.'

'How do you know you're not deceiving yourself? You've created a fantasy.'

'We had the kind of love that comes once in a lifetime. You must know that now, as well as I do.'

'I was a fool. You told me, in spite of everything, we'd be together, always. I believed you.'

'It was impossible.'

'I decided that if I was going to be used, I may as well be paid for it.'

'You can't blame me for that?'

'Who else can I blame?' she asked savagely. Her desire for revenge ebbed as quickly as it had risen. 'What difference does it make now?' she asked wearily. 'Go, Edward, please.' As she turned her back on him, he retrieved the necklace from the carpet.

'I never said, Esme. You're just as beautiful as you ever were.' She hesitated as she opened the door. 'I didn't have the courage. All those years ago. I was young, and you know what a bully my father could be. You have every reason to hate me, but I had to come and see you. And at last, we've been given the chance we were denied all those years ago. I charged in here, without considering how you might feel. I should have courted you. Earned the right to ask you. I couldn't wait; it was like the first time we made love. I wanted you so badly. You remember, don't you?'

'I remember,' she murmured reluctantly. 'At your father's house.'

'My life has been wasted,' he confessed wretchedly. 'If you never want to see me again, tell me now.' He handed her the necklace. 'But please keep this.'

Esme took the gold chain from him. As he walked away she pressed it against her cheek – remembering.

'Has it started?' Ruth asked Curzon impatiently as she paced restlessly from the living room of the apartment she had rented for Edith, into the bedroom.

'Not yet.' He sat back in his chair and pulled out his cigarettes. 'It takes time.'

'Can't you give her some more quinine?'

'There wouldn't be any point. Besides, we don't want to risk losing the baby.'

'Doesn't matter what happens to me though, does it?' Edith wailed from the bed. 'You two should be locked up. You're butchers, the pair of you.'

'I take care of my investments,' Curzon said coldly.

'But it could die, couldn't it?' Ruth asked apprehensively. 'What happens then?'

'Then it gets really expensive,' Curzon warned.

'So, you've had a good day?' Clive asked Maurice Lamb as he handed him a pint of brown ale.

'Ground them down. We'll get there.'

'You know, we work fourteen hours a day, more if they tell us. And we can do sod all about it.'

'Sorry, Clive. I've got my hands full at the moment.'

'I don't expect you to do anything. I think it's time we did something for ourselves.'

'You mean join a union?'

'Yes, why not?'

'You need to find out who else is interested. Some of them will be scared: they'll have heard all sorts of rubbish about unions. We're all bolshies. Waiting to start a revolution.'

'Sounds all right to me.'

'Take it one step at a time, Clive,' Maurice laughed.

'Haven't you finished yet?' Christina complained to Stephen as she wandered into the office of the Manhattan.

'Not quite.' He flicked through a roll of pound notes, counting them before placing them alongside six similar rolls on the desk.

'I want to dance, and then I want . . .' Perching on the side of the desk, she leaned over and whispered in his ear.

'You're impossible.' Forgetting about the takings, he pushed his chair back and looked at her.

'Of course I am.' Using the wings of his collar to pull him closer, she kissed him, slipping her tongue into his mouth. They separated as the door opened. Marcus darted in and grabbed a couple of rolls of cash.

'They've found Ruth in London. I'm going there now. Look after everything while I'm away.'

'How are you getting there?' Stephen asked.

'The milk train. It leaves at midnight. I can just make it.'

The lights in the Reading Room had been turned down for the night. The waiters had long since finished their shifts. Esme sat alone, waiting, until Edward walked through from the foyer carrying a bunch of flowers.

'You look lovely.'

'Thank you.'

'I came as soon as I got your message. I brought you these.' He handed her the roses. 'It's cold outside. I went for a walk earlier . . .'

'I've been doing a lot of thinking. What I've been, what lies ahead. I like it here. I live well and I can look anyone straight in the eye. You've made me feel more wretched than any man I've ever known. You've broken my heart, Edward, and you expect me to give all this up. Everything I've worked for.' As he turned away, she reached up and stroked his cheek. 'I thought I'd wear red. What do you think?'

'You mean . . .'

'Yes.' Standing on tiptoe, she finally kissed him.

Chapter Twenty-One

Collins hadn't finished dressing the next morning, when there was a sharp knock at the door. Before he could answer it, Esme Harkness walked in.

'Miss Harkness. What is it? You should have sent for me.' He reddened in embarrassment at the mess of clothes flung over his unmade bed, as he moved swiftly to the wardrobe and lifted out a jacket.

'I'm sorry to disturb you, but I wanted you to be the first to know. I've accepted Edward's proposal. He knows what I became, and it makes no difference to him.'

'I'm very happy for you.' He almost choked on the sentiment.

'It looks like I'll be leaving the Grand after all.'

'It won't be the same without you.' Until he actually said the words, he had no idea how much he meant them.

'Thank you.' She kissed his cheek. 'And don't worry,' she said, winking as she walked to the door, 'no one saw me coming down here.'

'Push, Edith,' Curzon urged as the woman finally entered the last stages of labour. 'Come on, that's it. Push harder . . . come on . . . Good! And again . . .'

Ruth stole closer to the bed, fascinated by the sight

of the baby coming into the world.

'A big push this time. Go on . . . .Good . . . And again. We're nearly there . . .' Tenderly, expertly, he delivered the child and cut the cord. Ruth watched as he washed the squalling, pink bundle of humanity in the bowl of warm water he'd prepared. As he wrapped it in a blanket, Edith held out her arms expectantly. But he turned to Ruth.

'Your baby boy, Mrs Bannerman.'

'Let me hold him.'

She was amazed by the strength of her feelings as she cradled the helpless child. A boy, her son. Totally reliant on her for everything from this moment on . . .

A banging on the outside door shattered the peaceful moment. Ruth froze. Curzon rolled down his sleeves and straightened his tie. Turning back at the door, he looked at the two women and placed a warning finger over his lips.

Closing all the connecting doors behind him, he walked down the flagstoned passage and opened the front door.

'Yes?' he enquired baldly of the two men standing on the step.

'My name is Lambert. And you are?'

'Jackson.' Curzon studied him for a moment before looking to the tall, dark, sardonic man standing behind him. He waited expectantly for an introduction. But none was forthcoming for Mr Marcus Bannerman.

'Do you let these rooms, Mr Jackson?'

'Are you looking for somewhere?'

'A friend of ours has been looking for lodgings in the area. We're trying to make contact with her.'

'I'm living here myself at the moment.'

'She might have called round.' Marcus delved in

his pocket. 'I have a photograph.' As he handed it over, he watched Curzon for any reaction. There was none.

'Not a face you'd forget,' Curzon commented as he handed it back.

'No. Perhaps I could take a look round. If this place ever becomes vacant . . .'

'It's not terribly convenient. I have a companion.' He lowered his voice. 'He's terribly sensitive. You understand?'

'If you should see her,' Marcus said as he gave him his card. 'I'd make it worth your while.'

'She must be a very close friend.'

'She's my wife.'

'I see. And she's looking for lodgings? Are you expecting to find a third party?'

'It isn't what you think. She's pregnant.'

'And she's left home? I find that very odd. When my wife was pregnant, she clung to me like a vine.'

Irritated by the way the man had manoeuvred himself into the position of interrogator, Marcus retreated. 'She hasn't been herself. I'm concerned for her.'

'With good reason. The Heath can be a dangerous place, especially at night. You might try the police station.'

'I might. Thanks for your help.'

'My pleasure.'

Curzon closed the door and returned to the living room, where Ruth had again succeeded in working herself into a state of near hysteria.

'What the hell am I going to do?'

'Resourceful fellow, your husband.'

'He's a bastard. You've got to help me, whatever it costs.'

'There's a nursing home less than a mile from here.

Very exclusive, very discreet. I do a lot of business there. You'll be among your own kind.'

'But what about yesterday?'

'You were there. That's what they'll say if you pay them enough. We can go there straight away. You'll need a few things for the baby. I'll send someone round.'

'Thank you.'

He shrugged his shoulders as he picked up his coat. 'It's business.'

'You've done more than you had to. I saw the way you delivered the baby.'

'You can send me the rest of the money.' He went to the bedroom door. 'I helped a woman like you. A long time ago. She was in trouble, so I broke the rules. I know what it's like to get found out.' Taking a couple of notes from his wallet, he walked through to the bedroom and placed them on the table next to Edith. 'Make sure you clean this place. Get rid of this lot.' He pointed to the medicine bottles.

Ruth opened her handbag and took out the extra money she'd promised Edith. She held it out, waiting until the woman had taken it before easing the baby from her grasp. Curzon led the way to the door.

'When you get to the clinic you'd better ring home. Let someone know where you are. Come on.'

Edith looked down as they left. Instead of her baby, she was holding a fistful of money. It was only then that the enormity of what she'd done sank in.

'I'd like a car bringing round, Jacob. We're due at a luncheon and I don't want to be late.'

'Very good, Mr Bannerman, Miss Lloyd-Price.' Before the concierge reached reception, Esme called him over.

'Mr Collins, I don't believe you've met Edward' She turned to her companion. 'Jacob's been a very good friend to me, Edward.'

'I've tried to be of assistance whenever I could,' Jacob replied evenly.

'I owe him a great deal. I would like you to shake his hand, Edward.'

'Esme's told you the good news?' Edward asked as he shook the concierge's hand.

'Yes, sir. I hope you'll be very happy.'

'I have no doubt about that.'

Edward escorted Esme into the bar, passing Stephen and Christina, who were sitting, waiting for the car.

'My parents want to have lunch with us tomorrow,' Christina was saying. 'They're getting in a bit of a flap about the reception.'

'The reception?' Stephen said in surprise. 'We haven't gone as far as the church.'

'They're completely out of control. They'll be choosing names for grandchildren next.'

'We need a bit more practice before we have any of those.' He glanced at his watch. 'We're going to be late.' He returned to the foyer. 'Is the car here yet, Jacob?'

Collins stared at him blankly. 'I'm terribly sorry, sir. It completely slipped my mind.'

'For goodness' sake. We should be leaving now.'

'I'm sorry, sir. I'll see to it right away.'

'So, Kate.' Clive stood back and folded his arms. 'I think we should set up our own union branch.'

'Can you do that?' she asked, stepping to one side so another maid could pass her in the narrow corridor.

'Once we've persuaded people to join.'

The Grand II: The Roaring Twenties

'Do you think they will?'

'They'd be daft not to. Once we're in the union we can start trying to change things. We should get paid if we do extra. And a day off should be a day off.'

'They should get someone to cover for us,' she agreed. Both of them started at a crash behind them. 'Lark, you all right?' she called as the girl stood in the middle of a mess of spilled coal.

'Handle broke on the bucket.' Lark lifted up the broken handle she was still holding. 'I suppose I'd better get a brush.'

'Let's talk to the others,' Clive suggested, 'and see what they think.'

'Who is responsible for this?' Mr Collins shouted furiously as he stepped into the coal.

'I was just going to clean it up, Mr Collins,' Lark apologised, emerging from the cupboard with a brush.

'It shouldn't be there in the first place. Look at the mess. I could have broken my neck. Clean up every last bit of it, or there'll be trouble.' Storming off down the corridor, he retreated into his room and slammed the door.

He looked around. What did he have? A few books and toilet articles piled neatly on the table beside his bed. A couple of photographs to remind himself of the life he'd once had. Who'd notice if he disappeared off the face of the earth right now? They might call his name once or twice, and when he didn't materialise, hire someone else.

As he took off his jacket, a button came off in his hand. He looked at it in disgust before opening his wardrobe door. There, in a neat row, were six identical jackets. Clothes he wouldn't wear of choice, but then what was his choice? After so many years of servitude, did he even know what he wanted?

* * *

Ruth moved behind the cot as she heard footsteps echoing down the corridor towards her private room. A nurse opened the door and Marcus walked in. Closing the door on the nurse, he went to the cot.

'Your son.' Ruth smiled tentatively as he stroked the baby's cheek with his finger. Was it going to be all right between them? When he lifted his head, she saw that his eyes were cold, angry. Raising his hand, he slapped her soundly across the face, sending her reeling across the room.

'Don't you ever walk out on me again,' he warned brutally, as tears started into her eyes.

It was almost one o'clock in the morning before Clive managed to assemble the staff in the kitchen. All the girls were in their dressing gowns, and the only ones in uniform were the porters who'd just come off duty.

'My dad says unions are nothing but trouble,' Lynne was whispering, although there was no one to listen in on them. Mrs Harvey had long since gone home.

'They're not,' Clive repudiated. 'They're full of people like us. Working people.'

'But what's the point of them?' Bob asked.

'It's like Lark the other night. You all stood together and she got to go home.' Clive looked to Kate for support.

'Clive says if we join, we can ask about getting more money and not working such long hours.'

The girls nodded agreement.

'But we can't do it on our own,' Clive warned.

'So how do we join?'

'You pay your subs, Lynne, and you get a membership card.'

'Subs? What are they?' she asked suspiciously.

'Subscription. You have to pay to be in a union.'

'I'm not paying to join—'

'You said you'd ask for *more* money, Clive,' Brenda reminded him, 'not take it off us.'

'It won't be much. It's so they can help us when we need them. It will be worth it.'

'They could help us get more time off,' Lark said hopefully.

'Why don't you give it a try? What have you got to lose?'

'All right then, Clive.' Lynne rose to her feet. 'But first you find out how much it is.'

Edward went to the bar of the Manhattan, but before he could order drinks for himself and Esme, a prostitute moved in. Shaking his head at her proposition, he left his order with Jim.

'Did you see that?' he asked Esme, as he returned to their table.

'I hope you turned her down.' She only just managed to keep a straight face.

'She was half my age. It must be the twinkle in my eye.'

'No, Edward, it's the bulge in your wallet.'

He took her hand and kissed the tips of her fingers. 'I've been thinking about where we might live after we're married.'

'Have you?'

'I think we should begin our lives together in a place we can call our own. Make a new start.'

'I agree.'

'Would you have any objections to leaving the area?' he asked.

'I could tear myself away.'

'Then what do you say to Brighton?'

'That would be wonderful.'

'I was hoping you'd say that. I've sent for details of a number of properties.'

'I'd love to see them.'

'I should have them tomorrow. In fact, come for lunch. Meet the children – they'd like to meet you.'

'And I'd like to meet them,' she murmured nervously. He smiled and squeezed her hand, wanting to reassure her that this time it really was going to be all right – for both of them.

'You'll wear those shoes out with polishing, Mr Collins,' Mrs Harvey warned as she walked through the back door the following morning.

'You can't beat a polished surface, Sylvie. That's what the guests expect to see in a place like this. If the mirrors gleam and the silverware sparkles, it doesn't matter what's underneath.'

'Yes, well, we're expected to sparkle ourselves this lunchtime.'

'Oh, yes?' he looked at her quizzically.

'A message from Mr Bannerman. He's coming back with Mrs Bannerman and their new baby. A boy. And he wants all the staff lined up to greet him.'

'It's the Bannerman way, Mrs Harvey. I remember seeing Stephen and Miss Adele make their first appearance.'

'I doubt we'll summon the enthusiasm there was on those occasions.'

'The surface, Mrs Harvey.' He looked down at his shoes. 'That's all that counts.'

'This is, Julia, my eldest daughter.' Esme shook the hand of a striking young woman, in her early twenties.

The Grand II: The Roaring Twenties

'Sophie.'

'How do you do?' Esme smiled at Edward's fifteen-year-old, younger daughter.

'And George.'

Esme shook the hand of the twelve-year-old.

'Children, this is Miss Harkness. And I think that's enough formality for one day,' Edward said decisively, opening the door of the drawing room. 'Let's sit down.'

'This is a lovely room,' Esme complimented, admiring the elegant furniture and décor, but most of all the simple paraphernalia of family life. The photographs, books, and vases filled with flowers from the garden.

'My mother chose everything.'

'She had exquisite taste, Julia.'

'Time for sherry.' Edward went to the decanter on the sideboard and poured three glasses. 'Julia, do the honours will you?' He handed her two cut-glass goblets and she passed one to Esme.

'How do you know my father?' Sophie asked.

'We're very old friends,' Esme said as she sipped her sherry.

'It must have been quite a surprise, meeting after such a long time.'

'Yes, Julia, a very pleasant surprise.'

'Here's to us.' Edward raised his glass.

'There's a few more, Lark, for when you've finished that lot.' Mrs Harvey dumped another pile of table napkins next to the mountain waiting to be ironed.

'Yes, Mrs Harvey.' Setting the iron she'd been using back on the block to heat, Lark took a fresh one.

'I heard you went home the other night, Lark.' Mr Collins handed Mrs Harvey a room list. 'I hope you made the most of it.' He nodded in the housekeeper's direction. 'It doesn't happen that often.'

'It's all going to be different in the future, Mr Collins.'

'Is it?'

'We won't be working long hours any more. We're all going to stand together. We're going to be in the union. Are you going to join?' she asked innocently.

Mrs Harvey rolled her eyes heavenwards before disappearing into her office, leaving Mr Collins to deal with Lark's revelation.

'Whose idea is this?'

'Clive. He's going to help us.'

Collins went to the cellar where Clive was stacking crates.

'Clive? What's all this about a union?'

'We're just going to make a few reasonable demands, that's all.'

'Of Marcus Bannerman?' Collins asked incredulously.

'It's happening all over the world, Mr Collins. Working people standing up for their rights.'

'What's given you this idea? Is it that lot upstairs?'

'I want to make things better, we all do.'

'If you march into Marcus Bannerman's office and start making demands and telling him what to do, he'll sack you. And if you lose your job, what's going to happen to you then?'

'But he won't sack me. That's the point of being in the union. The others will back me. He can't sack us all.'

'That lot out there? You reckon they'll risk their jobs for you?'

'If it came to it, yes.'

'Come with me.' He walked back into the kitchen where Mrs Harvey was issuing instructions to the staff.

'Mr and Mrs Bannerman are due back at one o'clock,' she was saying. 'I want you all in the foyer at five minutes to. In clean uniforms. And mind you scrub your nails.'

'I'd like a word if you don't mind, Mrs Harvey,' Mr Collins interrupted.

'Yes, of course.' She stepped aside.

'Clive tells me he's trying to start a union. So I've had no alternative but to give him his notice.' He had to raise his voice as the sound level escalated. 'He'll be leaving at the end of the week,'

'That's not fair, Mr Collins,' Kate shouted angrily.

'There's no place for unions at the Grand. Not with Mr Bannerman in charge. You'd better let me know which of you intends to go out in sympathy.'

In the silence that followed, most of the staff looked down at their feet, but Kate stared Mr Collins straight in the eye as she put up her hand. Lark followed Kate's example. Mr Collins looked round. After a moment's hesitation, one other maid joined them.

'I see – a minority of three. Don't worry, Clive's going nowhere. And we don't want to lose Clive, do we? But if Mr Bannerman had found out before me, it would have been him standing in front of you.'

Clive looked around, devastated, as the staff sheepishly filed away. Only Kate and Lark went to offer him their sympathy for what he had tried to do.

Esme picked up a photograph from the display on the piano. It was of a beautiful woman in her fifties, with the kind of contented expression that only comes from years of satisfied living.

'She's beautiful, isn't she?' Julia asked.

'Yes. Is it your mother?'

'That was taken a year ago. Just before her illness.'

'Really? I thought it must have been taken some time ago.'

'She was much younger than my father.'

'Where's Dad?' Sophie asked, closing the lid on the piano.

'He went to see how lunch is coming along. Why don't you see what's holding him up, George?'

'I'll come.' Sophie ran out behind him.

'Has he said anything at all about my mother?' Julia refilled Esme's sherry glass.

'Not a great deal.'

'Ever since she died, he's been running away. It's only fair that you should know that.'

'Thank you. I'll do all I can to help him.'

'We've been living with a stranger. He's like a different man.'

'He's trying to build a new life, so perhaps he's starting to come to terms with what happened.'

'I don't think so,' Julia demurred. 'He doesn't know what he's doing. He'll wake up one morning and he'll see you lying beside him, and then he'll despise you. He'll hate you, because you're not my mother.'

'I can understand your anger,' Esme sympathised cautiously. 'You've lost your mother, and I'll never be able to replace her. But your father and I love each other.'

'He wants to forget. You're a means to an end, and he doesn't even realise. He isn't ready for all this.'

'Julia, how dare you speak like that?' Edward admonished from the doorway.

'Have you talked about where you might live?' Julia asked Esme.

'Yes, as a matter of fact we have, last night,' Esme replied, looking to Edward.

'It won't be here?'

'We want to make a new start together.'

'And what about Sophie and George. Did he mention them?'

'I'll take care of them, you know very well.' Edward stepped into the room.

'You can't even look after yourself. I've been taking care of them since mother died. Stop deluding yourself.'

'I love Esme and I want to marry her.'

'We've loved each other all our lives,' Esme revealed.

Julia picked up the photograph Esme had replaced on the piano. She held it out towards her father.

'Tell my mother that Esme's the love of your life, and that you never loved her the way you love Esme.' She stared at Esme. 'He nursed my mother when she was dying.'

'Stop it!'

'He was absolutely devoted to her. He gave up his job to be with her. He used to sit by her side. All day, through the night. I used to worry he'd make himself ill. I pleaded with him to rest, but he wouldn't. He didn't want to miss a single moment of her precious life.'

'Julia!'

When she heard the anger in Edward's voice, Esme realised that his description of his marriage as 'a marriage much like any other' had been a lie.

'When she became very weak, he'd sit up and read to her. She couldn't listen for long. She hadn't the strength, so he'd read poetry to her.' Julia gazed intently at her father. 'Since she died, he hasn't allowed us to mention her name.'

'Please . . . I beg you . . . don't . . .'

Katherine Hardy

Julia put her arm around his shoulders. Convulsed by grief, he fell back on to the sofa.

'I couldn't bear to see her suffer like that,' his voice was harsh, cracked, clotted with tears. 'I couldn't bear it . . . and then . . . then . . . she was gone.'

As Julia murmured soft words of comfort and stroked the hair away from his face, Esme walked quietly out through the door.

'I wouldn't trust Marcus Bannerman as far as I could spit him,' Collins confided to Clive, who was sitting on the only chair in the concierge's room. 'I couldn't let you walk up there. I know times are changing, and I'm pleased you've found something to believe in. But now's not the time. They're not ready; you're not ready. Wait until it's something you really want to fight for. And make sure you've got them behind you. You never know' – he smiled wryly – 'even I might join then.' As Clive returned the smile, the concierge knew he'd made his point and the boy bore no bitterness. 'I'd best be getting upstairs. Shut the door behind you.'

Mr Collins saw Esme Harkness as he walked into the foyer. She didn't say anything, she didn't need to. One glance was enough to tell him how lunch with Edward Lawrence's family had gone.

'I don't want to see her flipping brat,' Lynne complained as Mrs Harvey marshalled the maids towards the front door.

'Can you imagine what it will be like with them two as parents?' Brenda sniggered.

'Yeah,' Lynne answered. 'Horns and a tail.'

The girls shuffled into line opposite the porters as Stephen left the bar.

The Grand II: The Roaring Twenties

'Stephen?' Esme called from the stairs. He turned, surprised to see her dressed so elegantly, early in the afternoon. 'Tell your uncle I'd like to discuss a business arrangement with him. He'll know what I mean.'

'He'll be here any minute. You can tell him yourself,' Stephen answered politely.

'The emperor returns,' Esme whispered to Jacob.

'Yes, miss. Things will soon be back to normal.'

'They are already, Jacob.'

Collins inclined his head. The doors opened and Marcus swept in, followed by Ruth holding the baby. At a cue from Mrs Harvey the staff applauded in a desultory, unenthusiastic fashion. But it was enough for Marcus. Taking the baby from Ruth, he lifted it to shoulder height. Ruth stood at the foot of the stairs and smiled at the assembled staff, afterwards they all agreed, it was a smile of pure triumph.

Chapter Twenty-Two

The well-built man hovered at the entrance to the bar until an elderly couple claimed the full attention of the concierge. Slipping over to Tom, one of the junior porters, he drew him away from the reception area.

'I've a message for Miss Harkness. Could you tell me what room she is in?'

'I think she's out at the moment, sir,' Tom replied politely, trying to recall Mr Collins's directives respecting guests' privacy. 'You can leave a message here.'

'I'll deliver it to the room.' The man tipped a wink. 'It's personal.'

Tom smiled, flattered by the confidence. 'Of course, sir. Room forty-four.'

The man stepped behind the concierge and ran up the stairs. He walked quickly down the first floor corridor checking the numbers on the doors. When he reached forty-four, he tried the door. It was locked. He took a screwdriver from his pocket and slipped the blade into the locking mechanism. Hearing voices, he concealed the screwdriver in his hand and retraced his steps.

'Get a move on, Lark,' Brenda shouted impatiently. 'If Mrs Harvey catches you napping, she won't let you on the bus. You'll have to run along behind.'

'What's it like, this Morton Sands?' Lark pushed her trolley towards the next room on their list.

'Sandy,' Brenda replied succinctly.

'Bunch of sand dunes, a filthy dirty café and a little old man who invites you to come and see his kittens,' Lynne teased. 'Keep clear of him.'

'Why?'

'Brenda, tell her.'

The man hiding in the alcove at the end of the corridor watched them open the door of room forty-six. Too close. But then, he was prepared to wait.

'Here you are, miss.' Kate carried a bowl of water and a cloth into the Bannermans' private living room.

'I told you Kate would have the answer,' Stephen reassured Christina, who was staring at an ugly stain on the back of her coat.

'It's definitely rust. It must have been that taxicab. Bloody thing.'

'Salt and lemon juice. That'll shift it,' Kate promised. 'Mix them together, rub it in, leave it a bit, then dab it off.'

'I thought you could do it.'

'I'm sorry, miss, I can't. We're all on double shifts. It's the staff outing tomorrow, and if we don't get everything done, Mrs Harvey's likely to cancel.'

'Where are you going, Blackpool?' Stephen asked.

'You're joking. Blackpool's forbidden after what happened in 1913.'

'The great disaster,' he laughed.

'Hush now. It's been removed from the official history.'

'Well, remind me to be out tomorrow. It's murder putting up with relief staff.'

'Don't worry about that, sir – half of us will still be on duty. It's your uncle, the new regime. We can't *all* go on a trip. He's not having that. Half of us tomorrow, half of us next month, so he doesn't have to buy in relief staff. Saves all of, ooh, three quid.'

'God, he'll be counting out the tea leaves next.'

'We're doing that already.'

'Come on, Stephen,' Christina prompted, irritated at being excluded from their conversation. 'Kate's said she's busy. Don't keep her.'

'Sorry,' Stephen apologised. Kate gave him a smile before hurrying out of the door.

'So what happened in 1913?' Christina asked.

'Long story, hotel joke, it's not that funny, really . . . it's a bit . . . dodgy. I'll send down for coffee.' He went to the telephone, leaving Christina with the salt, water and lemon. Picking up her coat, she sighed and set to work.

'Morton Sands, it's a swizz.' Lynne pulled the trolley to the end of the corridor. 'The staff in the Midland get Blackpool, a hamper for lunch, two shillings for tea and a hat.'

'What do you mean, a hat?' Lark asked.

'I don't know – a hat.'

'What sort of hat?'

'Do I work at the Midland?' Lynne checked the list and opened the door of room sixty-seven. 'Come on, let's make a start.'

The man hiding in the alcove stepped out. The corridor was empty. As he darted back to room forty-four, he palmed the screwdriver. Barrelling the lock was the work of a moment, although the door refused to latch when he tried to close it behind him. Without wasting any more time, he went to the wardrobe.

The Grand II: The Roaring Twenties

Taking a cut-throat razor from his top pocket, he opened it and began to slash at the clothes.

When the entire contents of Esme's wardrobe had been reduced to rags, he set to work on the bed. Not content with shredding the sheets, blankets and counterpane he began on the mattress.

Kate hurried down the first-floor corridor listening for the maids. Thinking that they must have moved on to the second floor, she headed for the lift. Used to the vagaries of guests, she ignored the strange noises coming from forty-four, but as she passed, the door swung open and she saw a man attacking the bed with a blade.

'Oi! What the hell are you doing?' She stared, horrified, at the jumble of ruined clothes on the floor. 'What are you *doing*?' Without thinking, she ran towards him intending to make him stop. The man blocked her path.

Catching her by the waist, he shoved her aside. As she crashed into the dresser, her head connected with the side of the mirror. The man picked up an ornament and threw it towards her, but she ducked and it smashed into the mirror. His intended target. She fell to the floor, protecting her head with her hands as shards of glass cascaded around her.

'That sounds like Mrs Harvey's dropped her teeth,' Lynne joked as they heard the sound of breaking glass. 'Go and look.' She pushed Lark out of the room. 'We'll only get the blame if something's broken.'

Lark saw the man emerging from Esme's room. Red-faced, he paused to straighten his jacket and tie.

'Sir, what's all the noise?' Ignoring her, the man walked on. 'Sir? Sir?' She ran on down the corridor.

Seeing Esme's door open, she looked in and saw Kate lying on the floor. 'Oh my Lord!' She dashed towards her. 'Kate, what's going on? What's happened?'

'I'm all right,' Kate mumbled thickly, struggling to focus.

'Look at you! Was it him? Was it that man?'

Mr Collins greeted the young couple leaving the Reading Room.

'Good morning, sir, ma'am.' Hearing a clatter on the stairs behind him, he was furious when he saw Lark charging towards him.

'Mr Collins, sir, Mr Collins . . .'

'For God's sake girl, keep your voice down. You're not allowed in the foyer.'

'There was a man, sir, and he tried to kill her. He tried to kill Kate Morris, sir, he did. She's up there and she's dying an' everything.'

'What man?' he demanded urgently.

'Tall, and a big coat . . .'

'Clive! Man just walked out, tall, dark hair, get after him. Stan,' he shouted to the duty porter, 'go with him.'

Clive and Stan raced across the foyer and out through the door, as the concierge ran up the stairs.

'Where is she?'

'Room forty-four, sir,' Lark called back breathlessly as she followed. 'Miss Harkness's room.'

Esme sat back in the chair behind the desk in the office of the Manhattan and studied the girl sitting in front of her. She wasn't beautiful in the accepted sense of the word, but she certainly knew how to make the most of what attractions she did have.

'You have your own accommodation?' Esme asked.

'Baveystock House. But you'd know that already. You wouldn't interview girls who sell themselves along the canal. You'd want professionals.'

'Do you own the apartment?'

'Yes.'

'Then you've no financial connection with Mr Scott?'

'I'm independent, in as much as a woman in this profession can *be* independent. He's certainly not my pimp, if that's what you mean. I find my own clients, word of mouth and a discreet arrangement with the railway hotels.'

'Then you've absolutely no connection with Mr Scott?'

'It's impossible to operate in the south of Manchester without knowing Mr Scott.'

'Louisa, do you pay him?' Esme questioned bluntly.

'It's protection money.'

'How much?'

'Half. Fifty per cent of my earnings.' She watched Esme scribble a note. 'Esme, if the rumours are true – I can call you Esme?'

'Miss Harkness.'

'If it's true, Miss Harkness, that you're back in business, I'd be interested, with certain conditions. You'll have noticed that most of the girls you've summoned haven't turned up, in case Mr Scott hears of your plans. I'd want my safety guaranteed.'

'I've got backing. The owner of this club has considerable influence.'

'Marcus Bannerman, now there's a puzzle. You allowing a man to hold the purse strings.'

'I'm working *with* him, not *for* him.'

Louisa laughed. 'We've all said that.'

'I don't say things lightly.'

Katherine Hardy

'What would be your commission? Twenty per cent?'

'Oh no. Mr Scott's no idiot. I'd be taking half as well.'

Marcus glanced at the two women through the glass door of the office as he sat at the deserted bar, sipping a whisky.

'Simple procedure, Jim. If a man's new in town, or new to the game, he usually heads for the barman. A quiet word and a nod in the right direction, that's all you have to do. Miss Harkness can take things from there.'

'If you don't mind my saying, sir, it's a bit small beer isn't it, turning money out of tarts? What you going to make? Ten quid a week?'

'Twenty, which is one thousand and forty a year. By the time my son's an adult, that's an inheritance of more than twenty thousand pounds.'

'God, you can adopt me if you want. Most men, they start a family, they slow down a bit.'

'And that's why most men fail.' He left his seat as Esme and Louisa walked out of the office.

'It's been a pleasure, Miss Harkness,' Louisa said as she buttoned her coat. 'I think we'd work together rather well.'

'I'll decide that.'

Louisa smiled at Marcus. 'Hello again.'

'Louisa.'

The office phone rang.

'I'm there,' Jim shouted, racing to answer it.

'She gets my vote,' Marcus said to Esme, as Louisa left.

'Unfortunately, Marcus, you don't have a vote. The girls are my business, and if any of them catches your eye, you'll have to pay.'

'I'm a happily married man,' he protested.

'Aren't they all?' Esme reminded.

'He's here, they're both here, hold on . . .' Jim looked out of the office. 'Excuse me, sir, Miss Harkness, it's the Grand. You'd better get back.'

'Honest, I'm all right,' Kate remonstrated as Mrs Harvey led her to bed. 'It was a bump, that's all.'

'We'll wait for the doctor, thank you, Kate,' the housekeeper said, using briskness to conceal her concern.

'What was he doing, that bloke?'

'What do you think in Harkness's room, Brenda?' Lynne sneered. 'It's bad enough putting up with her. Now we get thumped by her clients.'

'Lynne, that's enough speculation,' Mrs Harvey ordered.

'They should sling her out,' Kate murmured as Mrs Harvey folded back the sheets.

Stephen walked in, showing more confidence and concern than Christina, who hovered behind in the doorway.

'I've only just heard. They told me in reception. Are you all right, Kate?'

'I'm fine, really, no one believes me.'

'What happened?'

'I'll tell you what's happening now,' Mrs Harvey snapped. 'This young girl's in her bedclothes with a gentleman in the room. Could you please leave?'

'But you're really all right?' Stephen looked to Kate.

'Really, yes.'

'If you could, sir, quick as you can,' said the house-keeper as she stepped in front of him.

'Stephen, come on,' Christina pleaded.

317

Katherine Hardy

'Right, well, Kate, you just get some rest.'

Christina addressed the housekeeper. 'If there's anything we can do . . .'

'It's all under control, thank you.' Mrs Harvey ushered both of them out before her.

The moment they left, Brenda and Lark began giggling.

'If there's anything we can do . . .' Lynne stuck her nose in the air, mimicking Christina.

'He can see me in me bedclothes,' Brenda sighed. 'That's worth a good bashing any time.'

'It's ridiculous,' Stephen complained as the maids' laughter echoed after them. 'She needs peace and quiet.'

'They're her friends, sir,' Mrs Harvey reminded. 'I think she's glad of a little company.'

'You can't just leave her in there,' Stephen said forcefully, as another burst of laughter echoed down the corridor.

'The doctor's on his way, sir.'

'That room is freezing. She needs proper care.'

'It's freezing down here all year round, if you could get them *all* better accommodation, injured or otherwise, I'd be the last to complain, sir.' Mrs Harvey looked him in the eye as they reached the staircase that led up to the foyer.

Esme and Marcus stood side by side in the centre of her room, surveying the damage. To Collins's amazement, neither of them looked particularly surprised. It was almost as though they'd been expecting it to happen.

'I didn't see him come in,' the concierge apologised. 'I sent Clive to look in the street, but he'd gone.'

'And Kate?' Esme asked. 'How is she?'

'She's not so bad, more of a shock I think. She's being looked after.'

'If you could apologise, and' – Esme opened her purse and took out a pound note – 'perhaps you could give her this.'

'I don't think so, Miss Harkness,' he said gently, aware of the animosity Kate still felt towards Esme Harkness for the part she'd played in Monica's downfall. 'She might not appreciate the gesture.'

Esme nodded as she returned the money to her purse.

'Have you called the police?' Marcus asked.

'I would, sir, in normal circumstances. But I was thinking of Miss Harkness. If this man had some grievance with you, miss, you might not want the authorities alerted to your . . . activities.'

'Quite,' Marcus replied for her. 'Well done.'

'Though I have to think of the staff. If there's any danger he might come back . . .'

'He won't,' Esme broke in.

'We can handle this, Collins. It won't happen again,' Marcus assured him.

Collins looked from Marcus to Esme.

'Thank you, Jacob.' Esme smiled, but it was still a dismissal. Collins went to the door.

'Mr Scott?' Marcus asked Esme after Collins left.

'Evidently.'

'What do you want me to do?'

'Nothing – yet.'

'All the colleges at Oxford have got charitable status, so they've got pots of money,' Christina informed Stephen as they sat drinking tea in the Reading Room. 'They must have accommodation for people like us,

married quarters, but St Hilda's won't allow gentleman callers, not even husbands, so I'd have to live
out.'

'Oxford,' Stephen mused. 'I'd be closer to my
parents.'

'You could become a student. Why not? You'd get
in. And be honest, you don't want to run a nightclub
for the rest of your life. I'd be a student with a husband. It could be rather glamorous.'

Stephen rose to his feet. 'Look, it's stupid. Kate
works for the Grand, so the Grand should look after
her. We've got dozens of beds. There's bound to be a
room free. Excuse me, this will only take five minutes,
but if I don't get it done, no one else will.' He walked
out, abandoning Christina to her resentment – and
jealousy.

Kate leaned on Mrs Harvey's arm as she walked down
the guest corridor, Lark trailing behind, her arms full
of Kate's things.

'They'll be laughing, Lynne and that lot. I'll never
hear the end of this. Me in a guest room, Lady Muck.'

'If I was you, I'd make the most of it,' Mrs Harvey
advised as she opened the door to room nine. 'I've
never slept in one of these beds meself. Suppose I
never will. Still, by all accounts, a soft bed leads to
problems in the lower back.'

'Don't you and Mr Harvey have a proper bed?' Lark
asked.

'There's more to a marital bed than comfort, Lark
Rothery.'

Lark looked around the room before dumping
Kate's things on the table. 'I could stay with you, Kate.
Tomorrow I mean. You'll need someone if you're feel-
ing dizzy and that.'

'I've never been dizzy in me life.'

'I don't mind, though. I'll miss the trip, but you've looked after me, so now it's my turn.'

'Don't be daft.' Kate kicked off her shoes.

'The coach is booked, Lark, and you're on the list,' Mrs Harvey reminded her. 'You can't go changing lists. Takes a lot of planning, a good list.'

'I'd sooner look after Kate.'

'The last thing Kate needs is your fussing.'

'Is everything all right?' Stephen opened the door.

'Very kind of you, sir,' Kate answered, 'but I'd rather not. There's no need.'

'Of course, there is. You've been hurt, this place should be looking after you.'

'Your timing's almost supernatural, sir,' Mrs Harvey snapped irritably. 'She may not be in her bed-clothes, but she's a second away from divesting herself, so off you go.'

'If you need a meal or anything, just call down, Kate. You're one of the guests now.'

'She'll have a lamb chop like the rest of us,' Mrs Harvey said flatly.

'Just take care. It's yours for as long as you need it.'

'You could stay all week!' Lark sighed enviously as Stephen left. 'It's like having a guardian angel.'

'I hope his motives are that divine. Quite the little favourite, aren't you, Kate?' Mrs Harvey pronounced in a cooler tone. 'Into bed.'

Collins waited until the porters had carried the damaged furniture out of Esme's room before approaching her.

'If you don't mind me saying, Miss Harkness, if there's something going on, it's better that I'm told, so I can help. Does it involve Mr Bannerman?'

Katherine Hardy

She scooped up an armful of shredded, crimson wild silk that had been her favourite evening gown. 'Why do you ask?'

'You seem to be spending a lot of time with him.'

'It's a business proposition. It might not work out. Early days.'

'It's not my place, Miss Harkness, but I've seen what happens to those who put their trust in Marcus Bannerman.'

'Thank you, Jacob, but you needn't worry. It's not a matter of trust. If Marcus and I can use each other's talents, then it's a good alliance.'

'What would those talents be?'

'I've only the one.' She smiled sadly.

'Miss Harkness,' a porter knocked on the door. 'There's a gentleman downstairs waiting to see you, a Mr Scott.'

'I'll come down, thank you.'

'Mr Leonard Scott?' Collins asked after the porter had left.

'Yes.'

'Miss Harkness, do you really need to do this?'

'He's waiting, Mr Collins.'

Jacob Collins saw Scott standing, waiting in the foyer, as he escorted Esme down the stairs. His reputation belied his appearance. A thin, weedy little man of middle height, foppishly dressed, with an effete look about him.

'If you need me, Miss Harkness, I'll be on duty,' Collins said loudly for Scott's benefit, as they reached the foot of the stairs.

'Thank you, Jacob. Mr Scott?'

'Miss Harkness.' He gestured towards the Reading Room. 'I hope you don't mind, I ordered tea.'

'The bar is open.' She walked in, leaving him to follow.

'So, I'm told you had a spot of trouble,' Scott said after the waiter had brought their drinks.

'It was nothing.'

'Really? Good. *Good.* I mean, it might seem this man . . . whoever he was. Perhaps he got a little carried away. What I mean is, if he was meant to deliver a warning, he . . . improvised, shall we say. Made it more of a threat.'

'Is this an apology?'

'Good stuff,' Scott commented, sipping his whisky to avoid answering her question.

'These tactics are nothing new to me. I've lived my life playing this game, but this time it's attracted the attention of Mr Bannerman.'

'Yes, I'd rather hoped we could sort this out between ourselves.'

'Too late.'

'Miss Harkness, I've got bills to pay, I've got debts, I've got employers of my own. I couldn't sit back, I had to take action, it was expected. They were waiting for me to do something.'

'Mr Scott, you almost sound out of your depth.'

'Marcus Bannerman needn't be a part of this. You stay here, in the Grand. Leave the girls to me and we can forget this ever happened.'

'Or what? Am I supposed to be in danger?'

'Not at all. With Mr Bannerman's protection, there's little I can do. Although it's strange – who'd have thought? We seem to be enemies, when in fact I could help you, Miss Harkness. I could make things so much better, with just one small piece of information.' He played with his glass, twirling it on the table. 'We're all tired of these little wars, and I'm not one to

strike terror. Look at me! I'd rather work by coopera-
tion. That's why the girls trust me.'

'How could you possibly help me, Mr Scott?'

'Just think back. London, the old days, both of us
chasing money. Though I didn't cut such a dash as the
famous Miss Harkness, so I had to find other skills. I
kept quiet and listened, and remembered every single
name. Thank God for the one strength I have, a good
memory.'

'Blackmail, is that it?'

'Of course not, I wouldn't dare.'

'My past is an open book. I can't think of any secrets
that might cause me harm.'

'Miss Harkness, it's not blackmail, I swear. I could
help you, I really could, if you tell Mr Bannerman
you're cancelling the partnership. He couldn't run the
girls on his own – they'd be too scared of him. They'd
much rather stay with me. Cancel the partnership,
keep my name out of it, then we can talk.'

'About what?'

'Wonderful things, Miss Harkness, just waiting to
be told. You'll be grateful, I promise. You'll bless the
day we met.'

'Then tell me now. If we're striking a bargain, I have
to know what's at stake.'

'Make the decision, *then* we'll talk. It's been a pleasure. Good day.'

More rattled than she would have cared to show
Scott, Esme wondered exactly what he meant.

Chapter Twenty-Three

Marcus handed Esme a sherry, before sitting beside her on the sofa.

'He used all manner of delicate phrases, but it amounts to blackmail, Marcus. He'll soon learn: there's no blackmail for the shameless. So' – she raised her glass – 'time you made your presence felt.'

'It's been a while since I conducted this sort of business. Rather invigorating.'

'Marcus, no one's to be hurt. A small gesture is all it takes. It's like swatting a fly.'

'Miss Harkness, what brings you here?' Ruth enquired ungraciously as she walked in with the baby.

'I thought it was time I passed on my congratulations.' She looked at the child. 'Isn't he splendid? Have you thought of a name?'

'Charles,' Marcus informed her.

'Your father's name. That's inspired. At last, a Charles Bannerman under your control.'

'That wasn't quite the point,' Marcus laughed.

'Then it's a bonus.' She turned to Ruth. 'I'm told you've employed a wet nurse.'

'I have, yes, I find it more convenient.'

'Very wise, but you'll take care, Mrs Bannerman. I'm told the physical effect can be rather traumatic, if your own milk isn't expressed.'

'Thank you! It's hardly a matter for public discussion.'

'I suppose not. Society would rather women gave birth quietly and discreetly, almost by osmosis.'

Amused by the women's sparring, Marcus took Charles from Ruth.

'Nothing quiet about this. I could shout it to the world. Charles Marcus Bannerman. Everyone keeps saying he's got my eyes. What do you think?'

'Actually he looks nothing like either of you.' Esme left her seat and went to the door. 'Congratulations.'

As Ruth watched Marcus cradling the baby, a small shiver of fear crawled down her back.

'Excuse me, sir.' Clive stopped Mr Collins as he passed the back door. He pointed to the broken mirror from Esme's room. 'Bob was asking, are we chucking this out? It's from Miss Harkness's room. Bob's got a cousin who runs a stall on the market and he reckons he could flog it.'

'You didn't ask, I didn't know, so long as it's gone.'

'Sir, how come you didn't call the police?'

'Miss Harkness didn't want to take it further.'

'It's not just her, though, is it? Kate got hurt. Any other guest, you'd have done it. Different rules for Miss Harkness, isn't it?'

'Thank you, Clive, the matter is closed,' he replied swiftly, concealing his own uneasiness at the situation. Seeing Mrs Harvey, he held up the papers he was holding. She nodded, and he went into her office. The housekeeper took two mugs from the dresser and picked up the teapot.

'Now, that's the schedule on the wall, Brenda. Lark' – she frowned at the maid, who was picking at a pimple on her face – 'don't do that. And while I think of it, Mr Bannerman's given permission: one bottle of beer each, for the journey.'

'Just the one?'

'Just the one, Bob, or it's Blackpool all over again. You and Clive get the crates first thing, put them in the boot. The rest of you, the coach arrives at five. I want you on board by half past.'

'How come when we're working it's up at six, holiday, it's up at five?'

'It's not a holiday, Lynne, it's a treat. And treats need supervision.' Taking the mugs, she headed for her office. 'And it's best clothes, remember, not any old rags. Out there, on Morton Sands you're not day-trippers, you're . . .'

'*Ambassadors!*' the staff shouted in unison before she could say the word. Smiling, she joined Mr Collins.

'These trips come round in the blink of an eye,' she commented as she handed him one of the mugs. 'Another tick on the calendar, another year gone.'

'Not much to show for a twelvemonth is it, if the highpoint's a trip to the sands? As Mr Eliot said, I have measured out my life with coffee spoons.'

'Yes, but he didn't leave the maids a tip, did he? Birth, marriage and death, that's what Mr Harvey says. The stages of a life: birth, marriage and death.'

'We've both had the first two. I don't fancy the third much.'

'Oh, a long way off. All sorts of things could happen before then. Years ahead of you, Jacob. You could marry again.'

'What, find meself a lass on Morton Sands? There was enough of that in Blackpool.'

* * *

'Coming to the club tonight?' Stephen asked Christina as he walked her to the door.

'Stephen I'm getting a reputation as a bar fly. I'll see you tomorrow.' She turned her back as he helped her on with her coat. 'It worked, look.' She pointed to the spot where it had been stained. 'She's very clever, that Kate. Worth looking after.' She kissed him. 'Bye.'

'I'll come round tomorrow.'

Christina waved to Marcus and Jim, who were leaving the office, then walked out through the door.

'Afternoon, sir,' Jim greeted Stephen.

'Jim, what are you doing here?'

'Bit of business, sir.' He glanced slyly at Marcus. 'All done.'

'What's that about? Is it the club?' Stephen asked, as Jim left.

Marcus eyed Stephen. 'Now here's a young man in need of a rest. I've been working you like a slave. Tell you what, take the evening off, I'll look after the club tonight.'

'Really? I'm fine, I don't mind.'

'No, I insist, leave it with me.'

'All right. I wish you'd told me sooner – Christina's just left.'

'If you run, you can catch her.'

Stephen looked at the door for a moment, then remembered Kate. He went to the stairs.

'I'll see her tomorrow.'

Kate sat in front of the dressing table in room nine feeling lonely, and faintly ridiculous. Like a little girl who'd sneaked into forbidden adult territory. Picking up her plain, deal hairbrush, which looked distinctly downmarket on the highly polished mahogany surface, she brushed out her hair, twisted it into a thick rope and piled it on top of her head. Then she pulled a face.

It was no use: she couldn't even pretend to be a lady.

Mrs Harvey checked her office one last time, then picked up her coat and bag and locked the door. As she went towards the back door, she heard a scuttling in one of the linen cupboards.

'Who's there?' she called.

'It's me, Mrs Harvey.' Lark stepped out.

'In your nightclothes! You lot, it's Sodom and Gomorrah.' She smiled, belying her pretence of anger. 'Go on, off to bed before you give Mr Collins a convulsion.'

'I was just . . . I was talking to Connie Baines, and she'd much rather go tomorrow.'

'She's on the list for next month.'

'But I'll swap with her. I don't mind. She'd love to go, and she's nice Connie . . .'

'Lark Rothery, I'd swear you're trying every trick in the book to wriggle out of this. What is it?' she probed gently, concerned by the downcast expression on the girl's face. 'Don't you want to go?'

'No.'

'Why ever not?'

'It's all the stories, and the others. They keep talking, like people go missing and things . . .'

'With me in charge? Is that likely?'

'No, but . . . Mrs Harvey, it's the sea. I've never been to the sea. Seen pictures and things in books and that, and me mam says she took me to Southport, but I was tiny, I don't remember. And people drown, they do, all the girls are saying. People get drowned.'

'Well if they do, they'll have to answer to me. Now

then, Lark,' the housekeeper said as she wrapped her arm around the girl's shoulders, 'you come with us tomorrow and take a look. If you don't like it, you can stay on the bus.'

'They'll be laughing at me.'

'It's *my* day out. I'll decide who laughs and who doesn't. Will you do that though? Just take a look?'

'S'pose,' Lark conceded reluctantly.

'Good girl. Now off to bed.'

'You going home?'

'Of course I'm going home. Mr Harvey's waiting. Off you go.' But she stayed long enough to watch the girl scamper off down the corridor that led to the bedrooms.

'I'm sorry about this,' Marcus apologised to Ruth as he walked into their living room in his evening suit. 'Just this one night. It's rather important. I promise, the rest of the week, I'll stay with you both.'

'On your way out, could you tell Mr Collins I'd like to see him?'

'Why?'

'I can't move the furniture on my own. I thought I'd move back into your room.'

Marcus smiled. Kissing the baby's head, he turned to Ruth, embracing her with more passion than he'd shown since she'd first become pregnant. She caressed the baby as he left. Little Charles, her son, the solution to all their problems, and a source of more love than she would have believed possible.

'Come in.' Kate wrapped her dressing gown around her as she sat up in bed. Clive walked in carrying a champagne bucket.

'The house finest, for madam.' He set it on the table

beside her.

'Clive, you'll get the boot. That's four guineas a bottle.'

He lifted it out of the bucket. 'It got left at the bar. You might get two glasses if you wring it out.' Putting on his best mock-posh accent, he said, 'Do call down, Madame, if you require anything else.'

'Thank you, Evans, you're dismissed,' she answered, falling in with his mood.

He was still laughing when he closed the door. Then he saw Stephen Bannerman walking towards him.

'Evening, sir.'

'Clive.'

'Everything all right, sir?' he asked as Stephen passed.

'Yes.'

Clive scowled as Stephen knocked on the door of room nine, but his disapproval was wasted. Stephen didn't even look in his direction.

'Don't tell me,' Kate called out, 'the bottle's gone missing, and they want it back.'

Stephen popped his head around the door. 'Sorry?'

'Sir.' Kate coloured in embarrassment. 'I thought you were Clive.'

He raised his eyebrows when he saw the bottle. 'Clive will be in trouble, bringing you that.'

'Oh, don't tell on him. He's just being nice.'

'Of course I won't. Who do you think I am? How are you?' He walked in and sat on the bed.

'I'm fine and sick of saying it. Bump on the head, everyone thinks I'm dying. Stephen, you'd better go.'

'Yes.' But he made no effort to leave. Instead he went to the champagne bucket and poured her out a glass.

'I told Mrs Harvey that I didn't want to stay in a guest room. I made a fuss, but not too much of one in case she whisked me back downstairs.'

'You deserve it, my father would have done the same.'

'He'd be shocked, though, if he walked in now. Kate Morris with proper sheets, glass of the ninety-six.' She took the champagne he handed her. 'I'm getting a taste. Wouldn't mind living like this.'

'You could have done.' He'd meant to sound light-hearted, but it came out anything but. He closed the curtains, anything other than look at her. 'Christina's been to Oxford for the interview. They should let her know this week. Quite a procedure – she had to stay overnight. They pass you from one tutor to the next; they've even got moral tutors. I can't imagine what a moral tutor has to say . . .' He turned to see her crying. 'Kate . . .'

'How come?' she babbled tearfully. 'Good education, you, good school, and you're stupid.'

'What have I done?'

'Why did you put me in here? Why did you do it, because it's not fair, you don't stop, all these months and you never stop.'

'What?' he asked in genuine bewilderment.

'Looking. You don't stop looking. I walk past and you're looking.'

'I don't, I've got Christina. We just talked this morning. I'm going with her, to Oxford.'

'And I let you. So, what does that make me? Sitting here, in me bedclothes, you all but married, and I *let* you. What sort of a girl does that?'

'You ended it,' he reminded her. '*You* did. I didn't want that, I told you. But you said what you wanted and I did the right thing, for your sake, because that's what you wanted. I found Christina, and she's perfect. She is perfect,' he reiterated as though he'd only just realised it. 'She's perfect for me. And that only makes it worse.' His voice wavered with emotion. 'Because I turn round, and you're there. *Not* looking. Making such a point of not looking.'

'You're engaged.'

'I am. Yes I am.' He walked out, slamming the door behind him, leaving her sitting in bed, still holding the champagne and crying her heart out.

'Mr Scott, you received my invitation.' Marcus left his table as Scott entered the Manhattan with Louisa.

'More of a summons, I thought. I hope this won't take long. I'm a busy man.'

'Miss Harkness,' Louisa greeted Esme. 'A pleasure to see you again.' She looked up at Scott. 'As you can see, there are one or two details I left out of my story.'

'No, they were perfectly evident. As a means of spreading information, you were faster than the Royal Mail, and considerably cheaper. I've reserved us a table, Mr Scott. Louisa, you can leave your belongings in the cloakroom.' Turning her back, she walked to the table, confident that Scott would follow.

Marcus waited for Jim to appear before joining them. The barman was out of uniform. He nodded, and Marcus nodded back, understanding the signal. Disregarding Louisa, who'd been abandoned at the bar, he joined Esme and Scott.

'It's a simple proposition,' Esme explained. 'We'll run the best dozen girls from here. We're hardly denying you a trade: the canals, Piccadilly, the railway station will still be yours.'

'The lower end of the market.'

'You're lucky I'm leaving you with that. Mr Scott,

your girls aren't clean, they aren't kept, they aren't
safe. My intervention's all too late, and all too
necessary.'

'All the same, that's fifty pounds a week taken out
of my pocket.'

'More like twenty pounds. Men always exaggerate
the contents of their pockets.'

'And let's say, let's speculate: what if I'm not willing to cooperate? What then?'

Esme deferred to Marcus. Taking a cigar case from
his pocket, Marcus extracted a cheroot, and lit it.
Puffing smoke in Scott's face, he murmured, 'I'm
sorry, I've got nothing to say. Absolutely nothing.' He
glanced at the bandleader, who switched from a slow
to a jaunty number. 'You see, it's already done, Scott.'

'Meaning what?'

'The Cross and Jameson warehouse, Lower Moseley
Street. You own it?'

'Yes.'

'I'm afraid you'll find it's burnt to the ground – no,
perhaps I should use the present tense: burn*ing*. Now
run along, don't let me keep you. Oh, and thank you
for the drink. If you could pay at the bar . . .'

Scott rose from the table. Pushing his way through
the dancers, he stormed across the room to Louisa.

'Get the coats! I said *coats*! For God's sake, get the
bloody coats, girl.'

'I said no one's to be hurt,' Esme reminded Marcus
as they followed Scott.

'It's uninhabited, I swear. Just property.'

Louisa handed Scott his coat warily, fearing
another outburst. Pushing his hand into the pocket,
he pulled out a few coins and slammed them on the
bar.

'Mr Scott,' Marcus said, eyeing the little man

coldly, 'you brought damage to the Grand Hotel, and that *never* happens. I trust our business is concluded.'

'Miss Harkness, a word in private?' asked Scott.

'It's all right, Marcus.' Esme went to Scott as Marcus moved to the bar.

'Oh yes,' Scott sneered, 'so proud of your independence, and here you are, being led by Marcus Bannerman, and I told you, I *told* you, I could help.'

'Then prove it,' she challenged.

'There's still time. You could pull out, if you knew what's at stake.' He leaned closer: '*I know where your children are.*' He stepped back to Louisa who was waiting at the door. 'Good night.'

'What are you doing here?' Lark asked as Kate crept into the maids' bedroom in the early hours of the morning.

'I felt stupid up there, so I came back where I belong.'

Lynne's voice floated out of the darkness. 'Oi, Morris, we're up at five, shut up.'

Lark turned over and went back to sleep. Kate stared up at the ceiling, knowing there'd be no sleep for her, not tonight.

Stephen was sitting in the living room, drink in hand, thinking about Christina, and about Kate, and about something he hadn't allowed himself to consider for a long time: his future. Hearing footsteps, he looked up expectantly, but Marcus walked straight past the door and into Ruth's bedroom.

Ruth sat up in bed as her husband walked in. It had been a long time since they had shared a room – and a bed. He sat next to her. Lifting his hand, he stroked her hair, then he leaned down and kissed her.

She pulled him closer, invoking a passion that roused her own. He released her for a moment to pull off his jacket. Kicking off his shoes, he climbed on to the bed and eased himself on top of her. A new, yet familiar sound rent the air, the high-pitched wail of a baby crying.

Frustrated, Marcus pulled away. Ruth looked at him and they both laughed, suddenly realising that the sound was the best in the world.

'You're just in time, Miss Harkness. I'm locking up.' Collins dimmed the light in the foyer. 'Good night.'

'I take it you don't approve. You'd rather I stayed in retirement?'

'I'm not one to judge.'

'Oh, but you are.'

'I can't see *why*, that's all. You've a fine life, here in the Grand, why go back?'

'Why not? I sailed past the police, the courts, the judges, not caring what they said. Then passed sentence on myself. Locked myself away, guilty as charged. But they kept calling,' she said bitterly. 'The men kept calling.'

'Then turn them away. Just give me the word, I'll do it, I'll stop them.'

'But they were right. They knew I couldn't change. Retirement! Sitting in that room. Counting the days, drinking more than I used to. Even when I tried to find friends, look what happened to her.'

'You've at least one friend, Miss Harkness.'

'It's good work,' she murmured not listening to what he was trying to tell her. 'It *is*. Protecting those girls, turning them away from my mistakes.'

'Miss Harkness, what's wrong?'

The Grand II: The Roaring Twenties

'You're a decent man, Jacob Collins. Why the hell should you care about me?' She walked up the stairs leaving Collins more concerned than ever.

'Five o'clock, up you get.'

At Mrs Harvey's knock, Lynne tumbled out of bed.

'Come on, Brenda Potter.' She had to shout to make herself heard above the din Mrs Harvey was making to wake the maids in the other rooms. 'We're on the back seats, we are.'

'It's freezing. We'll catch our deaths. Big Lucy said the Midland, they get trips in midsummer, middle of the season.'

'Thank your stars Big Lucy's not coming. Last time she had the back seats, the front wheels were in the air, spinning.'

'You coming, aren't you?' Lark asked Kate.

'Try stopping me.' She grimaced as she left her bed.

'You'll cope without me, Sylvie?' Mr Collins asked as they met in the chaos of the staff kitchen. 'I'll take the second lot, next month.'

'But they've called in your relief, Mr Rose. He's on his way. Cathy Broderick!' she yelled at a maid who was running across the room in her nightdress. 'Put some clothes on.'

'I've never trusted Mr Rose. I'll double up with him. There's one or two things happening upstairs I'd best keep an eye on.'

'Well, it won't be the same without you. Hetty Blake,' she called after another of the maids. 'Am I blind? You're not coming looking like that. What is that? Rouge? Off with it!'

Lynne dropped her breakfast roll on to her plate,

pulled a face and adopted a 'posh' voice. 'Clive said that Mr Bannerman said, "Do enjoy your little trip. Some of us don't get a holiday."'

'That's just like him, you're the image!' Brenda egged her on. 'Go on, do your Mrs Bannerman.'

Lynne stuck her nose in the air. '"Kindly refrain from making a noise in the corridors."'

'Which Mrs Bannerman's that?' Lark asked.

'All of them.'

'Do your Mr Collins,' Brenda nagged.

'"Get back on duty, bonny lad."'

'What did Mrs Harvey say?' Clive asked Bob innocently as they left the table and headed for the crates he'd carried up from the cellar earlier. 'Was it one bottle each or one crate?'

'Got me there.'

'We'll take them all, just in case.'

'Here you go.' Tom joined them. 'Give us one.' Taking a crate, he hauled it past the maids.

'Oi,' Lynne shouted, 'what you doing here?'

'Flying a kite. What's it look like?'

'He's not staff, he's upstairs staff,' Lynne declared disapprovingly. 'He doesn't live in. Standing behind reception all day: "There's your key, sir". Call that work?'

'He's a bit nice, though, him,' Brenda sighed dreamily.

'Oh, she's started. Lark, put the muzzle on her. She'll be frothing next.' Cramming the last of her roll into her mouth, she climbed off the bench. 'Hurry up, you lot.'

'Lark, love, get your things. You need to grab a good seat,' Brenda advised. 'If you sit on the axle, you'll be sick all the way.'

'That's why they give hats at the Midland,' Lynne

said solemnly, 'in case someone's sick on your head.'

Lark paled – Lynne had just given her one more thing to worry about.

'I'm not sure, Kate,' Mrs Harvey wavered indecisively, 'the doctor said to rest.'

'And he said there's nothing wrong with me. Honestly, Mrs Harvey, I'm back to normal, and it will do me good: seaside, fresh air.'

'In the middle of November?'

'I can suffer with the rest of you.'

'Go on, get your things,' Mrs Harvey smiled. She turned to the rest of the staff. 'We're leaving. All aboard, and quiet as you can. There's folk asleep out there. Lark Rothery, since Mr Collins won't be coming, you can sit with me.'

'Ooh!' Brenda, Lynne and half a dozen of the other maids pulled faces at Lark as they ran out of the back door and up the steps.

'Don't worry about them,' Mrs Harvey said encouragingly. 'I'll look after you. You'll enjoy it, Lark, I promise. There's all sorts of things to see on the way. Cows in the field. Ever seen a cow before?'

'Yes, Mrs Harvey.'

'Some folk have never seen a cow,' she mused putting a protective arm around Lark as they went through the door.

Still wearing the clothes he'd worn the day before, Stephen left the living room and took the lift to the first floor. He hadn't slept all night, but he had made a decision, the first he'd made for himself since he'd left the army. Walking swiftly to room nine, he knocked on the door. When he didn't get a reply, he opened it. The room was empty. She'd tidied it before she left, even making the bed up with fresh sheets.

After running full pelt down the stairs, he charged down the back corridor into the staff quarters to find Mr Collins sitting alone, drinking tea.

'Morning, sir. Just got in?'

'No. Have they gone, Jacob?'

'Just listen to that.' The concierge stopped and smiled. 'Peace and quiet. Anything you need, sir?'

'No, I just wanted to . . . see them off.' Stephen retreated back down the corridor.

For once Mr Collins took his time over his breakfast. Then he walked up the stairs, went to the foyer, and nodded warily to the relief hall porter.

'Mr Rose.'

'Mr Collins.'

They stood at opposite ends of the foyer. The door opened and Leonard Scott walked in. Mr Collins took care to reach him first.

'I'm here to see Miss Harkness.'

'Mr Scott, isn't it? I don't think that will be possible.'

Marcus left the office. 'Now, Mr Scott, there's a surprise. Thank you, Collins. Jacob, thank you,' he repeated when the concierge made no attempt to move.

'I don't think there's anything more we have to say,' Marcus said to Scott, as Collins finally walked away.

'I need to see Miss Harkness. It doesn't concern you.'

'She can be the judge of that.' Marcus led the way up the stairs and along the corridor to Esme's room. He knocked the door, waiting for her 'come in', before entering.

'A visitor, Miss Harkness, he seems rather keen.'

The Grand II: The Roaring Twenties

'Like most of your callers, Miss Harkness,' Scott joked badly as he followed Marcus into the room. 'Though I can profit you in other ways.'

'Don't think I'm leaving you alone with the lady.' Marcus leaned back against the closed door. 'Say your piece, whatever it is, then get out.'

'Oh, you've not told him, Esme? Some partnership. I'd ask him to leave. You don't want your lord and master listening to this.'

'He can hear it. I don't care – we're partners and equals.'

'Fine.' He sat down. 'Then you'll both understand me better when you see what I'm offering.'

'Which is what?'

'Salvation, not for you, Mr Bannerman: you're past that. But would you deny it to a lady such as this?'

'Tell me,' Esme demanded, bored by his play-acting.

'Dr Renwick, very good doctor if you paid him enough. Oh, and discreet, too clever to write anything down. But there were always those lads. The lads you'd walk past, the lads mopping the floor, cleaning up the blood. They'd meet up, those lads, sit in the pub and pass on stories, and one of them listened. Little lad called Scott.'

'You've got proof?'

'And it's yours, Esme, if you cancel the partnership. Mr Bannerman, you've a thousand other ways of earning money, you don't need this. You could set her free.'

'It's my decision, not his. You said you know where they are?'

'A boy and a girl, alive in the world. The Harkness children. At twenty-one, you gave birth to a girl, then at thirty-six, I'm told a boy. Dear me . . . what happened that night, Esme? Get a bit drunk? They were passed on for adoption, to agencies, and interested parties. All the while carried by the lads, those little chattering lads. The girl's called Elizabeth, the boy's Richard. What did you call them?'

'I didn't give them names.'

'Plenty of Richards out there, thousands of girls called Elizabeth. But I can give you the surnames. Let me do that. Surnames can be traced, the children can be found.'

'A certain flaw in your stratagem, Mr Scott. Why on earth would I want to find them?'

'What else have you got? You must be so tired of all this.' He waved his hand around the room. 'Just look at yourself. You came up here, far away from all your friends and contacts. Trying to escape. And I'm sorry, Mr Bannerman, you'll just lead her back to the same old ways. Don't do it, Esme.' He rose to his feet. 'Now, you'll need some time to sit and think. This is a lovely room, very nice, if a little lonely. Mr Bannerman, good day.'

Chapter Twenty-Four

Marcus watched Esme carefully as she poured herself a drink.

'It's always the little men, they're always stronger than you think. Mr Scott, the powerful magician, he can produce a family out of thin air.'

'Esme, do as he says,' he urged.

'You see? Such magic! Changing even you.'

'He's right, though. I've got other ways of making money; the girls are just a sideline. I'll manage without.'

'We're a good alliance. Now I've at least six girls I can trust. I suggest you meet them tonight. We can start business with six. I'll keep looking for others . . .'

'You could have both. I could force the information out of him. I've got men . . .'

'*No!*' she broke in vehemently. 'Absolutely not. You've brought enough violence into this, and I won't have it. I won't conduct business on those terms. I *won't*.'

'Then I'll do nothing. I'll let you go.'

'How sentimental! You'll have me in tears.' She held up her glass. 'Join me?' Marcus nodded. 'The fairy tale,' she murmured as she filled another glass. 'Let's dispense with that. A handsome man and a fine young lady, their mother running towards them.

Katherine Hardy

Happy endings. But when the story's done, what happens then? When I tell them what I am?'

'For all you know, they'd love it! Look at me, I'm from a fine God-fearing household, and I've no problem with you.'

'Then you'd like a whore? As your *mother*?'

'Might have livened up Sunday lunch.'

'They could be dead.'

'Then find out!'

Marcus flung the door wide at a knock, expecting Scott. It was Collins.

'Yes?' he demanded in exasperation.

'I just wondered, sir . . . if there's anything you need . . .'

'We're fine, thank you. Leave us alone.'

'Miss Harkness . . .'

She didn't even look up when he called her name.

'It needn't concern you, Jacob,' Marcus said pointedly. 'It's business.' He closed the door on the concierge.

Feeling tired and unaccountably wretched, Collins made his way downstairs. Mr Rose was presiding over the foyer. Slipping off his jacket and loosening his tie, Jacob declared, 'You can have it, it's my day off, and I'm wasting it.'

'I'd go to the pub, if I were you.'

'Who with?' Collins asked acidly as he walked away.

'It's too easy, Esme.' Marcus sat back as they started on their second drink. 'Reducing your family to nothing, making them count for nothing. It's the work of a moment. I've done it. Betrayed my own brother, and drove him out.'

'And you're so sorry?' she asked caustically.

'What if I am? All that came before I had a family of my own. A son. Next to him, the Grand means nothing.'

'The family man? It doesn't suit you.'

'It's a surprise to me. You can't turn Scott down just because I've offered you a partnership. I won't be responsible for that. Find your children. Just to *see* them.'

'I've had this all my life. Men, talking, thinking they know best. I tried so hard, but they still hold the power.'

'I'd help you. I would, I'd help, I've always admired you. We're equals in many ways.'

'You can go now, thank you.'

'Esme, a daughter and a son . . . '

'I said you can go.'

'Just tell them the truth, tell them all about yourself, tell them everything, and let *them* decide.'

'Marcus Bannerman, you're a gambling man. Cards? Poker? Yes, look at you, a fine poker face. Shall we play? It should be night . . .' Summoning a burst of energy, she crossed the room and drew the curtains. 'Cards should be played in the dead of night. The night's drawing in, Marcus, a winter's night. Cards, I've got a set of cards, here, look!'

'It's hardly the time . . .' he began hesitantly, thrown by her strange mood.

'A game. I've no time for reason. A Parliament of men, with their debates. Leave it to chance. We'll play each other.'

'What for?'

'If you win, I'll do as you say.' She pulled a small table between their chairs, setting the bottle next to her glass; she handed him the deck.

'You'd better deal. I'm rather good at cheating.

There's only one stake. Just keep playing until one of us is ready to call. A bastardised version of the game, but that's rather appropriate.'

Marcus shuffled the pack.

Stephen was sitting in the office, still thinking about Kate, when Christina walked into the foyer. He shrank back behind the filing cabinet as she collared Mr Rose.

'I'm here to see Mr Bannerman, Mr Stephen Bannerman.'

'Who shall I say is calling?'

Christina removed her glove and smiled as she showed him her diamond ring. 'His fiancée.'

'Certainly, miss. If you could wait in the Reading Room, I'll find him.'

Stephen made no effort to move as Rose reached for the telephone.

The coach drew up at Morton Sands. Pulling on the handbrake, the driver shut off the engine. Vast expanses of sand dunes and bleak, cold, grey sea stretched as far as the eye could see, grim and uninviting beneath dark November skies.

'Back at one o'clock,' Mrs Harvey shouted down the bus. 'Listen for the church bell! It's only the one chime, so keep an ear out!' She smiled at Lark sitting beside her. 'Now, not so bad is it?'

'It's . . . wonderful!' Lark gasped wide-eyed and open mouthed.

'Morton sands. A dirty old beach in the bitter cold, and the likelihood of rain, but who's to say you're wrong? Go on, you don't want to stay with me.'

'Thanks, Mrs Harvey. Thanks ever so much.' To the housekeeper's embarrassed delight, Lark kissed her on the cheek before running after the others. Racing past Kate to catch up with Brenda and Lynne, she shouted back, 'Isn't it brilliant?'

Clive and the boys wandered slowly in the opposite direction to the maids.

'God, brass-monkey weather,' Clive complained. 'Where are we going?'

'Thought we'd find that café,' Tom suggested. 'Bob says they've got girls serving there.'

'Three of them,' Bob chimed authoritatively.

'Fancy your chances?' Tom asked. 'Everyone's heard of the Grand Hotel, even out here. That should impress them.'

'Don't fancy it,' Clive said, hanging back.

'Clive, one of them's blonde,' Bob persisted.

'Better off blind, if you're having a go.'

'Race you, Bob,' Tom shouted, tearing off across the sands.

Clive looked towards the shoreline. Kate was standing alone at the water's edge. He smiled at her and she smiled back.

'At last, there you are.' Christina left her seat and kissed Stephen as he walked into the Reading Room. 'I've booked lunch, we're going out. The club must have been busy,' she said, noticing his clothes. 'Look at you.'

'Up all night, I'm worn out.'

'Maybe I should cancel. We don't want you falling asleep in the soup.'

'It's been months, working all night, then up in the mornings, every morning, to spend time with you . . .'

'Oh, that's a hardship,' she quipped.

'I haven't slept, not for months. It's like a fog. I've just been walking through the days, walking and walking because it's easier than stopping . . .'

'Then resign,' she cut in impatiently. 'I've told you often enough.'

'I just made it easy. I wanted it to be easy. And you were there, and I needed you. I needed you so much.'

'Of course you did.'

'That's what it was. I *needed* you.'

She shivered, suddenly realising what he was trying to tell her.

'I got in. Oxford. The letter arrived this morning. I thought we could celebrate.'

'You see? You don't need me. I always knew that, and so did you.'

'Actually, no,' she agreed quietly.

'I've been so tired.'

'There's someone else.'

'There isn't.'

'I could start all sorts of rows. I'm entitled to that. You're the one who proposed. You did it.' She bit her lip in an effort to contain her emotion. 'Though I didn't stop you. Still, I could wait. Just wait. But there's no point, if there's someone else.'

'There isn't, really, I swear it. It's me. I'm so tired. I haven't slept for years and years. And I didn't mean . . . it wasn't . . . it was *me*.' A tear fell from his eye. 'I'm so sorry, I'm so useless. Hurting you. It's all I do, hurt them . . . years and years . . . if I could just *sleep*.'

Christina left her seat and reached for her coat. Anger, like bile, was rising in her throat.

'I should go.'

'Don't . . .'

'Plans to make. Next September.' She took a few steps and turned back. 'The Oxford student, the clever one, but she didn't see this. Though it was always coming.' Removing her engagement ring, she laid it on the table in front of him. 'Look after her.'

Stephen waited only as long as it took Christina to leave the hotel. Tearing out of the Reading Room, he ran across the foyer and up the stairs. He burst into the living room and found Ruth sitting there with the baby.

'Where's Marcus?'

'I don't know.'

'The car.' He pulled at the drawer where Marcus kept his keys. 'I need to borrow a car.' Grabbing the bunch, he ran out of the door. He charged back down the stairs, through the foyer and out of the door.

Mr Rose watched him go. When he was certain Stephen wouldn't return, he walked over to the table Christina had been sitting at in the Reading Room. Looking around to make sure no one was watching, he picked up the engagement ring and pocketed it, before returning to the foyer.

Esme discarded one card and picked up another. She considered her hand for a moment, then laid it in front of Marcus. He shuffled his cards together and laid them, face down, in a pile on the table.

'Well done,' he congratulated.

'Could I do it?'

'I'm sure you could do anything.'

'Just surnames. What if I couldn't find them? And if I did, what could I show them? One solitary room.'

'Excuse me, in rather a fine building.'

'But it's enough. We manage, so why change it? It's not as if I'd become their mother, not now. But if I met them, just once, you'd help me?'

'Partners.'

She leaned back, exhausted. 'Then you win.' Rising to her feet, she opened the curtains. Marcus picked up his cards and shuffled them back into the pack, a small smile of triumph on his face.

'Come on! All aboard!' Mrs Harvey shouted at the top of her voice from the platform of the bus. 'It's off to the village for a plated meal, then you can come back and play.'

'Play!' Lynne sneered. 'You, Tom Corbett,' she called, as the boys drew alongside them. 'I saw you chasing that girl. Better-looking donkeys out there.' She shuffled into line with the rest of the staff and climbed on the bus. 'What the flipping heck!' she dug Brenda in the ribs. 'That's not fair, can't they leave us alone?' she griped as Stephen drew up in Marcus's car.

'Stephen Bannerman!' Tom exclaimed in disbelief.

'What's he doing here?' Brenda asked no one in particular.

Lynne looked at Kate, who turned to see Clive staring at her.

'He might have come to give us money,' Brenda suggested hopefully. 'His dad did that, last Christmas.'

'Mr Bannerman, is there something wrong?' Mrs Harvey asked, stopping him from walking on to the bus.

'I'm sorry, I've come to see Kate. I have to see her.'

The entire staff with the exception of Mrs Harvey stared at Kate, who shrank back into her seat, mortified.

'What for?' Mrs Harvey demanded imperiously.

'I've just come to see Kate. Could you let me . . .' He tried to push past her.

'I could not, sir! This is staff, the one day of the year that's staff. We're at no one's beck and call. Could you please go, sir? You're spoiling it.'

Looking over Mrs Harvey's shoulder, Stephen finally spotted Kate. 'Kate!'

'You can find her back at the Grand.'

'Mrs Harvey, let me past, I have to see her. Kate!'

'For what good reason, Mr Bannerman?'

'Because I love her,' he said, simply and devastatingly.

In the massive silence that followed, Kate left her seat. Keeping her head down, she pushed her way to the front of the bus. For a second, Stephen thought she was heading for him, but she walked past and kept going.

'Kate!' He ran after her. 'I'm sorry, just listen to me, please. Just give me a chance . . .'

Mrs Harvey followed them off the bus.

'Shame on you, sir! God in heaven, for *shame*. You're engaged, had you forgotten?'

'But I'm not . . .' Kate finally stopped and looked at him. 'It's over, she's gone. Christina's gone.'

'You leave me *alone*!' Running, Kate raced down to the sea, getting as far away from Stephen as she could.

Marcus escorted Esme down the stairs. Both of them were blinking, finding it strange to discover that it was still daytime. Handing the receptionist a note, Esme asked, 'Could you have this delivered to Mr Scott? Right away. I need to see him.' She watched the receptionist summon a porter and hand the note over, then she walked into the bar. Marcus followed.

'They all talking about me?' Kate asked as Clive joined her at the edge of the sea.

'Forget Blackpool, it's the new great disaster.'

'Where's Stephen?'

'Washed out to sea, drowned.'

Katherine Hardy

'Good. Have to go, won't I? Can't stay at the Grand. What am I going to do, Clive? Two years back, there were jobs on every street corner. There's nothing now.'

'Still be talked about. Legend.'

'What *did* happen at Blackpool?' she asked suddenly.

'I don't know, it happened years back. Ask Lynne. She says one thing, Mr Collins says another. It's just a story. You just wait, ten years time, they'll say, Kate Morris, she ran off with him, both of them naked on the beach.'

'Shut up.' But she couldn't help laughing in spite of her misery.

'Me dad had these stories. He'd been to Canada, worked on the railways. He had a hundred stories, and not all of them funny. Christ, he saw some things. But he *did* them, Kate. They were real; he'd lived them. Doesn't matter how bad it gets, it's just a story when you're old.'

'I can't, Clive.'

'Scared?'

'Yes,' she whispered in a small voice.

'You like him, though?'

'Yes.'

'Well then?'

'What will they say? All the others, and me mam, and me sisters?'

'Find out.'

'What if it doesn't . . .? He's mad, he's . . . It won't last, it can't . . .'

'Then you'll have to leave. Move on. You're doing that anyroad, so what's the difference?'

'I can't.'

'Don't, then. Just sit there, not one mistake, keep

nice and quiet, you and me both.' He smiled. 'Did you see him, though? Climbing on that bus, shouting? Always thought he was a right idiot, but fair do's. I'll never do that.'

'You might though. I could see you running about after some poor girl.'

'He's waiting, Kate. Go on, if they're all talking, sod them. There's some of us want you happy. One mistake is better than having nowt. It is, Kate, I'm telling you, it's better than having nowt.' Taking her arm, he pulled her back from the sea. 'Come on.'

They walked up the beach towards the bus. Most of the staff had gathered outside the door. Stephen was standing further down the beach, on an outcrop of rocks.

'You can stop staring and all,' Clive admonished Lynne, Brenda and Lark.

'She never is!' Lark gasped as Kate left him and headed for Stephen.

'She is though. Wish she'd hurry up, I've had no dinner,' Brenda moaned.

'I had a bloke. Good bloke, my sort of bloke, and I did nothing wrong, and where's he gone? Why does bloody Kate Morris get it all?' Lynne asked, envy making her vicious.

Kate stopped a few yards from Stephen. He looked up at her, not daring to say any more.

'What about me job?'

'I don't know. You could leave. I'd look after you.'

'Not doing that. You like me, so I'm stopping as I am, hard worker, me.'

'All right.'

'Right.'

'Is that it?' He ventured a smile.

'Banged me head. Everything's spinning.'

Stepping towards her, he took her in his arms and kissed her, the way he'd wanted to for a long, long time.

'I don't want any trouble,' Scott asserted as Marcus opened the door of Esme's room to him. 'I'm doing you a favour, remember that.'

'I've underestimated you, Mr Scott,' Marcus replied. 'It's quite a talent of yours, listening. Now that Miss Harkness will have other things to occupy her mind, perhaps we should all think of working together.'

'We could, yes,' Scott replied doubtfully. He handed Esme an envelope. 'If you don't mind my saying, the best of luck, really.'

Taking the envelope, Esme threw it on the fire.

'For God's sake.' Marcus dived towards it, but he was too late: the flames were already licking at the paper.

'Let it burn.' She turned to Scott. 'Stick to the canals, Mr Scott. We'll be watching.'

'Miss Harkness, welcome back.'

'Just wait there.' Marcus reached the door before Scott and blocked it. 'You've still got it, the information?'

'And it's useless.'

'Give it to me.'

'What? Out of the goodness of my heart?'

Marcus slammed him against the wall.

'Marcus, I've warned you, leave him alone,' Esme warned. 'It was a game, that's all. The same old games. I told you, I'm a cheat.'

Marcus released Scott. 'Get out.'

Trying to recover his dignity, Scott went to the

door. 'As a matter of fact, Mr Bannerman, I'm still listening. I hear all sorts of things about all sorts of children.'

'Meaning what?'

'Nothing . . . I wouldn't dare.' Opening the door, he fled the room.

Marcus looked to Esme.

'Now we're equals,' she said briskly. 'We've paid the same price. So, the club, tonight, eight o'clock. I'll have the first six girls ready and waiting. The start of a new enterprise.'

She stared into the flames as Marcus went to the door. There was a thin film of powdery ash coating the top of the unburned coals. It could have been almost anything.

Stephen and Kate wandered slowly back over the sands towards the coach as Mrs Harvey ushered the last of the staff inside. Kate looked indecisively from the coach to the car. Stephen held out his hand.

She glanced at the faces glued to the windows. Brenda and Lark grinning, Lynne openly hostile, and Clive, who winked and gave her a thumbs-up as she went with Stephen. But it was the expression on Mrs Harvey's face that terrified her as they drove away. Cold, damning, like ice. Not even Stephen's smile could thaw the apprehension she felt as they headed back towards the village.

Chapter Twenty-Five

'Thanks very much for everything,' Kate said to Marcus and Ruth. 'That was lovely.' She rose to her feet as the waiters walked into the Bannermans' private living room to clear the table.

'There's no reason the evening should end, Stephen. I have to keep an eye on the club, but you're welcome to join us,' Marcus invited.

'Kate didn't apply for a late-night pass: she's got to be back in her room,' Stephen said swiftly.

'Well, no need to rush. Stay for another coffee. I'm sure Mrs Bannerman can keep you entertained.' Marcus turned to his wife. 'If you wouldn't mind, Ruth?'

'Of course not,' she replied stiffly in a tone that belied her words.

'No, really,' Stephen interposed. 'I'd better walk Kate home. All of five floors. I'll meet you outside, Marcus.'

'Goodnight, sir, ma'am, thanks again.' Kate and Stephen walked out of the door.

' "Mrs Bannerman can keep you entertained"!' Ruth glared at Marcus. 'I could kill you.'

'I thought she acquitted herself rather well.' He smiled broadly at his wife.

*   *   *

The Grand II: The Roaring Twenties

Kate and Stephen ran down the first two flights of stairs. Laughing too much to go on, Kate sat on a step and attempted to get her breath back. Stephen crouched beside her.

'That was a nightmare!' she giggled. 'A bloody nightmare, start to finish! God, he went on and on. I'm sorry, I know he's your uncle, but he just went on and on!'

'Geneva! He talked about the banking laws in Geneva!'

'And me with ten bob saved in the Post Office. I'm never doing that again, ever!'

'You will, though.' He pulled her close. 'I'm so proud of you, I want the whole world to see. We'll have to go to London and visit my parents.'

'Oh God, you'll have to meet mine.'

'Oh God!' He looked at her and they both started laughing again. 'We can, though, we can do it. I always thought this would be such a problem, but it's fine. People don't care these days.'

'Your people might not, but it's different for me. You should hear the talk downstairs. Then you pop your head round the door, and I think: Sod them.'

He bent his head and kissed her, gently at first, but as she responded, with a passion inappropriate to the time and place.

'Excuse me.'

'Sorry, Mr Collins.' Kate jumped up, patting her hair and straightening her skirt, as the concierge appeared on the stairs.

'Kate, you've got five minutes. If you're late back, you'll have to sign the book. It'll be docked off your wages.'

'Sorry, sir, just going . . .'

'Oh, for goodness' sake, I'm not serious.' He

winked. 'I can remember what it's like. Now don't mind me.'

But Stephen still waited until the concierge turned the corner above them, before kissing Kate again.

Ruth lifted the baby out of his cot, cuddling him while Marcus put on his coat.

'He waits until you're gone, then he starts crying.'

'Just like his mother.'

'Thank you,' she snapped sarcastically.

'Mrs Bannerman.' Mr Collins knocked at the open door. 'There's someone to see you. She says she's a friend of yours, from London. She didn't give her name, but said she's a colleague of Dr Curzon.'

'Who's Dr Curzon?' Marcus asked.

'He's the specialist I went to see, when I was expecting Charles.'

'In that case, I'd like to meet her. I'll walk you down.'

He offered Ruth his arm, leaving her no choice but to return the sleeping baby to its cot, and accompany him downstairs.

Marcus frowned at the sight of the shabbily dressed, young woman waiting in the foyer.

'And you complain about Stephen's companions?' he whispered, as Ruth stared, horror-struck, at Edith, who looked even more down-at-heel in the foyer of the Grand, than she had done in the grubby little rooms in London.

'I'll deal with this. You go to the club.'

'Without an introduction?' He tightened his grip on her arm as he led her towards Edith.

'I'm Marcus Bannerman. How do you do?'

'How do you do, sir?' Edith replied awkwardly.

The Grand II: The Roaring Twenties

'Edith West, my husband.' Ruth tried to edge Marcus closer to the door, but he stood his ground.

'So you're to blame for what happened?'

Ruth froze, too terrified to speak.

'I'm sorry?' Edith stammered in bewilderment.

'You're with Dr Curzon?'

'Yes, sir,' she faltered.

'He should be on report for unprofessional behaviour.'

'How do you mean, sir?'

'His way of handling the birth, what do you think?'

'I don't know, sir. What have you been told?'

'Thank you, Marcus. The car's waiting. You should go.'

But Marcus was not to be dissuaded by Ruth, or anyone. 'My wife disappears to London, gives birth without my knowledge, all arranged by this Dr Curzon. The man should be sacked.'

'Good evening, Marcus.' Esme sailed towards them in a crimson, silk evening gown. 'Are we ready?'

'On my way.' He looked at Edith. 'You can tell Curzon he's lucky I'm not taking him to court.'

'Yes, sir . . . Oh, Mr Bannerman, sir.'

Ruth clutched the banister for support as Edith called him back. 'Congratulations.'

Marcus nodded. The second the door closed behind Esme and Marcus, Ruth turned furiously to Edith.

'What the hell are you doing here?'

'I had to come—'

'Not in public, for God's sake.' Ruth strode across the foyer and pressed the handle on the office door. But when the door refused to open she felt herself walking right into it with a bump. 'Mr Collins, it's locked. Why is it locked?'

'It's always locked after ten o'clock, ma'am.'

Katherine Hardy

'Well, open it!' she commanded imperiously.

Collins pulled out his keys. As soon as he'd opened the door, she swept past him, beckoning Edith to follow.

'Now, what do you want?' she asked, closing the door on them.

'I'm sorry, Mrs Bannerman, I couldn't think what else to do. I want to see him, that's all.'

'You can't.'

'He's my son.'

'His name is Charles Bannerman. He's mine. I didn't just buy him: I made him mine. He's absolutely mine. That was the deal. How did you find me?'

'It didn't take a genius. If you want to keep hidden, don't live in a palace.'

'It's money, isn't it?' Ruth enquired coldly, hoping against hope that was all the woman wanted. 'But if I pay you now, what's to stop you coming back, every year, every month?'

'I don't need money.'

'You've spent it, haven't you?'

'Most of it,' Edith confessed. 'If I wasn't in debt, I wouldn't have sold him to you in the first place. And there's the other kids, me sons: they're growing up, they're eating money.'

'And where are they now? You're a wonderful mother, abandoning her children.'

'Me mum's looking after them. I just want to see him, then I'll go back. Charles?' she murmured softly. 'It sounds like a gentleman.'

'You can't see him,' Ruth refused flatly.

'It was all so fast. It was such a panic, and I was looking at him. I looked so hard because I thought: I've got to remember. But I can't. I was so scared. I'm looking and I can't see, Mrs Bannerman. And his eyes, they don't get proper colour in their eyes, not until they're a few days old. That's all I want. His face.'

'His eyes are brown. Anything else?'

'Just once, please,' Edith begged.

'We broke the law, you, me, and Dr Curzon. Take this further, and what do you think Curzon will say? You've seen the world he lives in. For his own sake, he'd have you stopped, and he's no gentleman.'

'Oh, you're a fine lady, in your fine hotel, and here you are, threatening me . . .'

'You came here, to my home. If that's not a threat, what is? Do you want me to call Dr Curzon? Is that what you want?'

'No!'

'One telephone call, that's all it would take.'

'I don't have to hold him,' she pleaded, 'if I could just look.'

'Your children, Edith, two sons, what would happen to them? I'm following the conditions of sale, conditions we all agreed. You can't see him, you can never see him. He's mine. The matter's closed, the contract is at an end. Thank you, Edith. I don't expect to see you again.' Opening the door, she held it until Edith finally walked out into the foyer.

Collins saw Edith out. When he looked back to the office, Ruth was sitting, white-faced, fists clenched, staring into space. He did the kindest thing he could think of. Turning his back, he continued with his duties.

'How did you manage up there?' Lark asked as Kate washed her hands and face at the washstand. 'All them knives and forks, I'd be lost.'

'Oi, I'm the one that lays them out,' Kate reminded her. 'I could do knives and forks blindfold.'

'Did you call him Mr Bannerman?' Brenda asked. 'You never called him Marcus! I'd give anything to call him Marcus to his face.'

'I just called him sir.'

'That's not fair, you're a guest.'

'That man would be happy for his own wife to call him sir, never mind me.'

'Did you have name cards written out, telling you where to sit?'

'No, Lynne, there was only the four of us.'

'Just wondering in case yours had Christina Lloyd-Price crossed out, and Kate Morris scribbled over.'

'Don't be so mean,' Lark reprimanded.

'I'm just saying what everyone's thinking. Last week it's Christina, this week it's you. That's all you are, Kate, this week's girl.'

'You've a nasty turn, you,' Brenda chipped in.

'They always say that about them that tells the truth, Brenda,' said Lynne. 'Now stop your noise. Some of us are working in the morning, not swanning about with management.'

Knowing how vicious Lynne could get in a quarrel, Brenda gave Kate a sympathetic smile and snuggled down in her bed. Kate dried her face and donned her nightdress. But even in bed, she couldn't stop thinking about what Lynne had said. Was that really all she was: 'this week's girl'?

'Next time you invite people to the club, give it some thought first,' Stephen admonished Marcus as he joined him at the bar of the Manhattan.

'I thought Miss Morris would enjoy it.'

'Do you think she'd enjoy seeing that?' Stephen indicated Miss Harkness's table, where she was introducing an elderly man to one of her girls. 'With her opinion of Miss Harkness, she'd better not find out.'

'Stephen.' Marcus raised his eyebrows. 'Lying already?'

'It's not a lie, it's . . . an omission. I run the bar and the ordinary clientele. If you've chosen to make it a den of prostitutes, that's nothing to do with me.'

'But you don't mind the extra profit rolling in?'

'No, I'm just saying could you please be careful? Back at the Grand.'

'Lies, omissions and secrets. A fine way to start a relationship. It's always done me proud.' Grinning at Stephen, Marcus crossed to Esme's table as the couple left. 'Busier than ever. Our estimate of twenty pounds a week looks a little conservative.'

'On the contrary, I'm turning away more than two-thirds of these men. The vital part of my job is protecting the girls. You promised me they'd have rooms.'

'I offered you the rooms upstairs.'

'What are you suggesting? We put up a couple of hammocks? Without rooms, those girls have to disappear to the gentleman's accommodation. Once they're out of my sight, Marcus, they're not safe.'

'You need bedrooms?' His smile broadened. 'I own a hundred.'

'How was it?' Clive asked Kate as she worked her way through a pile of ironing. Lynne and the other maids sniggered behind her back.

'I survived, just about.'

'Kitchen said you had best side of beef. Very posh. We had sausages down here. Made out of bread, with bread mixed in. And on the side a slice of bread.'

'Don't you start, she's bad enough.' Kate gave a backward glance at Lynne.

'Staff announcement,' Mrs Harvey shouted, as she walked into the kitchen with Mr Collins. 'Everyone listening, thank you. Put that bucket down, Susan. Lark' – she frowned at the maid who was biting her nails – 'don't do that. Special news! From the King himself!'

'The papers have just come in from London,' Mr Collins explained. 'There's an announcement from Buckingham Palace. Last night, Princess Mary was engaged to Viscount Lascelles.' A couple of the maids applauded politely. Not to be outdone, three porters wolf-whistled and cheered. 'There's going to be a public fund so that one and all can subscribe to a wedding present. Mrs Harvey will be handling that, if you'd like to chip in.'

'I'll have sixpence off all of you,' she said briskly.

'When's the wedding, sir?'

'Not confirmed as yet, Lark, but it's said they'll get married before the Prince of Wales gets back from India.'

'Bit of a rush – she must be pregnant.'

'Wash your mouth out, Lynne!' Mrs Harvey's face turned purple with rage. 'You'll have extra duties for that.'

'Just in case you were planning a little celebration tonight, I should warn you: half of Manchester's planning the same. The restaurant's flooded with orders; both the Lancaster and York suites have been booked, so it's double duties. All leave's been cancelled.' Mr Collins held up his hands to silence the groans. 'If you want to complain, write to the palace.'

'Normal duties until midday,' Mrs Harvey cautioned. 'I'll be busy interviewing new girls as Janey Birdsall's run off with the milk boy. I'll publish a new rota at twelve o'clock. And oh, yes, Kate, there's one job needs doing straight away. The lavatories, ground floor, I want them scrubbed, top to toe.'

'Right you are, Mrs Harvey, Lark, give us a hand?'

'You stay there Lark Rothery.' The housekeeper glared at Kate. 'Did I mention anyone else?'

'But it's a job for two, that . . .'

'Then you'll have to work twice as fast. I trust you find that suitable employment, or are you above such things now?'

'No, Mrs Harvey,' Kate replied, resigned to her fate.

'Then off you go, quick sharp.'

Mr Collins gave Kate a sympathetic smile as she grabbed a mop and bucket, but it didn't make up for the burst of victorious laughter from Lynne and her cronies.

'Jacob?' Esme waylaid Mr Collins as he returned to the foyer. 'It's been some time since we took morning tea together. I've missed it.'

'We're rather busy, Miss Harkness. It's the royal wedding. Everyone seems to have abandoned the working day.'

'Ah, but you also made some excuse yesterday, and the day before.'

'Well, if you'll pardon my saying, there used to be a certain freedom in visiting your rooms. Nowadays there's every danger of finding Marcus Bannerman in your company since you entered into partnership.'

'It's the same old job, Jacob,' Esme murmured sadly. 'You never disapproved in the past.'

'I think you'll find it's never quite the same, once Mr Bannerman's involved.'

'Then good luck with your celebrations,' she replied acidly, taking offence. 'A splendid young man, Viscount Lascelles, as I recall.'

Katherine Hardy

As Esme headed for the bar, a middle-aged woman dressed in immaculately tailored mourning walked into the hotel, two porters laden with luggage trailing in her wake.

'Mrs Delaney,' Mr Collins beamed, 'welcome back.'

'Mr Collins, you haven't changed.'

'You can rely on that, ma'am. Can I say, on behalf of the Grand, my every sympathy regarding your husband.'

'Thank you. It happened almost twelve months ago now. Mr Bannerman wrote me the kindest letter. I must thank him. Is he here?'

'I'm afraid Mr Bannerman has left. His brother's in charge.'

'Really? Quite a revolution. I trust it was bloodless.'

'Not quite, ma'am. It's the usual room, Mrs Delaney, just as you asked.'

'I wonder if . . . I don't want to impose, but it's rather strange, coming back here on my own. I just thought – and please say no if it's an imposition – could you find time for tea, Mr Collins? Later on?'

He glanced at Esme, who'd joined an elderly man at his table. 'Of course I've time. Anything for you, ma'am.'

'Thank you.' She smiled at the concierge, as the receptionist left the desk and handed her a key.

'If you've not heard by second post Wednesday, then take it as a no, but thank you for coming.' Mrs Harvey glanced at the candidate for the maid's job sitting on the chair she'd set in front of her desk. 'And one word of advice: we don't wear stockings. If you could send in the next one . . .'

Mrs Harvey crossed the girl's name off the list as she walked out of the door.

The Grand II: The Roaring Twenties

'Sit yourself down,' she said automatically, not even bothering to look at the next girl. 'Now,' she said, picking up an application form, 'Charlotte Baines, two years' experience at the Cheltenham, is that right?' She finally raised her head. 'References?'

'My name's Edith West. You can get a reference from Mrs Bannerman, Mrs Ruth Bannerman.'

In the main office, Ruth Bannerman quaked inwardly as she looked first at Mrs Harvey, then at Edith West, who was standing behind her, then back at Mrs Harvey.

'For all I know, she's the best girl in Christendom,' said the housekeeper, addressing Ruth. 'But I've a procedure to follow, and she's not on the list.'

'Mrs Harvey, good.' Marcus breezed in. 'I wanted to see you. Miss West?' He turned to the girl. 'What brings you back?'

'The job, sir. New chambermaid.'

'I see, you're a friend of the entire family,' Mrs Harvey observed caustically. 'If I can ask Mrs Bannerman, where did you meet the girl?'

'London,' Edith answered smoothly. 'Mrs Bannerman used to come down to stay. Private hotel. You wouldn't know it.'

'I'm asking Mrs Bannerman.'

'I don't recall offering you a job.' Ruth stared coldly at Edith.

'Then what did you say, Mrs Bannerman? What exactly did we discuss?'

Cornered, Ruth found herself with no real choice. 'Give her the job.'

'Begging your pardon, ma'am, but it's not that simple . . .'

'Sorry, sir, just got your message,' Kate apologised,

as she ran into the office.

'Kate, good. Right, Mrs Harvey, have you finished?' Marcus waved his hand dismissively towards Edith. 'She's got the job. If she had the initiative to approach my wife first, then so much the better.'

'Sorry to bother you.' Mrs Harvey's voice was brittle with indignation.

'No, stay there. I want a word with you and Kate.'

Mrs Harvey glared at Edith. 'Back downstairs,' she commanded. 'Wait by the office, and don't touch a thing.'

'Excuse me.' Ruth left the office and ran straight up the stairs, away from Edith.

'Tell me, Mrs Harvey?' Marcus smiled. 'How often have I refused the budget for an assistant house-keeper?'

'Three times this year.'

'Here she is.'

'What, me?' Kate stared at him in dismay.

'Starting today.'

'I'm sorry, sir, I didn't ask for this . . .' Kate stammered.

'I've begged an assistant, sir,' said Mrs Harvey, 'begged one, but I've had my eye on a very good woman, ten years service, Cheadle . . .'

'But no experience of the Grand, which can't be said of Kate.'

'Mrs Harvey,' Kate broke in urgently, 'I didn't know anything about it, I promise . . .'

'For God's sake,' Marcus interrupted impatiently. 'I'm doing you both a favour. You need an assistant, and Kate, if you need a late-night pass, you can write it yourself. I'm sure it's quite a shock, seeing my generous side. Now off you go before I change my mind. Thank you, Mrs Harvey.'

Kate looked after the housekeeper as she stormed off. 'Sir,' she pleaded, 'there's no need. I'm happy as I am.'

'Good, then you won't ask for much of a rise. Now, to begin with, you can sort out this nonsense with the restaurant.' Pushing a pile of papers into her hands, he left the office.

'One minute I've come to dinner,' Kate complained to Stephen as he sat in the living room, 'next I'm promoted and made to look an idiot.'

'I didn't ask him, I swear . . .'

'Just like you, though. Buying presents. You did that with Christina. We all saw. She's walking in with a new coat, then a new necklace, but you can't do that for me, can you? I'd look stupid in a new necklace, so you give me a job instead.'

'Hey, come here. What's this got to do with Christina? It wasn't me,' he protested. 'Look at me, Kate. I had nothing to do with it, why would I lie?'

'Honestly, though?' she reiterated, too upset to determine whether he was telling her the truth.

'Honestly. Look, do you want me to tell him?'

'That'll make it worse, you stepping in.'

'Then what do you want?'

'I want it back as it was.'

'Just tell Mrs Harvey. She'll put it right. You can solve it together. Go on, she's always liked you, she'll listen.'

'I knew it.' She smiled despite her misery. 'Stepping out with you. Disaster beginning to end.'

'But worth it?'

'Maybe,' she answered contrarily. He laughed and gave her a kiss. She hugged him, then broke free. 'Right, Mrs Harvey here I come, and God help me.'

Katherine Hardy

* * *

'Mrs Harvey . . .' Kate stood back, dumbfounded as the housekeeper left her office wearing her coat and carrying her bag. Walking straight past Kate, Mrs Harvey marched into the staff kitchen.

'Now,' the housekeeper addressed the startled staff, 'here's the second announcement in one day, and no doubt a far more joyous occasion than the royal wedding. You've all been ignoring me for years, and now management's doing the same. I know when I'm not wanted. So, thank you and goodbye, every single one of you. I wish I could say it's been a pleasure. If you've any questions, address them to the new housekeeper.' She pointed at Kate. 'From assistant to head of the household in one morning. Amazing what a kiss can do.' Turning on her heel, Mrs Harvey strode out of the back door.

'Told you,' Lynne crowed as everyone stared at Kate.

Chapter Twenty-Six

'She'll come back,' Clive reassured Kate as she watched the excitement over Mrs Harvey's sudden departure with increasing dismay.

'If Mr Bannerman finds out, she won't have the chance. We'll have to cover, all of us. It's a mess, Clive: there's all the rotas, and they've ordered three sittings for the restaurants. We haven't got the staff.'

'Call the agency, get extra girls.'

'Who's going to sign for it?'

'Miss Kate Morris,' Clive grinned.

'Stop laughing, you. Where's Mr Collins?'

'Disappeared. I'll try again.' Winking at her, he ran up the stairs that led into the foyer.

'Anything I can do?' Lark asked.

'Any good at using a pen?'

'Yes.'

'Copy that out.' Kate thrust a rota into her hands. 'Thanks, love.'

'I've become bored with tea,' Mrs Delaney confided as she poured two sherries for herself and Mr Collins. 'My husband wouldn't allow alcohol until six o'clock, and then in moderation.'

'He certainly had his standards,' Mr Collins observed politely.

Katherine Hardy

'Oh, Mr Collins, he was a bully, as well you know. Bless him. If I could ask: how long is it since Mrs Collins passed away?'

'Getting on for eight years now. Influenza. She was as strong as an ox, then gone. Took five days.'

'It's like Alfred's with me. A ghost at my shoulder. I thought I could lay him to rest, visiting all the places I went with him. But at my age, Mr Collins, there's nothing to do, other than sip sherry.' She raised her glass to his as she sat down. 'And play bridge.'

'I had the Grand. Once Eileen was gone, well, I just stayed. There was Peter of course. Looking after him took all my time. That's not quite true. The Grand took all my time, still does. Peter became one of the staff. I shouldn't have done that. I should have moved on. Stay in this building too long, you become fixtures and fittings. Bit of a waste.'

'We're not too old, are we?'

'It's *feeling* old, that's the problem.'

'I spent last month in London, Mr Collins. The young girls, you should see them, such a future! I can't help but look at them and . . . It's jealousy, it really is. A sharp little spike of jealousy. Doing whatever they like.'

'Oh, I've read the papers. I think a man in my position is supposed to disapprove. But I say good luck to them.'

'The Grand always was my favourite place. It's rather silly, but I had thought, tonight, given the celebrations . . . well, I've got something planned. A little adventure. Are you on duty tonight?'

'As always.'

'Then you won't mind – no I won't tell you, if you'll be there. Tonight, Mr Collins, I'm stepping out of his shadow. I think I can promise you a surprise.'

The Grand II: The Roaring Twenties

*　*　*

'So what brought you up here?' Lynne asked Edith as they walked along the downstairs corridor towards the storerooms.

'Work, innit? Nothing to be had in the capital, and I've got kids to feed. Me mum's looking after them.'

'How many?'

'Three, all boys.'

'You could at least look busy,' Brenda grumbled as she pushed past with a loaded trolley.

'I'm thinking, and thinking's me work today.' Lynne turned her head to watch Brenda go. 'They don't care. They're falling at Kate's feet – it makes me sick. I loved Mrs Harvey. She's a rare treasure, that woman, and look at her: chucked out with the rubbish. Poor soul.'

'How come this Kate's the favourite?' Edith asked.

'The Bannermans' friend, isn't she?'

'Then she's no friend of mine.'

'Good for you. Stick with me: we'll give her hell.'

Ruth took the hundred pounds she'd drawn from the bank that morning and pushed it into an envelope. Before she was able to return it to her handbag, Tom knocked on the door.

'Sorry, Mrs Bannerman,' he apologised. 'We're that busy . . .'

'I called down twenty minutes ago. There's a new girl, a chambermaid, Edith West. Find her, and send her to me immediately.'

'Yes, ma'am.'

Kate pushed her way through the throng of working girls towards Brenda and handed her four lists.

'We're fine for now, but eight o'clock it goes mad.

That's when we're splitting shifts. That's the staff list.'
She tapped the first one. 'Cross-check them, copy
them twice and pin them up. Ta.'

'Cutlery?' Brenda reminded.

'Oh heck, I forgot.' As Kate dashed off to the butler's
pantry, Lark dropped a plate.

'Lark Rothery, of all the nights . . .' Brenda went to
help her clear up. Lynne waited until Brenda's back
was turned, then swooped on the lists. Taking them to
the larder, she pulled out her pencil and began alter-
ing them.

'Mrs Bannerman said immediately, Edith,' Tom
warned. 'She's waiting upstairs, go on.'

'Why should I?' Edith asserted. 'I'm not at Mrs
Bannerman's beck and call.'

'I think you'll find you are.'

'Tell her anything she wants to say she can say in
public, and see what she says. Make her sweat.'

'You'll not be staying long.'

'That's fine by me, Tom,' Edith shouted after him.

'You tell 'em, Edith.' Lynne slapped her across the
back as she emerged from the larder.

'Everyone, pay attention,' Mr Collins bellowed as
he walked into the kitchen with half a dozen girls in
waitress uniform. 'The agency staff are here. Sally,
Lynne, Molly Harris, show them what's what. And
keep the noise down – it's like a zoo in here.'

'Minnie Hobson,' Lynne called to one of the girls as
Mr Collins went into the housekeeper's office. 'Look
at you, over here, come on.'

'Blimey, Lynne, it's a madhouse. Bloody royals. I'd
chuck 'em in the tower. Go on, where's the silhouette?'

'Sacked!'

'Never!'

'Telling you!'

'Well, sod the royals. That's reason to celebrate.'

'Guess who sacked her.'

'Bannerman?'

'Kate Morris,' said Lynne.

'Never in this world.'

'Pushed her out, took her job, all because she's canoodling the Bannerman boy. Thinks she's queen bloody bee, all four foot six of her.'

'Well, I'm sitting down, I am. That's a shock. Never trust a redhead. Me sister always said that, and she's dead.'

'It's not fair, and it's not right and it's not Christian. She needs scuppering, that girl. You with me?'

'Show me what to do!'

'Just follow the list,' Mr Collins advised Kate calmly. 'They won't notice a thing up there.'

'I can't, though, Mr Collins, me head's in bits. There's Mrs Harvey, saying she's taught us the lot. She hasn't. She's kept half of this quiet.'

'Well, I've got to admire that. Wise move, making yourself indispensable. Any trouble, just call for me.'

'Thanks, sir.'

He went to the door. 'In times of crisis, Mrs Harvey tends to call me Jacob.'

'I'm not Mrs Harvey, sir.' The smile died on her lips as yet another crash echoed through from the kitchen.

'If you could wait at the bar, sir, ma'am, we'll call you through as soon as your table is ready.' The smile on Mr Collins's face grew more fixed as the door opened and another dozen people flooded into the crowded foyer. 'I'm sorry about the car, Mr Curtis. It will be here in another fifteen minutes.' Seeing Clive hovering at his elbow, he murmured, 'Can't it wait?'

'Thing is, sir' – Clive glanced sideways at Marcus, who was standing in the doorway of his office, surveying his empire – 'if Bannerman finds out Mrs Harvey's done a bunk, he'll sack her.'

'I know. I'd go round to see her, but look at the place. Up to me eyeballs.' He greeted a young lady. 'Miss Adams, your party's waiting at the bar. Thank you.'

'I could go,' Clive suggested.

'Oh, just the night to take an hour off.'

'Stan could run the bar. He's doing it now. He knows it all, does Stan. You don't want to see her out of a job.'

'Quick as you can,' the concierge agreed decisively. 'Thanks.'

'Evening, sir, ma'am.' Mr Collins bowed to the Mayor and his wife. 'Oh, indeed, sir, wonderful news. What is it now, Tom?' Collins asked, responding to frantic signals from the reception desk.

'Mr Bannerman just gave me this, sir. Rooms one to five, booked out for the next month.'

'What about it?'

'Look at the names, Broad, Woodcock, Browell, Barns, Murphy. That's the Manchester City forward line.'

'More a United man myself. Why would Manchester players be staying in a Manchester hotel?'

'Exactly, sir. Bit odd, isn't it?'

'It's got Mr Bannerman's signature, so it must be confirmed. For God's sake, Tom, it's hardly the night to quibble. Just set the rooms aside, and warn Kate: they'll need the mattresses turned. Mr Lonsdale,' he said, nodding to one of the hotel's regular diners, 'a pleasure to see you again. I'm afraid there's a slight delay . . .'

'Who wants the chairs?' Bob shouted to Kate across the staff kitchen.

'Lancaster,' she called back, not noticing Edith sidling into the corridor that led to the service staircase.

'I've done rooms one to five. What you want me doing next?' Lark asked.

'It's on the list. Brenda, what are you wearing?'

'Me clothes.'

'You should be in waitress uniform, because you're Potter. Surnames after M, waitress until nine o'clock.'

'Not on the list.'

'Read it again,' Kate bit back, as five other staff tried to claim her attention.

'Said so.' Brenda nodded her head as she checked the list. 'I'm ten till midnight.'

'Never mind what's written down,' Lark advised one of the agency staff, as she carried a heavy tray of glasses into the kitchen. 'Just ask Kate. She knows what's going on.'

'Oh, whoops-a-daisy.' Minnie said, deliberately barging into her and sending the tray and its contents flying. 'You clean that up, small fry.'

Incensed, Lark fell to her knees and started piling the pieces of broken glass on to the tray.

'Kate?' Brenda charged down the stairs. 'They've started that meal in the Lancaster, and there's no one on silver service.'

'Why not?'

'How should I know?'

'There's nobody wants these bloody chairs.' Bob hauled them out of the service lift. 'I've tried them all.'

'Right, let me look.' Kate pushed her way through to the office. 'Just wait there, Bob, don't move.'

Closing the door on the chaos and noise, she rummaged through the piles of papers on the desk.

'Just off to the Manhattan,' Stephen said as he stuck his head around the door. 'Everything all right?'

'No.'

'Anything I can do?'

'Actually, you can do me a great big favour.'

'What?'

'Get out.'

He laughed and kissed her cheek. 'Good luck.'

'I need it.'

Lynne was in the corridor weighed down by an enormous tray of wine-filled glasses. As Stephen approached her, she lurched forward, almost colliding with him, slopping some of the wine out of the glasses on to the tray.

'Mind yourself! Nearly had that down your nice clean suit, sir.'

Suspecting that she had engineered the incident, Stephen turned away in embarrassment, only to bump into Minnie.

'Ooh, mind yourself!' Minnie cried as the wine splashed out of her glasses. 'Nearly had that down your nice clean suit, sir.'

Only too glad to get away, he raced up the stairs, taking them two at a time.

'Hope you don't mind, Mrs Harvey.' Clive looked around as she showed him into her front parlour. The heavy, Victorian, mahogany furniture and Rexine-covered suite gleamed, immaculately clean, cold and totally cheerless.

'Just passing, were you?'

'Yes,' he lied.

'Long way to come, just passing. You could have

given warning. I'm not one for visitors.'

'Well, I just thought I'd pop in . . . you know . . .'

'I know why you've come. And it won't do any good, Clive. I've made up my mind. Still, it's quite a walk. I'd be no sort of hostess if I didn't offer a cup of tea. I'll put the kettle on.'

As Mrs Harvey hadn't invited him to sit down, Clive stood in the centre of the room for a few moments. Seeing a photograph frame lying flat on the mantelpiece, he picked it up. It was empty. He replaced it quickly, feeling as though he were prying into forbidden territory.

Wishing Mr Collins would return from wherever he was hiding, Tom did his best to fill in as hall porter.

'Mr Berridge, if you could move to the restaurant, the table's ready. Thank you, sir. Sorry about the delay . . .'

'Oi.'

He turned to see Lynne behind him, in chambermaid's uniform.

'Wrong uniform, Lynne, you're not allowed in here wearing that.'

'She's falling apart down there. We're twenty minutes behind. I've had grown men weeping on me shoulder.'

'What am I supposed to do about it?'

'Tell Mr Collins. He should see it . . . I'll tell him meself. Where's he gone?'

'Wish I knew! The Rotary Club's just walked in, and he's gone and disappeared.'

'Mr Collins?' Mrs Delaney stood in front of the cheval mirror in her room. 'I want your honest opinion. Tell me the truth: do I look ridiculous?'

'Not at all, ma'am,' he replied sincerely.

She glanced back in the mirror again. 'I do,' she contradicted. 'I'll just stay here. I'll have a meal in my room. I wouldn't want to embarrass you.'

'Mrs Delaney, it would be my pleasure to escort you to the foyer, on this very special evening.' He extended his arm. She hesitated. He smiled and she allowed him to lead her out of the room.

'Look, the soup's getting cold and the salad's getting hot,' Brenda griped to Tom. 'Who's in the next sitting?'

'Stop asking me. Kate's supposed to be in charge. Good evening, sir,' he greeted a guest, 'if you'd like to make your way to the bar, you can study the menu there. Thank you.'

'Whatever you do, don't let Mr Collins downstairs. Where is he?' She looked around the foyer.

'Oh, good God above!' Tom gasped, staring at the stairs.

'I never did!' Brenda's mouth fell open as Mr Collins escorted Mrs Delaney down the stairs. 'She's got bleeding trousers on.'

Drawing confidence from Mr Collins's composure, Mrs Delaney walked on, but she couldn't help noticing the reaction in the foyer.

'Mr Collins, they're looking,' she murmured, hearing a couple of sniggers.

'Surely that's the point, ma'am.'

'I'd feel a bit more confident if I was twenty years old.'

'Older and wiser, Mrs Delaney. Like the best of us.'

Mrs Delaney waved to a group of middle-aged women who were staring at her. 'My friends, Mr Collins.'

The Grand II: The Roaring Twenties

The concierge bowed and stepped back as she joined her party. To his delight, they burst into applause as Mrs Delaney met them.

The silence closed in around Mrs Harvey and Clive as they sat across from one another in the freezing cold, formal room listening to the inexorable tick of the grandmother clock. Feeling the need to do something to ease the strain between them, Clive pulled out his cigarettes.

'You don't mind?'

'Of course. I'll get an ashtray.' Leaving her chair, Mrs Harvey looked around but she couldn't see one.

'It doesn't matter.'

She handed him a saucer from the Victorian dresser that dominated the room. 'Saucer, just this once.'

He patted his pockets fruitlessly. 'Matches . . . I must have left them on the bar.'

'I've got some.' She hurried out of the room. Minutes ticked past before she reappeared. 'There.' She handed Clive a box.

'More fuss than it's worth.' He finally lit his cigarette. 'I thought Mr Harvey was a smoker.'

'He is.'

'He's not back yet?'

'Working late.'

'What, late shift at Cranston's?' he asked in surprise.

'That's right,' she said evasively.

'I didn't think haberdashers did late shifts.'

'Well, now, Clive,' Mrs Harvey said as she began gathering the cups together, practically forcing him to leave. 'Much as I'd like to stop and talk, I've never been a night owl. My bed's calling. It was very kind of you to call round. Next time a bit of notice wouldn't go amiss . . .'

'Mrs Harvey, it's about Kate,' he began, deciding to take the bull by the horns.

'Never mind that. Off you go. They'll be screaming for you at the bar and my pillows are ready and waiting.'

'It's not just her, though. Past few weeks, you've been a bit . . . I dunno . . .' Embarrassed at the thought of talking to Mrs Harvey about personal matters, he fell silent.

'I'm perfectly well, thank you,' she interrupted sternly.

'Well, then. I don't know when I'll see you again.'

'You'll see me. Tomorrow morning, first thing, on duty, as ever.'

'Great!' He smiled, pleased with his success. 'Give my regards to Mr Harvey.'

'Off you go, quick sharp, see yourself out. I don't want the night air giving me a chill.'

'Good night.' Clive glanced back as he closed the door. Mrs Harvey was sitting like a statue in the comfortless room, listening to the endless tick of the clock.

'I'll stay with him.'

'You can't keep locking yourself away like a Spanish wife, Ruth,' Marcus argued forcefully, lowering his voice for the sake of the sleeping child. 'The whole town's celebrating. People expect to see you at my side. Half an hour – what difference can it make? He's fast asleep.' Taking Ruth's hand, he led her out of the nursery, closed the door behind them, and guided her to the lift.

At the opposite end of the corridor, Edith stepped out of the shadows and trod carefully towards the nursery. After the chaos below stairs, it was quiet in the Bannermans' living quarters – too quiet. She found herself starting at every creaking board and rattling windowpane.

Turning the knob on the nursery door, she slipped into the room. It smelled expensive. Of baby powder, and special baby bath preparations, things she had seen and smelled in shops, but never been able to afford. She crept to the cot. He was lying there, his eyes closed. She reached down and lifted him to her breast.

He snuggled close, seeking warmth, and she pulled a blanket from the cot and wrapped it around both of them, before stroking his face, his hair, his minute fingers, revelling in the feel of his soft, delicate baby skin. His eyes opened, he looked at her. Unbuttoning her blouse, she lifted him to her breast, smiling, as she began to feed him for the first time.

Champagne in hand, Ruth stood among the guests, smiling, nodding to friends and acquaintances, but no one lingered at her side more than the few moments it took them to realise that she hadn't listened to a word they'd said to her. So she continued to stand and smile, alone, not really part of the festivities, watching the waitresses' every move, waiting for first one, then another, to turn her head, but none of them was Edith.

'Collins?' Marcus called the concierge over to his party. Drawing him aside, he nodded towards Mrs Delaney. 'Have a word with her. She looks ridiculous.'

'No, sir, I don't think she does.'

'Perhaps if she had youth on her side . . .' Marcus crossed the room, and took the lady's arm. 'Mrs

Delaney, enjoying yourself?'

'Very much.'

'If I could just have a word. About the dress code.'

'It's all the fashion in London,' she faltered, her confidence shattered.

'This is Manchester. It's for your own sake, Mrs Delaney. People are laughing,' he glared at one group who were openly tittering.

'I'm sorry . . .' She rushed out of the room. Furious with Marcus, Mr Collins followed.

'I made a fool of myself,' she muttered tearfully, as he caught up with her in the lift.

He nodded to the lift boy to close the doors. 'Mrs Delaney, stay as you are. It's not over yet.'

Kate shoved a handful of cutlery at Lark.

'Give them a polish,' she said frantically, darting towards the kitchens. Lark laid the cutlery on the table and pulled up a chair. Before she could sit down, Minnie whipped the chair out from under her, and she bumped unexpectedly and extremely painfully to the floor.

'Look at her,' Minnie smirked. 'She's a dizzy piece. Can't sit down straight!'

Lynne burst out laughing as Lark climbed stiffly to her feet.

'See, that's the kitchen list.' Brenda tore it from the noticeboard and showed it to Kate. 'It's completely wrong.'

'I didn't write that . . .' Kate looked around the room, seeing Lynne and Minnie laughing in the corner, Lark crying at the table as she valiantly began to polish the cutlery, and suddenly she understood exactly what had been going on.

'Oi, little Katey, I'm standing idle, I am,' Lynne

shouted.

'They've moved out the Lancaster,' Brenda warned. 'Tom said it needs the once over.'

'Kitchen says they're two girls down.'

'Bannerman's furious,' Bob informed Kate as he dived into the cellar. 'He was shouting.'

'What you gonna do?' Lynne mocked. 'Two girls down . . .'

'I should be in Lancaster, but they want me back in York . . .'

'It's a mess, the whole bloody thing,' Minnie sang out derisively.

'Right!' Kate grabbed a chair and climbed on it. 'The lot of you, shut up. I said shut up,' she screamed. 'No one's talking, just me. Stand still a minute, all of you, hush a bit.' Desperate, she turned to Bob. 'Bob?'

'*Shut up!*' he roared at the top of his voice.

'Orders from the housekeeper. This is the list.' She held up her original list. 'One list in my writing, don't read any other.'

'That's because the rest are wrong,' Lynne said knowingly.

'Lynne Milligan, you're off duty. I'm putting you on report. Get to bed.'

'Why?'

Kate brandished the second list. 'Because that's your handwriting. Are you leaving, or do you want me to call Mr Collins? And you, Minnie Hobson, get out of this hotel. You're not getting paid a penny.'

'I'm owed two shillings, me—'

'Out that door, lady, right this minute, or I'm telling the agency you're not fit for duty. Both of you, out!'

'That's you, that is, Lynne.' Minnie punched her as she went to the back door.

Lynne stared at Kate for a moment. She looked to

the rest of the staff, then headed down the corridor that led to the bedrooms.

'The rest of you, we'll get this done a lot quicker if you stop the chat and buckle down. One list.' She waved it in front of them. 'My list. Now get to work. Lark?' The girl looked up, terrified by this new, authoritative Kate. 'Keep doing that, good girl.'

Lark beamed as Kate stepped down.

'Mrs Harvey always says "quick sharp".' Brenda broke the silence.

Kate smiled. 'Quick sharp.'

The room burst into life as everyone moved back to work. Two of the girls began clapping, while a few of the boys cheered. Kate grinned as she went into the office. She *could* do it. It wasn't that hard after all.

Chapter Twenty-Seven

Finally free of Marcus, Ruth ran frantically along the corridor of the top floor. She opened the door of the nursery, and closed her eyes, terrified of what she might find. Then she heard the baby gurgling.

Charles lay on his back in the cot, his tiny arms waving in the air. He looked plump, happy and contented. Ruth leaned back weakly against the door, composing herself, before going to him. Picking him up, she cradled him close to her, wishing – and hoping – that she could hold on to him for ever.

'Miss Harkness?' Mr Collins smiled in relief as she opened her bedroom door to him. 'Excellent. I thought I might have missed you.'

'Everyone's out to dinner, their wives at their side. There's precious little business for my kind.'

'I've an apology to make. I'm sorry, I've been . . . Esme . . . I'm set in my ways, it takes me a while to catch up with the world. Except tonight. I've discovered that I'm more advanced than I thought.'

'What's happened?' she asked, intrigued by his smile.

'If you don't mind, you can do me a very great favour.'

* * *

Katherine Hardy

'Mr Collins.' Tom pounced on him as soon as he left the lift. 'Where have you been? There's not a taxicab to be found . . .'

'Not now, Tom.' Walking past the porter, he went to Marcus.

'Mr Bannerman,' he said, indicating the stairs. 'Regarding the dress code, I trust you have no objection.'

Marcus turned to see Esme Harkness and Mrs Delaney walking down arm in arm, both wearing trousers. Mrs Delaney's outfit had been lifted by the addition of a crimson silk scarf, expertly tied in the French fashion. And Esme looked like a fashion plate – as always. One of Esme's many male acquaintances applauded the ladies as they passed. Esme smiled graciously at him, as she took Mrs Delaney across the room to Marcus.

'Marcus, my companion, Mrs Delaney. It was all her idea. She's an inspiration. Marcus and I are in business together,' she explained. 'It's a fierce debate, in our relationship, as to who wears the trousers. I think I've answered that tonight, thanks to you.'

'Ladies.' Marcus nodded, a gracious loser

'If I could ask, Miss Harkness?' Mrs Delaney enquired as they walked away. 'I'm rather amazed you could find the necessary clothing at such short notice.'

'I've had these trousers for years. They're part of my headmaster's outfit. A long story,' she replied to Mrs Delaney's bewildered look.

'Thomas, you saw the bedlam last night,' Mr Collins complained as the porter knocked at his door while he was reading the paper and enjoying his mid-morning cup of tea. 'Can't I have an hour with the morning paper?'

'Sorry, sir, it's those bookings: the Manchester City forward line.'

'What about them?'

'Well, the Mr Murphy turned up, but he's not playing for City. Must have been seventy at least, coughing his lungs up.'

'Is there a point to this?' the concierge asked wearily.

'Right, so, half past one, another Mr Murphy turns up, and I said, "Mr Murphy's already booked in," and he says, "Oh, I must be the other one, Mr Barns." So, I gave him Mr Barns's room. It's not their real names, sir, but they all know Mr Bannerman.'

'Must be a corporate booking, or something. Thank you, Tom, good lad. I'll look into it. Later,' he added as Tom left and he returned to his paper.

'And we did it,' Kate announced triumphantly to Stephen, who was breakfasting in the Bannerman living room in his dressing gown. 'We caught up. Third sitting was bang on time, and the Rotary Club left five pounds in tips.'

'I didn't get in till three. I looked in downstairs and everything was spotless, like it never happened, not a cup out of place.'

'Oh, I made sure of that. They were all in bed, no talking, and lights out.'

'Remind me never to get on the wrong side of you.'

'Remind you? I'll order you,' she teased.

'Excuse me,' Clive said from the door.

'Clive, come in,' said Stephen.

'Kate, you know what a nightmare it was, Mrs Harvey walking out?'

'Yes.'

Clive smiled. 'It's nothing compared to the

nightmare now she's back.'

'Right, Kate.' Mrs Harvey picked up a pile of papers
from her desk and began to sort them. 'This is a dream
come true. My own assistant. I want the receipts done
by midday.' She piled a bundle of small tags into
Kate's hands. 'Double-check them, or you'll have the
wrath of Mr Bannerman. That's the grocer's, the fish-
monger's, the linen,' she explained, sorting them in
order. 'We need to restock with carbolic, microlene,
boracic and snowfire.' She passed the stock list on to
her. 'And we're nine shillings out on the Marks and
Spencer's Penny Bazaar account. Sort that out, Kate,
there's a good girl. Me? I'm having a cup of tea.'

'I can do the orders,' Kate said as she followed the
housekeeper into the staff kitchen. 'But the thing is,
I'm going out tonight. It's in the book. I wrote it down
two days back.'

'With Stephen Bannerman?'

'Yes.'

'Then thank the Lord he's related to management.
He'll understand you're busy.' She looked at the girls.
'How are we all? Did we cope last night? Kate, any
girls on report?'

Kate eyed Lynne before replying. 'No, Mrs Harvey.'

'Then you must have had your eyes shut. Work to
do. Off you go. Use my desk. Make yourself at home.
Lynne?' She sat next to her at the table. 'Is that tea
dead or steeping?'

'Just brewed up, Mrs Harvey. Don't you move.'

'Not often we get the chance for a chat. It's a godsend, this. Now, last night, tell me the worst.'

'Disaster, Mrs Harvey. Fell apart without you.
They'll look back on it as the Grand Hotel catastrophe.'

Mrs Harvey glanced across the room as Brenda

slammed down the bucket in which she was rinsing floorcloths.

'Do you know?' she took the tea Lynne handed her. 'I think I'll have a sugar with that.'

Esme kissed Mrs Delaney on the cheek after she'd checked out of the hotel.

'Don't forget: next time you come, give me time to prepare. I've a couple of outfits that would get us tarred and feathered and run out of town.'

'Miss Harkness! If you're not the cheekiest woman I've ever known.'

'I'll take that as a compliment. Goodbye. If you'll excuse me, I'm meeting a friend.' Esme left them for a woman who was waiting in the Reading Room.

'And thank you ever so much, Mr Collins.' Mrs Delaney shook his hand. 'I'll come back soon, I promise.' She watched as Esme and her companion sat at a table. 'If I might ask, how long have you known Miss Harkness?'

'Almost two years, ma'am, why do you ask?'

'You're very good friends.'

'I like to think so.'

'*Very* good friends?'

'I think you might have misread the situation,' he muttered coyly.

'It's been eight years since I saw that look in your eye.'

'Thank you, Mrs Delaney, that's hardly possible,' he replied, flustered by the implication.

'A new age, Mr Collins. Anything can happen, anything at all.'

'Mr Collins?' Tom called from reception as the concierge closed the door on Mrs Delaney. 'Did you have a word about rooms one to five? Because we've just opened the book for December, and it's the same: rooms one to five booked out solid.'

Collins leaned on the desk and watched Esme in the Reading Room. 'Tom, stop your fussing,' he ordered, too busy gathering bricks for one very small castle in the air to concern himself with football teams.

Ruth ventured warily down the stone steps that led into the basement. It was the first time she had been below stairs since she had moved into the Grand, and she felt as though she were entering alien territory. She looked into the staff kitchen to see a couple of maids hard at work, and Mrs Harvey sitting at the table with a cup of tea in front of her.

'Mrs Bannerman.' The housekeeper jumped to her feet. 'And here's me first break of the day. Lark, put that down,' she ordered as the girl picked up the tin of biscuits she'd asked her to open. 'Can I help you, ma'am?'

'I need to cancel the car for this afternoon. I won't be going out.'

'Surely that's a job for reception, ma'am.'

'They were busy.' Ruth glanced sideways at Edith. 'So I'll be home for the rest of the day, though my husband is going out. I'll be on my own, in case anyone needs me.'

'I see,' Mrs Harvey answered, confused by Ruth's sudden confidence.

'Thank you.' Turning, Ruth retreated upstairs.

'If she's acting funny, Mrs H, it's indigestion. The Bannermans were second sitting last night,' Lynne informed her solemnly. 'They didn't get their soup until midnight.'

'Can't say I'm surprised.'

'I said, "They're starving up there."' Engrossed in

the story Lynne was weaving, neither she nor the housekeeper saw Edith leave. 'Kate, though, she's with Stephen, all lovey-dovey. Told me to push off.'

'She's young. She knows no better.'

'I said to her, I said, "Mr Collins is run ragged." She said stuff him . . .'

'She did not!' Throwing down the floorcloth she'd wrung out, Brenda stormed towards her.

'Oi, keep your nose out, Brenda Potter,' Lynne threatened.

'I will not. My nose is in. Right in, because I was there. Kate did a marvellous job. I'm glad you're back, Mrs Harvey, but she did, and she did it for you. But this one, *this* one' – she dug her finger into Lynne's chest – 'she was a disgrace, she was on report!'

'You! You're a flipping, bloody, nasty, little, bloody . . . traitor!' Lynne spat savagely.

'They always say that, about them that tells the truth,' Brenda retorted, throwing Lynne's own phrase back at her.

'I thought you were me friend.'

'I used to be.'

Close to tears, Lynne ran out of the room. Brenda followed. Totally unperturbed, the housekeeper turned to Lark.

'So, tell me, Lark: how is your mother?'

'You can shove off,' Lynne ordered as Brenda joined her in their bedroom.

'Go on then, shove me.'

'Will, an' all.'

'Put it this way. You've never been nice, that's why I like you. You've had all the nerve to say things I never would. But Kate, though, she's done no harm. She's head over heels, that's all. Lucky beggar.'

Lynne plunged her hand into her apron pocket. 'Got to wear these.' She slipped on a pair of cheap spectacles. 'Right little beauty, aren't I? I couldn't afford proper ones. Had to go to Woolworth's to pick up a pair of Ready Readers.'

'Can't you manage without?'

'I'm all fingers and thumbs.' She picked up a photograph of her parents and pulled out a second picture, tucked behind it. 'I can't see him.'

'Fred Willets!'

'Only bloke that ever liked me, and he couldn't bugger off fast enough. And I did nothing wrong. I was nice to him and all sorts, but off he went. Kate Morris, she only has to blink . . .'

'That's not her fault, is it? She's born lucky. Go on, leave her be.'

'Who's going to like me, wearing these?'

'Perfect eyesight, me. Still got no one.'

'Have to make do, won't we, with each other?' Lynne said acidly.

'If we must.' Brenda took Lynne's hand as she sat beside her.

Edith stole to the door of the nursery. She opened it to see Ruth cradling the baby. Ruth stared at her for a moment. Recognising the pain in Edith's eyes, she was beset by an uncharacteristic pang of conscience.

'Once,' she said, holding the baby out. 'Just once,' she warned as Edith took him.

'I came up here last night. I didn't take him, did I? It's all I want, Mrs Bannerman.' She gazed hungrily at the bundle in her arms. 'His face, that's all.'

'I suppose you'll be wanting an office key,' Mrs Harvey said as Kate walked into the housekeeper's office with a ledger. 'It was ten years before I had one. What is it now?' she asked, as Kate closed the door behind her. 'Bit beyond you, is it?'

'To be honest, I'm good at sums.'

'Oh, another little Einstein.'

'Me dad taught me daily accounts. It only took an hour, so I thought I'd help out. I looked at the weekly.'

'That wasn't part of your instructions,' Mrs Harvey broke in quickly.

'Mrs Harvey, what's the Cranston account?' Kate hated having to ask.

'We've all sorts of accounts, we've a hundred accounts. How am I supposed to know every account?' she bit back crossly.

'You're the housekeeper. There's five shillings a week going out to Cranston, with your signature, and I've checked. There is no Cranston account, but the money goes out, cash, five shillings a week, under your name.'

'What are you saying?' The housekeeper couldn't look Kate in the eye.

'I'm asking.'

'Are you calling me a liar? By all the saints! Called a thief in my own household. You're a snake in the grass, nothing but a poisonous snake . . .'

'I've not told Mr Bannerman, have I?'

'It's surplus cash.' Mrs Harvey struggled to concoct an explanation. 'It's in constant rotation. All comes back in the end.'

'Where from? Surplus to what? Where's it come back from?'

'Then it's a mistake . . .'

'You can't take money.'

'I've done no such thing.'

'I can't think why. Just tell me why. The Grand pays

tuppence, I know that, but you've got Mr Harvey: he brings in a regular wage. You can't be wanting.'

'Then imagine, Kate. Just speculate, for a moment. If, say, that regular wage had gone. If, say, the wage earner had gone. If he'd wandered off to someone else. If then, perhaps, a lady of certain means found herself . . . without. And if that woman worked like a dog her entire life, wouldn't she deserve it? A few shillings? To pay for the roof above her head, because her husband won't send her a farthing?'

'Why didn't you say?'

'I've said nothing, I'm saying *if*.'

'That woman, Mr Bannerman would sack her. He'd call the police – no *if* about it.'

'If she was reported.' Mrs Harvey's voice was small, desperate.

'I'm telling no one. They don't close the books till April, so there's five months to get the money back. Plenty of time. Oh, Mrs Harvey, you should have said.'

'Yes.'

'I'll not say a word, not to Stephen or anyone, because me dad just taught me sums. You taught me everything else, and I've never said thanks.'

'If that woman had no assistant, she'd have carried on. She'd have been caught. If she had any sense . . . she'd be so grateful.'

'There you are!' Stephen pounced on Kate as she left the office. 'Tamed the dragon, yet?'

'Come here.' She hugged him tight.

'Hey! In public!' he joked, loving every minute of it.

'Don't you run off, don't you ever.'

'Damn,' he teased, 'I've just packed me bags.'

* * *

Edith persisted in holding on to Charles, knowing Ruth was impatient to see her gone.

'I could, Mrs Bannerman,' she pleaded. 'You've employed a wet nurse, I could do it. He'd still be yours. I'd just see him, that's all.'

'You've got two children back in London. What about them?'

'We could find rooms in Manchester. You could pay. I'm not asking for money. But you could, though.'

Ruth opened her purse and took out the money she'd withdrawn from the bank. She held out the envelope to Edith.

'Of course I'll pay,' she assured her. 'I owe you that. A hundred pounds, and then, Edith, then, twenty pounds a month. The first of every month, twenty pounds to your London address. For your sons, if you promise never to come back.'

'That's not fair.'

'Is it fair on them to turn me down? Feed them and clothe them and keep them safe and I'll keep him.' She reached out and touched Charles's hand. 'Because he is mine. I bought him, yes. I thought I'd hate him, but I can love him. I do love him.' She pushed the money into Edith's hand. 'As you must love your own. Help them.'

'I could come and see him,' Edith cried, clutching the money Ruth had pressed on her. 'Once a year.' She backed towards the door. 'I could take him, I could run,' she threatened suddenly. 'Who's to stop me running?'

'Keep three in poverty, or save them all?' Ruth waited, knowing by the expression on Edith's face that she had won.

Edith kissed the baby's head, handed him to Ruth and ran, crying, from the room.

'To Mrs Delaney.' Esme raised her glass to Jacob Collins as they sat sipping whisky in her room. 'And to think my original suggestion was tea. You were right, Jacob: your imagination's advancing with the age.'

'Well,' he conceded, 'in fits and starts.'

'I thought you'd have a problem with the rooms.' She refilled both their glasses. 'And I hope you understand, it's certainly not for the money. Once upon a time, it was the glamour, yes, a little excitement, all of which fades away. Now it's to protect the girls. Not exactly Langham Court, but the Grand's a good enough substitute.'

'Sorry, Miss Harkness, what do you mean? The rooms?'

'Marcus hasn't told you?'

'Which rooms?'

'One to five. A permanent booking, for the girls.'

'For prostitutes . . .'

'Marcus promised to tell you, Jacob. I'm sorry, he did say. And you came to my room last night, you were . . . different, you were . . . I thought you'd agreed.'

'What? You thought I was excited? At the idea of turning the Grand into a brothel?'

'I thought you were glad to help. You've always helped me, and it's a service, a vital service . . .'

'Jesus Christ almighty!' He leapt to his feet. 'Standing there! Every day of my life, and what am I? A pimp! How could you? How the bloody hell could you do that?'

'And the men who come to my room? Oh, you'll let them pass. You're happy to watch, so long as you're not part of it. Is that what you like, Jacob? Watching? Are you that sort of man?'

'I'm supposed to stand there. Give the key, take the money? If you can't see the difference! And for Marcus Bannerman? What do you think he cares about? The girls, or the money?'

'The money, of course. That's why it needs you and me, together . . .'

'This is my life. My son was born here, my wife died in a bed downstairs, and you've made it . . .' Speechless, he wrenched open the door and walked out.

Angrier than he'd ever been in his life, Jacob stormed downstairs. Tearing the register from Tom, he ripped out the offending pages.

'Men, you said! Men! Rooms one to five! God, but you're a stupid kid. Did you not think to mention the women? The girls on their arm, did you not see them?'

'Of course I did, sir, but you've always said discretion, turn a blind eye.'

'I did, didn't I?' Collins said quietly, subduing his anger. 'I taught you well. Gave you just the education for the Grand Hotel. You'll do well in this place. You'll go to hell with the rest of them.' Leaving Tom, he walked to the bar.

'Whisky,' he ordered abruptly.

'Right you are, sir,' Clive lifted down the bottle. 'Who's it for?'

'Jacob Collins.'

'You sure about that, sir?'

'Clive!' He slammed his fist on the counter. Clive poured out a glassful and handed it over, watching as the concierge knocked it back in one.

'Best watch out, sir,' Clive warned. 'Mr Bannerman's in.'

Collins turned his head and saw Marcus walk

through the foyer and head up the stairs.

Red-eyed, heavy-hearted, Edith pushed the last of her belongings into a battered carpetbag. She looked around. Her roommate was fast asleep. She sneaked out without waking her. But, as she was halfway across the staff kitchen, she was startled by the stentorian cry of Mr Collins.

'Where do you think you're going?' he yelled.

'Sorry, sir.'

Pushing his glass of whisky aside, he looked at her, seeing the bag for the first time. 'Getting out? Run, fast as you can. Edith West didn't last a day. Good for you. Stay one day, thirty years have gone.'

'Yes, sir,' she answered warily, realising he was drunk.

'That was my room.' He pointed down the hall. 'It was different then. They've built on since. But down that end, Mr and Mrs Collins. The Collins suite, they called it. Oh, they'd laugh at us, a married couple in service. We didn't mind. We had a boy, Peter. Lost him. There you go, never mind.'

'Is something wrong, sir?'

'Marcus Bannerman. Of course, you're friends with his wife. I feel sorry for her. He's the bastard, and what can I do about him? Nothing. Thirty years and there's nothing I can do.'

Edith took the chair opposite his. 'She's not my friend, Mrs Bannerman, she's just as bad.'

'Both of them, damn 'em.'

'Because it takes a while. Like she's talking and it's all sweet and honey, she could have you crying. Because it's so clever. Then you realise what she's done. She's bought them all. Not just the baby, all three of them, because I'm so stupid. They belong to her.'

'What does?' he asked, not understanding a word she'd said.

'Of course I want him. I'm no sort of mother, but her? And him as a father? Oh no!'

'Who's bought what?'

Reaching into her bag, she pulled out the hundred pounds Ruth had given her, opened the envelope and dropped it on the table between them.

'Where did you get this?' he demanded, sobered by the sight of so much cash.

'You want to get him, sir, Marcus Bannerman and his lady wife? Because I can tell you how.' Leaning closer, she began to whisper in the concierge's ear.

Chapter Twenty-Eight

The short, undistinguished, middle-aged man standing at the bar of the Manhattan looked ill at ease and out of place. His evening suit was tight and frayed at the cuffs, and he looked somehow uncomfortable in it – as though such attire was rarely, if ever, worn by him, and there was nervousness in his gestures that betrayed his discomfiture.

'Yes, sir, what can I get you?' Jim asked.

'A pint of mild.'

'Sorry, sir, it's only wine and spirits. There's a pub down the road.'

'No, no, I'll have a glass of wine.'

'White or red?'

'Red.'

'Right you are. That will be sixpence halfpenny.'

'Good God!'

'Do you want it, sir?' Jim asked, wondering if the man had wandered into the wrong club.

'Of course.' He delved into his pocket and handed over the money.

Stephen left the office and beckoned to Jim. 'Marcus should be on his way. He was asking for this. It's a list of surplus stock. Anything we've got spare, he wants taking to the Grand tomorrow for the christening.'

'Right, I'll make sure he gets it. You'd better run.'

Stephen glanced at his watch. 'God, late again.'

'Excuse me,' said the man at the bar, waylaying Stephen as he headed for the door. 'I'm sorry – who's in charge here?'

'You've asked the right person: I'm the manager.'

'Right. Um . . . I don't know . . . I mean I'm not sure how it works. I've been told there are girls. This is the place to come, if you want a girl.'

'If you could talk to that lady . . .' Stephen pointed out Esme, 'Her name's Miss Harkness. She can find you what you want.'

'So I just walk up to her?'

'It's all right. Tell her you've spoken to me.' He offered his hand. 'Stephen Bannerman. How do you do?'

'How do you do.'

'Don't worry, just talk to Miss Harkness. I do apologise, I've got to go. You've caught me on my one night off.'

'Thank you for your time, Mr Bannerman.'

'Good luck.'

Jim waited until Stephen had walked out of the door before tearing the list he'd given him in two and dropping it into the bin.

The off-duty staff who were sitting at the table in the kitchen looked up in surprise as Mrs Harvey walked through the back door and dumped down two suitcases.

'Now, don't let me disturb you. As you were. Clive, there's three more cases at the top of the steps. Fetch them now, quick sharp.'

'I'm just off duty. The porters can shift them.'

'Three cases, right!'

Realising he might as well do it first as last, Clive headed out of the door.

'So, this is what happens as soon as my back's turned.' Mrs Harvey picked up the teapot from the table. 'That's the best teapot. It belongs on the shelf, Kate.'

'I thought you'd gone home for the night.'

'And here I am, home.'

'What's in the cases?' Brenda asked.

'Cases are for clothes, Brenda, and clothes are what I wear of a day, unless you'd rather I did my job naked, and judging by standards in this place, you'd be happy with wilful nudity in the corridors. But from tonight, my back will be turned no longer. Not ever.' She walked to the office, unlocked it, and went in, closing the door behind her.

'What's going on?' Lark asked. 'What's she doing?'

'Who's naked?' Bob asked, bewildered by the conversation.

Lynne stared at the cases. 'She never has. Tell me she hasn't.'

Leaving the table, Kate walked into the office to see Mrs Harvey taking things from her bag and stowing them in the desk drawers.

'It was a mistake from the start, that house. Ridiculous size. We aimed above ourselves, buying property. Mr Harvey wanted his little castle. Well I can't afford it. He can move back in, with his new princess.'

'Mrs Harvey, I'm sorry,' Kate sympathised.

'You look nice.'

'Going out, taking Stephen to meet me parents.'

'Found myself at the stove tonight, cooking a meal for two, and him gone six weeks. Now accommodation: that shouldn't be too difficult – I spend my life looking after bedrooms.' Mrs Harvey left the office just as Clive humped the last of her cases through the door. 'Lark, fetch Mr Collins. We might as well make this official. Well?' She glared at the hapless girl. 'Don't stare, get it done! Now, a room. We could fit an extra bed into your room, Lynne. Would you like that? Go on, it's not like you to be so quiet. Tell me, would you like that?'

'Yes, Mrs Harvey,' Lynne whispered, appalled at the thought of sharing a bedroom with the house-keeper.

'Course you would,' Mrs Harvey countered scathingly. Grabbing two of the cases, she headed off down the corridor.

'There you are, proof, did you see?' Brenda asked the stunned maids. 'She's not wearing her wedding ring.'

'You're kidding,' Clive said in disbelief.

'What's that mean?'

'It means Mrs Harvey isn't Mrs any more, Bob. And if the Mrs has gone, the Harvey's gone too.'

'Gone where?'

'Where any husband goes: another bed.'

'Never mind him, Brenda. I'll tell you what this is – the worst day in the whole of history,' Lynne announced dramatically. '*Mrs Harvey's living in.*'

'Oh my God!' Brenda gasped.

'Mrs Harvey,' Kate was saying, following the house-keeper down the corridor, 'just give us a minute.'

Mrs Harvey flicked through the keys on her ring. 'The nightwatchman's room. Hasn't been used since the cutbacks. Perfect. One little room, that's all I need.'

'Have you tried . . . have you talked to Mr Harvey?'

Katherine Hardy

'Letters have been exchanged, there's no more to be said.'

Lark ran down the corridor towards them. 'Mr Collins has gone out, Mrs Harvey. Tom said he's coming back by midnight.'

'Well, out enjoying himself. Nice for some. Fine, I'll cope on my own, always have and always will.'

'Mrs Harvey, what's wrong?' Lark asked.

'Nothing. It's not for you to know, Lark. You're fourteen years old, you shouldn't hear such things.'

'Is there anything I can do?'

'Lark,' Kate warned quietly, 'come on . . .'

'I just want to help.'

'I'll cope. Always have.' As Mrs Harvey burst into tears, Lark dared to give her a hug. 'You couldn't know, Lark. Fourteen years old, you stay as you are, just fourteen.'

'Had a bit of a shock, walking in here.' The young man dug the girl he'd just been introduced to in the ribs. 'I said bring on the women. Up comes the old bird.'

'What? Miss Harkness?'

'I thought *she* was on offer. Nearly ran out through the door. I'm not that desperate.'

They both turned away laughing, neither of them seeing Esme behind them.

'Sorry, sir,' Jim apologised to Marcus as he walked up to the bar. 'I've not seen a list. Chasing me tail tonight. I turn up, everything's locked up.'

'He's having a night off. Didn't he tell you?'

'Not a word, sir, and that's the third time this week. It's half my job, chasing his mistakes. Still, never mind. All runs a bit better without him.'

'Good Lord!' Marcus exclaimed in amazement as the concierge walked in. 'Mr Collins, you should have said. I'd have brought you in the car. Welcome to the Manhattan.'

'I've come to have a word with Miss Harkness,' Mr Collins answered uneasily.

'Really? Excellent!' Marcus grinned. 'I though you were above such things. I hope your wallet's full.'

'Sir.' He walked past Marcus to the office where Esme was sitting behind the desk.

'Miss Harkness?'

'Mr Collins, if you've come to continue the argument, I'd rather keep the discussion out of working hours.'

'It's not that. I need a word. I have to talk to you, Miss Harkness. You're the only person I could think of who'd *know*. I thought I'd seen it all, but this . . .' He looked back at Marcus. 'God, I don't know any more. Where do I start?'

'What is it, Jacob? Sit down, please. Can I get you a drink?'

'Oh aye, one I can swim in.'

Kate stole quietly down the Bannermans' corridor. She opened the door to the living room, closing it again when she saw that the room was in darkness. Suddenly the nursery door flew open and Ruth appeared.

'Sorry,' Kate apologised.

'I thought I heard someone . . .' Ruth smoothed back her hair, conscious that she looked unkempt.

'I was just looking for Stephen. We're late. Are you all right, Mrs Bannerman?'

'There you are,' Stephen said as he walked out of the lift. 'I've been up and down the back stairs. Come on, we're late.'

'On me way. Goodnight, Mrs Bannerman.'

Katherine Hardy

'Kate, that new girl, the chambermaid, Edith West, has she gone?'

'I think so, yes.'

'You *think* so?'

'Well, she was sharing with Molly Harris, and Molly said she's packed her things and gone, not a word to anyone. Disappeared.'

Mrs Harvey opened the door to the nightwatchman's room, expecting dust, cobwebs, spiders, and possibly a mouse, but what she found was very different.

'Edith West? What are you doing here? Why are you crying?'

Mrs Harvey led her to a chair. As she sat beside her, Edith began to talk, and she listened, at first in doubt, then horror.

'There's a girl by the name of Edith West,' Mr Collins explained to Esme. 'She came to the Grand and took a job as chambermaid, but she hadn't come to work. She'd come to claim what's hers, what she *says* is hers. Edith West says she's the mother of the Bannermans' child. She says Mrs Bannerman went to London, employed a doctor called Curzon, and he found Edith. Mrs Bannerman told her she couldn't conceive, said her husband wanted children more than anything on this earth. And Edith was already pregnant, some lad who came and went. So, Mrs Bannerman paid her. Kept her in lodgings, and when the child was born, took him. To bring him up as her own. And Marcus Bannerman knows nothing of the deal.'

He and Esme both looked to the bar, where Marcus had stood a round of drinks to celebrate Charles's birth and christening.

'His wife deceived him, then,' Collins continued,

'and deceives him to this day. He thinks the child is his. They had separate bedrooms. Mrs Bannerman said she feared for the child's safety. She wouldn't be touched throughout the pregnancy – we all saw that.' Downing his drink, he muttered, 'It's madness, Esme, it has to be. But the girl knows so much. The dates Mrs Bannerman went to London, even the clothes she wore. If it's a story, then how could she know so much?'

'It's not a story.'

'You knew about this?'

'Not until now. But it makes such *sense*. Ruth visited London, disappeared for the birth. A wet nurse . . . a wet nurse, Jacob, of course! Good God almighty, it was always there. And she had ignorance on her side. Men are taught so little, and wonder even less . . .'

'And is that the world you live in, Miss Harkness? Newborn children up for sale. But Ruth Bannerman? How would she know? How would she find these people?'

'I might suggest, if she's had cause to seek an abortion in the past, she'd know certain doctors. Men who could find other men, for the right price. That world you talk of, Jacob, that shocking world, it's never more than two conversations away.'

'And you're so proud of it?'

'I accept it. Deny it exists, and look at you. Lost. I'm sure I know, but tell me: why has Edith West come back?'

'She wants her child.'

She looked again at Marcus, receiving congratulations and celebrating.

Stephen shook the raindrops from his coat as Mrs Morris opened her front door.

Katherine Hardy

'Pleasure to meet you, Mrs Morris.' He offered her his hand as they stepped inside her front room. 'Sorry, I'm soaked. It started just as we left the Grand.' He gingerly removed his coat. 'Where shall I put this? Thank you.' He smiled as she took it from him.

'Never seen the house so empty,' Kate commented. 'They've packed me sisters off for the night, or they'd be yapping away. You'd not get a word in edgewise. Is Dad home?' she asked her mother.

'Got back early this afternoon. He'll be down in a minute.'

'What's wrong?' Kate asked, seeing the expression on her mother's face. 'Oh heck, he's in a mood, isn't he? Just what we need.'

'Sit yourselves down.' Mrs Morris indicated the chairs. 'Mr Bannerman.'

'Stephen, please.'

'Your father wants a word, Kate.'

'Oo, that sounds serious,' Kate joked.

'Look, I'll go if it's not convenient. I don't want to get in the way . . .'

'Is it work?' Kate interrupted. 'What have they told him now?' She turned to Stephen. 'They're always doing this to him, mucking about with his hours . . .'

'Mr Bannerman?' The man standing in the doorway looked familiar. Stephen searched his memory, then paled as he recalled the man in the Manhattan, the small man in the rather drab and ill-fitting evening suit.

'Now mind out,' Kate said as she went to kiss her father's cheek. 'I'm wet, it's still pouring down. Dad, this is Stephen. Stephen, my father.'

'We've met,' her father informed her abruptly.

'When?' She looked from one to the other in surprise.

410

'Tell her, then. Go on, tell her about it, Mr Bannerman.'

'Sylvie, this is a bit late for you,' Mr Collins said, surprised to find her sitting in the staff kitchen after nine o'clock.

'I've been listening to stories. In the nightwatchman's room.'

'The guest list has gone up, there's another twenty for the christening.' He didn't want to think about the implication of what she'd said.

'It's all lies, of course. She has to be lying.'

'Every word of it is true. He'll have to be told.' He sank down wearily on the chair next to hers. 'The mother wants her child. It's the only decent thing we can do. I've waited, Sylvie, I've waited for the day I could bring Marcus Bannerman down. But I can't. I'll take away his son. It's like death. He'd lose his son. His only son.' He buried his head in his hands, not wanting her to see the pain he knew was etched in his eyes.

'I'd heard talk.' Mr Morris looked at Stephen. 'The lads at the docks, laughing away, the Manhattan club. The girls. And I'm thinking I know that name, the Manhattan, run by Stephen Bannerman.'

'It's not run by me, sir. I'm not in charge of the girls . . .'

'And I gave you the benefit,' he continued as if Stephen hadn't spoken. 'I went there to prove them wrong. And you're surrounded by a ring of whores.'

'They're nothing to do with me.'

'You're the manager.'

'I didn't know about this, Dad.'

'Of course you didn't, love, we never thought that

for a second,' Kate's mother reassured her.

'Did he take you there, Kate?' her father asked. 'Did he ever take you to his precious club?'

'No.'

'Mr Morris, I swear, I'm not the owner. It's my uncle, Marcus Bannerman. It was his idea, he brought the girls in.'

'The man who runs the Grand Hotel?'

'Yes.'

'Well then, that makes it simple. Because I did worry. I thought: What happens to my girl after this? Still have to work for Stephen Bannerman's family. How is she going to cope? But you're all the same. I'm sorry, Kate, you'll have nothing to do with that family, that entire building.'

'If you'd just listen to me,' Stephen persisted, 'if you'd let me explain: I wasn't even consulted – it was my uncle and Miss Harkness, they decided—'

'*Harkness?* Oh Jesus, you and her.' Kate looked at him in disgust.

'Look, it was a job. I was doing my job. We've all done that. Even in your job, sir, you get on with it, even if you hate it . . . and I'll give it up. You're right, I shouldn't have let it happen . . .'

'Oh, so it was all a mistake?'

'Yes!'

'Running a brothel, by mistake? By God, that's one hell of an accident! And chasing my daughter, court-ing her, making her part of that? My own daughter? Was that a mistake? Or just a good joke?' he shouted, raising his voice for the first time. 'I think my wife and my daughter have heard quite enough. If you could go . . . You're not welcome in this house.'

'Kate, I'm sorry,' Stephen pleaded. 'But just listen. Let me tell you how it happened . . .'

The Grand II: The Roaring Twenties

'Come on, lad, I've told you once.' Mr Morris rose to his feet.

'Stephen,' Mrs Morris said. 'Best be gone.'

'Kate?'

She turned away, refusing to look at him.

'I knew all about it,' he began quietly, 'right from the start. Of course I did. Because you were bound to find out, then you'd hate me and that's . . . fine.' Grabbing his coat, he walked out of the door.

Kate sat with her parents for a few minutes, then she went after him. She ran full pelt down the street, the rain lashing down on her bare head and shoulders.

'Why?' she wailed as she cannoned into him, pushing him back against a wall.

'I let things happen. I'll even make them happen,' he confessed wretchedly. 'I'll invite them. So it all gets spoilt. Because when things are going fine, I'm just waiting for the bad news, and it always comes.'

'But why, though?' she repeated, wanting to understand.

'Because I met this kid once. He must have been sixteen. He had glasses, and he was eating away, eating a pie or something, stuffing his face. You know when you're really hungry and you're shoving it down? You can't even taste it and it's great.'

'So?'

'So, I killed him, before he killed me. Because that was my job, a soldier's job. The things I did, Kate. And now I've got all this, I've got you, and I don't deserve it. No wonder it all goes wrong: it has to. Strange thing is, the army, we were all the same, we'd all done things like that. I was forgiven, because of the uniform. I hated it, I hated it so much. But what I did was because I was a soldier, not Stephen Bannerman.'

Katherine Hardy

'You deserve better. You do, and I could help you. I could, because I love you. It doesn't matter what you've done, I still love you. But what about me? That's all I become. Stephen's help. It's like a job, like a nurse. It doesn't matter who I am.' And slowly she walked away, taking a street that didn't lead to her father's house, or the Grand.

Chapter Twenty-Nine

'Baths run at midnight,' Brenda grumbled as she returned to her bedroom. 'Some guests need slapping. So?' She turned to Lynne, who was sitting up in bed, cigarette in hand. 'What's new?'

'I've taken up smoking, does it suit me?'

'Nope, owt else?'

'Let's see, Molly Harris, her foot's gone again, she's had no feeling since tea. It's gone midnight and Kate Morris isn't back, and there's someone in the night-watchman's room because I heard snuffling, and it's not the ex-Mrs Harvey, because she's in with Big Lucy. Oh, and Mrs Bannerman's mad.'

'Same as usual, then.' Rinsing her face and hands at the washstand, she began to undress. As she buttoned on her nightdress, she realised Lynne was studying her photograph of Fred Willets – again. 'Really, Lynne, you should chuck that out. You'll find better than Fred Willets.'

'Won't.'

'I mean, he was a nice lad and that, but he walks out, not a word. He's never written. He's as bad as the rest of them.'

'He's not, though. He wasn't like that. He must have had good reason. Must have,' she insisted.

'Listen to that.' Brenda changed the subject, not

wanting to argue any more. 'It's not half raining.'

'Good for the allotment.' Lynne automatically used one of her father's favourite phrases.

'You got an allotment?'

'No.'

Brenda reached out and gently prised the photograph from Lynne's fingers.

Kate stood outside Esme's room, dripping water over the corridor carpet.

'Kate Morris!' Esme said in surprise as she opened the door. 'It's a long time since you called at my room.' She stepped aside, inviting Kate in.

'Almost a year to the day,' said Kate. 'Just tell me, yes or no, then I'll be gone. Your . . . work, your business, the prostitutes at the club, was any of that Stephen Bannerman's idea?'

'No.'

'Was he happy working with you lot?'

'No, I don't think so.'

'Really, though?'

'Would I lie?'

'He really didn't like it?' Kate reiterated, seeking more assurance.

'You'd know that already. What do you really want?'

'I want you telling me, Miss Harkness, because you've excelled yourself this time. Me, Stephen, me parents, the whole lot of us, poisoned, and all because of you.'

'Then I'm glad to earn your contempt. Because it's girls with Sunday-school minds, girls like you, that cast me out. And I like it out here. We're fighting, we're changing, we're moving on. Left to you, we'd still be living in caves! It must be a fine view, standing on your pedestal, looking down on the rest of us. But lonely, I'd have thought.'

'You're right there.' Kate hesitated, unable to check the tears that were trickling down her cheeks. 'Clever, aren't you?' she snapped, allowing her contempt for the older woman to show. 'Because I do, I push them away. Pass judgment and push them away. Look at me, soaked to the skin.' Physically and emotionally drained, she collapsed on to the sofa. 'I dunno, I'm just doing what I was taught. Sunday-school kids' talk.'

'I was never taught. I had to learn things on my own. Who knows? Perhaps I've got things wrong, and you've been right all along.'

'Oh, yes?'

'Poison, I can see that. I carry a certain poison, yes. A good man like Jacob Collins, not able to look me in the eye. Monica, Clive Evans, now little Kate Morris. If I could have helped just one of you . . .' Her voice trailed, then she turned to Kate with a fixed, determined smile on her face. 'You'll be glad to know, I'm moving on. Tired of the fight. I've got money, there's a thousand hotels, Paris, Rome, anywhere. I'll go somewhere where I can't speak the language. Keep the poison bottled up.'

'Miss Harkness.' Kate steeled herself to ask the question she'd been wanting to all along. 'You'd know, you've seen them all. Is it all right to love a bloke? If he needs you? I mean, that's not love, is it, if he needs you?'

'These are different men, Kate, the ones we sent to war. To be needed by a man who's survived that. I could almost envy you.'

'Really?'

'Would I lie?' She smiled and Kate laughed. 'And if

it's not perfect, then look around you. What is?'

'I should go.' Kate rose to go to the door. 'What am I going to do? I can't go home. Can't go downstairs, they'll be laughing. I've nowhere to go.'

'Both of us.'

Esme moved towards her. Gingerly, tentatively, she reached out, and when Kate didn't push her away, she held her, offering what little comfort she could.

Marcus went straight to the nursery when he came home. As he'd expected, Ruth was there, standing over the cot, watching the baby.

'He's fast asleep,' he whispered, so as not to wake the child. 'How long have you been standing here? Come on.' He dropped a kiss on to her forehead. 'One last drink before bed.'

'You're out every night. This is all I've got,' she said as she followed him into the living room. 'Walking these rooms, with all their ghosts.'

'I'll spend more time with you, I promise.'

'You can do more than that. Sell it. Sell this hotel, we'll move away.'

'I don't think so,' Marcus smiled, amused at the suggestion.

'This building contains everything you've ever done. It follows me round, things we've both done, they're here, soaked in the walls. We should go where none of it can find us.'

'Funny, I thought the same tonight looking at Stephen when he turned up at the club, drunk again.'

'Then move on.'

'Rather move him. I've given his job to Jim Craig. Stephen can find his way back to his parents.'

'Can't you do something for *me*? I won't bring up that child in the Grand.'

The Grand II: The Roaring Twenties

'Ruth, it's impossible. This is my son's inheritance. I'm not about to give it away . . .' He stopped talking as Stephen walked in. He headed straight for the decanters.

'That's more like it.' Stephen lifted the glass stopper on the brandy. 'This stuff's free.'

'Don't you think you've had enough?'

'Oh, no, Marcus. No, no, no.' Pouring out a generous measure, Stephen downed it in one, then refilled his glass.

'Stephen, Marcus has sacked you,' Ruth said flatly, 'did you know?'

'Thank you, Ruth,' Marcus broke in, giving her a warning look not to trespass any further.

'Fine,' Stephen mumbled, not caring.

'He's sacked you because he can't bear to look at you, because he looks at you and he remembers what he did. He remembers sleeping with your mother.'

Stephen burst out laughing. 'God, I have been drinking!'

'Tell him,' she demanded of Marcus.

'Sorry.' Stephen picked up his glass and went to the door. 'You're in the middle of a row. I'll leave you alone.'

'Tell him!' Ruth commanded Marcus furiously.

'That's enough!'

'He seduced your mother, and bedded her, and it was easy. And your father, he knew, Stephen, he *knew*. They were driven out in shame. They'd abandon their son, rather than stay. It was the end of a campaign Marcus had conducted for years. All your mother's married life, he chased her. The entirety of your life on this earth, Stephen, every day and month and year in the Grand, that's what was happening.'

Stephen looked at his uncle. Unable to meet his

gaze, Marcus turned away, and then Stephen knew. It was true. Dropping his glass to the floor, he hurtled out through the door.

'That's your son's inheritance,' Ruth smiled triumphantly. 'And we can survive it, please, if we get away. Just leave and not look back, tell no one where we've gone, or it will find us. It will always find us. We have to get away or he's not safe. The child's not safe.'

Perplexed by her train of thought, Marcus held her. 'All right.' He stroked her hair. 'All right . . .'

'What's more important? Your son or the Grand Hotel? Sell it!'

'All right, yes,' he murmured, still trying to calm her, but once he'd agreed he began to think of the possibility. 'Yes,' he reiterated softly.

Stephen didn't stop running until he reached the foyer. He charged forward slamming into the doors, scrabbling at the handle. They were locked. Reaching for his keys, he opened them, and he carried on running, down the street and into the sleeping city.

Kate woke with a start. Looking around at the unfamiliar surroundings, she finally focused on Esme sitting at her dressing table.

'Oh my God.' She leapt from the sofa. 'Bloody hell, it's the christening. What am I doing? I'm on duty, sorry . . .'

'I think you've got more important things to do,' Esme suggested. 'Go and find Stephen.'

'Do you think—'

'If he's done anything wrong, it's only because he works for Marcus Bannerman, but so do you. Tell your father that.'

The Grand II: The Roaring Twenties

'Me dad's always banging on. I've not listened to him since I was twelve. Sorry about, you know . . .' She pointed to the sofa. 'Did you mean that last night? You're really leaving?'

'I thought Paris, first. You remember Madame Euphrasine De Bourg D'Oisans?'

'Poor sod.'

'She left me this.' Esme held up the trinket. 'Russian, genuine Fabergé, though it's more than jewellery. It's history. Part of a vanished world, the legacy of the House of Romanoff. Worth eighty thousand pounds.'

'God!'

'Enough to pay for my escape. Wherever I go, it will be the same solitary room. But the view will be so much finer.'

'Good luck,' Kate said sincerely.

'And you actually mean it. Who'd have thought?'

'A year to the day,' Kate said, thinking of Monica. Leaving Esme to her pendant, glittering and sparkling in the morning sunlight, Kate finally opened the door and left.

'Fat lot of good you are,' Edith railed at Jacob Collins. 'Look, if Mr Bannerman needs telling, I'll do it myself. Come on, come with me, I'm not scared, watch me tell him . . .'

'I'm warning you, Edith,' Mr Collins cautioned, 'you've dealt with his wife, but you don't know the man. Marcus Bannerman, he'd as likely turn around and break your neck. For your own sake, stay here. I'll put things right.' Leaving the nightwatchman's room, he went into the staff kitchen.

'He's got to be told, Jacob,' Mrs Harvey insisted. 'There's guests arriving from all over the country,

Sylvie. There's the cars, the reception . . . Let's cope with that, give him that at least. One day, tonight, when it's over, I'll talk to him then.'

'It's a *christening*,' Mrs Harvey reminded him. 'Naming the child in the eyes of God, naming the parents. If we let that happen, we're committing a sin.'

Worn out by the situation, Mr Collins nodded agreement. 'He's upstairs, I'll find him.'

As Mrs Harvey watched him walk away, she didn't believe for one instant that he would actually tell Marcus Bannerman.

'I did Stephen Bannerman's room, first thing,' Lark confided to Kate. 'His bed's not been slept in.'

'In some gutter, knowing him.'

'How come you stayed out?'

'One of those nights. Seems like nowt when the sun's up. He'll come back.'

'Suzie Hatcher,' Brenda gossiped to Clive and Lynne as they walked down the corridor, 'she says Mr Harvey ran off with a dancer from the music hall. One of them as does nude tableaux. He gets his own private performance nightly, though she still makes him pay.'

'Have you heard, Clive?' Lynne announced, not to be outdone. 'Mrs Harvey spent the night in Big Lucy's room.'

'Well, you can stop your trouble, you lot,' Clive lectured, unaware that the housekeeper's office door was open behind him. 'The last thing Mrs Harvey needs is you taking the rise. Bit of sympathy, or can't you manage that?'

'Oh, aye?' Lynne sneered. 'Me heart's bleeding. Just you think, Clive, think of all the girls she's sacked over the years: Olive Clegg, Jean Taylor, Claire Miller. Where are they? Out on the street. All Harvey's doing. It's her chickens coming home, and about time too.'

'Upstairs, all of you, this minute,' Mrs Harvey shouted from her desk. 'I want that foyer gleaming, top to toe.'

'They did the foyer, first shift,' Lynne said. 'We're not allowed there in the day.'

'This day, Lynne Milligan, this day is different. Upstairs now!' she ordered brusquely. 'Every last one of you. Clive, the bar, Bob, the chairs. Out!'

'I've been meaning to say, Jacob,' said Marcus, 'you can step out of uniform. Attend the christening as a guest. It's about time. You've done enough for this family.'

'Thank you, sir.' Jacob hovered in the office doorway. 'But there's one or two problems. I'd rather be on duty. I might be needed.'

'I'm asking you to come as my guest. Is that so difficult, Jacob? It's meant as an apology.'

'What for?'

'Do you want the list? It was brought home to me, last night. That moment when you see yourself as others see you.' Marcus left his chair. 'It's a fine morning, the rain's passed on. A new beginning.'

'Mr Bannerman . . .'

'The offer's there. It's your decision. If you can't accept, I'll understand.' He reached for his coat. 'Was there anything else?'

'No, sir.' Jacob returned to the foyer, amazed to see staff pouring out of the corridor, mops, buckets, polish and cloths in hand. 'What's all this?' he asked Tom.

'Mrs Harvey, apparently. New instructions.'

Katherine Hardy

* * *

Ruth put the baby in the cot and tenderly tucked the blankets around him.

'I'll look after him.'

She turned to see Mrs Harvey behind her. 'It's all right, there's plenty of time.'

'I'll look after him.' Mrs Harvey repeated her offer. 'You take your time, get the maids to run a bath. You want to look your best. Special day. I can cope, Mrs Bannerman. It's not the first time I've held a child in my arms. I had one of my own, but it wasn't to be.'

'I'm sorry.' For the first time, Mrs Harvey heard sincerity in Ruth's voice. 'What happened?'

'She was taken. Fourteen years ago. God's will, all part of the plan. That's what we're told: there's a plan.'

'How did she die?'

'She's not dead. Whatever makes you think she's dead? She was a mongol. They took her away. Mr Harvey said, "How can we look after a thing like that?" Though we could have tried. She might still be alive, I don't know. All in the plan,' she smiled. 'Now you treat yourself. I'll look after him.'

'Thank you.' Ruth walked down the corridor to her bedroom. Mrs Harvey waited until the door closed before picking up the baby. Wrapping him securely in a shawl, she carried him out of the nursery and down the corridor towards the back staircase.

She almost bumped into Clive as he hauled crates of beer out of the cellar. He stopped for a moment, wondering why she'd brought the baby to the staff quarters, then Tom called down from the foyer and he quickened his pace.

Walking quickly, Mrs Harvey went into the night-watchman's room.

'Take him.' She thrust the baby towards Edith. 'There's money, a ticket to London, and don't you come back, girl. Don't ever come back to this god-forsaken place.'

'Thank you.' Edith felt that the words were totally inadequate, but she didn't have any others.

'Get out,' the housekeeper ordered.

Clutching her baby, Edith rushed out of the back door.

Ruth wrapped herself in her dressing gown. Returning to the nursery, she opened the door.

'If he needs—' She turned, surprised to see the room empty. Thinking Mrs Harvey must have taken him to another room, she walked down the corridor. The living room was empty. Panic began to build as she opened door after door – the seven bedrooms, the study . . .

'The christening gown,' Marcus said as he ran up the stairs. 'I've had it cleaned. It's been in the family a hundred years. No harm in a little tradition. Where is he?' he asked, looking into the empty nursery.

'Mrs Harvey. Mrs Harvey's got him.'

'I left him in the nursery,' Mrs Harvey insisted as she faced Marcus and Ruth in the staff kitchen.

'You were looking after him . . .'

'I was called away, Mrs Bannerman. I didn't see the harm.'

'I trusted you.'

'But Mrs Bannerman, tell me: where do you think he could have gone?'

'Now come on, he hasn't gone,' Marcus said angrily. 'He's a month old. He didn't walk out of the door. Mrs Harvey, are you quite sure?'

'I left him in the nursery.'

'But he's not there!' Ruth was close to hysteria.

'What do you mean exactly?' Marcus loomed over the housekeeper. 'You were called away?'

'I was called away,' she repeated, trying to put on a brave face.

'What for?'

'It's a very busy day, sir. I'm the housekeeper, I'm needed all over . . .'

'Where did you go?' Marcus cut in abruptly.

'I came here.'

'What for?'

'All sorts of things.'

'Then who was it who called you away?'

'I did, sir.' Clive came forward.

'For what reason?' Marcus demanded coldly.

'The wine list, sir. Mr Collins was busy so I asked Mrs Harvey to check it. She came straight down.'

Marcus stared at Clive before looking back at Mrs Harvey and the assembled staff.

'The rest of you, then, come on, someone must have seen something . . . Mr Collins,' he shouted as the concierge walked into the staff kitchen. 'The man who knows everything! Now come on, this is upsetting my wife . . .'

Ignoring Marcus, Mr Collins went straight to Mrs Harvey. 'She's gone. Edith West has gone.'

'What's she got to do with this?' Marcus asked.

'Mrs Bannerman?' The concierge looked expectantly to Ruth.

'Edith West was here?' she whispered dully.

'Jacob, if you're using my son in some ridiculous prank against me, then I'll make sure you regret it . . .'

Summoning a courage he hadn't been aware he possessed, Collins said, 'Edith West is the mother of the child, sir.'

'What child?'

'The boy, sir. Your little boy. I'm sorry, sir, he's not yours.'

'All right, very funny. Now, wherever my son is, there's no one looking after him. You could show some concern. For God's sake.' Marcus stared at half a dozen plants that had been taken out of the public rooms. 'I told you, get rid of those plants, I'm sick of the sight of— Very funny, laughing behind my back. Now you've had your fun, let's—'

'Ask your wife, sir,' Mr Collins suggested.

'She doesn't know where he is.'

'Ask her.'

Ruth shrank back, terrified, as Marcus turned to her. Turning, she fled up the back staircase.

Chapter Thirty

'Better get dressed, I don't imagine you're wearing that,' Marcus said calmly to Ruth, pointedly looking down at her dressing gown as he walked into their bedroom.

'Dressed for what?' She was more terrified of him in this mood than when he was in a temper.

'The christening.'

He closed the door, leaving her trembling.

Edith stood on the edge of the platform, waiting as the train pulled in. She was third in line to board it when she saw them. Three huge, burly policemen closing in on her from the left. She turned, intending to run back into the ladies' room, and three more moved towards her from the right. Clinging to her son, she bent her head over his. Wanting, needing, to protect him, she fell to her knees.

'Didn't I say?' Lynne crowed to the maids who were working alongside her in the staff kitchen. 'I said ankles. Look at her ankles. No woman gives birth with ankles slim as that.'

'And me mam, she saw Mrs Bannerman in town,' Kate chipped in. 'She said it didn't look right. It's bloody scandalous.'

'Do you think Marcus Bannerman's the dad, though? Oh my God,' Lynne gasped, 'he's slept with Edith West! I can feel me breakfast coming back up. Do you think he did, really?'

'Don't ask me,' Brenda frowned, confused by their conversation. 'I've not followed a word of this.'

'You shouldn't be laughing,' Lark scolded. 'It's awful. They've broken the law. It's dirty, the whole thing . . .'

'Oh shut your face, titch.' Lynne flicked a towel at her. 'This is the best working day of me life.'

'Kate?' Clive called her from the door. 'It's Stephen, he's come back.'

'He always does.'

'You been rowing, you two?' Lynne goaded. 'Wait until you tell him about his uncle.' She gave Kate a push as she dropped her iron back on to the range.

'Give him my love,' Brenda teased.

'Yeah, after I've given him a good thump.'

'He's upstairs in the foyer.'

'I can't go in there, Clive. The cleaning's done. Ask him to go upstairs . . .'

'He's in the foyer.'

'Clive, what is it?' she asked, realising something was wrong.

He opened the lift doors and she stepped inside, alongside him. 'What's he done? Is he in trouble? That's my fault, walking off. I should've stayed with him.'

'I'm the one told you. I said, yeah, walk out with him, give it a try. Can't do any harm.'

'If there's owt wrong, I want to know.'

'I'm sorry, love.' The lift stopped, he opened the door. 'He's out there.'

She walked into the staff corridor. Pushing the glass door, she stepped through into the public area of the foyer. Mr Collins gave her a sympathetic look. She looked around. There was no sign of Stephen at the bar or in the Reading Room. Then Mr Collins nodded towards the front doors. They opened and she saw a porter place two suitcases alongside a soldier. He turned and her heart stopped. Stephen was back in uniform. He waited for her to come to him, as though he was afraid to set foot in the Grand.

'Twelve-month commission. Back to Germany. I suppose they're still clearing up. Work to be done. A good job, proud of it. You're the one that usually says that. Now it's my turn.'

'You can't have . . .' She shook her head. 'What have you . . . have you signed?' she asked urgently. 'Oh God, you haven't signed the papers?'

'Signed and dispatched. Can't change my mind. It would be against the law. They'd come and get me.'

'You hated it, Stephen; it drove you mad.'

'It's the only thing that ever made any sense.'

'One argument, we had one argument, and you're running away. Don't listen to me dad, sod him . . .'

'What would we have, Kate?' He looked intently into her eyes. 'Even if you came back to me . . .'

'I *have* come back,' she insisted vehemently. 'I never left.'

'Even then, what's it for, Kate? Marriage, nice little picture-book wedding, like our parents before us, an imitation. My mother and father. My own mother,' he repeated acidly, 'and none of it's real. One big lie, every second in the Grand, my entire life. It doesn't happen, Kate, happy ever after and . . .' He struggled to keep his emotions at bay. 'Love, there's no such thing,' he said finally.

'I love you.'

He saw the tears in her eyes. 'Then grow up, Kate,'

he advised gently.

'I do, though, I love you, Stephen.'

'I love you, but that's how it starts.'

Stephen Bannerman picked up his cases and walked down the steps.

'Sir, sir,' Tom shouted as he ran through the staff door. 'They've brought her in, sir. Came in the side entrance. Police and everything.'

'Who?' the concierge asked.

'Edith West, sir, they've taken her upstairs.'

'They've what? Here?' Checking the lift and seeing the doors closed, Collins charged up the stairs. He stopped to catch his breath when he reached the Bannermans' floor.

'It was Highgate, flat six, Victoria House, on the lane,' Edith's voice, high-pitched in fear, echoed from the living room. 'Go and look. I lived there for three months; she paid for it. Just go and look. Dr Curzon, ask him, find him and ask him . . .'

Collins walked into the room to see Edith flanked by two uniformed constables. The Chief Constable was standing in front of the fireplace with Marcus and a man he'd never seen before. Ruth was next to Marcus, already dressed for the christening with the baby in her arms.

'He went there.' Edith pointed to Marcus. 'Mr Bannerman, he almost found us. I was *there*. Tell them, Mr Collins,' she appealed, seeing him for the first time. 'Tell them it's true.'

'Thank you, but I think my wife's a better judge of the origin of her own child. Ruth?' Marcus prompted sternly.

'He's mine.'

'Excuse me,' Mr Collins addressed the Chief

Constable. 'Whatever the facts, this woman should be at the police station. What is she doing here? There are statements to be made. We can all tell the story, but in the proper place. What are you doing?'

'They're all his, Mr Collins. He's paid them off, every last one of them.'

'Chief Constable, that woman's made something of a slur on your reputation,' Marcus commented. 'As I told you, she's mad.'

'He's paid them,' Edith repeated angrily.

Both the Chief Constable and the man with him avoided Mr Collins's eye.

'I might be a layman, but even I know the procedure,' Mr Collins reiterated. 'Take her to the station. With the child that's rightfully hers.'

'Dr Spencer?' Marcus turned to the stranger.

'I've got the papers. They're all signed, though they'll need verification.'

'I'll provide that,' Marcus said shortly.

'That's not the family doctor,' Collins protested. 'I've never seen this man in my life. The Bannermans' doctor is Dr Lewis, St John's Street. Call him . . .'

Taking the papers from Spencer's hand, Marcus held them out.

'Chief Constable?'

'What are you doing? What are those papers?' Edith questioned, suddenly afraid.

'Mr Bannerman, you can't do this,' Mr Collins warned.

'What are they?' Edith reiterated.

'The necessary documentation,' Marcus explained coldly. 'They're all I need to have you committed to the County Asylum.'

'You bastard!' Edith lashed out, and the two constables moved in, holding her away from Marcus.

'You filthy bastard!'

'Take her.'

At Marcus's cue, the Chief Constable nodded to his men and they dragged Edith towards the door.

'You can't!' Edith screamed. 'Mr Collins, tell them, tell them! Let me go, let go of me, you bastards!'

'Mr Bannerman, I'm sorry, I'm sorry this has happened, but you've got to stop it,' Mr Collins insisted.

'He's mine!' Edith wailed as the policemen pulled her into the corridor. The Chief Constable and the doctor followed, but Marcus and Ruth remained in the living room with the baby. Mr Collins ran after them, watching helplessly as the girl was dragged away.

Lark Rothery was standing outside Stephen's room, a pile of towels in her arms.

'Someone's going to listen,' Edith shrieked, loud enough for the Bannermans to hear. 'He can't buy the whole world! He can't do this, he sodding well can't! Let me go! Mr Collins! For Christ's sake, tell him! The boy's mine, he's my own child, he's mine . . .'

Lark looked to the concierge, expecting him to do something to help Edith. When he didn't, she ran off crying down the corridor.

Collins turned back to the living room. He stared contemptuously at Marcus and Ruth.

'Better make some space,' he said. 'Move the chairs back, make a space in the centre of the room, because there must be tons of it, piles and piles of money to buy me off. But understand this,' he warned earnestly, 'you could give me all the money on this earth, and it won't silence me. I'm not for sale. I won't have this happen. I'll stop you.'

'The cars should be here soon.'

'For God's sake, Mr Bannerman, you can't keep the child.'

'I don't want him,' Marcus said softly.

'Then why have you sent that woman—'

'Everyone is arriving for this reception, everyone,' Marcus spat back, finally showing his anger. 'They're travelling the country to celebrate my child, and by God, they'll do it! The boy's good for one day,' he said calmly, regaining control of himself. 'Then I don't care: they can find him dead.' He looked at Ruth for the first time since Collins had returned to the room. 'And you alongside him.'

'We could try again. I'll put it right. I'll conceive again. We could try . . .'

'Call the asylum, Jacob, book a room for two. She's talking like she actually was pregnant.'

'I was.'

'Oh, and I'll believe anything you say?'

'I carried the child for six months, a whole six months. Edith said she spent three months in my pay, just *three*. She said so, you heard her.'

'You'll have told her to say that.'

'Would she keep saying it now? It wasn't my fault. I couldn't tell you. That's the only reason you married me, to bear children. But she died.'

'A girl?'

Even after all that had happened, Jacob was affected by the sudden pain in Marcus's eyes.

'Your daughter.'

'My child died, and you didn't tell me?'

'I broke the conditions of our marriage. But I did all this, all of it, for you.'

'Where is she?'

'There was nothing we could do, I did try . . .'

'Where is she now?' He repeated sternly.

'I couldn't have told you.'

'Where?'

The Grand II: The Roaring Twenties

'She's gone Marcus.'

'Where?'

Ruth hesitated for a moment. 'Burnt,' she revealed cruelly.

Saddened and shocked to the core, Collins looked at Marcus.

'Cars,' he barked abruptly, 'the christening gown.'

'It's over, sir. You *know* you can't get away with this. I'll talk to the guests. They don't have to know. I'll think of some story . . .'

'The ceremony is going ahead.' He glared at Ruth. 'No wonder she died, trapped inside you.'

'I did want her. I did . . .'

'Our guests will be waiting,' he cut in frostily. 'On schedule, exactly as I planned. Ruth?'

She looked at Mr Collins, then, carrying the child, she followed Marcus out through the door.

'I dunno, you lot.' Jim looked over the bar at the party in the reception area. 'You keep saying you got good jobs. At the Midland Hotel, they're laughing. Look at the staff, here.' He indicated the long, hostile faces staring at Marcus. 'Not a smile among them.'

'Welcome to the Grand,' Clive murmured as he piled another half a dozen dirty glasses on to a tray.

One of the guests shouted 'speech' and half a dozen others took up the cry. Marcus shook his head, but they persisted, almost carrying him to the stairs. Raising his arms for quiet, he unconsciously repeated the phrase he had used the night of the Grand's reopening.

'Right, thank you for coming. Thank you for drinking me dry.' He waited for the laughter to subside. 'Now the last thing you need is a speech. We're here to celebrate a new life in the world. Although it looks the same as ever. Mr Collins, didn't I say? Get rid of those plants. My father bought them, forty years ago.' Unable to think of anything else to say, he looked at the expectant faces of the guests. At Kate and Mrs Harvey, hostile, watching his every move. At Mr Collins, saddened, pitying. He turned to Ruth and held out his hands for the child. She lifted the baby up. Marcus took him and held him high. 'Charles Marcus Bannerman. Do you know what he was? An investment, a long-term financial plan. But he's more than that. The firstborn. A clean slate, all those years ahead. The future, he's the future. One month old with the potential to be everything I'm not.' His voice wavered. 'But he can't. He's the past. All the things I've done, the child I deserve. Oh yes, he's mine.' He saw Ruth, crying. 'My daughter,' he whispered hoarsely. 'We made far more than a child together, we made our own world. A stinking, dirty world, and all of it mine. I made you, Ruth. Found you, trapped you and turned you into this. I'm sorry.'

As he stepped down the band began to play again, a sad, mournful ditty, a fitting epitaph to his speech, while the guests, stunned into silence at first, began to mutter to each other in bemused embarrassment.

'I never thought to help you, Ruth. I'm helping you now: get far away from me.'

'I'll never leave you, Marcus.'

'I know, so I'm leaving.'

She reached out for the child but Marcus handed the baby to Mrs Harvey. Pulling an address book from his jacket pocket, he flicked through it, his eyes blinded by tears. Tearing out a page, he gave it to Mr Collins.

'Dr Spencer. He'll know what to do. Let her go. Give Edith West her child.'

'Thank you.'

'I'll talk to the police, I'll ... good ... fine. Anything else? Mrs Harvey, if the maids could pack . . . Mrs Bannerman and I will be leaving. Separately.'

'What about the Grand, sir?'

'Is that all you've got to care about, Jacob?' Marcus asked wearily. 'It's consumed us all. Remarkable child' – he stroked the baby's cheek for the last time – 'to bring this place tumbling down. It's up for sale.'

'To whom?'

'Offices, that's where the money is. Quick sale. They can turn it into offices.' He shook Jacob Collins's hand. 'Jacob, thank you.'

'Marcus.'

Marcus looked around the room for the last time. It was the way he wanted to remember it, filled with guests and staff, but there was also Ruth.

'Where will you go?' Esme asked.

'I think I might try the Midland.'

Three days later Mr Collins assembled all the staff in the kitchen and told them the news.

'So . . .' – he took a deep breath before saying the words he'd hoped he'd never have to – 'the Grand's being sold as fast as possible. It's likely they'll tear it down. It's the land they want, not the hotel. There's nothing we can do about it. We'll give you references.' He nodded to the housekeeper. 'Mrs Harvey and I will try to find you work.'

'There's nothing out there, sir,' Clive said grimly. 'You've seen them, the unemployed, queuing up at the drill hall. Where are we going to go?'

'I don't know,' Collins conceded wearily.

'Mr Collins, I gave me life to this place,' Kate protested. 'It's all I've got left. They can't close it.'

Katherine Hardy

'They can, and they have, Kate. Of course we could all chip together and raise a hundred thousand pounds,' he joked harshly. 'Now off you go, leave it tidy. Let's have the old girl looking her best.'

Mr Collins started at the top floor. He watched the removal men strip the Bannermans' living room. They took the pictures, the rugs, the ornaments, the smaller pieces of furniture. When there was only the dining table, chairs and sideboard left they covered them with dustsheets. Unable to bear the sight a moment longer, he walked down to the second floor, where the bedrooms were being given the same treatment. Dustsheets covered the wardrobes and dressing tables; the windows had been covered with cleaning white, the fittings in the bathrooms wiped with a disinfectant that lent the whole place a forlorn, antiseptic smell. Finally, he reached the foyer, where Bob was piling the plants on to a trolley. In the bar, Clive was stacking the last few bottles into cardboard boxes. He waited until they'd finished, then switched off the lights.

Only the staff quarters left. The girls were wearing their own clothes; the maids' and waitresses' uniforms were packed away in the cardboard boxes that held the accoutrements of the hotel.

Lynne took the last dress from the wardrobe the four of them had shared, and folded it into her case. She looked around the room. There was only one thing of hers left. The photograph of Fred Willets. Picking it up from the chair next to her bed, she laid it on top of her dress and slammed the case shut. Pushing past Kate, who was standing in the doorway, she put her head down and walked quickly away.

The Grand II: The Roaring Twenties

Sitting alone in a strange room at the Midland Hotel, Esme spun her Fabergé pendant, plotted . . . and dreamed.

Epilogue

Kate was sitting at home looking out of the window when Lark ran along the street. There was a smile on the young girl's face. Kate rushed to open the door.

Just as it had been the first to be covered over, so the Bannermans' apartment was the first to be opened up. Mr Collins supervised the men as they flung the casements wide to air the rooms. He watched as they rolled back the dustsheets. Light streamed in for the first time in weeks.

As the concierge walked down the guest corridors, he saw the scene being repeated a hundred times over. From his station in the foyer, he could hear Clive slamming bottles back on to the shelves in the bar.

Downstairs the staff streamed in through the back door. Brenda stood to one side, clutching her suitcase tight, biting her bottom lip as she watched and waited. Lynne was one of the last to walk in. She looked at her, then rushed over and hugged her tight.

Mrs Harvey presided over the chaos in the staff kitchen. She clapped her hands for silence, but no one noticed – and for once, she didn't care.

The following morning, Mr Collins stood in the foyer.

The Grand II: The Roaring Twenties

The staff lined up either side, and Mrs Harvey moved next to him. They waited in silence. Ten minutes later the doors opened. Two men held them back, and Esme Harkness walked in. She nodded and smiled at the concierge and the housekeeper, but Lynne could only stare at the younger of the two men. She couldn't believe her eyes. Fred Willets!

Esme walked slowly along the lines of staff, emulating a colonel inspecting his troops. She stopped in front of Kate. Kate smiled and Esme smiled back. It was going to be all right. Mr Collins handed her the keys. Esme took them and stood on the stairs.

'Staff,' she said, 'let's get to work.'

'Yes, Miss Harkness,' the staff chorused.

The concierge and the housekeeper stood back and watched the new owner of the Grand walk up the stairs.